C000260566

"I was kept guessing as to who and wl
and the reappearance of a voice from th
illustration of the title of this volume. All three volumes form a whole to
be savoured and treasured."

—*Pat Nevin*
Swansea. United Kingdom

"*Master and the Commander* meets Robert Lewis Stevenson in the
final instalment of this three-part adventure story. The polite and formal
Victorian dialect conjures a former era of duty, service, and honour—and
heroes."

—*Dr. Ronald D. Klein*
Professor
Hiroshima Jogakuin University, Japan

"I have had so much pleasure from this historical novel, and with the
final volume set partly in NZ, it has had a special impact for me as New
Zealander. I have again been held in anticipation of the adventure and
did not want the adventures to conclude."

—*Michelle Simpson*
Bank Manager
Wellington, New Zealand

"Nostalgia, the sense of adventure, and truly lively characters are the
ingredients that make this novel a true pleasure to read! One cannot help
but admire Langdon's stamina to create such a wide-spanning series of
books! A truly gripping novel!

—*Martin B. Stanzeleit*
Elizabeth University of Music
Hiroshima, Japan

"As in the first two volumes, the author surprises, using unexpected twists and not only interesting, but well-researched technical and historical details. A book full of adventures and emotions that cannot be put down, right from its very first pages."

—*Katharina Ferris, M.A.*
Bari, Italy

"Langdon's style has mellowed and matured with earlier novels, and it was enjoyable and easy reading."

—*Richard Wardopper*
Senior Civil Engineer, Abu Dhabi

"Having read two volumes and already familiar with the hero *Jason Smiley Stewart*, one is used to his very detailed descriptions of even minor events and things. The dramatic climax is a crime story and its solution, and the reader, now caught in suspense as to the outcome does not drop the book until the riddle is solved."

—*Dipl.-Ing. Edgar Bublik*
Technical University, Vienna, Austria

Dear Sid
My best wishes
John Milton Langdon

FULL CIRCLE

FULL CIRCLE

Volume 3

Jason Smiley Stewart - My Life Story

John Milton Langdon

TATE PUBLISHING & *Enterprises*

Published by Tate Publishing & Enterprises, LLC
127 E. Trade Center Terrace | Mustang, Oklahoma 73064 USA
1.888.361.9473 | www.tatepublishing.com

Tate Publishing is committed to excellence in the publishing industry. The company reflects the philosophy established by the founders, based on Psalm 68:11,
"The Lord gave the word and great was the company of those who published it."

Published in the United States of America

ISBN: 978-1-60247-787-2
1. Fiction: Historical   2. Action: Adventure

07.08.13

To my wife,

Dietlinde

ACKNOWLEDGMENTS

I would like to thank Herr DI Dr. Gernot Pirker for introducing me to the *Frigate SMS Novara* and some European history that was previously unknown to me. I must also thank his brother Herr DI. Dr. Ulfried Pirker for continuing the development of my home page.

Many relations and friends have offered suggestions and words of support. There isn't space to mention everyone individually, so I hope that a global thank you will be acceptable.

CONTENTS

PREFACE

My novel is fiction based loosely on fact, and all the characters, companies, and events described are figments of my imagination. Any resemblance to persons living or dead, companies extant or closed, and historical events are coincidental. I hope students of history will forgive me if some of the events I mention are not strictly in chronological order.

AUTHOR'S NOTE

When I was attending Grammar School in South Wales between about 1948 and 1953, our history lessons concentrated upon "English" kings and didn't extend beyond the early 1800s. It was not until I visited Austria in the late 1960s as a tourist that I learnt of the existence of the Austro-Hungarian Empire, but I had no idea how far the Empire extended or that it had access to the sea at Trieste and a deep-sea Navy based at Pula at the southern extremity of the Istrian Peninsula.

Consequently, it was something of a surprise when my stepson, Herr DI. Dr. Gernot Pirker, introduced me to the Frigate *SMS Novara* and its circumnavigation of the world for scientific purposes between 1857 and 1859. This was such an important scientific expedition I could not resist the temptation to include mention of the voyage in this book although it is chronologically incorrect to do so.

The *SMS Novara* left Trieste on 30 April 1857 and sailed 51,886 sea miles in a voyage that lasted 551 days and took the ship to Rio de Janeiro, Capetown, Ceylon, Madras, Singapore, Hong Kong, Sydney, Auckland, and Valparaiso, amongst other places. The ship had a complement of 345 officers and men under the command of Captain Freiherr von Pueckh and seven scientists who reported to Dr. Karl von Scherzer, who was the scholarly leader of the exhibition. In overall command of the expedition was Commodore Bernhard von Woellersdorf-Urbair.

The expedition was considered to be so scientifically important that the *SMS Novara* was able to return to Trieste without being attacked despite the fact that war had broken out between the French and Austrian Empires during her voyage.

Much more detail can be found on the Internet by searching for *SMS Novara*.

ONE

A New Life

I stopped close to the foot of the first class gangway of the ship that was to carry me in luxury to Australia, in a horse-drawn carriage with the blinds partly down.

It wasn't that the light hurt my eyes, it was just that I had no wish for my haggard features to be seen and remarked upon by "Joe Public."

I waited and watched the other passengers boarding. Some were clearly excited at the prospect of a voyage on a luxury liner and were chatting animatedly to those around them. Others were clearly dreading the prospect of weeks at sea in a metal box and climbed the gangway as if they were going to their executions. I wondered if they had been sea sick before and knew the trauma awaiting them if the ocean was as rough as it could be.

As sailing time approached, the number of passengers coming to the gangway became less and less, and my chances of an unwelcome conversation reduced in step.

When I decided it was time to climb down from the carriage and board the ship, it wasn't exactly the last minute, but crewmen had started to release the lines securing the end of the gangway to the quayside. I was the last person to board and felt there was now no possibility of unwelcome conversation with a potentially inquisitive passenger. At the head of the first class gangway a senior officer was on hand to welcome each boarding passenger, and I realised that if I had been earlier I would probably have been greeted by the captain in person.

Not that I was concerned about my apparent demotion. I didn't desire publicity.

The officer said interrogatively, "Mr. Smiley Stewart?"

I nodded, but didn't respond verbally. I don't think I responded to his welcoming smile either and it was switched off like a light.

"You're just in time, sir. We have started to bring the gangway on board."

"I had noticed that activity," I said.

After taking a few moments to consult the papers attached to his clipboard, he turned the smile back on and said, "I see your baggage has already been loaded, sir. Your cabin is A25 on the port side, and you have been placed at the captain's table for dinner this evening after we sail."

"I'll dine in my cabin," I said. "Where is it?"

The smile switched off again. "Sir, it is an honour to dine at the captain's table, and Captain Osborne will not be very pleased if his invitation is rejected. A place at the captain's table is much sought after, sir."

"I will be sorry to displease Captain Osborne, and I am fully aware of the honour he does me, but I am not accepting his invitation for dinner tonight. I'm not in the mood to be sociable."

I had started to speak in a conciliatory tone but by the end was sounding quite irritated. *Unusual for me,* I thought. In all honesty, I had to correct myself and admit that the irritation I was starting to feel was a relatively normal experience these days. I hadn't always been so prickly but recent events had changed my previously cheerful disposition for the worse.

Unfortunately, that thought didn't modify the terse way I repeated, "Where is my cabin?"

There was no vestige of a smile now as the officer turned to a steward and ordered, "Stevens, take Mr. Stewart to A25."

"Yes, sir," responded a black-bearded steward who was clad in an immaculate white, perfectly pressed uniform. He turned to me and said, "Please come this way, Mr. Stewart."

Without comment I followed my guide along several passageways and after a few minutes found myself outside Cabin A25. He opened the door and allowed me to precede him into the cabin.

In the doorway he stopped and said, "If you will excuse me for a moment, sir, I'll go and tell your cabin steward that you are on board."

"Thank you," I said, quite politely.

A few minutes later there was a discreet knock on the cabin door and another steward entered in response to my call. He was a tall, slim, clean shaven young man and like Stevens he was clad in a carefully pressed and immaculately clean white uniform.

He spoke in a faint accent that reminded me of Birmingham and said, "Good evening, Mr. Stewart. My name is Edwards, and I am your cabin steward during the night. I see that you are dining at the captain's table tonight, so with your permission I will just prepare your evening clothes."

"No!" I said.

He was probably so used to an affirmative response that he ignored my refusal and had the wardrobe door open and was reaching inside for my dinner jacket before he heard me say angrily, "Confound you, I said no!" at a volume that would have registered on deaf ears.

He flushed, closed the wardrobe door as quickly as he could, and said plaintively, "Sir?"

I took several deep calming breaths and then said as politely as I could manage, "I will not dress for dinner tonight, Edwards, as I will not be dining at the captain's table. I will eat here in my cabin. Please ensure that Captain Osborne is advised that I am indisposed and then bring me a dinner menu."

"Yes, Mr. Stewart. Immediately, Mr. Stewart," he responded as he opened the door and hurried away.

Five minutes later he returned with a menu card and waited politely whilst I made a selection. He went away with my order and then came back and finished unpacking my cases and laid out my night attire. A steward from the dining room brought my dinner and then waited on me. When I had finished eating, he cleared and took everything away, and I changed into my night clothes.

I lay down on my bunk more in the hope of sleep than any real belief that I would achieve the blessed state of unconsciousness that provides restoration of body and spirit. As had been the case for so many weeks now, I slept for an hour or two then woke with my brain churning over past events, desperately trying to find a way to put the clock back.

Just as the decks were becoming visible in the dawn of a cloudy grey day I dressed and started to walk around the boat deck. The physical exercise was good for my body but did nothing to improve my jaundiced outlook on life. I went back to my cabin, washed, changed, and walked to the dining room to get some breakfast. It was still early and I was able to enjoy a substantial but happily solitary breakfast and then return to my cabin. I didn't bother with lunch and again had dinner in the cabin much to the distress of Steward Edwards, who tried to persuade me to join the captain's table once more.

In the morning and after another largely sleepless night, I went to the boat deck once again. But the motion of the ship was becoming steadily worse as we progressed south and west toward the Bay of Biscay, and my walk degenerated into a series of short runs from one hand hold to the next.

As I finished my solitary breakfast, a man in naval uniform stopped by my table. He was a big, thickset man, and I noticed the four gold bars of a captain on his sleeve. I looked up into a pair of bright blue, twinkling eyes set in a face tanned to the colour of mahogany where it was not obscured by bushy white eyebrows and a full beard and moustache.

He said with a smile, "Good morning. My name is Osborne. I'm pleased to see that at least one of my passengers is not affected by the motion."

"Thank you, Captain," I responded civilly. "I am also pleased about that as I have no desire to add mal de mer to my other troubles."

"May I ask your name, sir?" asked Captain Osborne.

"Smiley Stewart," I responded without elaboration.

"Ah!" he said. "The gentleman who is unable to have dinner at my table. Thank you for the message you sent with Steward Edwards, but I usually get such a message from passengers who are suffering from sea sickness, and that is clearly not your condition. I have to go to the bridge, Mr. Stewart, but if you will excuse me saying so, you are not like the other passengers we have on board. If you would care to come up to the bridge when you finish your breakfast, I think I would enjoy a conversation with you."

"I should be pleased to accept your invitation, Captain," I responded, as I couldn't think of a plausible excuse for refusing it. I would have preferred to go back to the solitude of my cabin and metaphorically hide under the blankets, but this morning I would be unable to indulge myself.

I finished breakfast and went to the bridge.

The motion was slightly worse than a few hours earlier but still nowhere near as bad as the storm conditions I had previously experienced at sea. I knocked on the port side bridge door and when Captain Osborne beckoned, I opened it and went in. Automatically my eyes scanned the horizon, the ship's heading on the compass, and the settings on the engine room telegraph.

I wasn't aware that I had done so until Captain Osborne asked, "When were you last on watch, Mr. Stewart?"

"Some years ago, Captain. I was a cadet and then third officer on the *Earl Canning*. It was one of the Gold Star Line ships."

"Yes, I've heard of the line. You had a service between Liverpool and Bombay, if I remember correctly. May I ask why you gave up the life of a sea officer?"

"Essentially, the governor of Bombay asked my captain to release me to help with the installation of the underwater telegraph cables between India and Iraq. He agreed, but only under pressure from the governor, and I have had no desire to return to sea full time since then."

"I confess, I'm intrigued by that statement, Mr. Stewart, as I can see no obvious connection between a young naval officer and the telegraph system."

"Normally, Captain Osborne, there would be no connection. In this case I knew the manager of the telegraph company, and as he had taught me about the telegraph, he thought I would be a good choice to help him whilst he recovered from dysentery. It changed my life," I added, but this last comment reminded me of things I didn't want to remember, let alone discuss, so I changed the subject.

"Do you anticipate a bad storm, Captain?" I asked.

"The glass has been falling since yesterday afternoon and it's looking very threatening ahead of us. I think it is going to be very uncomfortable for the passengers for the next few days. I will probably have to reduce speed and alter course later tonight if it continues to worsen, but we have plenty of sea room at present."

Captain Osborne turned from me to order the Officer of the Watch to rig safety lines and to screw down all the porthole deadlights. He then ordered a slight alteration of course to keep the bows heading into the worst of the oncoming waves and made an appropriate note in the log.

As he turned back to me, I said, "If you will excuse me, Captain, I'll return to my cabin. Thank you for your courtesy."

He said, "Not at all, Mr. Stewart. Everything has been done that can be done to prepare the ship for the storm that's coming, and now it is necessary to be vigilant, as you know from your own experience." Then quite unexpectedly he said, "May I make a personal observation, Mr. Stewart?"

I was so surprised by the question that I said, "Yes," without thought.

"Your appearance and demeanour suggest that you have suffered a very bad personal tragedy, Mr. Stewart. If you would like to talk about it to an older and more experienced man, I am prepared to listen. It may help you to talk about it."

"Thank you, Captain," I answered, "but I'm not yet ready to discuss my private feelings with a stranger."

"I understand," said Captain Osborne as we shook hands preparatory to me leaving the bridge, "but if you change your mind, please send your steward to make an appointment with me. Sometimes a stranger can be more help than family."

I went back to my cabin and found that my bunk in the first class was bigger than the bunk I had "enjoyed" on *Earl Canning*, and consequently I was unable to brace myself so effectively against the motion of the ship. Nonetheless, I made myself as comfortable as possible and tried to read, but Captain Osborne's suggestion held my attention more strongly than the book. I knew that my demeanour had changed recently, and I didn't like the bitter and bad-tempered man I was starting to become. I had never been like this previously so perhaps talking about my tragedy might help, and I acknowledged that Captain Osborne had been exceptionally perceptive in his assessment of my situation.

There was a knock on the cabin door and Edwards opened it in response to my shout of, "Enter."

He looked at me and said, "You do not appear to be affected by the weather, sir. Can I get you anything?"

"Not at present. Thank you, Edwards. Will I be able to get dinner later?"

"Yes, sir," he responded. "Will you come to the dining room? I imagine you will have the room to yourself tonight except for the captain, of course. Shall I arrange for you to eat with Captain Osborne, sir?"

"Yes," I said, knowing as I did so that I was going to accept the captain's invitation to talk about my tragedy. I don't know whether it was the solitary confines of my cabin or the well-remembered movements of a ship pitching and rolling as it rode the gale-driven seas, but I suddenly knew that I had to talk to someone or be driven mad by my thoughts.

"Edwards, please inform the captain that I would like to talk to him this evening if the storm permits him to leave the bridge."

"Yes, sir," said my slightly puzzled steward.

I dressed for dinner and made my way to the dining room. I was pleased that I hadn't entirely lost my sea legs but even so the safety lines proved a blessing.

At seven thirty I was the only passenger in the dining room, and fifteen minutes later Captain Osborne arrived. We decided to eat immediately and since the food remained on the plates and the plates on the table, we managed quite well with a very nice steak and kidney pie with vegetables. We had decided not to have soup, for obvious reasons, and chose not to have the pudding as the helping of pie had been substantial.

Captain Osborne leant back in his chair and said, "The glass is still falling, Mr. Stewart, but not so rapidly, so perhaps we are already near to the centre of the storm. The steward intimated that you would like to talk to me. I will not go back to the bridge for several hours, so if you wish to tell me what has blighted your life, I am more than prepared to listen."

"Thank you, Captain. I must talk to someone before my thoughts drive me insane. As I mentioned earlier, I joined the telegraph company in Bombay at the request of the governor. I was very much involved with the installation of the underwater part of the telegraph cable between Fao in Iraq and Gwadur in India. During that time I came into conflict with the local Omani fishermen and ended with a life-threatening bullet wound in my leg. Only the courage and tenacity of my fiancée…"

The emotions evoked by my memories swamped my ability to speak for several minutes, and we sat in the dining room listening to the sound of the sea and sensing the ship riding the waves. Captain Osborne didn't move or speak, for which I was grateful.

I took a deep breath and said, "Excuse me, Captain."

"Naturally, Mr. Stewart," Captain Osborne responded.

"As I was saying, Captain, only the courage and tenacity of my fiancée pulled me through, and when I had recovered sufficiently we sailed for Britain."

TWO

The Homecoming

The Anglo-Indian Telegraph Company had been very generous to Joanna and me, as they had provided us with adjoining cabins on a new steamship bound for Liverpool. I was so weak when I boarded the ship that I had to be helped up the gangway and into my cabin. But over the next weeks the combination of good food, good air, and daily exercise on the boat deck soon started to replace the muscle that had wasted from my bones during my illness, and I was able to discard the few suits I had commissioned from the tailor after my discharge from hospital and resume wearing my normal apparel.

Joanna was a tower of strength during the early days, just as she had been during my hospitalisation, and was instrumental in preventing the weakness and continuing pain from my leg dragging my spirits down too far. The fracture knitted itself back together in time and I discarded the splints and crutch. The former went over the side and the latter into the hold with my baggage as it was too nice to throw away and reminded me of the old shipmate who had made it for me. The bullet wound healed but left a scar and a deep, angry looking depression in my flesh that was much more sensitive to touch than the surrounding skin.

As my strength returned so my desire for Joanna mounted in concert and it was just as well for both of us that Joanna had the support of two homeward-bound Army wives as chaperones.

Even so, it was difficult for us not to anticipate the joys of marriage.

It was so difficult in fact, that Joanna seriously suggested that it would be better if we travelled on different ships. This was a notion I didn't take kindly to, so I promptly changed my ways and became less demanding.

We arrived in Liverpool after an uneventful voyage in purely nautical terms, and after disembarking I escorted Joanna to her home in Caernarfon by train and then by carriage.

Mrs. Evans heard the carriage stop outside her house and with a maid close behind came rushing out of the front door to greet us as we climbed down from it. She threw her arms around Joanna and embraced her warmly.

Then, with her arm still around Joanna's waist, she said, "I am very pleased to see you, Jason. I was so worried about you when I received Joanna's letters. She wrote that you were at death's door and now all of a sudden here you are and looking almost as good as I remember."

I said seriously "I'm very pleased to see you again, Mrs. Evans, and I have to tell you in all sincerity that I would have been dead and buried long ago if Joanna had not arrived in Bombay when she did and then nursed me so effectively. I owe your daughter my life, Mrs. Evans. And I have had the chance to recuperate on the voyage home, which is why I look well."

"Come in to the house," said Mrs Evans, "and the maid can bring coffee to us in the morning room," and a few minutes later we were all sitting down.

Mrs Evans sat in an armchair, and when she noticed Joanna and me sitting hand in hand on the sofa, she asked, "Have you made any plans for your wedding yet?"

"No definite plans, Mrs. Evans, but we have some ideas we would like to discuss with you when it is convenient," I said.

"Is anything wrong with now?" she asked.

"No!" I said, and turned to Joanna and asked, "Would you like to speak for us, Joanna?"

"No! Jason. Please go on," and she gave my fingers a little squeeze of encouragement.

I said, "Perhaps I should say first that I have been granted leave for a year at my full salary and can then return to the telegraph company if I wish. I have also been given a reward of one thousand five hundred guineas by the company and that has been invested for me by my solicitor. Consequently, I am confident that I can provide a good standard of living for Joanna if we marry soon, which is what we both desire."

We both coloured slightly as my unfortunate use of the word "desire" conjured up emotions we had been trying to suppress for some months.

Mrs. Evans appeared not to notice.

I went on, "On the voyage from Bombay we had some time to talk about when and where to marry and where we should live after the ceremony. I have few friends or relations in Lincolnshire, whereas Joanna has many in North Wales, and we decided it would be better to be married here at St. Peblig's Church if the Reverend Eli Jones will agree to officiate."

"I like that idea," said Mrs. Evans. "I'll speak to Reverend Jones. Please go on, Jason. Tell me when you would like the ceremony to take place."

I restrained the almost overpowering urge to say, "Tomorrow, please," and said, "We haven't fixed a date because there is so much to arrange, but we would like to marry as soon as possible and certainly within the next two to three months."

Perhaps my enthusiasm caused me to be a little too vehement because Mrs. Evans appeared to be rather shocked by my words.

She scanned her daughter's belly and then looked quizzically at her but didn't say anything. She didn't need to because we realised immediately what she had concluded. We were obviously very much in love and had been together for some time possibly without adequate supervision. One plus one can very soon equal three!

Joanna coloured and said firmly and more than a little angrily, "It's not *like* that mother! We *wish* to marry soon, but we do *not* need to! Jason is a gentleman and we both know how to behave with propriety."

"I'm sorry, Joanna," said Mrs. Evans contritely.

There was a short embarrassed silence that I sought to break by saying, "We haven't decided where to live yet. As I will be a gentleman of leisure for a year, we can live anywhere that is congenial, but when I work again we may have to move home even to a foreign country."

"I don't like that idea," said Mrs. Evans, probably imagining grandchildren growing up without the benefit of Mamgu's spoiling.

"We have a little time to decide that, Mother. More important now is to decide on a wedding date, and then everything else will fall into place. If at all possible, I would like to have the ceremony on a Wednesday. It's the luckiest day of the week for a wedding after all," said Joanna, practical as always.

"Why don't you live here after the wedding?" suggested Mrs. Evans. "This house is much too big for me, and I would enjoy having your company. Please think about it and let me know what you wish to do."

"I think that is a very good idea, Mother," said Joanna. "Jason and I will discuss it over the next few days, won't we, my dear."

"Yes," I said. "It's a capital idea," and there the matter rested.

I moved back into the bedroom I had occupied previously and rejoined the routine of the Evans family.

Two days later in the early morning I said goodbye to Joanna and set off for Lenton, promising to return as quickly as possible. It was the first time that Joanna and I had been apart for some months, and I was stunned by the loneliness I felt.

It was a new and not very welcome experience.

The journey to Lenton with the usual overnight stop in Grantham was just as tedious as it always had been, and I arrived outside the Vicarage in the middle of the following morning tired, hungry, and wet through from the rain that had fallen incessantly for hours. All the curtains were drawn and I wondered who had died in the village.

I walked up the path and tugged on the bell pull.

After a few minutes the door opened and the maid started to say "Good morning, Mr.—" then screamed and collapsed onto the doormat at my feet.

I shouted up the hall, "Mrs. Perceval. Quickly! Come here!" then bent down to see if I could help the girl lying at my feet. She was conscious again, but as soon as she realised I was looking at her, she crossed herself then made a sign between us as if to ward off an evil spirit. I started to straighten up just as Mrs Perceval hurried along the hall with another maid just behind.

With the light behind me, my Aunt didn't recognise me immediately but as soon as she did she froze and her face went quite white.

She said, "Jason?"

"Yes, Aunt Mary."

"But you're dead," she said.

"No I'm not," I responded. "I nearly died, but Joanna made sure I didn't," and wondered what had prompted this bizarre conversation.

Aunt Mary moved a step closer, reached out, and very tentatively touched my arm, as if she expected her hand to pass through it. When it didn't, she squeezed it.

"You feel solid enough and you look like Jason. I don't understand! Yesterday we received a letter from Bombay. It was from an acquaintance of your father's, a Mr. Samuels, expressing his condolences to us following your untimely death. You had better come in and tell my husband and me what has been happening," and she bent down, helped the maid stand up, closed the front door, and lead me to her husband's study. She knocked on the door, opened it, and started to enter the room.

She stopped, motioned me to stay outside, and said quietly, "Wait here a moment. There have been enough shocks this morning," then walked on into the study leaving the door open.

She said to her husband, "My dear, I am pleased to tell you that the letter informing us of Jason's death is not correct."

"That's wonderful news if it's true."

"Yes, it is," said my aunt calmly.

"How do you know?" asked the reverend a little sceptically.

"He has just arrived," said my aunt in ringing, joyous tones.

"What!" cried the Reverend Perceval. "Where is he?" and there was the crash of a chair falling over backwards as the Reverend Perceval ejected himself from his seat by the desk. He didn't wait for his wife to answer. He rushed across his study and into the hall where he grabbed my hand and shook it as he slapped me on the shoulder with his other hand.

He said with vast enthusiasm, "I'm so pleased to see you, Jason. I didn't want to believe what I read in the letter but had no choice. We had no other news of you." My aunt joined us and put her arms around me. She held me as tightly as she could and wept tears of relief as we stood there in a group with the maids staring open-mouthed at us.

She said emotionally, "Thank God it wasn't true."

"Come into my study and tell us what has happened," said the Reverend Perceval, and his wife sent one maid for coffee and the other to open the curtains again. Normality was starting to return, thank heaven.

My aunt asked, "Does my brother know that you are safe?"

"I don't know," I said. "Joanna said he came to the hospital to tell me he was about to sail. I don't remember his visit, but I was so ill then everyone thought I would die. If he receives the same letter that you received, he will believe it. He would have no reason not to."

"It has been bad enough for us these past hours and I dread to think what agony my brother will go through until he knows the truth," my aunt said, thoughtfully, "I wish there was something we could do. I feel so helpless here."

"There's a telegraph office in Grantham," I said. "I can send a message to Captain Downing in Liverpool and another to Mr. Fairweather in Bombay and ask them to contact my father and tell him the truth. There is nothing else we can do."

"That's a very good idea, Jason. I would never have thought of using the telegraph. But before anything else, you must please tell us what happened to cause Mr. Samuels to write as he did."

"I was shot in the leg by an Omani." I pointed to my right thigh. My aunt and Reverend Perceval looked serious and concerned by turns as I explained how near to death I must have been before Joanna arrived and undoubtedly saved my life by nursing me in such a devoted fashion.

"As far as Mr. Samuel's letter is concerned," I said, "I cannot imagine why he should have written as he did, because my recovery and departure for Britain with Joanna were well known to the hospital staff and to Mr. Fairweather. Perhaps he heard one of the exaggerated rumours that fly about through the expatriate community. Anyway, what is important now is to ensure my father knows the truth as soon as possible."

"I agree," said the Reverend Perceval. He added, "Has your wound completely healed, Jason?"

"Yes, thank you. It's still a bit sensitive and angry-looking, but it has healed. It's left me with a dent in my leg but that's all."

"Would you think me insensitive if I asked to see your wound?" he asked. "I have never been injured and I have never seen damage such as you describe."

"Of course, Reverend," I said, thinking what a strange request it was.

"Perhaps you would like to come to my room later, although I'm afraid you will be disappointed by what is left to see."

"No!" he answered. "I don't expect to be disappointed. To see the wound and too understand more clearly the agony you have endured might enable me to help a member of my flock more effectively in future."

"I understand, Reverend, and I will help you as much as I can."

We sat in silence for a few minutes whilst I finished my coffee and decided what to do first.

"If you will excuse me," I said to them both, "as the carriage is still outside I'll go back to Grantham and send the telegraph messages."

Later in the day I returned to the Vicarage colder, wetter, and hungrier than I had been when I arrived the first time. I rang the doorbell with some trepidation, half expecting a repeat of the morning's drama, but I need not have concerned myself as the same maid opened the door and said, "Good evening, Mr. Smiley. I'm truly sorry about this morning, but I thought you were a ghost. I'm so pleased the letter was wrong. Please come in, sir."

"Thank you," I responded. "I'm pleased it's wrong as well."

"You are in the same room, sir, and I have put your bag there."

"Thank you," I said again.

"Reverend and Mrs. Perceval are in the study, sir, if you would like to see them."

I just managed to avoid another "thank you" and said instead, "I'll go and see them immediately," and did just that.

"Hello, Jason," said Reverend Perceval. "Did you have a successful trip and would you like a sherry before dinner?"

"Yes and yes, please," I said.

With a sherry glass in my hand and my rump warming nicely in front of a roaring log fire I said, "I sent messages to Captain Downing and to Mr. Fairweather, as I had suggested, and I also sent one to the Harbour Master in Bombay and the shipping line's agent there. I have arranged for the telegraph office in Grantham to deliver any replies to me here. I hope that will be acceptable to you both."

"Perfectly," he said on behalf of himself and Mrs. Perceval.

My aunt asked, "How is Joanna?"

"She is very well and safely returned to her mother's house in Caernarfon. We hope you will both attend our marriage."

My aunt looked quite stunned at my news. "I didn't even know you had an understanding with Joanna," she said, "and now you are talking of marriage. Please tell me everything."

"I'm very sorry, Aunt Mary, I had forgotten that you didn't know. With Mrs. Evans's blessings we were engaged before I went back to Bombay. Then on the voyage home after I was discharged from hospital, we agreed to marry as soon as we could arrange it, and we expect to have the banns read in about two months' time in her local church in Caernarfon. You will come, won't you?" I asked.

"Of course we will, and I'm so pleased for you both, but you must try and arrange the date so that your father can attend. It will be a very important event in his life as well as yours."

"I will, Aunt Mary, but first I must find out where he is," I said.

"Hopefully we will receive an answer to one of the messages you sent," Reverend Perceval suggested. "We are not changing for dinner tonight, Jason, so if you would like another glass of sherry before we go in, I should be happy to get it for you."

"Thank you, Reverend, I would like another sherry," I said as I moved away from the fire, sat down in one of the arm chairs, and immediately stood up again as my overheated trousers made contact with unprotected skin. It was a reflex action that was observed with some amusement by Reverend Perceval.

"It's a very good fire tonight, Jason," he said with a chuckle, and I couldn't help joining his amusement with a smile of my own despite a singed backside.

We enjoyed a good dinner and went to our rooms to get ready for the night.

I slept well.

By next morning the rain had stopped, and when I leant out of the window, I was entranced by how clean and sparkling bright everything looked after being thoroughly washed. I filled my lungs with cool, clean air and thought how lucky I was to be alive and blessed Joanna for her strength and courage. And I missed her company enormously and felt the pain of our separation. I wanted to go back to Caernarfon desperately, but I couldn't leave my aunt and her husband so soon after coming to Lenton. There was the added complication, of course, that I needed to wait long enough in Lenton for a reply to my telegraph messages to arrive.

My thoughts turned back to the previous evening when Reverend Perceval came to my room to look at the wound on my leg. He stood by my bed, stared at the scar on my leg, shuddered, and said, "You must have been in agony, Jason. How did you manage to withstand the pain?"

"It was very painful, Reverend. It was so bad that I wished for death, as that would have been preferable to living with the constant pain."

"If the memory is not too painful, Jason, I should be grateful if you could tell me everything that happened to you."

In accordance with his request, I described everything that had happened from the time I was shot in the leg when I boarded *Earl Canning*, up to the time I left hospital. More accurately, I related what I remembered from my periods of consciousness whilst in the hospital. He was very interested in the use of opium by the Arab doctor and later ether by the doctor from Harley Street. When I had finished, he thanked me and started to leave my room with a very serious expression on his face.

In the doorway he stopped and turned back to say, "You were an extremely fortunate young man to have had Joanna there to nurse you. God moves in mysterious ways, Jason, and I wonder what he has planned for you. I shall pray for you."

"Thank you, Reverend, and also for Joanna if you will," I said.

"Of course," he responded as he left my room.

I realised in the silence that followed the departure of the Reverend Perceval that my attitude toward my wound and subsequent illness had changed. Talking about it in an objective way had made the memory less painful and consequently less important.

There were no messages that day or the next, and by the dawn of the third day I was becoming frustrated and irritated by my enforced idleness. After breakfast I saddled one of Reverend Perceval's horses and rode into Grantham to the telegraph office. I didn't expect to find a message there, but I felt that activity was better than sitting in the vicarage simply waiting.

I dismounted and tied the horse to a convenient post outside the telegraph office. I went in but didn't have time to enquire before the duty telegrapher said, "Good morning, Mr. Smiley. How are you, sir? I'm sorry, but there are no messages for you, sir."

"Very well," I said. "If you receive any messages, please send them to the vicarage in Lenton as we arranged."

"Yes, sir. We will dispatch them as soon as we can."

"Thank you and good day," I said, as I stepped out into the street.

I unhitched the reins and was about to mount when I heard a voice call out, "Mr. Smiley. Wait a minute, sir," and as I looked for the source of the voice I saw the operator dodge back through the telegraph office doorway and disappear inside. I tied up the horse again and went back to the telegraph office. The operator was busy receiving a message, and I was just in time to hear and understand the last few words of the transmission as they were being received in Morse code. I waited whilst he finished transcribing the message onto a message sheet and carried it over to me.

As he handed it to me, I said without thinking, "It's from Captain Downing in Liverpool, I believe."

The operator looked surprised and said, "That was a good guess, Mr. Smiley."

"It wasn't a guess," I said.

"Can you read Morse code?" he asked.

"Obviously," I answered, and as he seemed too surprised to hand over the message, I said, "May I have my message please?"

"I'm sorry, Mr. Smiley, here it is."

I took the message, signed the receipt pad, and walked back into the sunshine of a Grantham morning to read what Captain Downing had written. It was direct and to the point as one would expect from a senior captain.

> Dear Jason
>
> I cannot tell you what a shock I had when I received a telegraph message from someone I believed to be dead and how very happy I am to know that the report of your demise is untrue.
>
> Just before he sailed, your father also received a letter

saying that you had died in Bombay but he refused to believe it. He left Liverpool a very worried and unhappy man and intends to find out the truth when he reaches Bombay. I have sent messages to all the ports he is due to call at, telling him the joyous news and wait impatiently for an answer.
I will advise you when I have more news.

I stood by the horse stroking its neck in an absentminded way as I thought about the news I had just received. *So far, so good* I thought to myself. *If my father is on his way to Bombay at present, he will be home in time for the wedding.* I walked in to the telegraph office again and wrote out a message for my father telling him about the wedding and sent it to the Gold Star Line's agent in Bombay.

There was nothing more I could do now except wait once again, so I climbed back on the horse and rode to Lenton.

I told my aunt and Reverend Perceval what I had learned from Captain Downing and said, "I have sent a message to my father via the company agent in Bombay so we can do no more than wait for him to reply. I hope you won't think me rude, but I would like to go back to Joanna in Caernarfon as soon as possible."

"We quite understand, Jason, although we will be very sorry to see you leave so soon. What shall we do with any messages that arrive for you from the telegraph office?"

"Please read them. I do not expect any replies, but if there are any I imagine that they will do no more than inform us that my father knows I'm alive."

"When will you leave us, Jason?" asked my aunt a little sadly. "I sometimes think I will never get to know my nephew if he doesn't spend more time with me," she said in a plaintive aside to her husband.

I felt badly, as you can imagine, but I could do no more than say, "I'm sorry, Aunt Mary, but I really would like to go back to Joanna tomorrow. Perhaps after we are married Joanna and I can come and stay in Lenton for a time, if you will have us."

"Of course you can. We will be delighted to have you both," she answered more cheerfully.

I left them and went upstairs to my room to repack the clothes and other items I had arrived with not many days before. Next morning, I said goodbye to my uncle and aunt and set off for Caernarfon.

As I had not been able to tell Joanna exactly when I would return, I decided to spend a night in Liverpool so that I could see Captain Downing and my solicitor, Barnaby Williams, in the morning before travelling on to Caernarfon.

As I had on a number of previous occasions, I stayed in the Albion Hotel and after breakfast I only sent the bell boy to the solicitor's office, as it was more important to speak to him than to Captain Downing on this occasion. I would try to get an appointment with Captain Downing at the Gold Star Line office if I had time later.

The boy came back with a note from Barnaby Williams, giving me an appointment at half past nine. I set off about thirty minutes before the appointment to give myself adequate time to walk to the offices from which the prestigious firm of Williams, Henry & Compton practiced. The offices were in an imposing building in Dale Street and reached up a lino covered, dark, and dusty staircase. As I climbed the stairs, my footsteps echoed in the gas-lit stairwell and even though I knew the feeling to be false, it felt as if the building was totally uninhabited except for me. On the landing at the head of the first flight of stairs was the familiar door and there was a light from inside the office shining through the frosted glass panel set into the top half of the door. On the glass in a semicircle of black letters was the name William, Henry & Compton and horizontally, lined up with the "W" and the "n" was the word *Solicitors*.

I knocked and on receiving no response, knocked again a little louder and then opened the door and went in. A balding little man in a dingy frock coat looked up from a ledger then jumped to his feet with a smile of welcome.

"It's very good to see you again, Mr Smiley. Mr. Williams is expecting you so please come this way," and he lead me into the office used by Mr. Barnaby Williams, then turned and walked out again, closing the door quietly as he left.

I noticed that the piles of legal papers stacked on the carpet had not materially diminished since my previous visit but couldn't detect whether they were the same files or new ones as I stepped between them to reach the desk. Barnaby Williams stood up and came out from behind his desk to greet me very cordially.

"I am very pleased to see you are still in one piece," he said. "You don't look quite as well as the last time I saw you, so I hope you are in good health."

"I was quite ill, Mr. Williams, but I am recovering very well now. You should be aware that a so-called friend of my father has written to various people who know Captain Stewart and me and told them that I died in Bombay. As you can witness, I am still very much alive, but the letters have caused considerable distress."

"I can imagine they would," he said and asked who had sent the letters.

I told him what I knew, and at the end of my recital I said, "The really sad thing is that my father received the letter just before he sailed for Bombay and probably doesn't know the truth, although we have been sending telegraph messages to everyone we think he might come into contact with."

"That's really a dreadful act, Mr. Smiley. Why anyone would decide to write such a letter without first checking the truth of the situation I cannot imagine. Anyway, I assume that you have done everything you can to correct this distressing state of affairs."

"Yes," I said, "but I will not be easy in my mind until I know that my father has learnt the truth."

"Indeed!" he said, then added, "Please sit down, Mr. Smiley, and tell me how I can help you this morning."

I sat where he indicated and said, "First of all, perhaps you can tell me if my father received the letter I left with you and did he agree to my proposal to use Smiley Stewart as my new surname?"

"Yes, he agreed, and consequently I have made the necessary arrangements to legalise your change in name. I think you can safely use Smiley Stewart from now on if you haven't already started to do so."

"That's very good news," I responded. "The second subject concerns the money I sent to you from Bombay. I think I explained that it was a gift from the telegraph company."

"Yes, you did, and I thought it was not an overly generous amount considering the risks you took on their behalf. As you requested me to invest the money for you, I took advice from one of the partners in a brokerage company here and invested it over a wide range of companies who trade steadily if not spectacularly. I opened a bank account for you at the local branch of Lloyds Bank and the dividends are mounting up nicely. I will give you all the relevant papers to study and then you can decide whether you wish to change anything."

"That's also very good news, Mr. Williams," I said. "I'll certainly study the papers, but as I do not believe I can better the advice of a professional, I expect it will all remain as you have established it."

"Thank you, Mr. Smiley" he said, obviously pleased by my trust in his abilities and judgement.

"Now," I said, "I have some very good news to impart."

"Really?" said my solicitor, "I do enjoy hearing good news. More often than not in my profession the news is far from good, so I'm all agog to hear yours."

"In a month or so I hope to marry a beautiful and intelligent young lady, and I should be very disappointed if you are not able to attend the ceremony."

"That's very good news indeed, Mr. Smiley," said my legal advisor with a beaming smile of pleasure. "And may I know the name of the lady who has honoured you so?"

"She is Miss Joanna Evans and the only daughter of Captain Evans. You remember, the man who tried to charge my father with the murder of her brother." I saw his expression change but before he could make a comment that was sure to be condemnatory, I said, "My father has met Joanna and thought she was a lovely young woman. She has apologised to both my father and me for the behaviour of her father, so it would be churlish to harbour a grudge, now wouldn't it?"

"Yes, of course," he said and a smile replaced the frown that had appeared on his face.

Shortly afterwards I took my leave of Mr. Williams after promising to send him an invitation to the wedding as soon as possible.

I decided not to waste any more time by visiting Captain Downing, as the urge to be reunited with Joanna was becoming too insistent to ignore.

I walked to Lime Street Station, caught the first available train to

Caernarfon, and then hired a carriage to take me to Joanna's home. I reached there in the late afternoon and Joanna must have heard the carriage arrive as she appeared in the hallway moments after the maid had opened the front door. She came into my arms and embraced me with a lack of reticence that took my breath away. When we recovered our sense of decorum and moved apart, we went in search of Mrs. Evans so that I could say a polite "good evening."

Mrs. and Miss Evans had been busy during my absence. They had seen Eli Jones, the vicar of the local church, and he had agreed to officiate at our wedding on a Wednesday in six- to eight-weeks' time. The actual date was to be confirmed within two weeks.

When the three of us had finished talking about wedding plans, Joanna said, "How are your aunt and the Reverend Perceval?"

"Well enough when I left, I'm pleased to say, but not so well when I arrived."

"Were they ill, Jason?" Joanna enquired.

I said, "No, they were not unwell," and went on. "Please let me explain. As usual, I spent the night in Grantham and then took a carriage to the Vicarage. It was a wet, gloomy morning, and I was surprised to find that all the curtains were drawn as if they were mourning for someone. Anyway, I knocked on the front door and when the maid opened it, she collapsed in a faint on the doorstep as soon as she saw me. I called my aunt and when she saw me standing in the doorway she was clearly very frightened and became deathly pale. I'm sorry to relate that my unexpected arrival was something of a shock for the whole household."

"Why was that?" asked an incredulous Joanna.

"The previous day they had received a letter from Bombay. It was from a supposed friend of my father's, and he wrote that I had died and as a result he offered his condolences. My appearance was so unexpected that they thought I was a ghost and even Aunt Mary, who is a very down-to-earth lady, had to pinch my arm in order to be sure that I wasn't."

"How dreadful," said two wide-eyed ladies almost in unison.

"Yes, it was," I answered. "And what is much worse is the fact that my father received a similar letter from the same man and is somewhere between Britain and India believing that I died in Bombay. I have been sending messages by telegraph to everyone who might be able to contact my father and tell him the truth, but I don't know whether he knows yet."

"Oh! Jason," cried Joanna, "how could the man have been so stupid? He only had to ask at the hospital to have found out the truth."

"I know," I responded. "One day we might find out what motivated him, but for now we have our own lives to lead and much too much to arrange to waste time on speculation."

"That's very true, Jason," said my sensible wife-to-be.

Over the next six weeks, what appeared initially to be a series of intractable obstacles to the organisation of our marriage were resolved without apparent effort, and we were left wondering why we had been so concerned about them in the first place. The wedding dress, the bridesmaids' dresses, the "should young cousin David be a page boy?" questions were all addressed and answered, but to Joanna's "who will be your best man, Jason?" I had no favourite candidate to propose.

Joanna had a similar dilemma, as she couldn't think of anyone she could ask to give her away at the ceremony either—two vital supporters at the wedding and there was no one to audition for the parts and time was getting short.

One morning twelve days and only a few hours before the ceremony was scheduled to commence, a messenger boy arrived at the front door just as I was going out. I took the proffered message, gave the lad a few pence, and walked past him in an absentminded way.

"Excuse me, sir," he said meekly, "but the gentleman who gave me the message said I was to wait for a reply."

I took the hint, slit the envelope, and took out a sheet of Royal Hotel paper and found myself looking at a few lines of very familiar handwriting. The writer said,

> Dear Mr. Smiley,
>   I should be very pleased to call upon you if you are not too busy.
>   Yours sincerely,
>   Neil Fairweather

A reply in the affirmative was soon on its way back to the Royal Hotel, and an hour later Joanna and I took very great pleasure in greeting Neil Fairweather and then introducing him to Mrs. Evans.

After the usual interchange of who he was, what he did, and where Neil Fairweather fitted into my life and, more recently, Joanna's, my wife-to-be said, "Mr. Fairweather, I hope you will be able to stay in Caernarfon and come to our wedding. Jason and I would be thrilled if you are able to agree."

"I should be honoured to attend," he said. "I don't know about staying in Caernarfon until the wedding, but as I'm home on leave, I am a free agent for several months and will come back in good time."

I had an inspiration and said, "Mr. Fairweather, do you think you know me well enough to be my best man? I should be honoured if you would consent."

Before he had time to answer, Joanna had squeezed my arm and said, "What a marvellous idea, Jason!" To Mr. Fairweather she said, "Please say yes, Mr. Fairweather. I cannot think of anyone I would rather see as Jason's best man."

Fairweather said, "I should be honoured Mr. Smiley," and then added with a grin, "If you hadn't asked me, I would never have spoken to you again."

Later over dinner the subject of Joanna's supporter became the main topic of conversation.

As an outsider, Neil Fairweather very quickly focussed our thoughts by saying, "Don't you have any male friends who are old enough to act instead of your father, Miss Joanna?"

"The only man I know who is old enough is Jason's father, and I'm not sure he could be described as a friend. In any case, he will be too busy keeping an eye on my future husband."

"I agree," said Fairweather and looked at me with a grin. "Tell me, Miss Joanna, do you have no male relatives in all this vast county of Caernarfon?"

"Well! Yes, I do," Joanna answered, "but my father managed to offend Uncle Tudor and Uncle Gwyn during the last years of his life and they have kept their distance since. Uncle Tudor was a particular favourite of mine. He is the headmaster of the grammar school for boys in Bangor."

"Don't you think that your wedding could be a heaven-sent opportunity for a reconciliation?" asked Fairweather of Mrs. and Miss Evans.

"Yes," said Mrs. Evans. "It would be so nice to be a family again. When your father died," she reminded Joanna, "only your uncles came to the service, and they left as soon as the coffin was in the ground."

"But how do we manage to rebuild the bridges with so little time left?" asked Joanna, clearly enamoured of the idea but taking a practical view of the difficulties.

"We will have to go to visit them and personally invite them to our wedding," I said.

"Exactly," agreed Fairweather. "There isn't time for an exchange of letters, and the personal touch might be better in any case. If you both go to see them and deliver the wedding invitation with an appropriate apology for the rift your father caused, if that's appropriate, it might start the family on the path to reconciliation,"

"That's a lovely idea," agreed Mrs. Evans. "Will you go and eat humble pie for the sake of the family, Joanna?"

"Of course I will, and with Jason's support, I'm sure we will be successful. We'll try to see them tomorrow. Both families live in Bangor, so we should be able to visit both of them during one day."

After dinner and just before Fairweather went back to his hotel, I arranged with his coachman to come back early the following day to take Joanna and me to Bangor and, as we were unsure about our reception, Joanna and I decided to take a wicker basket containing food and drink with us in case we were not received as cordially as we hoped.

At eight the next morning the coachman stopped at the front gate. Joanna and I climbed aboard the coach, and we set out on the two-hour drive to Bangor with our picnic basket on the seat opposite us. Mrs. Evans had carefully penned the invitations in her very best handwriting after Mr. Fairweather had departed the previous evening and Joanna equally carefully placed them in her handbag for safekeeping. The weather was quite pleasant and the countryside more so, but Joanna was not in a casual, chatty, look-at-the-view frame of mind. The role of peacemaker worried her, and she couldn't make up her mind how she should begin or what she should say.

"Should I say, 'Good morning, how are you? I'm sorry my father offended you,' or 'Good morning. I'm sorry my father offended you. I hope you are well,'" Joanna postulated. "I really do not know how to begin, Jason, and it will be so important to make a good first impression."

"Will they recognise you?" I asked.

"What?" said Joanna, deep in worried thought. "I don't know, but it's probable. Why do you ask?"

"Only that you may need to start with 'Good morning my name is' if they don't, and then you could introduce me and that might distract their attention long enough to start an icebreaking conversation," I suggested.

We hadn't come to a conclusion before the coachman started asking for detailed directions to the headmaster's house and then we were in St. Paul's Terrace and dismounting from the carriage in front of a lovely cottage with a thatched roof, leaded light windows, and pink-coloured walls. It looked like something from a picture book. There was a woman in the garden weeding between some enormous hollyhocks. She straightened up and arched backwards to stretch her spine as she heard us dismounting.

I had no idea who the lady was, but it was a reasonable assumption that she was the wife of Joanna's Uncle Tudor, so I looked over the gate and said, "You have a beautiful cottage, Mrs. Evans, and I haven't seen hollyhocks as nice as those since my mother died."

"Thank you, sir, that's very kind of you," she said cheerfully, then a frown darkened her face. "I don't know you, sir, and I'm sure that I have never been introduced to you."

"You are correct, Mrs. Evans; we have never been introduced, but I know your name because my fiancé has come here with me. She wishes to apologise for her father's behaviour toward you and your husband and also to ask you to honour us both with your presence at our wedding in two weeks' time," and I reached back to pull Joanna forward into Mrs. Evans's view.

"Joanna!" she said. "I didn't ever expect to see you in front of my door after what your father did," and her face darkened with angry memories.

"Aunt Emily," said Joanna, "it cannot be easy for you to see me on your doorstep, but it is not easy for me either. As Jason said, I have come to apologise on behalf of my mother and also myself for my father's actions. We would like to invite you and your husband to our wedding in the hope it will begin the reconciliation of our families."

"I don't know!" she said and turned away toward her front door and the sanctuary it offered from an upsetting visitation.

I said, "Mrs. Evans, it cannot be easy for you to face such a situation alone, but perhaps it would be possible for us all to wait until your husband comes home so that we can talk it over with him as well."

Reluctantly, grudgingly, she said, "You'd better come in then," and led us into the cottage and through to the kitchen. "Wait here!" she said, indicating two chairs beside the scrubbed wooden kitchen table, "and I will go and see if Tudor can leave the school and come home now." She left the cottage through the back door.

Joanna looked at me for a moment and said, "That was very clever, Jason. There I was worrying about how to start a conversation and you made the opening for me."

"I was lucky that the cottage looked so well. It would have been much more difficult if it had been a hovel."

"The Evans do not live in hovels, Jason," she said sternly, "but I understand what you mean."

I reached across the table and took Joanna's small but capably strong fingers into my hand and was thrilled by the gentle pressure of her grip in return. We sat hand in hand for only a few minutes before the kitchen door banged open and a man strode in with Mrs. Evans trailing a few steps behind. My assumption that he was Uncle Tudor was confirmed by Joanna's polite greeting and an enquiry after his health. Both were ignored.

He said angrily, "After all these years why have you come here to upset my life? Didn't your father do me enough damage without you coming here to cause another upset?"

Joanna was so upset by this angry outburst that her mouth opened and closed a few times but she was unable to utter a word.

I said into the angry silence, "We came here to hold out an olive branch, Mr. Evans. We hoped that you and your wife would accept an invitation to our wedding. We have no intention of causing you discomfort or damage, and if your opinion is not open to persuasion then we are wasting our time here, and we will return to Caernarfon immediately," and I stood up to leave and held out my hand to Joanna to help her up from her seat.

As Joanna stood up, she said, "Uncle Tudor, it is a matter of great personal sadness to realise that you are as stubborn and pigheaded as my father. My mother and I have no knowledge of this great wrong that you claim my father did to you, and I am sure she will be as sad about your intransigence as I am. We all hoped that you would do me the honour of escorting me down the aisle on my wedding day, but clearly that is quite impossible in the circumstances."

Joanna turned and with her head erect and her back as straight as a guardsman's, she swept out of the kitchen and down the hall to the front door. She paused momentarily at the front door so that I could open it for her and then continued her dignified withdrawal from the house of her estranged uncle and aunt and climbed into the waiting coach. I called to the coachman to proceed as I climbed into the coach, and moments later the carriage lurched into motion.

As I stretched out and put my arm about Joanna's shoulders to offer her a modicum of comfort in her disappointment, we heard Tudor Evans shouting, "Stop, Joanna! Please stop!" I looked back and saw him rush out of the garden gate and start to run along the road behind us. I called up to the coachman and he quickly brought his horses to a halt.

When he came to where Joanna and I sat in the coach and had recovered his breath, he said, "Miss Joanna, please forgive me for my rudeness. I hope you will come back to the house and talk with us again."

We went back and explained again why we were there. As the atmosphere started to thaw, Mrs. Emily Evans made tea and produced homemade cakes and a strawberry jam that was at least as good as any my mother had made. Tudor Evans agreed to give Joanna away, and after an hour of increasingly friendly conversation we told them that we had to go to see Mr. Gwyn Evans.

"I'll come with you," said Tudor Evans, "and then I can explain why you are here and hopefully we'll avoid unnecessary bad words."

Joanna thanked him for his thoughtfulness, and we drove across Bangor to the home of Uncle Gwyn and Aunt Llynos in Victoria Avenue near to the Infirmary.

Following Uncle Tudor's advice, Joanna and I sat outside in the carriage and watched as Mr. and Mrs. Tudor Evans walked along a short, crazy paving path to a solid-looking front door adorned with a big brass knocker. We saw and heard Tudor Evans beat a tattoo with the knocker. After a pause, the door opened but we could not see who had done so. Mr. and Mrs. Evans stepped inside and the door closed again. After a silence that must have lasted several minutes and had Joanna and me sitting on the edges of our seats and straining our ears for the slightest sound, we heard more distinctly than we wished the unmistakeable sounds of grown men quarrelling. The angry sounds went on for a few minutes and then there was silence. After a moment or two, we started to breathe a sigh of relief, only to hear the quarrelling start again. It was a shorter argument this time and the next period of silence was longer and we started to hope for a peaceful conclusion to our day.

The front door opened and Uncle Tudor beckoned to us to come to the cottage. At the doorway I stood back to let Joanna precede me and immediately realised that I had made a mistake when I heard a female voice shout, "Is that you, Joanna? Trust your family to send a woman to do a man's work."

Instinctively I pushed in front of Joanna and confronted the woman who had spoken. I said angrily, "There are no male Evans left, now that Joanna's father and brother are both dead. She has no idea what has offended you, but she is doing her best to correct a wrong done to you by her dead father."

"Be quiet, Llynos," ordered Tudor Evans, then in a calmer voice he added, "The dispute will not be resolved by behaving rudely to Joanna."

I said, "Everyone talks about a dispute or disagreement, but neither Joanna nor I have any knowledge of it. Would one of you please explain?"

"Who are you?" the woman called Llynos asked aggressively.

"I am Jason Smiley Stewart, and I have the honour to be Miss Joanna's fiancé," I answered.

"Jason Smiley Stewart is it?" she mimicked. "A very upper-crust man you've got for yourself, Miss Joanna. I can hear that he's English. Welsh boys not good enough for you, I see."

"Yes, I'm English" I answered, trying to deflect the conversation from Joanna, who I could feel trembling at my side, and then I strained the truth a little by saying, "I'm sure my blacksmith father would have been thrilled to hear me described as 'upper crust' if he had been alive to hear it. I asked a few minutes ago for an explanation of the dispute but have only been insulted." I let the anger I was feeling creep into my voice as I said, "I have no stomach for further acrimonious conversation with people who cannot see that Joanna is making a genuine effort at reconciliation. Good afternoon to you," and once again Joanna and I walked out of someone's house, climbed into the carriage' and drove away.

This time no one followed us and for that I was thankful.

After a long silence Joanna turned to me, took my hand' and said, "I'm so sorry you were subjected to such a display of bad manners by my relations."

"Well it was only one relation, and as I imagine that Mrs. Llynos Evans is only related by marriage, you need not feel guilty on her account. I'm sorry her husband did not make more of an effort, but at least your Uncle Tudor has accepted the invitation, and that was the main purpose of our journey."

"I wonder what the disagreement is about," Joanna wondered. "My mother doesn't know, and I did hope my uncles might tell us but they only complained without being specific."

"I don't think there is anything we can do now, but after the wedding we will have time to try again."

"That's true, Jason," Joanna said. She relaxed against me, leant her head against my shoulder, and slept for the rest of the journey to Caernarfon.

It had been a tiring and stressful day and recounting the events to Mrs. Evans during dinner did nothing to ease our low spirits. We all knew that the key to resolving the problem between the various branches of the family lay in discovering what had caused the rift in the first place.

But Joanna and her mother did not know and both uncles seemed to be too angry to explain the problem to us. It was an impasse!

Not surprisingly, we went to bed very early that night.

In the morning Joanna went with her mother to the seamstress for another fitting of her wedding dress, and I settled down with a newspaper forlornly hoping that I would be entertained by it until my love returned. About thirty minutes after their departure, the maid came to me with a note on a silver tray.

She said as she proffered the tray, "A gentleman delivered this note, Mr. Stewart, and said it was to be delivered into your hands alone. He wouldn't wait for a reply."

"Thank you, Mary," I said, and took the note from the tray. I opened it and read.

> Dear Mr. Stewart,
>
> I would like to talk to you but not at Joanna's home. I shall be at the White Feathers for the next hour if you are able to come there.
>
> Yours faithfully,
>
> Gwyn Evans

I read the letter a second time to make sure I had understood the contents correctly, and my surprise was in no way diminished by reading it again.

After yesterday's charade, I couldn't imagine what he had to say, but there was only one way to find out and that was to go to the Feathers. I jumped up, went into the hall, and put on my coat and hat. I picked up a stout walking stick, told the maid I would be out for about an hour, and set forth on the fifteen-minute walk to the inn Gwyn Evans had named. I walked into the taproom and there immediately in front of me was Mr. Gwyn Evans, and I was struck by the strong resemblance between him and Tudor Evans.

"Good morning, Mr. Evans," I said.

"Good morning, Mr. Stewart. Thank you very much for coming here at such short notice."

"What is all this about, Mr. Evans?" I asked.

"Please come and sit down and I'll explain" and he led the way into a small private room where we sat down on opposite sides of a small, square table.

"First of all," he said, "I must apologise for the way my wife spoke to you yesterday. Llynos feels our loss of station rather more than I do, although there are times when it is difficult to be philosophical about our lives. Tudor was not hit so badly and also kept his post as the headmaster."

"It would be of great benefit if you would tell me what has happened," I said bluntly.

"Yes, of course," he said. "Stupid of me."

With some difficulty, I managed to restrain the impulse to voice my agreement with his sentiment, but I did point out in very strong terms that I wasn't clairvoyant and if he wanted my help he should explain exactly what had happened to cause the estrangement.

He said, "Not long before his son died, Captain Evans came to Tudor and me and suggested that we put some money into a company that he knew was doing very well. We could expect to accrue some nice dividends if we followed his advice. I didn't have the savings required to pay my share, but I allowed my Llynos to persuade me to borrow enough money. Tudor invested his entire life savings. Between the three of us we expected to own about half the company. Captain Evans took our money and undertook to make the necessary arrangements for the purchase of the shares, but then his son died and he started his vendetta against Captain Stewart.

"After a decent interval, we asked him what he had done with the shares, but he was already ninety percent mad with grief and denied all knowledge of the agreement. Tudor lost his money but kept his employment and self esteem. I lost everything. I had to sell our house and all our possessions to pay off the debt, and I lost my position in the bank because I had shown such a lack of judgement. I work in the infirmary now. I'm a clerk in the office, and my wife has to take in laundry so that we can make ends meet. Can you wonder why we feel so bitter?" he asked in a sombre tone of voice.

"No," I responded. "Thank you for taking me into your confidence,

Mr. Evans. I wish there was something I could do to help you and your wife."

"Thank you, Mr. Stewart, but there is nothing that you can do for us. For our part all we can do is count the cost of our greed. I'm sure that you can understand why we will not come to your wedding." With brutal honesty, he added, "We could not come even if we wanted to, as we have nothing to wear to such a grand affair, and we certainly couldn't afford a wedding present."

"I understand," I said, wishing that I didn't have to confront his poverty.

He said, "Please do not mention our meeting to anyone, as I do not want my Llynos to find out about it. She still has her pride and wouldn't want a stranger to learn about our shame."

"I understand," I said again, "I will do my best to comply with your wishes, but I may have to tell Joanna in confidence if she asks where I have been this morning."

He nodded in understanding.

I stood up, said a cordial good day to Gwyn Evans, walked out of the inn, and started the journey home deep in thought about what I had heard and what, if anything, I could do about it.

I was at home before Joanna and her mother returned, and as no one remarked upon my absence I chose not to say anything about my meeting with Gwyn Evans.

Early the next morning during breakfast Joanna said, "I'm surprised that we have heard nothing from your father, Jason."

"I am as well," I responded, "but there is nothing more I can do except possibly go to Liverpool and ask Captain Downing and Barnaby Williams if they have learnt anything since I last spoke to them."

"I think that might be a good idea, Jason. At least we will have the latest news or know there is no news. Either result is better than ignorance."

"Very true, Joanna, but when do you think I should go? I don't like leaving you when the preparations for the wedding are not complete."

"After they are complete, Jason, there will be no point going, as the wedding will be over."

"Very true," I responded. "I hadn't thought of that. I suppose I had better go today and try to come back by tomorrow night."

"I agree, my love," said my future wife.

An hour later I was sitting in a train rattling and smoking along the north Wales coast toward Liverpool.

I went to the Albion and took a room for the night with an option on a second and, after leaving my bag in the room, went to the office of Barnaby Williams. If he was too busy to see me or if he was appearing in court then I would have to make an appointment to see him at his convenience. I climbed the familiar stairs, spoke to the clerk, and five minutes later was back in the street with an appointment for nine the following morning. With Captain Downing I was more fortunate, as he was available and prepared to see me immediately.

As I sat down in the visitor's chair, he said, "Thank you for the invitation to your wedding, Mr. Smiley," then he paused and said, "I'm sorry. Mr. Stewart, I should say. I had quite forgotten that you have adopted your father's name. Anyway, I will be very happy to attend your wedding. Have you heard from your father yet?"

"No, nothing," I responded a little despondently. "I came to see you hoping that you might have some news. Has he not returned from Bombay yet?"

"Oh! Yes," Captain Downing responded, "more than a week ago and he knew that the announcement of your death had been somewhat premature. I gather he had some strong words to say to his erstwhile friend for spreading such a rumour. I wish I had been a fly on the wall at that discussion because when your father is filled with totally justified anger, he is a sight well worth hearing and witnessing. He would put the fire and brimstone preachers to shame when he is in full flow."

"I wonder, Captain, do you know if he has received his invitation to the wedding?" I asked.

"Yes, he has and he definitely intends to be there to see you safely wedded. Didn't he write to you?"

"I hadn't received a letter up to this morning," I said. "Is he still in Liverpool? If he is, I could arrange to meet him."

"He's not in Liverpool as far as I know," said Captain Downing. "He had a letter from Scotland and has gone rushing off up there. It was something to do with his brother, I believe, so he left his first mate in charge of the ship and was on a train north within the hour."

"It's good to know that he will come to the wedding, Captain, and I'm sure I'll hear all the news from Scotland in due course. Thank you for your time, Captain Downing. I look forward to seeing you at the wedding next week."

"I shall be there, Mr. Stewart, have no fear."

It was already late in the afternoon when I left the offices of the Gold Star Line, and as there was nothing more I could do until morning, I went back to my hotel. I read the newspapers in the hotel's first floor sitting room until dinner and then retired to my room intending to sleep. In the event, I lay in bed completely awake and wondering what had caused my father to rush away to Scotland as he had. Remembering what my Aunt Mary had told Joanna and me before I went back to Bombay the last time, I felt that it could only be bad news, but the whys and wherefores would have to wait upon the return of my father. I was glad that he was no longer grieving for me, and like Captain Downing I did wish I had been able to listen to the conversation when he confronted his letter-writing friend. I imagined that the language would have been distinctly salty, and with that slightly humorous thought, I went fast asleep.

Next morning, after a substantial breakfast of bacon, black pudding, and fried eggs, I set off to walk to Dale Street to keep my appointment with Mr. Barnaby Williams. I was punctual and as usually happened now, I was shown into Mr. William's office as soon as I arrived. There was no longer the clerk's, "I'll just see if he's in, sir," delaying tactic that I had experienced before previous meetings with my solicitor.

Barnaby Williams came around to the front of his desk hand outstretched in welcome and said simply, "As always, I am pleased to see you in my office, Mr. Stewart, and I hope you are in better health than when we last met."

"Good morning, Mr. Williams. Yes, my health is improving daily, I'm glad to say. I don't want to take up your valuable time, Mr. Williams, but I wonder if my father has been in touch with you over the past week?"

"No, he hasn't," was the instant reply. "I didn't know he was back in Liverpool."

That was a disappointment, and I said, "I'm sorry to hear that. I spoke to Captain Downing yesterday afternoon, and he was able to tell me that my father had returned to Liverpool about a week ago but had gone immediately to Scotland on family business. I have no idea why he has gone and hoped you might. Clearly, you are as much in the dark as I am, Mr. Williams."

"So it appears," Barnaby Williams said, "but if I hear anything, I will let you know, and I hope you will keep me informed of any news you receive."

"Of course," I responded and stood up to leave. Just as I was about to walk out of the office, I remembered the story Gwyn Evans had told me and asked, "Can you spare me some more of your time, Mr. Williams? I would like your advice about a strange story I have heard."

"Of course," he said and looked intently at the cartwheel of a watch he pulled from his waistcoat pocket. "My next appointment isn't until ten, and he is usually late, so you can have my undivided attention until he arrives."

"Thank you, Mr. Williams," I said and I sat down again.

"You remember Captain Evans, of course, but at the time we were involved with him during the enquiry, he was already showing signs of mental illness due to his grief for his son. What I have to relate this morning took place at least in part before John Evans died so tragically. It was like this. A few days ago I met both of Captain Evans's brothers," and I went on to describe the visit Joanna and I had made to Tudor and Gwyn Evans in Bangor and the subsequent meeting I had with Gwyn Evans in Caernarfon.

I went on, "Before John Evans died, and that is when this purchase of shares was supposed to take place, I think it is fair to describe Captain Evans as a competent and intelligent man. I have to assume he was also honest, as I know nothing to his detriment. I would like to believe that the shares were purchased, but before the details of the transaction could be revealed to the brothers, he received the news of his son's death. Captain Evans became progressively more senile due to his grief and denied all knowledge of the transaction as a result. As far as I know, Captain Evans died without recovering his faculties."

"It's a plausible explanation, Mr. Stewart, but I know nothing about it, as I was never Captain Evans's solicitor."

"I realise that," I answered, "but it might be possible to obtain information from his solicitor or someone who knew him. I think a very serious wrong has been done to two families whose only real fault was greed. It would be nice to put it right, and you may know someone who could help."

"I'll think about it, Mr. Stewart," Mr. Williams said as his clerk entered the office and announced, "Mr. Prendergast is here. Shall I show him in, sir?"

"Yes, but first escort Mr. Stewart out," and he stood up, shook my hand, and just as he reached out to pick up some papers from the corner of his desk, he hesitated for a moment, then said, "I'm very sorry, Mr. Stewart. I nearly forgot. Thank you for the wedding invitation. I will write, of course, to accept formally, but I will be honoured to attend your wedding, and I look forward to meeting the young lady who has chosen Mr. Jason Smiley Stewart as her lifelong partner. She is lady with good judgement. Good morning, Mr. Stewart."

"Thank you, Mr. Williams," I managed to say inadequately as I turned to follow the clerk from the room.

I walked back to the hotel and paid my bill. I carried my bag over to the station and caught the first train back to Caernarfon.

I explained to Joanna and her mother what I had learnt and Joanna summed up the situation quite neatly by saying about my father, "He knows you're alive. He has our wedding invitation and there is nothing more to be done until he contacts us."

"It must have been very serious for him to rush off to a place he hasn't seen for so many years," I said, "but I do wish he would enlighten us."

We had a quiet family dinner. Mrs Evans was there to be our chaperone, and we went to bed with the knowledge that there were not many more days before we would be man and wife and sleeping together. The desire to pre-empt that joyous state was very strong in me, and I think that either Joanna sensed my feelings or had similar feelings herself because next morning she came and sat beside me in the morning room where I was reading the latest paper.

She took my hand and said, "Jason, I think it would be more seemly if we lived apart until our wedding night," and her voice tightened up as the import of the words "wedding night" became a closer reality than ever. "I love you so much, Jason, and I want to make you a present of my body, but we have to wait until we are married. And that is the most difficult part. Just waiting another few days until we are man and wife will be purgatory but easier to bear if you are not so close to me all the time. Whilst you sleep here, I do not know how I manage to stay in my bed each night my desire to be with you is so strong."

I said, "Joanna, my darling wife-to-be, you are so brave to speak as you have and, of course, I will go away. I have to accept that it will be easier for me as well as you. It is difficult being a gentleman when your bed is only a couple of yards away. I'll go to the Royal and sleep there."

THREE

Marriage

So for the next seven days I spent the daylight hours with Joanna in her home and the nights tossing and turning in my chaste bachelor bed in the Royal Hotel. Fairweather arrived some days before the wedding, checked what had been arranged, and quickly organised everything that had been forgotten.

One wet afternoon he asked, "Do you ever think about Telegraph Island now, or is the memory still too painful?"

"Actually, I have been so busy helping Joanna with the organisation of our wedding I have given no thought to my previous life at all. Did Mustafa Kamal ever make contact with you?"

"No, not with me," Fairweather said. "Pollack went back to the island as superintendent, and Mustafa Kamal went to see him. Kamal was very distressed about your wound. I think the possibility of repercussions from Muscat when they learn that one of the fishermen tried to kill Jason Smiley, a trusted servant of The Queen, also exercised his mind. Anyway, a new agreement was concluded and the cable hasn't been damaged since. We still do not know what has happened to the missing operator. Ashton was certified as insane and his two companions insist they know nothing, and there the matter rested when I left Bombay for home."

"Thank you, Mr. Fairweather," I said, but my recollections of those days made my mood more than a little sombre for the rest of the day.

On the day before the wedding when it was deemed inappropriate for me to see my bride, Fairweather insisted that I show him around those parts of Caernarfon that I had visited with Joanna, and when we returned to the Royal, he read my speech and suggested several amendments.

Then, to my absolute astonishment, he said, "Now, Mr. Stewart, I want you to read your speech out loud. I will be your audience today."

"I don't think that's necessary, Mr. Fairweather. I wrote the speech after all and know what I've written down."

"As your friend and advisor for many years, have you ever known me ask for something unnecessary, Mr. Stewart?"

"No, never," I had to admit.

"Then please read your speech out loud in a voice that will reach to the back of a room, remembering at the same time that your new wife will be sitting beside you and there will be many people staring at you. You would not wish to make a mistake in front of Joanna now, would you?"

"No! Most definitely not," I said with feeling.

"Then please begin," said my cheerfully benign tormentor.

Thinking that this was the most ridiculous activity I had ever embarked upon, I stood up and said, "Ladies and Gentlemen," and stopped, as I couldn't remember what came next. Fairweather said not a word, but I felt his eyes upon me and my cheeks redden with embarrassment.

He handed me my speech and said calmly, "It's better to have this in your hands and read from it if necessary."

I started again and very quickly found that my breathing did not suit the construction of my sentences, and I ground to a halt halfway through a particularly flowery phrase as I had completely run out of air. It didn't create the impression I had been seeking. Over the next hour or so, I practiced and edited and practiced again under the constant tutelage of Mr. Neil Fairweather. In the end, I had a well-constructed speech that I could speak quite well and also a sore throat.

"Thank you, Mr. Fairweather," I croaked when he was satisfied. "I had never realised how difficult it is to prepare even a short speech."

"It's something that we all have to learn," he said.

Fairweather and I had dinner together but did nothing to commemorate my last night as a bachelor. I went to bed hoping to sleep but was kept awake for a long time by the realisation that in less than twenty-four hours I would be totally responsible for the welfare of another human being—someone who was bestowing her love and trust on me and I hoped I would always be worthy of both. More enjoyable, of course, was the realisation that I would never again willingly sleep alone.

I am sure that every bride dreams that her wedding day will be warm and sunny, but our wedding day dawned with thick, low clouds and torrential rain. As I looked out at the rainwater sluicing down my bedroom window, I did so want to go to Joanna and comfort her in her disappointment—to assure her that, in my eyes, she was the important element and not the weather—but I could not.

I washed, dressed, and then went downstairs where I joined my best man in the breakfast room. After a substantial breakfast, we went to our rooms and I made the final preparations for my entry into the state of marriage and tried to control my increasingly nervous demeanour. Fairweather came and inspected the end result and made a few adjustments to my clothing, admired the shine the boot boy had put on my boots, and suggested that the time had come to set off for the church.

As we walked out into the corridor, Fairweather turned to me and asked "I'm sure you have the ring in a safe place, but do you have your speech in your pocket?"

I felt in the pocket I thought I had put it in and found nothing and felt panic setting in as I searched pocket after pocket without success. We went back into my room and Fairweather picked the speech up off the dressing table and in so doing he uncovered the wedding ring, which had been lying underneath.

He gave me the speech and as I put it into my pocket he said, "I'll take charge of Joanna's wedding ring until the service. It's a little difficult getting married without it."

"Thank you, Mr. Fairweather," I said with heartfelt gratitude.

"Not at all," he said. "That's what a best man is supposed to do. Look after the groom when his nerves take charge."

We went out side and found that the rain had eased from torrential to heavy and the clouds were a little higher.

"Do you think this is an augury of better weather to come?" I asked Mr. Fairweather.

He looked out to the west where most of our weather comes from and said, "It's certainly possible. There is a small patch of blue out there."

We climbed into the coach with only a sprinkling of rainwater dampening our coats and settled down for the ride to the church. When we arrived at St. Peblig's, the rain had eased some more and the patch of blue had grown much larger. We hurried from the coach into the church and walked down the central aisle with our footsteps echoing through the whole building. We sat down on the front pew on the right-hand side of the church. There was no one else in the building, and the silence seemed to press down on us.

I whispered to Fairweather, "I wonder who will be first to come."

My companion was clearly not as awed by his surroundings as I was and said in his normal tones, "I cannot imagine—but I wish we had heard something from your father."

"Indeed," I said with a voice tightened by my nerves.

The big iron handle on the church door clattered as it was turned. The door swung open with a screech from rusty hinges then there was a *screech-bang* as it was shut again rather vigorously. Confident footsteps started to march down the aisle toward us, and Fairweather and I turned simultaneously to look along the church and saw a small slim man in a cassock approaching.

Fairweather and I stood, and as the priest reached us, I said, "Good morning, Reverend Jones. May I introduce my companion?" and when he nodded and extended his hand, I said, "Mr. Fairweather, I would like you to meet the Reverend Eli Jones, who will perform the marriage ceremony this morning. Reverend Jones, Mr. Fairweather is my best man and has been a friend and guide for many years."

"I'm very pleased to welcome you to my church, Mr. Fairweather. I gather from Miss Joanna that you have spent many years in Bombay. If there is time today, perhaps you could tell me a little about your experiences in such a distant land."

"I should be honoured, Reverend," said Fairweather, "but you should hear about my companion's adventures. He is not known as the Hero of Mussendam for nothing."

The Reverend Jones looked rather surprised at Fairweather's description of me and said, "As Mr. Stewart will stay in the area after his marriage, I will have plenty of time to find out about his heroics if he is not too modest to talk about his experiences. Now, if you will excuse me, I must prepare for the service," and he bustled away into the vestry.

The door rattled and screeched open but wasn't closed again, and we could hear the rattle and crunch of approaching coach tyres and the murmur of people softly conversing outside the church door. A beam of sunlight shone through one of the stained glass windows and lit up some of the pews in a rosy glow for a moment or two before disappearing again.

Perhaps Joanna will be blessed with sunshine after all, I hoped in my thoughts.

In ones and twos people started to file into the church and sit in pews somewhere between the middle and the back. *Like little school children trying not to be in the teacher's eye,* I thought. All the people who arrived early were clearly friends of the bride's family, as they sat on the left leaving my side of the church depressingly empty.

Captain Downing arrived in full dress uniform. He marched to the front of the church and said in his quarterdeck voice, "Good morning, Mr Stewart," as he shook my hand. "I hope you are well. I'm pleased to report that the weather has bucked up a little and should be just right for the arrival of your bride."

"Thank you, Captain," I said inadequately. "That's very good news. May I introduce my best man, Mr. Fairweather?" They shook hands and exchanged a few pleasantries.

Captain Downing turned back to me and said, "I have heard nothing from your father, Mr. Stewart, have you?"

"No, sir, nothing," was all I could say.

"I'm very sorry to hear that. We can only wait until he contacts us, I suppose," and he went and sat in the pew immediately behind mine.

My aunt and the Reverend Perceval arrived shortly afterwards, and they were closely followed by Barnaby Williams. Since the invitations had been sent out, I had recognised that my side of the church would look rather empty, but the reality was so much worse. I had only five people supporting me, and on Miss Joanna's side of the aisle there were about fifty.

Mrs. Evans and her sister-in-law, Emily Evans, arrived and went to a pew near the front of the church. It was nearly time for Joanna to arrive and it appeared as if she would be on time, for which I was thankful. We heard the wheels of a carriage crunching over the gravel outside the church; the verger shut the door, and we could hear nothing more from outside. The Reverend Jones marched along the aisle with his choir boys in ranks behind and they came to a halt in front of the porch door. Fairweather and I got up and moved to stand in front of the altar. With a great effort of will I managed to restrain my desire to turn around and see my future wife as the door to the church reopened. The schoolmaster's wife started to pump enthusiastically with her legs whilst her fingers flew across the keys of the harmonium to play "The Bridal Chorus". I heard the congregation stand as I stared at the altar and had to be content with the muffled sounds of appreciation as Joanna, on Uncle Tudor's arm, walked down the aisle toward the altar where I waited.

Then I was aware of a vision in white beside me, and our fingers found each other and gently squeezed. I stole a glance at her as she lifted her veil and whispered in her ear, "You look beautiful, Joanna."

"Thank you, my dear," she said with a radiant smile.

The Reverend Eli Jones had just taken his place in front of us when we heard a carriage crunch to a halt outside, then the church door rattled and creaked open and almost as quickly creaked shut. Eli Jones's eyes widened in surprise for a moment, but whoever it was who came in sat in a pew at the very back of the church and was soon forgotten about.

The Reverend Eli Jones started reciting the words of the marriage service.

I should have paid more attention, but I was so awestruck that some-one like Joanna would willingly tie herself to Jason Smiley Stewart and so ecstatically happy at the prospect that I remember almost nothing about the service at all. It passed like a dream except for the moment when I put the ring on Joanna's finger and a little later when I kissed her in front of the congregation.

At the conclusion of the service, the Reverend Eli Jones turned away from us to lead us into the vestry to sign the register.

As Joanna and I started to follow the Reverend Jones, I saw Mrs. Evans out of the corner of my eye as she got up from her pew to join the procession, but I could also hear the heavy, regular footsteps of some-one striding deliberately down the aisle toward us from the back of the church. Then there came the rustle of clothing as people in the congregation turned to look back, followed by the whispers of excited speculation about the identity of the newcomer.

Fairweather said in a voice just loud enough for Joanna and I to both hear, "It's your father, Jason."

Joanna and I stopped, looked back, and simultaneously gasped in surprise. I imagine that Joanna expected to see someone in naval uniform just as I had, but what we saw was Captain James Stewart's face surmounting the full tartan-kilted splendour of a Scottish chieftain.

I managed to close my mouth, which had dropped open from the surprise, and when he joined us, managed to say with remarkable calmness considering the circumstances, "Good morning, Father. I'm so glad you were able to come to our wedding. We were quite worried about you."

"Thank you, Jason, and may I congratulate you on your marriage. You are a very fortunate young man to have been able to marry such a lovely and capable young woman. Good morning, Joanna, I hope your marriage to my son is long and happy."

"Thank you, Captain Stewart," she said. "I am so pleased you are with us today. As my husband said," and she smiled at me, "we were quite worried when we heard nothing from you."

Reverend Jones said, "Perhaps we can go into the vestry and let the newlyweds sign the register?"

The statement was delivered as a polite question, but it had a steely quality that was obeyed immediately as if it was an emperor's request, and as we processed into the vestry my father greeted his relatives and friends and introduced himself to those he didn't know simply as "Jason's father."

Joanna and I signed the register and then it was the turn of our parents and witnesses. Mrs. Evans and Uncle Tudor signed, and then the register passed to Mr. Fairweather, who filled in his name and address before scribbling his signature. My father was next. He wrote something and then immediately passed the register to Reverend Jones, who looked at the entry, opened his mouth as if to comment about something, and then changed his mind and closed it again.

Joanna and I walked from the vestry and halted near to the altar so that the other principals could form up into a procession behind us. Then to a spirited rendition of the "Wedding March," Joanna and I set off along the aisle with Mrs. Evans and my father immediately behind. As we progressed along the aisle, we accepted the congratulations of the members of the congregation standing close to the aisle in the pews and then walked out of the gloom of the church, through the vestibule, and into a churchyard bathed in sunshine. The sky was a deep azure blue and somewhere above us skylarks were singing as if the world would end if they stopped.

My wife's dream had come true.

Aunt Emily came to us and embraced my new wife.

"You look as pretty as a picture, Joanna, and your dress is beautiful. Isn't it, Jason?" she asked me.

I hadn't really looked at Joanna's dress until then, and I had to admit it was the most attractive dress I had ever seen. Made from a gossamer, thick white net laid over a simply cut, white silk dress, it flowed from her shoulders to the floor in an unbroken sweep. The bodice was modestly cut at the throat and the sleeves reached to just below her elbows. The end of each sleeve was decorated with a short row of buttons made from mother of pearl, and just visible through the net I could make out a group of three tiny blue flowers appliquéd to the bodice of the underdress near her left shoulder. As far as I could see, Joanna wore only one piece of jewellery, and that was a ruby pendant on a thin gold chain. It was clearly very old and possibly belonged to Mrs. Evans.

Something borrowed, something blue, I thought as the old rhyme came into my mind, then wondered what Joanna was wearing that fitted the beginning of the poem. *Something old and something new,* I remembered.

"It really is a most beautiful dress, Mrs. Evans," I said inadequately, as I was much more interested in gazing at my wife of ten minutes and thanking heaven for my good fortune.

Joanna and I stood in front of the church in lovely warm sunshine and basked in the congratulations showered upon us by our friends and relations in the congregation and the good wishes of many people, mostly housewives, who had been attracted to the church by the sunshine and the joyous pealing of the bells. After a little while we were ushered to the postern gate of the church by the combined forces of Neil Fairweather and Mrs. Evans, so that we could be driven to the Royal Hotel, where we would have our wedding breakfast and later spend the first night of our marriage together. Joanna didn't comment on it, but I was very pleased to see that our carriage was drawn by a matched pair of grey horses.

We felt like royalty as we were driven in our open-topped carriage across Caernarfon, and we enjoyed waving to the unknown people who called out their congratulations as we passed.

The rest of the guests followed us in a cheerful procession of carriages and other horse-drawn vehicles.

At the Royal Hotel, Joanna and I stood with our respective parents and greeted the guests as they arrived.

As the last person passed into the dining room and with Mrs. Evans on his arm, my father beckoned to the Percevals and said quickly to the five of us, "I apologise for not telling you what I have been doing and for arriving so late this morning. There is nothing for anyone to be concerned about, but this is not the place or time for Stewart family explanations. First and most important, we must celebrate your marriage, Joanna, and welcome you to our family. We'll have time to talk later."

And with that we had to be content and went to our places at the top table relieved but also very mystified.

We ate Cawl Cannin followed by roast Welsh Lamb and for those who wished to wash the food down with something other than Adam's ale there were unlimited supplies of Welsh beer, French wine, and brandy.

After the meal and very much too soon, or so it seemed to me, it was time for the speeches. Fairweather delivered an off-the-cuff address that raised a few smiles. He praised Joanna in glowing terms, particularly for keeping me alive in a Bombay hospital, and then focussed on me for longer than I cared for.

In summary, he said, "Mr. Jason Smiley Stewart has been known to me for a number of years. We met on the *Earl Canning*, and I could not have imagined that the young officer I shared a cabin with when I went first to Bombay would, within a few years, receive a medal from our queen and be known with in our community of expatriates as a hero for his exploits. I have been honoured to act as Mr. Stewart's best man today, and it gives me great pleasure to invite him to address you."

I stood up beside my new wife, took my speech from my pocket, opened it, and held it out in front of me. To my horror and chagrin, I saw that my hand was shaking the paper to the extent that I could not read what I had written. I suddenly realised how very nervous I had become as soon as I stood up in front of the guests that Joanna and I had invited.

I opened my mouth with the intention of saying, "Ladies and Gentlemen," but was unable to utter a word, as my mouth had become as dry as sand in a desert.

Fortunately, Fairweather observed my predicament and passed me a glass of water. I took several sips and then took a deep breath and tried again. As I began to read the text I had prepared so diligently with Fairweather the day before and also to understand what I had written, I realised how little my words reflected my true feelings. I found I could not continue and stuttered to a halt, feeling the pitying gazes that were being directed at me from all sides and noticed the embarrassed droop of my new wife's head. I dropped the speech onto the table in front of me, took a sip of water and a deep breath.

"Ladies and Gentlemen," I said, and suddenly my brain was working and words started to flow over my tongue, "I spent some time with my best man yesterday preparing the short address that I planned to deliver this morning—but as soon as I started to speak to you, I realised that the words I prepared yesterday could not accurately reflect what I have experienced today. How could they? Imagination requires some experience to build from, and as I have never been married before I could not imagine how I would feel. There are so many emotions coursing through my body at the moment but predominate is a sense of awed wonder because this lovely lady," and I bent down to take her hand in mine, "has chosen me, from all the men in the world, to be her husband. I feel very humble, but also very proud, and I will honour the vows I made to my wife in church today for as long as I have breath in my body."

I sat down and was stunned by the applause. Joanna squeezed my fingers and said, "Thank you Jason."

Fairweather said, "What you said from the heart was much better than the speech you had written. Well done, Mr. Stewart."

And my ordeal was over.

Mr. Tudor Evans made a long and rambling speech that traced Joanna's life from baby stage to adulthood and included a number of anecdotes that gave the audience much cause for hilarity and my wife equal cause for embarrassment.

When he had finished his speech, the cake was brought in, and Joanna and I made the first cut to the accompaniment of cheers and applause.

Joanna and I were greeted and congratulated by all the guests and as we had to spend some time in conversation with all of them, the afternoon disappeared and the candelabra was lit before we realised what was happening. One by one, or couple by couple, our guests came to say goodbye and wish us health and happiness in our future life together, and then Mrs. Evans came to Joanna and whispered something in her ear. Joanna blushed scarlet but excused herself and disappeared out of the room with her mother and aunt.

The transition from centre of attention to the centre of a void was rather abrupt, but fortunately Barnaby Williams noticed and came to sit beside me. He congratulated me again on my marriage and drank my health enthusiastically with a substantial swallow of brandy. I thanked him and took a sip of mine in response.

"Do you mind if we talk business for a moment?" he asked.

"Not at all," I responded, wondering what on earth he could want to talk about that would be of interest at my wedding.

"If you remember you asked me about the investment Captain Evans was supposed to have made," he said.

"Yes, of course," I responded my interest quickening. "Were you able to find out anything?"

"Yes, I did," he said but didn't go on. Possibly he was waiting for me to take the initiative as he didn't want to affect my wedding night.

"Please go on, Mr. Williams. I am eager to hear what you have discovered and how you did so."

"The 'how' was quite simple in the end. I had to attend a dinner of the local bar association and the solicitor who used to act for Captain Evans was also there. After dinner, we chanced to be sitting together over brandy and cigars, and as we were alone I told him in confidence about your enquiry. He didn't know anything about the purchase of any stocks and shares, but he was able to tell me the name of a broker that Captain Evans knew. The broker is a man called Captain Roberts, but I think he was in the Army not the Navy. Not that it matters. Anyway, I have written to Captain Roberts requesting an appointment to discuss a matter of private business. I am waiting for him to respond."

"That's very good news, Mr. Williams," I said at the end of his recital.

"We know more than we did, Mr. Stewart, but we are no closer to finding a solution to the problem your new relations have. I will advise you if I find out anything, and now I must take my leave. Attending your wedding has been a memorable experience, and I wish you health and happiness for the rest of a very long life. But try to keep away from Arabs with guns, as I have no desire to attend your funeral. Good night, Mr. Stewart."

"Good night and thank you, Mr. Williams," I said and he got up and walked a little unsteadily to the door.

My father dropped into the chair vacated by Mr. Williams, and I noted that he had managed to find the time to change into his naval uniform.

He looks more like my father dressed like that, I thought.

"There is a lot to discuss, Jason, but tonight is your wedding night and neither the time nor the place for family discussions. Maybe there will be time tomorrow before my sister and her husband return to Lenton, but we will decide that in the morning."

He looked at me appraisingly for a moment and said, "I liked your speech. How do you feel?"

"Nervous," I responded.

"I can understand that. May I offer some advice as a father to a son?" he asked.

"Yes, of course, father," I responded.

"I'll be blunt, Jason. Because of the life you have led, you have had some experience in bed with a woman. Joanna has never been to bed with a man, and whilst she may know something about consummating your union, she will be afraid. She will be particularly afraid of being hurt the first time, as she will have heard all the old wives tales about wedding nights and brutal, lustful husbands. My advice is simple. Be patient, careful and above all, considerate of your lovely wife."

"Thank you, Father," I said quietly. "I will do my best to follow your advice"

"Good," he said, "and I think it's time for you to go to your bride, as I can see Mrs. Evans in the hallway beckoning to you."

I stood and said, "Good night, Father," and slipped from the room as quietly as I could.

At the bottom of the staircase Mrs. Evans took my hand and with a tear in her eye said, "Go up. Jason. Joanna is awaiting you," and pushed me toward the staircase.

I climbed quickly up the stairs and knocked on the door and said, "It's me, Jason. May I come in?"

A faint and slightly tremulous voice said, "Yes, come in, Jason."

I pushed open the door, walked into a bedroom smelling faintly of Joanna's perfume, and carefully closed the door behind me. I reached out to bolt the door, but changed my mind, as I realised it would appear as if I was locking my wife in rather than keeping intruders out.

Joanna was sitting in the middle of the bed with the clothes drawn up to her chin. She looked quite pale and very nervous, and I was thankful for my father's timely advice as I walked across the room and sat on the edge of the bed.

I said, "Good evening, Mrs. Stewart. Didn't we have a wonderful wedding?" and took her hand. It was cold and didn't respond to my touch as usual, and she didn't say anything either, but I noticed her lip tremble.

"Joanna, I have a confession to make," I said as seriously as I could, "I'm dreadfully nervous."

"You, nervous!" she said. "I don't believe it. What have you to be nervous about?"

"Three things actually," I said, and I was pleased to see a little colour return to Joanna's cheeks. "First of all, I don't want to offend you in any way. Second, I don't want to hurt you in any way, and third and most important, I don't know which side of the bed to use."

"What?" she said.

"Well, you're sitting in the middle, and I don't know which side I should try to lie on."

"Which side would you prefer to lie on?" she asked.

"I don't know," I answered. "I have never been married before."

"Idiot," she said with a laugh and moved over to one side and fortunately closer to me.

"Is that better?" she asked.

"Yes, Joanna, and we can always try the other side tomorrow and see which we like better."

"True, my husband," she said.

I put my arms around her and kissed her for the first time in private since our marriage and found it difficult to stop—but I did, and then undressed and climbed into bed for the first time as a married man. I am happy to record that the first night of our marriage passed in private, loving exploration that it is not necessary to describe in detail here.

Next morning, we came down the stairs hand in hand to a rather late breakfast and answered the polite good mornings and enquiries about our health from fellow guests equally politely, but there was no disguising the joy we were having in each other's company.

After we had eaten, my father invited us into the morning room where the Percevals were already sitting. Aunt Mary stood up and embraced Joanna, and they stood for a few moments exchanging woman talk in very soft voices that we were not expected to listen to, so we didn't.

When we were all seated around a table, my father said, "I have some news to impart concerning the Stewart family. First of all, I must apologise for failing to keep you all informed about my movements since I left my ship and particularly for failing to accept your wedding invitation, Joanna and Jason, and then nearly missing the ceremony altogether. I would have been most distressed had that happened."

"We were very concerned that we had heard nothing from you," said Joanna.

"Thank you, Joanna. As you already know, I received a message shortly after we docked in Liverpool. How he knew where to send the message I have no idea, but it was from the factor on the family estate.

"He wrote, *Please come as soon as possible, as your brother has had an accident,* so of course I handed over to my first mate and rushed to Lime Street to catch the first train north."

"May I ask what a factor is?" Joanna said.

"The factor is the man who runs the estate on a day-to-day basis under the direction of the owner," explained my father.

"Thank you, father-in-law," Joanna responded, and my father almost glowed with pride at Joanna's use of his new title.

"When I arrived at Strathmilton in the middle of the following day," my father continued, "I found that the situation was infinitely worse than I had expected from the factor's message. It wasn't an accident. It was a disaster. No one knows exactly what happened, but we believe that a fire started in my nephew's bedroom. Perhaps it was a spark from the coal fire. We have no proof, of course, but it seems a likely explanation. It appears that my brother tried to save his son after shouting for help, but he must have lost his sense of direction in the smoke and then been overcome by it as they were both found on the floor dead within a few yards of safety. It's possible that they might have been saved if they had been found immediately, but their bodies were behind the door and between it and a side wall and not found until the fire had been put out."

"How dreadful," said my aunt quietly. "So near but it was just too far."

Joanna and I stared at each other, and then Joanna said, "And all the time we were so happy, Jason," and started to cry.

Before I could say anything, my father intervened.

"You should not think like that, Joanna. It is a tragedy for some. For you, just starting married life and not knowing any of the people involved, it should be no more than a reason to say one more prayer next time you go to church. And if you pray for anyone, pray for those who are alive and might benefit. My brother and his son are beyond help now."

Joanna blew her nose daintily and said, "I'm sorry, Captain Stewart, but your description was a shock. I didn't expect anything like that."

Aunt Mary said practically, "So you are now the Laird Jamie. What will you do?"

"At this moment I have no clear idea, Mary, but let me continue with my story so that you all know everything that has happened.

"The tragedy I have described had taken place more than two weeks before I arrived, and my brother and his son had already been buried in the family vault under the chapel beside the castle. I went to see my sister-in-law immediately after I arrived and didn't receive a very good reception. She remembered the argument I had had with my brother and expected me to exact revenge for the wrong her husband had done all those years before and immediately expel her from the castle, as I was the rightful heir. When she finally understood that I was not about to send her out into the snow dressed only in her shift, her demeanour improved. I have agreed that she can continue to use the rooms in the castle she occupied when my brother was alive for the next six months and then she must leave the castle."

"I would have kicked her out without her shift, snow or no snow," said my aunt in such an uncharacteristic display of unchristian thought that the Reverend Perceval said, "Tut-tut," in disapproval.

I couldn't help grinning at the way Aunt Mary had spoken and received a not-too-gentle kick on the ankle and an admonitory glare from my lady wife, who was a very charitable person and not inclined to speak badly of others—whatever the provocation was.

My father suppressed his grin a little too late to be convincing but, in serious tones, he went on, "I went next to see the factor. I expect you will remember Duncan McAllister Mary. He was the assistant factor when I left home and he's very old now. He's really too old to be the factor and is only just able to keep things under control if nothing untoward happens. Without the guiding hand of the laird, he is like a rudderless ship, and I will have to go back and take over the reins until I can restore stability."

My father stood up, pushing his chair back with a screech of wood on wood as he did so, and then started to pace up and down. After a few minutes he came back and sat down again and said, "I have no option but to go back to Strathmilton. I owe it to my forebears to take control of the estate, and as a result I have decided to give up the sea so that I can concentrate on making the estate profitable again. It certainly isn't at the moment. I spoke to Captain Downing after the wedding, and he has agreed to accept my resignation with immediate affect. He didn't want to but accepted the necessity with good grace. So tomorrow I will return to

Strathmilton and become the captain of a castle. I think I'll miss the sea, and I'll certainly miss the challenges and triumphs of being the captain of an ocean-going ship."

"May I ask why you arrived at our wedding dressed in Scottish clothes?" I asked my father.

"It's quite simple really," he said. "I had to meet all the elders of the Stewart clan so that they could confirm the succession. It's a formality really, but we think it is a necessary one, as it helps preserve our heritage and it has the practical advantage that we meet at least once in a lifetime. But it takes a lot of time to prepare and then, when the meeting has been convened, a very long time to reach a formal and unanimous conclusion. The meeting was arranged for the morning of the day two days before your wedding, Joanna, but so many people wanted to air their opinions that in the end there was just time to jump in a coach and rattle my way to Carlisle to get a train south. There was certainly no time to stop and change from Scottish dress to my naval uniform as I had intended. There was no time to sleep or shave either, as a matter of fact."

Joanna asked, "Would it be possible for Jason and me to visit you at Strathmilton Castle, Captain?"

"I think you may have to do more than visit," my father said obscurely.

"Why is that?" I asked.

"Haven't you realised what the death of your uncle means, Jason?" my father asked.

Joanna and I exchanged looks, but she appeared to be no closer to understanding than I was and I said, "I have no idea what you mean, Father."

"Put simply, Jason, I have become the Laird of Strathmilton, and as my son you will be my heir and become laird when I die. For that reason I hope you and Joanna will spend a great deal of your time there learning about the management of the estate so that you can take over in the future."

There was silence for a moment as Joanna and I digested what we had just heard, and then with a great smile of delight Joanna cried, "I've married a rich landowner without knowing. My mother will be very pleased."

With a wicked little grin, she added, "And Jemima Woodley will be green with envy. She is already a little peeved that I married before she did."

"He's the heir and not so rich," my father said in order to keep things in perspective, "but he'll certainly have more than two halfpennies to rub together, and the estate is big enough to provide a good income if it's managed properly."

I was rather overwhelmed. The previous morning I was a bachelor, and in the space of twenty-four hours I had married and become the heir to a large estate. I knew next to nothing about being a husband, and my knowledge of husbandry was nil.

I suddenly felt rather inadequate.

Joanna saved the day by saying enthusiastically, "When can we go to Strathmilton, Jason?"

My practical mind woke up and I said to Joanna, "Since there has been a fire and my widowed aunt will continue to live there for a time, we may have to wait until the repairs are done and there is accommodation for us." To my father, I said, "Perhaps you could tell Joanna and me what you would like us to do?"

"Your assessment is essentially correct, Jason. However, the damage caused by the fire is being repaired, as I instructed the builder to start before I came here. He believes the work will be finished in about two weeks if we allow enough time for the new plaster to dry out thoroughly. Your aunt didn't sleep in the master bedroom and is content to continue to use her present small suite. She will have her meals with us or privately when she prefers solitude. I think I will need about two weeks on my own with the factor and then your assistance will be invaluable, Jason."

"I know nothing about farming, Father," I objected.

"I don't either, so we can learn together," he responded bluntly.

"Do you intend that we use the redecorated rooms, Captain?" asked Joanna.

"There are rooms in other parts of the castle I understand, but they are rarely used, as they are so far from the centre of the building. I can certainly make other rooms available for you and Jason if you prefer not to use the rooms where my brother died."

"No, it's not that. I hope you will not think me impertinent, Captain, but if Jason and I are to live at Strathmilton for any length of time, I would like to supervise the decoration of our first home myself."

"How very sensible of you, Joanna," said Aunt Mary. "I think that's a very good idea, don't you, Jamie?"

My father nodded, and after a moment's thought said, "I have no objection to your idea, Joanna, but you will have to come to Strathmilton much earlier than I suggested so that you can instruct the builder about what you want him to do before he makes too much progress."

I was a little surprised when Joanna excused herself and went upstairs to ask her mother to join the discussion. I hadn't realised that my mother-in-law had stayed the night in the hotel as well and wondered if she had stayed just in case her daughter required help on the first night of her marriage. I realised at the same time that I would probably never know. Joanna returned with her mother, and after explaining the change in our fortunes to many cries of amazement and wonder, the three ladies—my aunt was not going to be left out of a conversation about house decoration—settled down to a very serious discussion of fabrics, colours, candelabra, cutlery, and a myriad other items. We three men tried to be attentive and supportive, but the subjects were largely beyond our understanding, and we moved to another table to give Aunt Mary the space she needed to draw from memory the outlines of the rooms we were to occupy after Joanna had completed the decorating.

My father said, "I know you are supposed to be convalescing, Jason, but I don't think you will find the work on the estate too onerous, and the fresh air and exercise will be good for you. You said earlier that you have no knowledge about farming, and that's true, but you have grown up in a farming community and understand the rhythm of the seasons and how a rural community interacts. I think you will do well at Strathmilton once the people there learn that some Sassenachs are honest and trustworthy."

"I'll do my best, Father, as you know I will, but if the telegraph company wants me to come back, what should I do? I feel I have an obligation to them."

"That will not be for at least nine months, I believe. Joanna, you, or even both of you may hate the life in Strathmilton and want to leave, or you might want to stay and say goodbye to the telegraph. It's about crossing bridges, Jason."

"I understand, Father," I said.

At that point the remains of the wedding party broke up into its constituent parts. My father, together with my uncle and aunt, set off for the station in an open-topped coach and their long journey's to Scotland and Lenton respectively. Mrs. Evans went home, and Joanna and I found ourselves alone and with no specific tasks to occupy our minds until we went home the next day.

I suppose we did what every healthy young couple does in such circumstances. We went to our room and enjoyed the intimacy that marriage and privacy brings. Next day after breakfast we went back to the Evans's house where we were to live until we went to Scotland.

Several days passed uneventfully, and then I received a letter from Barnaby Williams asking if I could attend at his office the next day at twelve in the afternoon, as he had arranged to meet Captain Evans's broker. I decided that it was time to tell my wife what I had discovered in case she wanted to come with me.

I knocked politely on the door and went into the room where Joanna was sitting in front of an embroidery hoop on a stand. She was working on a floral scene of such reality that I wanted to bend down and sniff the roses every time I passed by.

"Joanna, my dear, I haven't mentioned this before, as I was asked to keep it a secret, but circumstances have changed—"

"Whatever is the matter, Jason?" she interrupted. She had gone quite pale.

"Nothing's the matter," I said.

"Then what circumstances have changed and what is it you've been keeping a secret from your wife?" She sounded more than a little miffed.

"Darling," I said, "I'm very sorry I have expressed myself so badly and upset you. Please let me start at the beginning."

"That would be a very good idea," was the blunt reply.

I said, "The day after we went to Bangor, your Uncle Gwyn came to Caernarfon and asked me to meet him at the White Feathers. You and your mother had gone to have a fitting for your wedding dress and were not at home when the message arrived. He told me privately what had happened between your father and his brothers but was so afraid of his wife's reaction if she heard about our meeting that I was asked to keep it a secret. I said I would if you did not ask where I had been that morning. You didn't ask, so I kept the confidence until now."

"So what has changed to make you tell me now?" Joanna asked, and she was clearly far from mollified by what I had said so far.

Why do I get involved in other people's problems? I thought to myself.

I said, "When I went to Liverpool looking for information about my father just before our wedding, I saw my solicitor and decided to tell him what your Uncle Gwyn had told me."

Joanna held up an imperious hand to stop me speaking. Obviously, she was becoming angrier rather than less so, and her cheeks had reddened because of her irritation.

In a voice that reflected her angry mood, she said bluntly, "You can break a confidence to tell your solicitor, but not your wife, even though she is directly involved. You haven't yet told me what my father is supposed to have done."

"Yes, Joanna, that is correct," I said and I must have sounded as tired of this unnecessary wrangle as I felt.

"Please let me finish," I said. "I became involved in something I didn't want to be drawn into, and I haven't told you what I have learned because I didn't want to be the one to tell you. And I didn't want to tell you because I didn't believe the story could be true. But since you insist upon knowing, I have to tell you that your uncles accuse your father of taking large sums of money from them to buy shares and ruining them by not returning the money or giving them the shares. Can you wonder that they hate your father's family as they do?"

Joanna went pale once again as the import of my statement registered, and she whispered, "That cannot be true. I cannot believe my father could cheat his own brothers."

"But that is the accusation that Gwyn made. I told my solicitor that it would be unlike Captain Evans to behave in such a manner and asked him to see if he could find out anything. After the wedding breakfast,

Barnaby Williams told me that he was trying to arrange an appointment with your father's broker. A man called Captain Roberts."

"I have never heard that name mentioned but my mother might know. I'll ask her later," said a more cooperative and less angry Joanna.

"The message I have just received is from Barnaby Williams. He has an appointment with Captain Roberts tomorrow at noon and has suggested I attend. I came to ask you if you would like to attend as well."

"I'm sorry that I misjudged you, Jason, and I apologise for doubting you," and she kissed me so warmly I would have forgiven anything.

"We'll have to leave quite early if we are to be there by twelve," said my ever-practical wife. "And, as we cannot return here tomorrow night, we can look at the shops in Liverpool in the afternoon and come back the next morning. Perhaps there is something on in the Playhouse. You could take me to the theatre, Jason. Wouldn't that be nice?"

"Yes indeed, Joanna," I said, hoping I sounded more enthusiastic than I felt about the prospect of shopping followed by a theatre performance.

Next morning, we travelled to Liverpool by train and took a coach from the station to Barnaby Williams's office in Dale Street. I was greeted like a respected client by the old clerk, but Joanna, who looked a picture of health and beauty, was treated more like royalty. We were shown into Barnaby Williams's office and given seats in front of the desk after being introduced to Captain Roberts. He was a short, well-dressed man with pomaded hair, and I took an instant dislike to him because of the speculative and appreciative way he eyed my wife. If nothing else, he certainly had plenty of self confidence.

Barnaby Williams said, "Perhaps we should start. I have asked you to be kind enough to meet us because there is a doubt about the outcome of a transaction Captain Evans was promoting shortly before his illness and death. We understand that Captain Evans was purchasing a number of stocks or shares in a local company, but nobody knows with certainty which company he was interested in or whether the shares were in fact purchased. So the first question I have to answer is simply this: Was anything purchased by Captain Evans? And my hope in asking you here, Captain Roberts, is that you may be able to provide an answer."

Captain Roberts cleared his throat with an unpleasant rasping sound that grated on my nerves and caused Joanna's eyebrows to rise quite remarkably.

He said, "Captain Evans certainly bought some shares, and I could look up the share numbers in my records if you wish. I remember it because the transaction seemed to be carried out quite secretly, which was unusual for Captain Evans. He arrived in my office with a black japanned cashbox. He opened it, counted the contents out in front of me, made me sign a receipt, and instructed me to purchase ten thousand ordinary shares in the Dafydd Boiler Works. This I did, and a week later he came to my office checked all the shares against my invoice, returned the receipt for the cash, and then put the shares and the invoice in the box. He locked it and carried it out of my office. I didn't see him again before he died, so I have no idea what happened to the shares."

"It's a relief to know the shares were bought so half the mystery has been resolved," I said, then added, "Do you have any idea what the shares are worth now, Captain Roberts?"

"Not exactly, as I do not remember how much Captain Evans invested, but the individual shares are worth about ten times what was paid for them," he answered.

"Captain Roberts, can you remember anything more about the box Captain Evans put the shares in?" I asked.

"It was a long time ago," he said but then gestured with his hands as he added, "It was about this long and this wide and so deep and it had a double gold band around the top of the lid about an inch in from the edge. I cannot remember anymore, and I have to go to another appointment."

He stood up, eyed Joanna as if she was a particularly luscious piece of fruit waiting to drop off a branch into his hands, and then left the room with cursory nods to Barnaby Williams and myself.

"Obnoxious little oaf," said Joanna as the door closed behind him.

"Agreed," I said and then, thinking out loud, went on, "I wonder where the box is now?"

"After my father died," said Joanna, "we found a lot of boxes like the one Captain Roberts described. Most were in my father's study and every one was locked. I don't know whether Mother ever tried to match the keys we inherited with any of the boxes we found, and as far as I am aware she has never had the heart to open any of them, even if she did make a match. I'm sure she has no idea that there might be something of value in one of them."

"I think we will have to ask you mother if she has opened any of the boxes when we get home, Joanna," I said.

Barnaby Williams said to both of us, "If there is a family argument about the existence of the shares, I think it will be necessary for the boxes to be opened in the presence of your uncles, or at the very least an independent person who can verify the contents when the box is unlocked. This will protect you and your mother from future criticism. You must remember that there is no guarantee that the box we want is amongst the boxes that are in your mother's house, Mrs. Stewart."

Joanna momentarily started to look over her shoulder until she remembered with a little smile that she was the Mrs. Stewart to whom he referred.

She said, "That's very true, and I cannot imagine where to look if it's not—I imagine Uncle Tudor will come to the house if he is asked but not Uncle Gwyn."

I said, "I think it might be kinder to assemble all the boxes in one place and have an independent person witness the opening and then inventory the contents of the box with the shares in it if we are lucky enough to find it. It would be a little cruel to raise your uncles' hopes and then find nothing."

"Very true, Jason," Joanna responded, "but who could be the independent person?"

Barnaby Williams said, "I think it should be someone of standing who has no family connection. I am Mr. Stewart's solicitor, so I should not participate except possibly as a witness. Perhaps the best person to ask would be the Reverend Eli Jones. He knows your family, Mrs. Stewart, but has no links to any of you."

"That's a very good idea, Mr. Williams. Jason and I will discuss all of this with my mother when we return home. Thank you so much for your help."

We left Barnaby Williams and went to investigate the delights of the shops in Liverpool, and I was more than a little impressed when my young bride gave the dresses and costumes only passing attention before concentrating upon furniture and then fabrics for curtains and bedspreads and so on. We didn't buy anything but came away with many ideas. We went to the Playhouse in the evening and, contrary to my gloomy fore-bodings, we watched "HMS Pinafore" with great enjoyment.

The following day we returned to Caernarfon, and as soon as we reached Joanna's house, we sat down with Mrs. Evans and Joanna described in detail where we had been, what we had discovered, and what action we proposed. Mrs. Evans was very pleased at the prospect of resolving such a bitter family dispute and immediately agreed to adopt the strategy agreed with Barnaby Williams, except that we didn't think it was necessary for the solicitor to make the journey to Caernarfon just to witness the opening of a box.

Next morning, Joanna and I went to the vicarage and fortunately found the Reverend Jones at home.

He listened to our request without comment and agreed to come in the afternoon to open the boxes and examine the contents. We went straight back to the Evans's house where we found that Mrs. Evans, with the help of one of the maids, had collected all the metal cashboxes they could find and lined them up on a trestle table in the downstairs sitting room. There were eleven, and most of them had the double gold banding that Captain Roberts had recollected. Also on the table was a heap of keys. Single keys, pairs of keys tied together with string, several bunches of maybe ten keys each strung on leather thongs. Clearly far too many keys for the number of boxes we had to open and no tags on the keys to link them to a particular lock.

After lunch the Reverend Eli Jones arrived.

Mrs. Evans greeted him like the long-standing friend he was and then took him into the sitting room. He looked at the boxes and then at all the keys and looked rather dismayed.

"This is going to take much longer than I thought," he said. "We have to match a key to a box before we can open it, and I can only spare about two hours this afternoon."

"Reverend Jones," I said, "if I select one of the boxes and test every key in its lock until I find a match, then you can open it and check the contents whilst I find the next match."

"Good idea, Mr. Stewart. Let's begin."

So I pulled the nearest box closer and started to test the keys in the lock. I began with a pile of keys near my right hand, tested them one by one in the lock, and built a reject pile near my left hand. When I found a key that would fit a lock, I passed both key and box to Reverend Jones so that he could open it whilst I started the process again and sought the next match. It was a slow, laborious process, but box by box I found the matching key, Reverend Jones opened the box, examined the contents, and said it was not what we sought. Every box was the same except one, and that was empty. We all looked at each other in open-mouthed, silent amazement, as we could not believe what had happened. We had been so convinced we were on the path to a solution that our failure to find one was very unwelcome.

"Thank God we didn't ask my uncles to be here," said Joanna, then, recollecting who was present, said, "Excuse me, Reverend."

"I quite understand, my dear," he said.

"What can we do now?" asked Mrs. Evans, and everyone looked at me for a solution.

"I suppose we will have to continue looking," was my initial response. "Clearly we have many more keys than boxes and whilst I would expect some to be duplicates, I think there may be other boxes that we have not yet found."

"But where could they be?" said Mrs. Evans rather plaintively.

"It may be unlikely but perhaps in the attic or the cellar. Maybe there is a cupboard somewhere in the house that hasn't been opened for a long time. All we can do is search and ask Reverend Jones to return if we find anything. I don't think he can do more this afternoon, and I, for one, would like to thank him for his patience."

"I was glad to assist," he said. "And I would be pleased to return if you need my support."

The maid brought his hat and coat and after exchanging cordial "goodbyes" with us all, he left the house to go back to his church and ministry. After the vicar had gone, we returned to the sitting room and surveyed the assembled boxes rather despondently.

What to do? I wondered.

Joanna put my thought into words, "What can we do now, Jason?"

"There is no easy solution to our problem. We have to search carefully and methodically room by room until we are certain that there are no boxes left in the house that haven't been checked. If we are still unable to find the shares, we will just have to look through all the papers in your father's study to see if there is any information there. I think the first thing I will do is to check the remaining keys to see if any of them are duplicates. That should tell us how many boxes we are looking for. What do you think, Joanna?"

"I have no better suggestion, Jason, but it will take some time to check everywhere."

"Until we go to join my father we have the time, and it will be time well spent if we can resolve the dispute."

"Agreed, my dear," said my wife.

I started comparing the remaining keys against the box locks and after about an hour of concentrated trial and error had been able to reduce the heap of unidentified keys to six. Unfortunately, they all looked different, which meant that we had to look for another six boxes on the assumption that they still existed.

I said a short, quiet prayer to the powers that be, requesting them not to lead us to anymore keys.

So what to do next, I wondered. *If Mrs. Evans doesn't know if any more boxes exist, then it is logical to assume that any boxes that do exist must be out of sight somewhere.*

It appeared to me that the attic was as good a place to start as any, and Mrs. Evans readily agreed to my suggestion that I made a search there and told me it was possible to get into the attic of the house using the hatch built into the ceiling in the corner of one of the bedrooms. Joanna and I took a chair to the bedroom and I placed it under the hatch. When I stood on it, I was just able to push up the hatch cover and, balanced on my upturned palms, slide it clear of the opening. Then with my hands grasping the sides of the opening I pulled with my arms as I sprang upwards with my legs. With a prodigious wriggle and a grunt of effort, I managed to get my backside through the opening where I sat gratefully on the edge of the hatch with my legs dangling into the room below. Joanna stood on the chair and passed up a rather smoky oil lamp. I was pleased to find that I was able to reach up and hook the handle of the lamp over a conveniently placed peg. Clearly, someone had been in the attic on more than one occasion before my visit and that was an encouraging sign in itself.

I looked around in the small circle of light cast by the lamp and could see some of the rafters in one small area of roof. I was sitting at the edge of the opening on one of the ceiling joists and between the joists I could make out the lath and plaster that formed the ceiling of the room below. When I stood up for the first time, all my weight was supported on one joist and it bent slightly, causing the lathe and plaster somewhere beneath me to crack with a noise like a pistol going off.

It gave me quite a fright and Joanna's, "Are you all right, Jason?" showed that the noise had been louder than I thought.

I said, "Yes, thank you," as nonchalantly as I could.

To move about in the roof space I had to step from joist to joist, which was bad enough but except immediately adjacent to the ridge timber, I had to progress bent almost double, as the height of the roof particularly close to the eaves was very restricted.

Naturally, I took the lantern from the peg and carried it with me as I stepped carefully from joist to joist. They all bent a little under my weight but there were no more alarming noises. I looked around carefully, but there was little to see apart from a couple of old wooden boxes that reminded me of sea chests. I carefully looked at the rest of the space under the roof and could see nothing else. There was a thick layer of dust over everything except in a single line of footprints that led to one of the chests and then back to the trap door again, and even these were being obscured by fresh deposits of dust. Clearly, it was a long time since anyone had been up in this attic.

I opened the box that was nearer to me. It appeared to be full of old uniforms. I lifted about half of them out to make sure there was nothing else concealed underneath, then replaced what I had disturbed and closed the lid of the box. Carefully, I stepped from joist to joist to the box that the footsteps led to and opened the lid. Inside were two black japanned money boxes just like the ones we had downstairs and both were locked. One by one I carried them to the trap door and carefully balanced them across the joists by the opening. I put the lamp down beside one of the boxes, lowered myself down to stand on the chair, and then lifted both the boxes and the lamp down after me. After turning out the lamp, I replaced the hatch and carried the boxes down the stairs to the sitting room with Joanna in close attendance. After a little trial and error, I was able to find a key for each lock, but I didn't know if I should open them or go on searching.

Hunger and fatigue supplied the answer, and I washed off all the dust, changed, ate a good dinner, and after a little inconsequential discussion with Mrs. Evans, Joanna and I went to bed.

Next morning, I went to Reverend Jones and he agreed to come and open the two new boxes after his early service. He was as good as his word and arrived just after nine. He immediately opened one of the boxes but found nothing of value and closed and locked it again.

He opened the other box and said, "There are three packages in this box sealed with red wax."

He lifted one out and said, "No, it's not a package; it's an envelope and there is some writing on it." He held it close to his eyes and said, "The ink has faded a little but it is clearly addressed to Mr. Gwyn Evans." The Reverend Jones took out another envelope and, after examining it very carefully, said, "This one isn't addressed at all, and this one," and he pulled out the third package, "is addressed to Mr. Tudor Evans."

"It's not conclusive," he said. "But it would be stretching coincidence a long way to imagine that these three packages do not contain the missing shares."

Joanna said in a breathless and excited voice, "Wouldn't it be marvellous if it's true and it's Jason we have to thank for not thinking ill of my father after what he tried to do. Thank you, my dearest," she said and gave me a hug that was all promise and a kiss that wasn't as chaste as it should have been in the reverend's presence.

Reverend Jones didn't appear to notice and said, "What do you think we should do now, Mr. Stewart?"

"I was wondering about that myself. I think the box should be locked again. Perhaps you would undertake to keep the box at the vicarage, Reverend, and Mrs. Evans can take charge of the key?"

They both nodded their affirmation.

"The next step is rather more difficult, as we have to meet your uncles and explain what we have done and then give them the envelopes to open. They will assume that they are receiving the shares, and it will be a cruel disappointment if it turns out to be something else. Although I cannot imagine what that something could be in the circumstances."

"I don't think we should meet here," said Joanna. "Perhaps we could meet at your vicarage, Reverend?"

"Of course you can, Mrs. Stewart. A neutral venue would be a sensible choice, I think," he said.

"Informing my uncles will be rather more difficult," Joanna continued calmly. "But I think Jason should write to both my uncles to explain what he has done and why and then invite them to the vicarage to open the envelopes to see if they contain the shares. If they know we have been trying to make amends, they may not be too put out if we have not been successful and have to search some more. Can anyone suggest anything better?"

No one had a better idea, and we agreed that I should write and ask them to be at the vicarage the following Sunday at three. This gave nice time for the letters to get to their destinations.

On Sunday Joanna, Mrs. Evans, and I arrived at the Vicarage at about a quarter to three and were shown into Reverend Jones's study where he was working on a sermon. After exchanging cordial greetings, we sat down quietly to wait for our visitors whilst the reverend continued his preparation. Just after three we heard a carriage stop outside and the housekeeper showed the newcomers into the large room just to the right of the front door that the Reverend used for meetings of the parish elders, Sunday school and similar functions.

Mrs. Evans, followed by Joanna and then me, left the reverend's study and walked into the meeting room. Reverend Jones followed close behind.

Mrs. Evans's pleasant, "Good afternoon, everyone," was overwhelmed by the voice of Mrs. Llynos Evans saying, "What's all this about then? Are you going to scam us out of more of our money? I see your daughter's fancy man is still here."

She drew breath and was about to launch another verbal attack when a stern voice from the doorway said, "Be quiet you foolish woman. Your tongue will cause *you* more harm than it can cause anyone else. We are here in the hope that we can give you good news. We are certainly not here to cause anyone ill. Now, Mrs Llynos Evans, will you be quiet and listen?"

"Yes, Reverend," said a subdued lady, and I thought it a pity that her husband had not taken steps to curb her vitriolic tongue a long time ago.

"Mr. Stewart has written and advised you about the enquiries he has made on your behalf," said Reverend Jones, "but I will ask him to tell you again in his own words so that everything is clear to all of you."

He said, "Mr. Stewart, if you please," and sat down.

I stood up and said, "I will try to be brief, but if there is anything you do not understand, please ask me to explain."

I started with my meeting with Gwyn Evans, which was a mistake, as Llynos Evans still didn't know anything about it and we had to listen in impotent silence as she gave her hapless husband a good tongue-lashing as a result. When quiet had been restored, I went on to explain about my meeting with my solicitor in Liverpool. After that I described the subsequent meeting with the broker that Joanna had also attended. The search for a box containing the shares or evidence about them was quickly covered and brought me to the present gathering.

I said, "As you gentlemen believed that your brother had embezzled the money you had entrusted him with, we thought it was necessary for an independent person to witness the opening of the boxes. In fact, Reverend Jones not only agreed to perform this task for the Evans family but actually opened and checked the contents of thirteen boxes before we found this one." I pointed to the box that Reverend Jones had brought in and put on the table before him. "We know that the box contains three envelopes but not what the envelopes contain. We decided to relock the box and place it in the reverend's care until we could arrange for you to be present."

"How do we know you haven't had your hands in the box?" accused the valedictory Llynos Evans to a chorus of "be quiets" from Gwyn and Tudor and a look from the Reverend Jones that would have turned a more sensitive soul to stone.

"In order to refute accusations of fraud such as you have made, Mrs. Evans," I responded and I couldn't help an angry edge creeping into my voice, "we arranged for the Reverend Jones to keep the box here at the vicarage and we, or rather Mrs. Evans, kept the only key we found that fits the lock in this box."

I turned to Mrs. Evans and said, "Do you have the key?"

"Yes, I do," she answered. "I hung it on a gold chain around my neck." She pulled it from her bosom and handed it to me.

"I think it would be difficult for someone to unite the key with the box without the reverend or Mrs. Evans being aware of the fact," I commented and was relieved to hear amused chuckles from both uncles.

"Now," I said, "if neither you, Tudor, nor you, Gwyn, have an objection about what we have done to reach this point, I would like to ask Reverend Jones to unlock the box and give you the envelopes that bear your names. Normally, opening your correspondence is a private matter, but on this occasion I expect you to open the envelopes and check the contents in front of witnesses. Do you agree to this?"

"Yes, of course," said Tudor.

"No," said Llynos. "I don't agree." She sat back in her chair and folded her arms across her bosom and the expression on her face was triumphant at the consternation she had caused.

"Are you totally unable to control your wife, Gwyn?" asked Tudor in a barely controlled fury.

Gwyn was white-faced with anger, but he said calmly enough, "I should be grateful if you would all leave Llynos and me together for five minutes." We did as he had requested. We all got up, filed out of the room, and crowded into the reverend's study.

We didn't hear anything and never found out what was said, but five minutes later a calm, normally complexioned Gwyn appeared at the door and asked us to return to the meeting room. We found Llynos sitting in the same chair, but her face was white and her lips were trembling.

She said in a shaky voice, "I apologise and will not interfere again," and leant back in her chair looking far from triumphant.

No one spoke for a moment, then I said, "I have your brother's agreement, so will you verify the contents of the envelope in front of us?"

"Willingly," said Gwyn.

Mrs. Evans pulled the key from her bosom again and handed key and chain to the Reverend Jones. As she did so, I wondered what would pass through his celibate mind as he took hold of a key that had been warmed between a woman's breasts. There was no visible sign that he thought anything.

He put the key in the lock, turned it, and pushed back the lid. He took out an envelope, read the name, and passed it to Gwyn, who took it with shaking hands. The next envelope was passed to Mrs. Evans and the third to Tudor Evans. The behaviour of the brothers was quite different. Tudor took his envelope, broke the wax seals, and had started to extract the contents whilst Gwyn turned his envelope over and over in his still shaking hands. It was as if he was afraid that opening it would bring a worse life than he already suffered, but in the end he ripped open the envelope and checked the contents.

Mrs. Evans just held her envelope and watched.

From his envelope Tudor Evans extracted what looked like a letter with a thick packet of papers attached. He read the letter, opened the packet, and checked the contents against the letter.

"It is all in order. I owe my brother an apology and wish I could apologise to his face," said a very upset Tudor Evans. "As it is, I can only pray for his forgiveness and ask my sister-in-law for hers."

Gwyn held up his envelope in hands, which had stopped shaking, and said simply, "I agree with everything Tudor has said. Please forgive us, Meg."

Mrs. Evans held one of each of the brothers' hands in her own and said with feeling, "I thank God that the trouble in our family is over, and, of course, I forgive you although your behaviour has been very hard to bear. At the same time, we mustn't forget how Jason has been instrumental in bringing about this reconciliation, and I'm so glad my daughter had the wisdom to marry such a commonsensical man.

After thanking me again, Tudor said, "We bought these shares some time ago. Do you think it will be possible to get some of our money back if we sell them?"

Joanna said, "Jason asked about that and the broker thought they would be worth about ten times what you paid for them. It's a very nice profit for you if you sell."

"That's incredible," said Gwyn. "I do not know what to do or say except thank you for everything you have done for us." Tudor agreed with his brother's sentiments with verbose enthusiasm.

FOUR

Scotland

About midmorning on the day after our meeting with Joanna's uncles, a telegraph company messenger delivered a message from my father. It was short and to the point.

> Rooms ready for decoration. Come at your convenience.
> Please send date and time of arrival.

When she saw the message, Joanna said, "We only have to pack a few clothes, Jason. I'm sure we can be ready to leave in two days."

"Yes, my dearest," I responded, knowing that I had so little to pack that I could have left the next morning if such haste had been necessary. I saw Mrs. Evans's eyebrows twitch upwards at Joanna's "few clothes" comment, but being a natural diplomat she said nothing.

As it turned out, it wasn't very much more than two days before we were able to set out on our journey by train and coach to the family castle in the borders of Scotland to the west of Carlisle.

The journey was remarkable only because of its length and the unexciting vista of rain-soaked countryside through which we travelled. At Carlisle we climbed down from the train hoping there would be someone to greet us, but apart from a group standing in a rough semicircle in front of one of the leading carriages, there was no one on the platform.

I took our cases from the train, helped Joanna to alight, and said, "If you wait here for a moment, Joanna, I'll go and find a porter." As I scanned the almost empty platform in vain, I added, "I cannot imagine where they all are this evening."

Most unusual, I thought, and then grumbled to myself, *There are usually as many porters as passengers when one doesn't need them.*

I started to walk toward the station exit, and in so doing I approached more closely to the group I had seen standing near the front of the train and noticed that they had changed their formation. It was almost a circle of people now, and they seemed to be agitated about something from the way they moved and gesticulated. I noticed several porters standing on the periphery of the group as I approached and walked up to the nearest of them.

I said, "Please collect my cases," and gesticulated along the platform toward Joanna's patient sentinel figure.

"Can't, sir" he answered, and his Scottish accent was very apparent. "'Is lordship is expecting someone," and he pointed with an inclination of his head at a man standing in the centre of the group.

As I looked where he indicated, I wondered who he meant by "'is lordship" and then forgot the question when I saw the familiar form of my father as he despatched one of the group to do something. As a result, I didn't immediately connect my father with the title "'is lordship."

I called out, "Father!" and he looked up, stared momentarily at me, and then shouldered his way through the group to stand in front of me.

"So there you are, Jason," he said, and fractions of a second later he asked, "Where is Joanna?" Within seconds of me pointing, two porters were hurrying along the platform with my father and me in pursuit and the rest of the group trailing several paces behind.

"My dear Joanna, I'm so sorry you have been left alone," said my father. "We expected you both to travel in the first-class coach and couldn't understand why you had not arrived on this train. We were discussing what to do with the stationmaster and hadn't considered looking in the other carriages."

"We hadn't even thought about the first class," said Joanna. "It's so expensive."

"There are a large number of changes to think about now, Joanna," my father said. "And travelling first class, for example, is something that we are expected to do."

"Can you tell me why that is?" asked Joanna.

Before my father could answer, one of the porters came back and, after coughing to attract attention, said, "The cases are all in the carriage, Sir James."

"Thank you," said my father and gave the porter some money.

Joanna had looked a little startled when the porter called my father "Sir James," and then she understood and said, "Of course, how silly of me. Now I understand. I'm very sorry, Sir James. I should have realised that you are now the earl—but surely that will not affect Jason and me."

"Jason is the heir to the title and the estate, Joanna. I'm sorry, but some changes in the way we conduct our lives are inevitable as a result of my brother's death. I expect it will be difficult for you and Jason to make the change from commoner to upper class, as it requires a completely new philosophy of life, but I hope it will not be too difficult, as it is expected of us. You can both count on my support and guidance always."

There was a profound silence for a moment as Joanna and I absorbed what we had just been told, and then to us both he said, "Perhaps we should start our drive to Strathmilton Castle. It's a good distance, and it will be getting dark before we get there."

He led the way to the exit from the station, and when we walked outside, we found various officials from the railway company lined up beside the carriage to wish us a safe onward journey. As the postillion opened the carriage door for us, I noticed a coat of arms emblazoned on the door.

"Is that the family crest, Father?" I asked, wondering if I should address my father as "Sir James" as well.

"Yes," he responded as we climbed into the carriage, and then my father called up to the coachman, "Back to the castle, Angus."

The coachman responded with a brisk, "Aye, Sir James," and cracked his whip. As the railway officials disappeared back into the station, we drove away from Carlisle Station in an easterly direction.

Some hours later the road started to climb up through the woods on the side of a steep hill, and suddenly we could see nothing around us but trees with a tiny scrap of sky visible through the thinning branches above us. The road flattened and dipped downwards for a time then started to climb again. Suddenly, we were on a flat section of road and the driver stopped to let the horses have a few minutes' rest. We climbed down from the carriage, grateful for a chance to stretch our legs after sitting for such a long time.

After about ten or fifteen minutes, the driver said, "I think the horses are rested enough now, Sir James," and my father nodded his agreement and ushered Joanna and me back into the coach.

We set off slowly down the slope with the postillions walking beside each back carriage wheel ready to push cast iron shoes between the iron wheel rim and the macadam road surface if it appeared that the weight of the carriage would take charge. As it happened, the only problem occurred when the inside hoof of one of the rear pair of horses suddenly slipped and it lurched sideways into its mate, almost knocking it over.

Fortunately, the coachman and postillions were quickly able to bring the team back under control, and we completed the descent through the forest without further excitement.

As the trees thinned, I noticed that the road was descending along and down the flank of the hill we had just come over. On the left side there was a cultivated and obviously fertile plain stretching away into the distance, and on the right the hillside was clad in ever-denser forest as one looked upwards. The road we were following turned left at the bottom of the incline and headed directly across the plain toward Strathmilton Castle, which we could see in the distance. The castle was set approximately midway between two ranges of hills. Even from a distance it was an imposing, dark coloured, powerfully squat building that had been constructed on what appeared to be a low grass-covered mound that was about three times the height of the castle towers. The plain appeared to be completely surrounded by hills covered in trees like the hill we had just traversed, and I could see why Aunt Mary had said she had been troubled by the cold when she had lived there as young woman. The castle on its mound was in the bottom of a basin formed by the surrounding hills, and in winter it would be submerged in freezing cold air that had no escape.

I almost shuddered at the thought of undressing in one of the castle's rooms one frigid winter's night.

As we approached the castle mound, I could see behind the sparse covering of poor grass, the rock that gave the castle its imposing position and realised that the builder had found a very good place to fortify. The castle had a tower at each corner that projected a little in front of the main walls, and the only openings I could make out were the arrow slits in the tower walls. The tops of the towers and the full length of the top of the castle walls were crenulated. The structure gave off an aura of invincibility, and I felt sure that many armies must have come here, examined its location, been awed and dismayed by its apparent strength, and had then moved on to attack castles that were less well fortified.

Before long we began to see the outline of the abandoned channel of the moat and the fixed bridge that had been built to carry the road over the moat and up to the castle gate. As far as I could see, that gateway was the only place where it was possible to enter the castle. The view of the castle gate disappeared as the road turned again and started to follow an inclined path that took us up the side of the rock mound toward the castle gate. At a good speed and with the clatter of iron wheel rims on cobblestones as a wild accompaniment, the coachman guided the carriage through an entrance that was only minutely wider than the wheel track of the vehicle with the confident skill that is born from years of practice. Inside the courtyard he brought the carriage to a gentle halt. Out of the right hand window I could make out a short flight of stone steps with an ornamental balustrade on each side leading up to an imposing but firmly closed wooden door.

The postillions rushed to open the carriage door and pull down the steps. I climbed stiffly down and turned to help Joanna alight in turn. As my father climbed out, the heavy wooden door creaked open and a man dressed in a morning suit walked down the stone steps from the front door and halted in front of my father.

"Good evening, Sir James, I hope you have had a comfortable journey," he said.

"Yes, thank you, Burke. Let me introduce my son and his wife, Mr. and Mrs. Stewart," and to us he said, "Jason, Joanna, I would like you to meet Burke. He is the butler and keeps the internal working of the castle running like a well-oiled machine."

"Thank you, Sir James," he said, then turning to Joanna and me he added, "Welcome to Strathmilton. If there is anything that you need, please tell me."

We said we would and then followed him back up the steps, through the big open doorway, and into a hall dominated by a blazing log fire crackling and smoking in a huge fireplace built of stone. We could feel the comforting heat on our faces at the same time as we could feel cold drafts on our necks. As I hadn't heard the door close, I assumed it was still open and looked over my shoulder to check. It was shut.

Thank God it's not winter, I thought and shivered. *Perhaps I was too long in India.*

"Perhaps we should plan to visit Bombay for the winter," I said quietly to Joanna, who looked quite startled for a moment.

"Are you reading my thoughts now, Mr. Stewart?" she asked in mock indignation.

"Not intentionally, Mrs. Stewart," I answered with a grin, "but it would be nice to be warm when Strathmilton is up to its sporran in snow."

Joanna laughed softly.

Nothing remarkable happened over the next two weeks or so.

Joanna was introduced to the local builder by my father the morning after our arrival, and she was an instant success when it was realised that she was not only Welsh but fluent in her native language.

Scottish Celt meets Welsh Celt.

The builder was quite a small man, but he was strong and wiry and a very good craftsman, particularly with wood. His name was Hamish McDonald, I recall. He employed two or three other men on a rather casual basis mainly to hold or carry or perform some unskilled task like nailing up laths before plastering started for example.

Joanna discussed her ideas with Hamish, and they were very soon in agreement with colours, materials, and so on. I was occasionally asked my opinion about something but generally had little to contribute and never managed to solve a difference of opinion between the two of them.

I spent my days partially in the estate office with Duncan McAllister and the rest of my time out on the estate with Malcolm McDonald, the factor's assistant.

I found it quite unnerving to be suddenly reading about bushels and pecks or rods, poles, and perches after many years during which I had dealt with the modern measurements of volts, amperes, and ohms that I had used in my daily work with the telegraph. The relationships between some of the different measurements that I had learnt by rote from the curate all those years ago in Pickworth came back to mind.

Two gills one pint,

Two pints one quart,

Four quarts one gallon,

Eight gallons one bushel,

Four bushels one peck

I was amazed that I still remembered any of it, as so many years had passed since I attended the village school.

It was a pity, but I didn't have Joanna's Celtic advantage.

Simply put, I was considered a Sassenach, even though my father was the rightful earl and born a Scot. I had been born south of the border, and my English accent clearly grated upon the ears of the people who had to listen to anything I said.

It was not a happy time.

I worked diligently and brought my limited knowledge of husbandry to bear on the problems that arose. I listened carefully to the explanations that were given, no matter how grudgingly they were enunciated in a form of the English language I could understand. To be able to support my father, I knew I had to learn as much as I could, as quickly as possible, but secretly I longed for the day when a letter would arrive from the telegraph company offering me release from an occupation that fitted me as well as a right hand fitted in a left-handed glove.

Most importantly, I think, I never once complained.

My opportunity to gain a little credibility amongst this community of farming people came about by accident.

I was with Malcolm McDonald. He had to visit several farmers and a village located about fifty miles from the castle, and my father decided I should go with him for the experience. We expected to be away for several days, and for the first time I would be separated from my wife and didn't relish the thought. Wherever we went I was introduced as the son of the earl, but the smiles of welcome were rapidly extinguished when the explanation continued and informed everyone that I was from "south of the border." No one was actively impolite, but I didn't feel welcome.

One of the people we had to meet was the local blacksmith, and I hoped I would be able to see him working so that I could compare his methods with those my father had used.

When we arrived at the forge, the blacksmith was hard at work. He had a working horse hitched to the rail outside and a second standing in the entrance to the forge. He was making the third shoe for this animal when McDonald and I arrived. I could see that the smith was too busy to talk to McDonald and suggested we should come back later, but a suggestion from a Sassenach, even a sensible suggestion was unacceptable, and McDonald started shouting. The noise frightened the horse, but it distracted the apprentice and that was much worse, as he became flustered, tripped over his own feet, and hit his head on the side of the anvil as he fell. He just lay there until I pulled him to one side and ordered McDonald to look after him. I threw my coat into the corner, pumped up the forge, and took over the apprentice's role. The smith looked startled but didn't miss a stroke as he continued the preparation of the third shoe—and the next and the next until both the horses had been re-shod. With impeccable timing the apprentice recovered his wits and returned to duties that had been already completed.

When I had picked up my coat, the blacksmith shook my hand and said, "Thank you, sir, but how does the son of an earl know how to shoe a horse?"

"In my youth I didn't know I was the son of an earl," I answered truthfully.

The blacksmith turned to McDonald and said bluntly, "Now, listen to me, McDonald. This man is not simply a Sassenach, and you would do well to look after him."

McDonald said nothing as we walked out of the forge, but I think he started to revise his opinion of me from that day on but it was an uphill struggle that my previous experience could do nothing to alleviate.

Duncan McAllister, I discovered, was a surprisingly well-read man for a factor on a Scottish estate miles from anywhere, and he seemed to be mainly interested in learning about the foreign countries he would never have the chance to see in person. Someone had obviously mentioned to him that I had been in India, because he mentioned it one day when we were together in the estate office.

"I understand that you have travelled to India, Mr. Stewart. I should be pleased to hear about the country if you have a mind to humour an old man," he said.

Malcolm McDonald, who was not in a mood to humour anyone, said with a gesture in my direction, "Before he starts reminiscing he has to finish checking those figures."

He was correct, of course, as I hadn't finished checking the totals of grain delivered to the estate granary. It wasn't urgent, but to keep the peace I said, "I should be happy to tell you something about India, Mr. McAllister, as soon as I have finished this for McDonald."

About thirty minutes later with my mind still reeling from the addition of quarts, bushels, and pecks, I went to sit opposite Duncan McAlister at his big desk.

"What would you like to know?" I asked.

"What can you tell me?" was the slightly unhelpful response.

I thought about that for a moment then said, "I was an apprentice on my father's ship and sailed many times from Liverpool to Bombay and stopped at many foreign ports during the voyages. I have lived in Bombay for several years and worked on the construction of the telegraph between Great Britain and India."

Joanna knocked at the door, and she came into the office and listened as I finished my initial recital and added, "He has also received a medal from The Queen and was shot and seriously wounded by an angry Arab."

In the silence that followed Joanna's statement, she said politely, "I hope you will not mind, Mr. McAllister, but I need to talk to my husband for a moment?"

"Of course not, Mrs. Stewart," he said but he sounded quite disappointed.

Joanna and I left the factor's office, and when I started to ask why she wished to talk to me, she put a finger to my lips and led me in silence up to our newly decorated living room. We sat on the sofa half-turned toward each other.

Joanna took my hands in hers and looked into my eyes.

"Jason," she said, "I think…No, I'm sure…You are going to be a father soon, and I'm so pleased."

I was so full of surprise and emotion at the news that I was struck dumb for several heartbeats but then found my tongue and said, "What wonderful news, Joanna," and then, full of concern, asked, "Are you feeling all right? Would you like to lie down? Can I get you a pillow?" and so on, until Joanna put her finger across my lips to silence my excited babbling.

"I feel well, Jason, so there is no need to be concerned at present," she said with a smile, then added quietly, "It will be some months before I need to be careful, and then I shall be very happy to be pampered by my husband."

"I hope the baby will be a boy," I said softly. "But a little girl would be nice also."

"You will just have to wait and see, my love," Joanna said matter-of-factly.

We continued to sit on the sofa for some time looking into each other's eyes, kissing occasionally, discussing favourite names and the many other topics that soon-to-be parents always discuss at times like this. Joanna's thoughts quickly moved forward in time and the need for a nursery became an important issue for her to discuss with Hamish MacDonald.

When we left our living room, we must have both been radiant with happiness because my father took one look at us and said, "Good news, I assume?"

Joanna and I looked at each other for a moment and then Joanna, blushing like a fifteen-year-old, said, "You are going to be a grandfather Sir James."

My father's shout of "Marvellous!" made the rafters ring and brought Burke at a dignified trot to see what his master wanted. The news of Joanna's condition was soon all around the castle and the high opinions that people had already formed about my wife rose even higher.

On the other hand, my reputation remained much as it had been since I arrived at Strathmilton Castle.

When Duncan McAlister had the time to indulge his desire for travel in his imagination, I was pleased to sit and tell him about my experiences. I think he enjoyed listening to my accounts and could appreciate the efforts I had made to achieve what I had. Malcolm McDonald, on the other hand, listened to me politely if he was in the office but was much less impressed, as he had the unshakeable idea that I had been successful only because I was the son of the earl. It was an attitude that I could not understand, as he knew very well the circumstances that had brought my father and me to the castle.

One day I mentioned to Duncan McAllister that the telegraph company had given me sick leave for a year.

"You don't look ill," said Malcolm McDonald in the sceptical tone of voice that people use when they think that they have detected a fraud.

"I don't feel ill now," I responded neutrally, "but it wasn't always so. In any case, the telegraph company will contact me before the end of the year to see if I wish to return to Bombay."

"You'll go, of course," Malcolm McDonald said eagerly, and I wondered if his attitude toward me was caused by a fear of losing his present position and the possibility of promotion to factor when McAlister stopped work. If I took over, there would be no need to employ a young assistant. I contemplated making McDonald squirm a little to pay him back for the unfriendly way he treated me but didn't have the stomach for it.

"When the letter arrives," I said, "I'll have to choose between living here and living in some foreign land. I am not a farmer, but as I am knowledgeable about matters relating to the electric telegraph, logic suggests I should go back to the telegraph company. But before making a final decision I will also have to consider the wishes of my wife and my father, the earl."

"How soon do you think you will know, Mr. Stewart?" he asked in much politer tones than he was accustomed to using when he spoke to me.

"In about six months," I answered. Then, flying a kite, I asked, "Why are you so interested? Are you hoping to get married?"

He squirmed on his seat in embarrassment for a moment, then answered, "Yes."

"You're a dark horse, Malcolm McDonald," said the factor rather indignantly. "We have been working together for a year or more now and you have never said a word about marriage. Who do you have your eye on then? You were sniffing after the miller's daughter at one time, I remember."

"No, it's not Annie from the mill," said a red-faced assistant factor. "It's Emily Carstairs from Sixty Acre Farm."

"Have you been bundling yet?" asked Duncan McAllister, clearly relishing the sight of his red faced and agitated assistant.

"No," was the strangled response. "Her mother won't let us until..." and his voiced trailed off.

"Until I let you take over as factor, is it? And you thought Mr. Stewart was additional competition for you?"

"Yes," said a thoroughly miserable Malcolm McDonald.

"Hah!" said Duncan McAllister in a disgusted voice. "Be about your business, Mr. McDonald, and leave Mr. Stewart and me to ours."

"Yes, Mr. McAllister," he said and walked quietly and very dejectedly from the office.

"What do you think of that, Mr. Stewart?" he asked when we were alone again.

"He's ambitious," I said. "And with the prospect of a good match if he can better himself, who can blame him?"

"That's true," said McAllister. "Do you think I should give up my post before I'm ready to, Mr. Stewart?"

"No," I responded. "I'm sure my father would agree when I say we need your experience to guide us for some time to come, but there would be no harm in telling the laird that you want to step down and hand over to Malcolm McDonald when your knowledge is not quite so necessary on a daily basis. The laird should decide when that will be, of course, but the knowledge that he will definitely take over running the estate should be enough to advance Malcolm's desires. I take it that you are satisfied with McDonald?"

"Och! Aye!" he said. "Picked him myself so he should be all right."

"Why don't you think about it and talk to the laird in the morning?" I suggested.

"Aye," he said. "I'll do that."

One morning a few days later I was on my way to the factor's office when I came across Malcolm McDonald heading in the same direction. He stopped to let me catch up and greeted me with a smile and a handshake that could not have been warmer.

"Thank you for advising the factor as you did, Mr. Stewart. Mr. McAllister discussed his retirement with the laird, and the laird called me to his office yesterday morning and confirmed that I would take over as factor before many more months have passed. I spoke to Emily's father and mother that same evening and have their permission to court Emily if she'll allow me to. I will be for ever in your debt, Mr. Stewart."

"I did nothing more than use common sense, Malcolm, and I hope it will all work to your advantage." I couldn't help adding, "And also to the advantage of Strathmilton Estate."

"You can depend on me making every effort, sir," said the jubilant assistant factor.

We went to Caernarfon the following week for a few days so that Mrs. Evans could be told personally about the baby. They quickly decided that Joanna would deliver the child in Caernarfon, as she would be much closer to the midwife and a doctor than she could be at Strathmilton.

They were so content with their decision that I didn't like to ask how the other mothers on the estate managed when their time came.

The weeks passed steadily and Joanna's girth increased in tune.

As time passed, I became more and more accustomed to the routine of the estate office. McAllister spent fewer and fewer hours at his desk and seemed quite happy to increasingly adopt the role of expert advisor to Malcolm McDonald. Once I had developed a reasonably clear understanding of the way that the estate office should function, I also stepped back from the day to day running of the estate and concentrated on helping my father with the longer-term decisions he needed to make if the estate was to prosper. He didn't like the loss of so many of the tenant farmers caused by my uncle's reorganisation, but he admitted sadly that the larger farms were more productive, and he had to plan many years ahead to keep them so.

I was physically and mentally active but could not find in farming the satisfaction I had experienced in Bombay as Fairweather's assistant. There was nothing I could do to change the situation and could only wait until I received a letter from the telegraph company.

At that time I would have a very hard decision to make.

About two months before Joanna calculated the baby would be born, I took her to her mother's home in Caernarfon, and after she had settled in I travelled back to Strathmilton and left my wife being mollycoddled by her mother—and clearly enjoying the experience, I noticed.

Over the next six weeks I did whatever I was asked to do, but clearly my father and Malcolm McDonald had everything running satisfactorily and my involvement was at best sporadic. I had time on my hands and worried about Joanna. Consequently, and about two weeks before the baby was due, it was a considerable relief to agree with my father that I could leave Strathmilton and travel to Caernarfon.

I packed a few clothes and set off on my trip south like a child let out of school early for a holiday; and like every journey at the start of a holiday it seemed interminable, although in reality it took very little longer than usual.

In Liverpool I had some hours to wait before I could continue my journey to Caernarfon, and I used the time to look for and then purchase presents for my wife and the child she was carrying, as I suppose every man in my position does.

For Joanna I bought a soft, warm shawl knitted from lambswool. It was a light beige colour with a slightly darker brown motif in each corner. I thought Joanna might appreciate something warm to put around her shoulders when she was nursing the little one. I also made purchases for the baby, but looking back I realise that I bought toys more suited to a child of five than a newborn and clothes of a size to fit an infant not much younger. I should have asked the advice of the sales assistant but was in too much of a hurry to get back to the railway station in case I missed my train. And, of course, when I got there, I stood with my packages at my feet and waited in frustrated impotence for the ticket collector to open the barrier at the end of the platform.

Eventually it was time, and I carried my impatience onto the train with the gifts and fidgeted for the whole of an apparently endless journey. It felt as if the driver and guard were conspiring to make the stop at each station deliberately longer than necessary just to delay my reunion with my lovely wife. I looked at my watch when we arrived in Caernarfon expecting to find that the train was hours late, but instead found that it was actually a few minutes early.

Outside the station there were normally five or more hackney cabs waiting on the forecourt for a customer at any time of the day or night, but I discovered to my chagrin that there were none. Once again I had to wait, and my impatience to be reunited with Joanna caused me to consider walking, until I recollected that I could wait fifteen minutes for a cab and still arrive at the Evans home at least ten minutes quicker than I could walk there. As it happened, a cab arrived after not more than five minutes had passed, and it took only a moment to climb on board with my purchases. When we arrived outside the Evans's house, I couldn't wait for the cab driver to look for small change and consequently sent him away with a disproportionately big gratuity. I ran up the path to the front door with my packages under my arms and managed to beat a tattoo on the knocker without dropping anything.

I stood back and waited in breathless anticipation for a reunion with my wife.

The door opened and I saw one of the maids with her eyes red from weeping standing in the entrance.

She cried, "Oh, sir!" She started to cry, threw her pinafore over her head, and rushed away into the back of the house sobbing loudly.

I stood rooted to the spot not knowing what to do except drop my presents onto the floor at the side of the vestibule.

Mrs. Evans came hurrying along the hall to the door.

She wasn't crying at that moment, but her eyes showed that she had only just stopped.

She took my hands in both of hers and said, "I'm so sorry, Jason, but I have dreadful news for you. Joanna miscarried and died last night trying to give birth to your child. The midwife and the doctor were both here, but they were unable to save Joanna or your baby boy."

I wanted to scream, "It's not true! It can't be true!" but knew in my heart that she wouldn't lie to me.

"I'm so sorry, Mrs. Evans. If only I had come sooner—"

Mrs. Evans interrupted me and said, "It would have made no difference if you had been here earlier, Jason. Even the doctor was powerless. Eli Jones will say it's God's will, but God can seem very cruel at times."

My mother-in-law burst into tears again and collapsed against my chest, racked with deep sobs. I wrapped my arms around her heaving shoulders and started to weep as well. I don't know how long we stood in the door opening in our tearful embrace, but eventually Mrs. Evans stood back from me, wiped her eyes, and blew her nose.

"You have travelled a long way today, Jason. Are you hungry?" she asked.

Food, I thought. *How can I think about food at a time like this? My world has come to an end, so what do I want food for?*

But I said politely, "I'm not hungry, thank you." I paused for a moment, then added, "I would be unable to stomach food even if I wanted something, but I would like to go upstairs." I stopped as an unwelcome thought crossed my mind and I asked, "Is Joanna…" and ground to a halt, as I didn't know how best to ask where my wife's body was lying without causing more upset.

Mrs. Evans must have had a similar difficulty as well as she said obliquely, "The undertaker has been to take care of that, Jason. You will be able to see her at the chapel of rest tomorrow," and she started to weep once again.

I excused myself, climbed the stairs to the room I had used before Joanna and I were married, and sat on the edge of the bed immersed in my solitary misery, mourning for what might have been. I didn't weep again. I think I was too stunned by the enormity of the tragedy that had befallen me to feel sufficient emotion to be able to weep.

I may have slept.

If I did, it was an unsatisfying slumber, and it was also a wonder that I didn't fall from the edge of the bed where I was perched. In the morning I made a rudimentary toilette and went downstairs to the breakfast room.

It was habit rather than necessity.

I was still too numb to feel simple things like hunger or thirst. There was food on the sideboard so I took some and picked at it for a while, then pushed the half-empty plate to one side. Mrs. Evans came in as I drank a cup of tea. We exchanged good mornings in voices that demonstrated the depth of despair we were both experiencing.

She selected a small plateful of food, and after a long silence, Mrs. Evans asked, "Will you go to the funeral parlour this morning?"

"Yes," I responded. "I don't want to, as I would like to remember Joanna as she was when she was alive—" and I stopped with a sob and had to wipe tears from my eyes before taking several deep calming breaths. "But I must confront the reality of what has happened."

"May I accompany you, Jason?" she asked in a tremulous voice.

"Of course," I replied. "I'll arrange a carriage for us as soon as you tell me you are ready."

Mrs. Evans pushed her plate to one side and said, "I have no appetite this morning. We can leave as soon as you can arrange a carriage, Jason."

"Very well," I said as I stood up. I went outside and waved down the first empty conveyance that passed. It was a cab rather than a carriage, but for the distance we had to cover, I felt that either vehicle would do. I told the driver to wait and went back into the house to find Mrs. Evans.

———————————

At the undertaker's premises we were introduced to the senior representative of the firm. I cannot speak for Mrs. Evans on this matter, and we never spoke about it, but I found it very difficult to politely shake the man's hand knowing that it was probably the same hand that prepared the corpses for burial. My repugnance was heightened by the cold, clammy feel of his fingers, and I was barely able to restrain a shudder of distaste.

He seemed not to notice, or else he was so accustomed to the reaction of his client's relatives that he didn't bother about it any more.

Unemotionally, he said, "Good morning, Mrs. Evans and Mr. Stewart. As you know, the funeral is the day after tomorrow at eleven. As the service will begin at your house, Mrs. Evans, I will bring the deceased there at ten. I take it we can set up the coffin on trestles in the morning room?" but Mrs. Evans rushed in tears from the undertaker's office, and I was left in my own emotionally charged state to make the arrangements.

When all was finished, he said, "Would you like to see Mrs. Stewart now?"

I wanted to say, "No!" and run from the place, but I knew that I should look upon my wife's face at least once before the coffin lid was screwed down and managed to make a half-hearted nod of agreement.

"This way, sir," he said and he led me out of his office. We walked along a short corridor. At the end he opened a door and led me into quite a large candle-lit room where I was astonished to find several open-topped coffins supported on trestles.

"Mrs. Stewart is here, sir," he said as he led me past two coffins and toward one at the back of the room.

He touched the wooden side of the coffin and said, "It's Welsh oak, sir," with such pride that I half-expected him to complete the sales pitch and add, "It'll last a lifetime, sir!"

I looked down into the satin-clad interior of my wife's coffin. She was wearing one of her favourite dresses. Her eyes were closed and her face was as peaceful as if she were asleep. The few laughter lines Joanna had acquired near the corners of her eyes had been smoothed away, and her face was as gently suffused with pink as if she was a vibrant and live person.

It looked as if she would awake with a kiss, but her forehead was cold and lifeless when I tried. I recoiled from the touch of dead skin and ran from the room wishing I had been content with my memories.

―――――――――――――

Two days later at about half past nine in the morning, Tudor and Gwyn, accompanied by their wives, arrived at the front door and were shown into the sitting room on the opposite side of the hall from the room where Joanna's coffin would rest temporarily. The men were dressed in dark suits and wore black ties and shoes. Llynos and Emily wore black costumes and hats and carried small, black handbags. Llynos and Emily went immediately to my mother-in-law and expressed their condolences about Joanna's untimely death, and all three ladies promptly coalesced into a tearful huddle. Tudor and Gwyn each shook my hand and said how sorry they were about the tragic event that had taken place, but mercifully we were freed from the necessity of further painful and emotional conversation by the arrival of a carriage and the hearse just before the hour. We went outside to meet the undertaker, who had arrived in separate polished black carriage together with four pallbearers. They all wore black morning suits and top hats and professionally mournful faces.

It was a beautiful, sunny morning with a gentle westerly breeze rustling the leaves, and somewhere above us a lark was singing.

Joanna would enjoy a day like this, I thought sadly and felt the tears prick my eyes again.

The hearse was drawn by a matched pair of geldings the colour of polished ebony and each had a tall plume of black feathers attached to its harness between its ears. The horses' tack was of black leather and it had all been polished until it gleamed. The hearse itself was a long, low vehicle with side panels made largely of thick glass with chamfered edges contained in wooden frames that had also been painted black and polished. I noticed that the roof had a low railing around the edge and wondered why it was necessary.

The undertaker walked to the back of the hearse and opened the end door. Two of the pallbearers reached into the hearse and, catching hold of the first pair of handles, pulled the coffin out toward them. The other two pallbearers and then Joanna's uncles stepped forward to grasp the other handles as they came into view, and in no time they had the coffin out of the hearse and then they lifted it up onto their shoulders and carried it into the house. Black-clad friends and neighbours of the Evans family started to arrive outside the house and handed their wreaths to the pallbearers before starting conversations with the people near them.

I knew no one and might as well have been invisible for all the notice that was taken of me. I suppose I could have tried to talk to someone, but I couldn't bring myself to walk up to a stranger and say, "Good morning. I was Joanna's husband." It didn't seem a very appropriate way to start a conversation.

I was very sorry that I hadn't received an answer to the telegram I had sent to my father to tell him what had happened, but there was nothing more I could do at present.

The Reverend Eli Jones arrived. I went back into the house, rejoined the family to listen to his words of comfort and support, and then it was time to go to the church. Joanna's uncles together with the pallbearers carried the coffin out of the house and placed it back in the hearse. The family wreaths including mine were placed on and beside the coffin whilst those that had been given by friends and neighbours were put on the roof. I understood then why the low rail was there. Joanna's mother and her uncles and aunts climbed into the carriage the undertaker had arrived in, and I climbed in after them and closed the door.

The undertaker walked to the front of the hearse and two of the pallbearers took position beside the coffin on each side. As soon as everyone was in place, the undertaker started to walk toward the church, and the hearse and our carriage followed him. I looked out of the back window and was gratified to find that most of the people who had stood outside the Evans's house were forming up into a procession behind us.

At the church Joanna's coffin was laid down with infinite care on a catafalque by the altar, and I was stunned to see that a tiny coffin already rested there. I realised that it must contain the body of my dead baby son and I felt the tears flow once again. I remember nothing of the service and came back to an awareness of my surroundings only when I stood at the graveside and watched them lower Joanna's coffin into the grave with our son's tiny coffin resting on top above her left breast.

As the first shovelfuls of earth clattered down on the wooden coffins below, I suddenly realised that I could at last understand the motives that caused a Hindu wife to throw herself on her husband's funeral pyre in the act known as *Suttee.* I did so want to be with Joanna that I almost threw myself down on to her coffin, but Tudor, possibly thinking I was about to faint, caught my arm and pulled me back and the feeling passed.

After the service we went back to the Evans's house for the wake, and the next day I left for Strathmilton.

I went straight to my father's study when I arrived at the castle and as soon as he saw me he said, "I have only just received your telegram and I cannot believe what I have just read. I didn't know if I should immediately start for Caernarfon or stay here until I could get more news." He paused to get up from his desk and take my hand as he added, "Jason, I can only say how very sorry I am that this tragedy has occurred. I assume that the funeral has already taken place, as you are here."

"Yes," I said. "The day before yesterday at eleven." I went on to describe everything that had happened. When I finished I asked my father to excuse me, and as I couldn't face the rooms that Joanna and I had spent such happy times in, I went to one of the guest rooms to grieve for what might have been. Over the next week I wandered from place to place and room to room too absorbed by my grief to be of use to anyone.

After allowing me what he considered to be sufficient time in which to wallow in self pity, my father, who had also been much affected by Joanna's sudden death, decided that enough was enough and told me in no uncertain terms to pull myself together. I hated him for his cruelty at that moment but looking back it was clear that someone had to bring me to my senses, and my father was by far the best qualified.

I followed my father's advice and wrote suitable messages to Fairweather, Barnaby Williams, and Captain Downing, but decided to go to Lenton to tell my aunt and her husband the bad news in person. I felt it would be better than an impersonal letter no matter how carefully phrased, as Aunt Mary and Joanna had been more like sisters than casually related women.

I packed a few things and said my goodbyes.

In retrospect, I think the inhabitants were as pleased to see the back of my miserable face as I was to be getting away from the painful memories of Joanna invoked by so much of the interior of Strathmilton Castle.

I set off on my long lonely journey south. I travelled all day and then all night and reached Grantham in the dawn. I had breakfast at the hotel I had stayed at previously then hired a pony and trap to take me to Lenton. I knocked on the door of the vicarage, and it was quickly opened by one of the maids. She said, "Good morning, sir." As her eyes took in the pallor of my complexion and the funereal black clothes I was wearing, she added, "Come in, Mr. Stewart, and I will get Mrs. Perceval immediately." She moved quickly to the morning room. I don't know what she said, but

Aunt Mary came hurrying into the hall with the Reverend Perceval close behind and they both looked very apprehensive.

Aunt Mary came quickly to me and, taking both my hands, said, "Whatever has happened, Jason?"

"Joanna's dead," I managed to say and tried not to give way to the emotion that was racking my body as I added, "She died trying to give birth to our child."

Aunt Mary's face crumpled in grief and tears started to course down her cheeks as she whispered in a shocked voice, "I can't believe it," then asked in the same whisper, "Is the child all right?"

"Dead also," I responded, and my voice wavered as all the emotion caused by my loss forced its way to the surface of my soul like an exploding geyser.

Aunt Mary dabbed at her eyes, sniffed, and said sadly "What devastating news. I can't believe it's true. Joanna was such a lovely young woman. Oh, Jason! I'm so sorry for you. You were both so happy together." Aunt Mary burst into tears once again and the maid who had been listening open-mouthed to our conversation quickly followed suit.

Reverend Perceval managed to keep his emotion under control. He took my hand and said simply, "I'm so very sorry this tragedy has occurred, Jason. I'll pray for you to find the strength of character necessary to overcome this heartbreak."

"Thank you, Reverend," was all I could say.

Life has to go on, and despite the tears and sobs I went back to the room I had occupied in the past and managed to sleep for an hour—then we had a sombre and largely uncommunicative lunch together.

Reverend Perceval tried to focus my mind on the future instead of the past and asked, "Do you think you will go back to Bombay, Jason?"

Without thinking I said, "I don't know, Reverend. I discussed the possibility several times with Joanna—" and ground to a halt as the pain of knowing that I would never, ever, discuss anything with my wife again screamed in my brain. It would have been so easy to give in to the emotion that was tearing me apart, but with my aunt and the Reverend Perceval trying not to observe my agony and the servant girl alternately sniffing and weeping, I knew I that I must not give in.

I took several deep breathes, blinked my tears away, and said as calmly as I could manage, "Joanna and I discussed the possibility several times, but we couldn't make a decision until I had an offer from the telegraph company, and until I'm asked to return I cannot go back to Bombay. I have no position or authority there. I do not need to work, but I must fill my waking hours if I am to keep my sanity, but I do not know what I can fill them with. I could go back to Strathmilton, but my father and the factor run the estate and there are too many memories of Joanna," and I had to gulp my emotion back again before saying, "for me to be happy there. I don't know what I will do, Reverend, but at present death is preferable to this continuing misery."

"Many people have felt as you do, Jason, but you have to try and have enough faith to accept that what has happened is God's will."

I choked back the angry responses that bubbled to my lips, stood up, and marched from the dining room. In my bedroom I threw myself on to my bed and stared through tear-filled eyes at the ceiling. What could I do now that my reason for living had been snuffed out like a guttering candle? Where should I go? Who should I talk to? Many, many questions but I did not have a single answer. After a time the fatigue of travel and emotion overcame my brain, and I slept fully dressed until morning and awoke to find that someone had covered me with a thick blanket.

I got up, shaved, washed, and dressed without conscious thought. I was just going through the routine motions of living. I went down to get some breakfast although I had no appetite and met Reverend Perceval in the breakfast room.

He said a polite, "Good morning, Jason," and continued with his breakfast. He didn't ask how I had slept and didn't allude to the emotional way I had left the dinner table the previous evening. He finished eating and said, "I should be grateful for your help this morning, Jason, if you have nothing planned."

I wondered how I could possibly help my uncle but said, "If I can help you, Reverend, I should be pleased to. What do you want me to do?"

"I have to go and visit one of my parishioners," he said in response. "She is a young woman and she is like you, very recently and unexpectedly bereaved. I think she might gain more comfort and support from talking to someone who is also suffering than I can give by prayer alone. It will be very hard for you to do, Jason, and I would understand if you decide to say no."

It was on the tip of my tongue to say no, but then I thought, *If the reverend thinks I might help, then it would be churlish to deny him the chance to help the woman even if it is by proxy,* so I changed my mind and said, "I'll help if I'm able to, Reverend. What happened?"

"The husband's name was Arnold Potterton, and he had just taken over his father's building company when he died. Old Mr. Potterton was a local man who had built up a fine reputation as a craftsman even outside the county. Because the company was so successful, they seemed to be quite a wealthy family, but for some reason the widow is in financial difficulties as a result of her husband's death. It's rumoured that she has to live on the little capital that's left now that there is no regular income. Her name is Emily, by the way."

"What did Arnold Potterton die of?" I asked.

"What?" said Reverend Perceval. "Oh? Didn't I say? He was renovating an old mansion on the other side of the county a few weeks ago when it happened."

"What happened?"

"A brick fell on his head and killed him stone dead."

"How old was he?" I asked.

"About your age, Jason, which is why I thought you might be able to help Emily better than an old man like me."

"I'll try, Reverend," was the only answer I could give. I then asked, "Where is my aunt today?"

"I'm sorry to say that she is too distraught by the news you brought yesterday to come down this morning," he answered bluntly.

"I'm very sorry to hear that, Reverend." It was all I could say.

A short time later the Reverend Perceval and I left the vicarage and started to walk to the other side of Lenton to visit Mrs. Emily Potterton.

Mrs. Potterton lived at the end of a grassy lane that had May and Hawthorn trees growing in the thick, high hedges. It was built of brick, had a slate-covered roof, and appeared to be the most modern house in

Lenton. As it should be, I supposed, as it was erected by the local builder for his own use. Reverend Perceval led us through the garden gate and up to the front door which he rat-a-tat-tatted on with the knob on his walking stick as there was no knocker.

The door opened and a young woman stood in the entry then stepped back and said, "Please come in, Reverend, and you, sir," and led us in to a room just to the left of the entry.

"I'll just go and tell my mistress you are here, gentlemen," and she whisked about and left the room, shutting the door gently behind her.

I looked around and noted the quality of the furniture that shone in the light from the big, leaded lights to the left of the door. The polished mahogany tables and bookcases, the leather upholstered chairs all spoke of wealth and good taste. I was rather envious, as it was very like the furnishing that Joanna and I had talked about. A lifetime ago! *Mrs. Potterton may have no income*, I realised, *but she could realise a good sum on the house and furnishings if her needs became desperate.*

The door opened and the maid came and there was a small boy about three years old clutching her hand. As soon as he saw Reverend Perceval and me, he let go of the maid's hand and retreated to a safer position where he was hidden behind her skirt. After a moment, I saw his big-eyed little face appear with his right hand clutching the fabric of her skirt and his right thumb firmly planted in his mouth. We looked at each other for a moment and then the face disappeared again. A woman appeared in the doorway behind the maid and walked listlessly into the room. That she was in mourning for her dead husband could not be doubted. Dressed in black from head to foot, the pallor of her cheeks could not have made a starker contrast with her clothing and I noted that her eyes were red from weeping. *What on earth am I doing here?* I wondered.

She walked over to Reverend Perceval without a glance in my direction and held out her hand, "Good morning, Reverend. I didn't expect to see you again so soon."

It was not a welcoming welcome, I thought, but Reverend Perceval, who seemed to be untouched by her tone, took her hand and said warmly but not quite accurately, "Good morning, Mrs. Potterton. We were nearby so I thought we would come and see if there is anything you need."

"Only my husband, but you cannot give him back to me, can you, Reverend?" she said acidly and my uncle winced.

"Mrs. Potterton," I said, "I was very sorry to hear about the untimely death of your husband. I would like to say how sorry I was to hear of your sad loss and how much I can commiserate with you in your grief."

She turned sharply toward me and said angrily, "Who are you and what could someone of your age possibly know about grief?"

"My name is Jason Stewart, Mrs. Potterton. My wife died trying to birth our child not two weeks back, so I have some personal knowledge of pain and suffering. My uncle," and I indicated Reverend Perceval, "thought that we might be able to help each other in our mourning."

"I'm truly sorry to hear about your wife, Mr. Stewart, and apologise for the way I addressed you," she said contritely.

"No apology is necessary," I said. "To the people who have had to live with me, I have been far from polite company for the past two weeks and for the same reason. When I return home, I will have to apologise to all the people I must have offended by my rudeness."

"Where is your home, Mr. Stewart?" she asked.

"Most recently I have been living in Scotland, but I come from Pickworth originally."

"I don't remember anyone by the name of Stewart living in Pickworth. Are there two villages called Pickworth?"

"I don't think so. I didn't know my family name was Stewart at the time, as I was brought up by Mr. Smiley, the blacksmith, and his wife."

"Are you Jason Smiley?" she asked, and before I could answer she added, "You went to India and got a medal for something, if I remember."

"Your memory is very good," I said and half-turned to Reverend Perceval, hoping that he would provide some excuse for me to escape from the questioning, but he just sat in his chair with a smile on his face and made a shooing gesture behind Mrs. Potterton's back to encourage me to go on. I did as I was bid, as I had no polite alternative.

"I don't remember the name Potterton from my childhood, and I have no idea what your maiden name was," I said.

"The Potterton family came to Lenton from Kings Lynn," she said. "My maiden name was Emily Beynon, and my parents and I moved here about fifteen years ago. That must have been about the time you went to India, Mr. Stewart."

She noticed that she and I were still standing and said, "Perhaps we should sit down, Mr Stewart, and continue our conversation in more comfort," and she suited her actions to her words. "Would you like to have some tea?" she asked, and when I agreed the maid was despatched to make it. The little boy was suddenly without his shield, and as his face puckered ready to cry, I managed to catch his eye and hold out my hand. Hesitantly, he toddled across and stood by my knees. When I bent down and picked him up, his whole body went rigid with fear, but I sat him on my lap and just supported him there. After a moment or two, tiredness overcame his fear and he leant against me and went to sleep. I looked down at the little boy sleeping on my lap and felt immeasurably sad.

If only things could have been different, I thought.

"His name is Malcolm," volunteered Mrs. Potterton, who had looked quite startled when her child had allowed a total stranger to pick him up.

The tea was brought in by the maid.

I noticed again the appearance of wealth in the silver teapot and sugar basin and the very delicate bone china crockery on a silver tray. The maid placed the tray on a low table beside Mrs. Potterton, who found she had to change from mourner to hostess whether she wanted to or not. The hostile, painful atmosphere of five minutes before was exchanged for something a little more domestic and less straining.

In an effort to keep our minds off recent tragedies, Reverend Perceval said, "You should encourage my nephew to tell you something about his experiences in India, Mrs Potterton. Quite hair-raising some of it has been. He is only at home now because he was badly wounded."

Mrs. Potterton's natural curiosity was aroused and she started asking questions. Out of politeness I had to respond, and as each answer seemed to provoke another question, we chatted about my life and experiences for a good hour before the little boy woke again and fractiously demanded food.

I cannot speak for Mrs. Potterton, of course, but for me that hour marked the beginning of my recovery. It was a turning point in my life. I had started to learn to control my grief so that it didn't affect other people quite so openly. I couldn't forget my loss, but I hoped it would no longer rule my life and my relationships with others.

I thanked Reverend Perceval for his thoughtful help as we walked back to the vicarage, but he said, "I don't need to be thanked, Jason. Seeing two very nice people start out on the road that leads to a recovery from a tragedy is reward enough."

Over the next few days the restoration of sanity that Reverend Perceval had instigated continued to prosper in the calm and loving atmosphere generated by my aunt and uncle. I knew that I should soon travel north again and try to make friends with the people I felt I had alienated by my overindulgent grief.

Reverend Perceval was convinced that everyone would understand the strain I had been going through and wouldn't expect an apology.

He said, "Jason, you should not underestimate the people you know. They are all aware of the enormity of the tragedy you have experienced and know that they would have acted in a similar fashion in the same circumstances. Going back and showing them that you are managing to control your grief will go a long way toward the reconciliation you hope to achieve. I should be astonished if there is any lasting animosity even if such existed before."

"I agree," said Aunt Mary, who had largely recovered from the shock of Joanna's death and was living with her normally robust outlook on life.

And so two or three days later I found myself on the back of a horse riding inexpertly along the track that lead from the foot of the hill to the castle gate. It was the last stage of my journey from Carlisle to the castle. I was tired, coated in dust, and my buttocks were so sore they felt as if they had been beaten with iron bars. I was tempted to get off the horse and walk the last mile but decided that the agony would be over quicker if I rode on. I walked the horse into the castle courtyard, stopped at the hitching rail by the main entrance to the castle, and dismounted with the grace of a sack of potatoes falling from a wagon. I had to clutch hold of the stirrup for support, as my legs buckled in protest and just managed to dodge a kick from the horse as I fell against its side. As I painfully straightened my legs and stretched my back, I heard the latch on the front door click and looked toward the entrance.

One of the maidservants stood on the step in the doorway and said, "Can I…" and, as she recognised me, changed what she had intended to say and said instead, "Oh! It's you, Mr. Stewart. How are you, sir?"

"I'm quite well and thank you," and in my mind I blessed the girl for not mouthing any of the "how sorry I was to hear about your wife" phrases. "Is my father here?" I asked.

"Yes, Mr. Stewart. The earl is in his office. Shall I tell him you're here, or will you go straight to him?"

It was still quite strange to hear my captain father proudly referred to as "the earl," and I realised it was a title that I would not only have to get used to hearing others use but would also have to employ at appropriate times when I was speaking with outsiders.

I said, "Thank you, but I'll go up immediately and tell him that I've returned. Please arrange for someone to take my horse to the stable."

"Yes, sir," she said.

I walked like an arthritic old man to the doorway and then upstairs and along the corridor to the room that my father had taken over as an office. I knocked and went in when I heard the familiar voice call, "Enter."

I went in and closed the door behind me. As I was about to speak, he looked up from the letter he was reading. Upon seeing me, he jumped to his feet and strode around to the front of his desk, wrapping his arms around me in a great bear hug of welcome.

"Welcome home, Jason," he said with enthusiasm. "I'm so pleased to see you again, and you're looking much better than I dared hope for. How are you?"

"I'm physically quite well, Father, thank you, and day by day the pain is easier to bear. Fortunately, Reverend Perceval was able to set me on the road to recovery. I don't know where I would be now if he hadn't taken charge on my first day in Lenton."

"The reverend is a very astute person," my father said. "You were very fortunate to have him to help you. How is my sister?"

"Aunt Mary was prostrated by the news, as you would imagine, Father, but she had recovered her sense of proportion by the time I left. She gave me a letter for you when I left. It's in my bag. I'll go and get it for you," and I turned toward the door.

"Later! Jason, later," he said. "You can give it to me after you have had time to wash and change after your long journey. I have some letters here for you," and he sat down again behind his desk and started to look through a drawer.

"They're in here somewhere," he said as he rummaged. "Please sit down, Jason, and tell me what you intend to do?"

"After riding a horse from Carlisle, I think I would prefer to stand a little longer, if you don't mind, Father?"

"No, please stand if that's more comfortable," he answered with a grin.

"As far as plans are concerned, Father, I don't have any. My life doesn't seem to have a point anymore, so why make plans? I expected to receive a message from Anglo Indian asking me to go back to Bombay. If Joanna," and I was surprised I could even think her name without having to choke back my emotion, "had been alive, it would have been very difficult to leave her here with a small child if I had received an offer. I suppose I should try and find something to do. Perhaps I should try to meet Mr. Fairweather to see if he needs an assistant again," I added unenthusiastically.

"In the mean time, if you would like to become involved in the running of the estate again, I'm sure Malcolm will be pleased to see you," suggested my father encouragingly.

"Thank you, Father, but I think it would be better not to become too involved until I know how long I am likely to stay here," I said, trying to postpone the need for a positive decision. "It would be a pity to start helping Malcolm and a week later stop again."

"Very well, Jason. You can practise being the idle son of an earl until you are bored or have a better offer."

"Thank you, Father," I said, grateful for his understanding.

By this time he had rooted out all of my letters and as he handed them to me he suggested we should meet again at dinnertime. It was a suggestion with which I was very happy to agree.

After dinner when I returned to my room I sat on the edge of the bed and looked at the small bundle of envelopes I had received. All the envelopes except one had a black band around the edge, and I realised that the contents would have something to do with Joanna's death. I put all these on the top shelf of the bookcase and told myself as I did so that I would read them later.

I never did and eventually threw them away unread.

The remaining envelope was quite large, made of stiff, white paper and had the emblem of the Gold Star Line embossed discreetly in the bottom left-hand corner. I realised that it could only be from Captain Downing and used my pocket knife to slit open the envelope. Inside was a note and an envelope addressed to Mr. Jason Smiley in handwriting that I didn't recognise.

I read the note first and it said,

> *Dear Jason,*
>
> *If I had not received the enclosed letter for you, I would not have written at this time, as I have found that a letter of condolence can exacerbate sensitive emotions instead of soothing them.*
>
> *You have been inflicted with a grievous loss, and my wife and I pray that your suffering will soon be reduced to a manageable degree. If I can help you at any time, please feel free to call on me.*
>
> *Yours sincerely,*

It was signed by Captain Downing, the Marine Superintendent of the Gold Star Line, and I appreciated the sentiments he had expressed with such sensitivity. At the same time I was suddenly very sorry that our wedding invitation had been addressed to Captain Downing alone. He and I had been together only in connection with shipping company business, and as a result I had never heard about or even considered the possibility that he might have a wife. They might also have children, I realised.

How sad that I do not know, I thought.

I picked up the other envelope and read that it was addressed to me, c/o Captain Stewart, Gold Star Line, Liverpool, as I slit the end open with a paper knife. *Someone's behind the times*, I thought. I pulled out a sheet of thick paper that crackled as I tried to unfold it and smooth it flat. Centrally placed at the top of the page, a colourful shield had been embossed, and I knew I had never seen one anything like it before.

The text was simple and to the point.

> *Dear Mr. Smiley,*
>
> *Sir David Tallboy has instructed me to write to ascertain your interest in coming to Australia to act as Sir David's personal assistant on matters related to the development of the electric telegraph in this country. I am also instructed to advise you that Sir David is mindful of the dreadful injury you suffered, and since much travelling in arduous conditions will be required if you agree to assist him, he will understand if you decide to decline his offer for that reason.*
>
> *Sir David would be grateful if you would send your reply by the most expeditious means.*
>
> *Yours sincerely,*

It was signed by someone of whom I had never heard and who described himself as the Secretary to the Governor's Office, which I thought to be a rather quaint title. Secretary to someone was normal, but secretary to an office was not—at least not as far as I was aware.

My spirits were raised a little as I realised how big a compliment I had received. To be asked to travel to the other side of the world and act as a specialist assistant to the governor of a state in Australia that was as big as many sovereign countries was something to crow about, but I decided it would be more appropriate to sleep on it. Besides, I didn't want to decide my future so quickly.

Next morning, I took the letter to my father's office and gave it to him to read.

He said, "That's a very good offer and a considerable compliment to your abilities, Jason. Will you accept it?"

"I don't know for certain, Father," I said as I tried to postpone the need for a decision. "It wasn't at all what I expected. Going to Australia instead of Bombay will take some getting used to, I think. Anyway, as I have to write back and then wait for a reply, I imagine it will be some months before I leave. I can afford the time to consider the proposal carefully; I'll think about it for another day or so before replying."

"If you think you are going to be here for a little while, there is something that you could do for me that will exercise one of your old and probably rusty skills."

My father's statement should have pricked my interest but didn't, and I was unable to match the note of enthusiasm apparent in his voice when I asked, "What do you have in mind, Father?"

"I was talking to Malcolm the other day, and he was complaining about the poor quality of the crops we get from the eastern fields due to the lack of water in the area. Then the next day I was near Milton Pool and wondered if it would be possible to pipe water from there. As you know, there is a small hillock between the pool and the fields, and that is where you come in, Jason. Perhaps you could use your surveying skills to see if the idea is practical?"

"It's a good idea, and I would like to help, but where can I get a transit?"

"You will have to ask the builder," my father responded. "If he doesn't have one, he will certainly know where you can get what you need. You will need two or three of Malcolm's men to assist you but you can arrange that."

"I'll go and see Malcolm in a little while," I said without enthusiasm as I left my father's room.

I'll write to Australia tonight, I decided as I walked to the factor's office, *but should I say "yes" or should I decline the offer.* I half wanted to go and at the same time, half wanted to stay where it was familiar. As one can imagine, writing the letter was postponed.

Several days of equivocation and frustrating delays later, I set out with my temporary assistants to make the survey my father had asked for. Finding a transit was not too difficult, but finding one that was in adjustment was a different question. In the end, I adjusted the one the builder had offered. Then it rained. Initially, the rain was torrential, but then it eased into what I believe is known as Scotch mist. It was just as wetting whatever it was called and certainly not suitable weather for surveying no matter how urgent. So here I was eventually, equipped with men and an instrument, blessed with fine weather and no longer able to find a plausible excuse to avoid starting when a stable boy riding bareback jounced up to the lake where I had decided to begin the work.

"Mr. Stewart, sir, the earl said please come back to the castle," the boy called out as soon as he was close enough for his thin, reedy voice to be heard.

"Did the earl say why I should come back?" I asked.

"No, sir, but someone has come to see you, I think."

"Very well," I said to the boy. "Please go back to the castle and send a message to the earl to tell him I will come as soon as possible."

The boy turned his horse and set off for the castle as I turned to my helpers and instructed them to take everything back to the castle and put it in the storeroom. I was quite ashamed that I felt so relieved. I should have been disappointed about the delay but wasn't in the least. I climbed onto my horse and set off after the stable boy, whose distant backside seemed to be bouncing up and down in a precarious if not an actually painful fashion.

About an hour later I was in the main reception room of the castle and found my old friend, Neil Fairweather, sitting there.

As he took and warmly shook my hand he said, "Your letter about Joanna's death came as a terrible shock, Mr. Stewart. I grieve with you and for you, my friend. But as you have found out already, I think, life must go on no matter how devastated we feel."

"Thank you," I said. "It has been the worst experience of my life." I took a deep breath to steady myself, pushed the unhappy memories into the back of my mind. I then asked, "How long will you be able to stay?"

"Only tonight, unfortunately," he responded. "I would like to stay and explore your castle because I have never been in a real castle before, but I have to return to duty in two days' time. And that's really why I came to see you. I am in need of an assistant again. My company has won an order to supply everything required for the overland telegraph cable between Darwin in the north and Adelaide in the south of Australia. We also hope to supply the armoured cable for the underwater link to the North

Island of New Zealand. Initially, I have to supervise the shipments in this country and then the installation in the Antipodes, and because it's such a great deal of work, I need a knowledgeable and trustworthy assistant.

"You are still employed by the telegraph company, but I could get you transferred to the cable company if you wish. Do you think you would like to rejoin me?"

"I think I would like that very much, Mr. Fairweather," I said hesitantly. "But there is a complication. I have been asked to go to Australia to be the governor's assistant on matters relating to telegraph."

"That would be a considerable honour for you, Mr. Stewart, and I can only congratulate you on your extreme good fortune. When will you sail?" Mr. Fairweather asked, having already decided that I would have accepted the offer immediately.

His eyebrows shot up in surprise when I said, "I don't know. I haven't accepted the offer yet."

"Why ever not?" was the astonished question.

"My life has been thrown into such turmoil following Joanna's death that I don't know what I want to do. I have been unable to make up my mind. I cannot decide if it is better to accept or to decline, and the result has been the achievement of nothing. And now you have arrived with a suggestion that further complicates my position by giving me another set of choices. My wish to hide in the corner of a dark room and let the world go by without bothering me further is so strong that I do not know how I manage to reject it. I don't mind telling you, Mr. Fairweather, that organising a little survey for my father has been a struggle against massive indecision, and you know how confidently I have made decisions in the past. I really wonder if I will be able to do what you want me to do."

"But at least you have started the survey, and that's a step in the right direction, isn't it?" asked Fairweather with a worried frown creasing his brow. "I'm quite sure that in a few weeks at most you will be back to the Jason Smiley Stewart we knew and respected."

"I suppose so," I answered unenthusiastically. "I certainly hope so, and I thank you for your confidence—but I would be a happier man if I shared it."

"But you will accept and come and help me, won't you?" he asked.

"I don't know, and that's the truth of the matter," I responded.

Fairweather pulled out his watch and, after opening it, he said, "I have to go and meet your father in five minutes. I expect we will reminisce about old times. Will you come as well?"

"No," I answered. "I'll go to my room and try to decide what to do."

I went to my room and tried to decide what to do, but every time I thought my future was settled, my brain sent me off on another cycle of inconclusive thought. The more I thought, the more muddled my thinking became and the more my recent tragedy affected my thoughts. I would go to Australia; stay at home; work with Fairweather; assist Sir David. Around and around my thoughts circulated until I thought I would scream with the frustration of not being able to decide. The dinner gong sounded distantly in the hall below, but I ignored it. A maid came and put a tray of food on the table, but I ignored that as well. I lay on my bed and was too remote from reality to take off my dirty boots. I wanted to decide but deciding was much too difficult. Eventually, I just lay on my bed too sorry for myself to move.

Next morning, quite some time after breakfast would have been over, my door slammed open and I opened my eyes to see water cascading from a bucket moments before it impacted upon my head. It was very, very cold. Moments later another deluge crashed in to my head and I started to sit up and say, "Why are you—" when a third bucketful landed and I erupted from my bed full of indignation, soaking wet and shivering.

"That's better," my father said. "A little emotion at last."

"Why are you dowsing me with cold water?" I spluttered.

"To wake you up," he said. "It's time to rejoin the real world."

"Why should I bother?"

He ignored my petulant comment and said bluntly, "You have to start behaving like a man again. We all know the enormity of the tragedy you have suffered, but life goes on and whether you like it or not, you have to be part of it. There are two very worthwhile opportunities open to you, and if you do not have the courage to choose one of them then I'll decide for you."

The determined set to his face made me realise that he meant what he said. "Now, Jason, you must wash and dress. I expect to see you in my study in half an hour. Is that clear?"

"Yes," I responded.

He walked to the door and then returned to the bed and pulled all the soaking wet bedding on to the floor then walked out, leaving the door open.

I washed, dressed, and exactly half an hour later I knocked on the door to my father's office. In response to his, "Enter," I pushed open the door, crossed the room, and stood mutely in front of the desk whilst he looked me up and down.

"Well, Jason, at least you are clean, tidy, and on your feet, and those improvements are major steps forward in their own right after your behaviour yesterday. You have procrastinated long enough, young man, and as I said upstairs, if you do not accept one of these exceptional offers yourself then I will choose for you. Now, which is it to be?"

I stood silently for a moment, then on the basis of "the devil you know is better that the devil you don't," I said, "I'll accept Fairweather's offer. At least he will know how I worked before Joanna died."

"Very well, Jason; sit over there" and he pointed at a table in the corner of the room, "and prepare suitable letters to Fairweather and Sir David Tallboy. When they are finished, I will ensure they are taken to Carlisle and posted today."

"Yes, Father," I responded.

I suppose I felt a slight feeling of relief now that one decision had been taken, but that relief was soon overshadowed by another set of worries as I contemplated going to Australia.

In fact, I wasn't allowed to worry about it, as my father took command and I simply had to do what I was bidden to do. I'm on this ship heading for Australia as my father has cajoled and bullied me every step of the way and has not given me the opportunity to dodge the issue.

"And so, Captain, you know now why I have been such a miserable individual," I concluded.

FIVE

A New Beginning

The ship lurched and the bows sank into a deeper trough than usual.

Captain Osborne picked up his cap and said, "Thank you for confiding in me, Mr. Stewart. I hope sharing the burden will make it easier for you to carry it, but now I must return to the bridge. Perhaps you would care to join me? It will be better for you than sitting on your own, I believe."

"Thank you, Captain. I think you may be correct."

We walked along the companionway together and up onto the bridge. Captain Osborne checked the course, tapped the barometer, and then looked at the chart with John Bartholomew, the first mate, for a few minutes. Captain Osborne told the mate, "Carry on," and came over to where I was standing behind the helmsman.

He said, "I am not a particularly religious man, Mr. Stewart, but I do believe that a tragedy such as you described earlier cannot be a chance happening. God must have had a reason for taking your wife and child away, and you have to be strong enough to live your life normally and find out what that purpose might be. You should not shun contact with your fellow man just in case they might ask painful questions. You will never understand why God acted as He did if you continue to cut yourself off. I can say without fear of contradiction that my faith in God's greater purpose sustains me when tragedies occur at sea that I cannot otherwise explain."

"Thank you for listening to me this evening and for your council, Captain. I will try to follow your advice."

I noticed the mate standing close to us and, thinking he wanted to talk to his Captain, started to excuse myself, but he said, "Excuse me, Mr. Stewart, but I would like to ask you a personal question, if I may?"

"Of course," I responded.

"I happened to see your name in the passenger list, sir. I have been to Bombay several times and I was told something of the exploits in the Elphinstone Inlet of a Mr. Jason Smiley who was working for the telegraph company there. I wondered if that was you."

"Yes, it was," I said without elaboration.

He held his hand out and said enthusiastically, "I should be very pleased to shake the hand of the gentleman who was known as the 'Hero of Mussendam.'" And he did.

Captain Osborne looked appropriately bewildered, as he had no idea what his first mate had been alluding to, but as soon as he did understand he wanted chapter and verse.

As requested, I gave Captain Osborne and John Bartholomew a brief account of the events that had led up to the award of my medal and then the evacuation of Telegraph Island.

When I finished my recital and had accepted their plaudits with polite good grace, I felt that it was high time to go to bed.

In the morning the weather had improved, and I decided to start following the captain's advice by going to breakfast at a normal time. Whether my few fellow diners had not remarked on my previous absences or had assumed I had also been afflicted with seasickness I do not know, but no one took any particular interest in me.

The number of times they had been sick or the number of bruises they had accumulated seemed much more important subjects of conversation.

After breakfast I sat on a steamer chair, as it was called by a steward. Essentially, it was a slatted wooden chair with an adjustable back rest and an extended seat to support the legs.

He brought me beef tea and a selection of books then wrapped me in a blanket, as the wind was quite chilly and the sun was still mostly obscured by clouds. There was no one on deck to bother me, so I reclined in the fresh air with a book until lunchtime.

There were only a few other passengers in the dining room at lunchtime, and I sat at what would be the captain's table later in the day. The only other person at the table was an elderly man with bad hearing who sat at the opposite end. We exchanged polite but distant salutes of greeting but nothing more.

After lunch I went back on deck with the intention of reading some more of the book the steward had given me but went to sleep instead and eventually had to be woken by him.

Later when I told Edwards that I would go to dinner, he took my evening clothes from the wardrobe with a smile of pleasure and said how happy he was that I was getting out of the cabin.

I dressed and then joined the captain's table for dinner.

That evening was probably the first time since we sailed when every place at the captain's table was occupied. During the meal conversation amongst my table companions covered a multitude of general subjects and didn't require my participation in any way. No one showed any particular interest in me for which I was thankful in one respect, but illogically I have to admit I was a little piqued to discover that my fellow diners could discern nothing of importance in me.

With one notable exception, my days entered a routine of breakfast, morning on the boat deck, then lunch followed by a siesta and then dinner and bed.

My fears that people would be inquisitive and pry into my recent tragedy proved unfounded. My fellow passengers in first class were mature people who had no need to enquire into the recent past of a fellow passenger who was much younger than themselves. When we conversed, which was rarely, it was about quite general subjects, as I had no knowledge of racehorses or the stock exchange, which were the conversational staple for them.

The exception was the chance discovery that one of my fellow passengers spoke Arabic.

I am sorry to say that I have forgotten his name, but for the sake of this discourse I shall call him Colonel Blunt. He must have been at least fifteen years my senior. At dinner one night Captain Osborne was participating in a discussion about the Arab world, and it was clear that Colonel Blunt had a comprehensive knowledge of several Arab countries and a high regard for the people.

Captain Osborne asked, "Do you know any Arabic, Colonel?"

"Yes," said the Colonel without elaboration and the conversation moved on to other more general subjects.

I remark on this conversation for two reasons.

The first is that it illustrates, in my opinion, how little thought is given by Government to the appointment of embassy staff. Here was a man with almost unique knowledge of the language and customs of the Arab world being sent as a military attaché to a colonial embassy in Australia where there probably wouldn't be an Arab within several thousand miles.

The other reason is more personal.

One morning, a day or so after the dinner I mentioned, I was walking around the boat deck and happened to meet Colonel Blunt, who was walking the deck in the opposite direction.

"Good morning, Mr. Stewart," he said as he came close enough to exchange greetings with me.

"Good morning, Colonel," I responded, then said, "Excuse me, Colonel. I was interested in your comments about Arabia and, as I have a slight knowledge of Arabic, I wondered if you would be prepared to utilise some of our time onboard to tell me where you have been and something more of your experiences?"

"I should be happy to talk with you, Mr. Smiley, but why, may I ask, do you know some Arabic?"

"I worked for the telegraph company in Bombay and one of our employees taught me some polite Arabic. I learnt some more vocabulary from the men laying the cable at Fao in southern Iraq and from the camel train drivers on a journey from Fao to Basra and back. I'm afraid some of the phrases I learnt would not be acceptable in polite society."

"Tell me one," he commanded.

So I did. It was a phrase used by one of the camel train drivers when a camel was more than usually stubborn, and I articulated it with all the angry enthusiasm I could muster.

The colonel hooted with laughter so loudly that he attracted the attention of the first mate as he passed us.

Answering the unspoken interrogative from the mate, Colonel Blunt said in a parade ground voice, "I've lived with the Arabs for twenty years and young Stewart here knows ruder Arabic than I do," and he hooted with laughter again.

"Get him to tell you about Mussendam," said the mate as he hurried on about his duties and left a slightly puzzled Colonel Blunt staring at his retreating back.

Over the remaining weeks of the voyage, Colonel Blunt and I could be found every afternoon walking around the boat deck. At the beginning I was largely listening, but I was soon able to build upon my rusty vocabulary so that by the end of the voyage several weeks later we were able to have quite long conversations in Arabic. We spoke about our experiences and in each other found a sympathetic listener because we each understood what the other had experienced.

And so the voyage continued day after day until there was the beginning of a buzz of excitement as we neared our destination.

We arrived in the port of Darwin just after midnight, and about mid-morning, just as I was about to disembark, the purser mentioned that someone was waiting for me and pointed out a tall, well built, bearded man standing near to the foot of the gangway. Behind him appeared to be a dockside bar with a small group of similarly dressed men lounging against the rail watching the passengers, particularly the female passengers if they passed close to where they stood.

I walked down the gangway, and as I stepped down on to dry land again, a voice said, "Mr. Stewart?"

I turned toward the sound and found the man who had been pointed out to me by the purser standing about a yard away. His clothes were roughly made and travel-stained. He himself clearly needed a bath. I could see him eyeing my clean, tidy clothes and polished boots with distain as he summed up his first impressions of me with the phrase "raw recruit."

I said, "Yes! I'm Stewart, and I presume you must be Mr. Carl Kopf. Mr. Fairweather told me to expect you."

My very English accent appeared to grate on his ears, but he answered civilly enough, "Yes, I'm Carl Kopf. I have been told to take you to Mr. Fairweather. Where is your luggage, Mr. Stewart?"

I pointed to the three small trunks the crew had brought down the gangway and placed on the ground at its foot.

"That's all of it," I said.

"In that case, there is no need to delay further, as we have a long way to go."

We had moved away from the end of the gangway and closer to the men lounging at the bar by this time.

"You will ride one of those," he said, gesturing along the side of the bar building. I detected a note of anticipation in his voice, and out of the corner of my eye I saw grins appear on the faces of one or two of the loungers.

I looked in the direction he pointed.

"Good Lord!" I said in astonishment. "Camels."

I heard a poor sotto voce impersonation of my voice repeating "Good Lord" in a strong local accent and the laughter that followed it.

Carl Kopf said, "You can pick any of the beasts that you fancy, but that dark-haired one is a placid animal."

To my eye it looked the least placid of the whole herd, but I said, "Thank you, Mr. Kopf. That's really very thoughtful of you. I'll just go and have a look at the beast, if you don't mind?"

"That's a very good idea, Mr. Stewart. I'll just wait here with the boys."

I noticed that the loungers had left the bar and were standing expectantly in a semicircle around Carl Kopf as I started to walk along the side of the building.

"Mr. Stewart," Kopf called, and I turned back. "You'd better take this with you," he said as he passed me a bamboo camel stick.

"Thank you, Mr. Kopf," I said again and tried to sound as though I meant it.

I had only covered about half the distance when I had my second surprise of the day. I glanced to my right into an alcove and saw two figures dressed in Arab clothing squatting in the shade. I ignored them and went directly to the dark-haired camel. As I undid the tether it tried to bite me, but a swift slap with the cane discouraged the attempt. I used my Arabic to order the beast to kneel, and with a groan of protest it did.

The two Arabs came after me, obviously assuming I was about to steal the animal, but Kopf shouted something at them I didn't understand and they desisted. I climbed onto the saddle and ordered the camel to get up. I urged it into motion, turned away from Kopf and company, and after about forty or fifty yards turned back and made the camel speed up as I headed directly for them. At the last minute I slowed down again and walked the camel forward until its loose lipped, slobbering mouth was so close to Kopf's face that he started to back away.

After a moment or two, I stopped and said quietly to Kopf, "Just because someone arrives on a liner direct from England doesn't automatically mean that they have no experience. I hope you will be more careful in future, Mr. Kopf."

"Yes, Mr. Stewart. I'm sorry, Mr. Stewart," he said contritely.

I ordered the camel to kneel and dismounted. I stepped over to Kopf and held out my hand and said, "Now that we are acquainted, Mr. Kopf, perhaps we should have a beer before we go and find Mr. Fairweather."

"That's a very good idea, Mr. Stewart," he responded with a grin of relief as he shook my proffered hand.

Almost as soon as we were in the bar with a drink he asked, "How is it you know about camels, Mr. Stewart?"

"I rode them in Arabia," I answered briefly, then asked, "How long will it take to get to Mr. Fairweather?"

"I expect we will have to camp out for four nights," he answered. "Do you want to leave today?" and contrary to his previous briskness he sounded as if he hoped I would postpone our departure for another day.

He was clearly disappointed when I responded with, "Of course. I came to help Mr. Fairweather, and I cannot achieve much sitting in a bar in Darwin."

"Very well, Mr. Stewart. I'll get everything ready. We can ride out in thirty minutes." And we did.

The cross-country journey to Mr. Fairweather's camp was, without any exception, as hot, dusty, and tiring as all my previous journeys on camelback had been. The saving grace was the many different animals that Kopf pointed out. For example, I saw kangaroos bounding away into the scrub one minute and ostriches running the opposite way the next. It was absolutely fascinating!

I was able to speak to the older of the two Arabs and ascertained that they came from a part of the Arab world about which I knew nothing. They were members of the tribe known as the Bani Yas.

When we reached the camp late on the fourth day, I took Kopf to one side and said quietly, "Thank you for meeting me, Mr. Kopf. I hope all goes well with you, but please don't forget what I told you."

"I won't," he said, "Goodbye, Mr. Stewart," and he turned and walked away after pointing out where Mr. Fairweather could be found.

I walked across the sand to the tent in the centre of the camp Kopf had indicated and found Mr. Fairweather in his office immersed in his plans and schedules, just as I expected.

I coughed to attract his attention as I stooped to pass under the tent flap.

As soon as he saw me, he jumped up and strode round to the front of the table he was using as his desk with his hand stretched out in welcome. "Mr. Stewart. How very good to see you again, and I'm happy to say that you look much more like the Jason Smiley Stewart I know from the past."

"Thank you, Mr. Fairweather," I responded. "I hope you are in the best of health. I'm very pleased to be with you again as your assistant and more than ready to help in any way that I can."

"Please come and sit down, Mr. Stewart," and he indicated a chair in front of the desk as he moved back around the table to resume his own seat.

He stared at me for a several seconds as if he was wondering where to start, then took a breath and said, "I would really welcome your assistance, as you know, Mr. Stewart, but there has been an unexpected complication. About a week ago I received a letter from Sir David Tallboy. You are welcome to read it if you would like to, but I can give you the gist of it immediately. He refers to the letter you wrote in which you respectfully declined his offer and informed him that you had accepted my proposal since your knowledge of the telegraph is essentially of a practical nature."

Fairweather went on after taking a swallow of water, "Sir David then wrote that Charles Todd can muster any number of practical men to help me deal with the problems of the telegraph, but his, Sir David's, need is for someone he can trust implicitly. Sir David concluded his letter by writing that I should arrange to send you to his office as soon as possible after you arrive here."

"Good heavens!" I gasped in surprise.

"Sir David has paid you a great compliment, Mr. Smiley, and much as I would like to keep you here, I have no doubt that Sir David's polite request would rapidly become an instruction if his wishes were denied. There's nothing for it; I'm afraid, Mr. Smiley, you will have to join Sir David's staff whether you like it or not."

"I see," I said, as I was still too stunned by the enormity of the change to think of anything more constructive.

Ever practical in times of crisis, Fairweather said, "I think the best thing is for us to have dinner and discuss how you are going to get back to Darwin so that you can get a ship south."

Dinner was probably much as one would expect to receive at a camp in the outback—filling certainly, and totally unlike the gourmet cooking I had experienced on the voyage out.

After we had eaten, Fairweather said, "I can't spare Kopf to escort you back to Darwin, as he is already late with an assignment he was working on."

"I don't need him," I responded. "I could manage quite well on my own, but it will be better to take one of the Arabs as a guide, as he knows the country. I would like to talk to them both and then ask one of them to volunteer."

"They speak almost no English," said Fairweather dubiously, and he was obviously wondering what sort of conversation I would have with two Arabs. "We don't have an interpreter here that you could use, and I am reluctant to let you go out into the bush with someone you cannot converse with," he added as an afterthought.

"I think I know enough Arabic to converse with them, Mr. Fairweather, and I had the opportunity to practise the language on the voyage here.

Please send someone for them, and if I cannot make myself understood I will accept an alternative suggestion from you."

"Very well," he said. "I'll send for them," and one of the cook's helpers was dispatched to bring them to the office.

Five minutes later two apprehensive, shuffling Arabs arrived at the open tent flap and peered in at Fairweather and me sitting at a big table.

"Salaam ali khum," I said as I started the usual ritual greeting.

"Alikumm as Salaam," they responded in a ragged chorus.

In Arabic I said, "What are your names?"

Unsurprisingly, they had typically Arabic names. One, the elder of the two, was Mohammad bin Mohammad, and the other called himself Ibrahim bin Mohammad. I didn't think they were related although the family name was the same.

I went on, "I have to return to Darwin tomorrow. I need one of you to come with me and bring both camels back to the camp here." Out of the corner of my eye I could see the look of astonishment on Fairweather's face as he listened to my unanticipated fluency.

Both Arabs immediately volunteered.

That's a pity, I thought. *Now I have to make a choice.*

When I explained the dilemma, Fairweather saved me the trouble of a decision.

"Why not take them both?" asked Fairweather. "I have no work for them until Kopf has finished his calculations and goes out into the field again."

"A very good idea," I said and told Mohammed and Ibrahim what had been agreed. The smiles that spread over their swarthy faces showed clearly that the idea of ten days on the back of a camel in the outback was infinitely preferable to inactivity in a camp full of infidels.

Both men were dismissed after they had been instructed to get water, food, and so on, ready for a start at first light in the morning.

"I think you may be facing a difficult time, Mr. Stewart," remarked Fairweather.

"Why do you think so?" I asked.

"For Sir David to openly say he needs someone he can trust means that he is unable to trust at least some of the staff he inherited from his predecessor. In turn, you will be unable to confide in anyone until you are confident of their loyalty to you and Sir David. I do not envy you, Mr. Stewart."

"I see what you mean, Mr. Fairweather. Clearly, I will have to be very careful what I say and to whom. Thank you for your insight; I could have been in serious difficulties without your timely warning."

"Not at all, Mr. Stewart. That's what a colleague is for. However, it's late, and as you have a long day ahead of you tomorrow, I suggest we go to bed."

"I agree, Mr. Fairweather."

Next morning, after a large breakfast I supervised the loading of my three unopened trunks onto the back of the pack camel and shook hands with Fairweather.

He said, "Don't forget all about me now that you are going into Government, Mr. Stewart."

"I won't do that, Mr. Fairweather, and if the situation is as complicated as you suspect, you will probably find me knocking on your door asking for some levelheaded advice."

"As you know, Mr. Stewart, you will be very welcome whether you come as a visitor for old time's sake or as an ex-colleague seeking advice."

I shook his hand again and said a heartfelt, "Thank you," as I climbed onto my camel. A few moments later I followed Mohammad out of the camp and joined the track we had arrived on only the evening before. Ibrahim and the pack animal followed behind.

It was not very many minutes before Mohammad started to diverge from the track we had followed to the camp under Kopf's direction. I was not surprised, as my sailor's training in navigation had indicated that we were following a rather circuitous route from the port to the camp. I was more surprised that a surveyor like Kopf hadn't noticed long before. However, I was quite prepared to let Mohammad lead and let my thoughts wander over the new task that faced me.

Not that it was a fruitful exercise, as I didn't have much material for my brain to work on, just Sir David's request and Fairweather's rather pessimistic forecast. I thought quite a good deal about it on my journey but always came back to the same conclusion. *I must keep my own counsel.*

When I arrived in Adelaide after a three-week voyage from Darwin in an old and smelly but surprisingly fleet schooner, I had my trunks taken to a respectable-looking inn near to the waterfront and booked a room for a few days. I washed and changed into my most respectable clothes before going to find the Governor's Residence so that I could report my arrival to Sir David.

I walked to the Residence, as I had been informed by the inn keeper's buxom wife, "It ain't far, luv."

She was correct in so far as it certainly wasn't worth hiring a coach to get to the entrance gate. However, she hadn't mentioned the length of the driveway, which was certainly worth the cost of a coach ride. Consequently, I arrived at the entrance hall to the Residence in a rather hotter and dustier state than I would have wished since I was about to meet my new employer. I contemplated retreating to the hotel and trying again in the morning, but that was too much like admitting defeat, and that was an action I wasn't prepared to countenance. Ignoring the sweat and dust that coated me, I walked in through the entrance doors as if I owned the place.

In an alcove, about a third of the way along the marble-floored hall on the right-hand side stood a desk with a man sitting behind it on a padded, backless stool. It was a little like a piano stool. He was wearing a typical English business suit made from a dark, worsted material, and this was surmounted by a tall, thin, long-nosed face. His small, dark eyes were close set and surmounted by thick, bushy, black eyebrows. I saw that his head was bald, except for a sparse growth of short, white hair that stretched around his head from temple to temple in a narrow strip. I noticed also that the bone structure of his skull showed through the tight, suntanned skin and looked like a model used by medical students. The desk surface was highly polished but totally devoid of anything that could be useful to a clerk. I assumed that pen and paper was probably kept in a drawer in the desk. He turned his attention from a close examination of his fingertips in order to look me up and down.

I could see from his expression that my hot and dusty appearance did not meet with his approval, and there was silence as we each waited for the other to speak first.

As I was here at Sir David's request, I decided that I couldn't really spend too much time waiting for this minion to open the conversation, so I said, "I would like to see Sir David, please."

"Most people who walk up the drive would like to see Sir David," he said in a rather squeaky but accent-free voice, "and generally they would like to borrow some money in order to sail home or pay a gambling debt. Which category are you in?"

"If I had known how long the drive is, I would have taken a carriage," I explained and realised as I said it that I didn't really need to make any explanations to the gatekeeper. "I don't belong in either of your categories," I went on. "I am here following Sir David's instructions, as I am to join his staff."

"Really?" he said in a disbelieving sort of voice as he stood, turned his back to me, opened the lid of his seat, and took out paper, pen, ink, and a printed schedule. He placed them neatly on the desk in front of himself, selected a pen, and carefully squared a sheet of paper with the edge of the desk in front of himself. "Name?" he asked.

"Jason Smiley Stewart."

He neatly wrote my name at the top centre of the paper in a nice, rounded hand, wiped the pen nib, and then slowly consulted the schedule.

"Your name is not on my list," he said. "Possibly you have a letter from the governor instructing your presence here?"

"No," I had to admit. "I received Sir David's instruction verbally. Perhaps you would be kind enough to see that Sir David is advised of my arrival?"

He stood again and turned away from me to restore everything except the sheet of paper in the stool. That done, he turned back to the desk, picked up the paper, said, "Wait," and walked away along the hall. He disappeared through a doorway at the far end.

I could feel my temper rising at the man's lack of courtesy but managed to stay calm, as he may have been instructed to behave as he had in order to discourage uninvited and unwelcome visitors. Shouting and metaphorically stamping my feet would relieve my frustration but would not necessarily achieve my objective and would certainly draw unwelcome attention to my arrival. I didn't think Sir David would appreciate an argument at his front door. To fill in the time, I turned my attention to a watercolour of a country scene that was hung on the wall near the desk. The view looked familiar, but I couldn't place it. There were several other similar pictures and also some seascapes that appeared to have been done by the same artist. There was no signature, but very faintly painted in a corner, I did detect two intertwined letters. There was a "T" and an "M." *A puzzle for another day*, I realised as the man came back.

"I have seen the governor's secretary and you should come back here tomorrow at nine," he said.

"I have an appointment to see Sir David?" I asked

"Certainly not," he responded with some asperity. "The appointment is with Sir David's secretary. He will decide if you are to see the governor."

With that he turned and walked away. Once again he disappeared through the doorway at the end of the hall leaving me standing alone but this time with no option left to me except to return to the inn for the night. I walked back along the hall, down the entrance steps, and then set off on the long, hot, dusty walk back to the town.

Next morning, I chartered a carriage to take me to the Residence, and consequently I arrived with a calm, cool, dust-free appearance in good time for my appointment with the governor's secretary.

As I walked along the hall, I received an off-hand nod from the "gate-keeper" in response to my cheerful, "Good morning," and before I could ask for directions, he gestured toward the door at the end of the hall. I knocked and, receiving no reply, opened the door and went in. It was obviously a waiting room, so I sat down just to the left of the door to wait for the time of my appointment. As I waited, I wondered if I was about to meet the man who had written to me and described himself as the "Secretary to the Governor's Office."

Promptly at nine the door on the opposite side of the room opened, and to my astonishment the person who walked in was Ignatius Montmorency, and his normally pious expression had been replaced with a big welcoming smile. Apart from the smile, he looked exactly the same as he had when I had last seen him, and that had been in Sir David's office in Bombay.

And that was the day my dreams about Mary Thomas were shattered by her father's intransigence, I recalled a little sadly.

As I stood up, he advanced across the room and shook my hand.

"I am so pleased to see you, Mr. Stewart, and I know Sir David will be delighted that you received the message he sent to Mr. Fairweather. Just wait a moment longer and I will go and tell Sir David that you have arrived." He disappeared back through the door, and I realised that this could not have been the person who had written to me in England, as I would have recognised the name and signature. I wondered if perhaps Ignatius was the governor's personal secretary.

Ignatius reappeared in the doorway, beckoned, and I followed him through an anteroom furnished with a big desk and then through a pair of very tall double doors into the governor's office.

As I walked through the entrance, Sir David did me the honour of coming around to the front of his desk with his hand outstretched in welcome.

As I grasped his hand, he said, "I am very pleased to welcome you to Australia, but first of all, Jason, I must commiserate with you over the loss of your wife and child. It is a tragedy that is inexplicable except to say that God moves in mysterious ways."

"Thank you, Sir David," I managed to say through a throat tight with unexpected emotion.

He continued, "I believe it is just as well that we cannot foresee what will happen in the future. Lady Megan and I both met Joanna when you were so close to death in that Bombay hospital and we developed a great regard for her—"

"I didn't realise that you had met Joanna," I interrupted.

"Not surprising really, as you were unconscious most of the time," he said sharply, slightly irritated by my intervention, then went on. "As a result, Joanna's death was a tragedy for Lady Megan and me as well. However, we are here to deal with the present and the future and no matter how hard the task may be the past must be left in the past."

"I'll do my best, Sir David," I muttered.

"Those members of my staff who should know of your tragedy do know but have been requested not to rub further salt in your wounds by offering their personal condolences when they meet you. They would like to make a personal gesture, of course, but I have requested them not to do so, as I have expressed their condolences with mine. I hope that is acceptable to you."

"Yes! Thank you, Sir David. That is very thoughtful of you," was all I could say.

"Now, to business," he said as he returned to his seat behind the desk. "Please come and sit here, Mr. Stewart," and he pointed to one of the visitors' chairs. Ignatius sat on another.

"As you will know from my letter to Mr. Fairweather, I need someone on my staff I can trust. There are staff members, like Ignatius for example, whom I trust implicitly, but they work in the Residence. They see the information that I see. We make our decisions based on the assumption that the information we receive is both accurate and honest, and from recent experience we are not sure that our basic supposition is still applicable. With your agreement, Mr. Stewart…"

I thought, *Can one refuse a request from a governor?*

He continued, "I plan to appoint you as my personal technical assistant for the telegraph and associated subjects. This is a general title covering a broad sphere of responsibility. Under my aegis, you will have freedom of movement in Australia and New Zealand and the authority to enquire into anything that you believe could affect the development of the telegraph system. Additionally, planned extensions to the telegraph or the construction of new lines as a result of increasing population and commerce might also indicate that the development of the roads or railways is being considered by the local authorities. Trustworthy information on any of these subjects is of immense value. I'm sure you realise, Mr. Stewart, that Her Majesty's Government relies on the intelligence they receive from their accredited representatives such as me, and if that intelligence is flawed, the decisions that are taken are equally flawed. Our need is for information that has been acquired by a man we trust, and I hope that, in turn, it will lead us to those who are attempting to mislead The Queen's representative for their own selfish ends.

"There is one particular man, John Darcy by name, who is trying to persuade me to persuade the Government to invest enormous sums of money in supplying telegraph equipment for various schemes in New Zealand. I have asked myself this question. With such a small immigrant population, can there really be so many developments planned or is he trying to hoodwink us for his personal gain? The task is not without risk, as you will realise, Mr. Stewart, but you've taken risks before. There is a lot of Government money at stake, and if the promoters of these schemes believe you have become a threat to their plans, they will try to discredit you at best and at worst dispose of you."

There followed a long pause whilst I was given time to digest the Governor's information and valedictory warning, then Sir David said, "Well, Mr. Stewart, will you join me?"

"Of course, Sir David," I responded. "I should be honoured to assist you."

"I'm pleased you are prepared to help us, Mr. Stewart. Ignatius will arrange for you to occupy a small villa in the compound and an office in the Residence with some clerical assistance. I suggest you familiarise yourself with the telegraph schemes that are currently being planned or considered and then make such enquiries as you see fit. I cannot give you more guidance than that."

"Thank you, Sir David," I said, and I followed Ignatius from the Governor's office.

Ignatius took me back to the entrance hall, which we crossed, and then down a corridor on the opposite side of the building. He opened a door about halfway along the corridor and preceded me into a large, sunny room with a high ceiling, looking out onto a close cut, green lawn. It was furnished with a big desk made of some highly polished dark wood, a comfortable chair, and the floor was of polished wood strips. There were several chairs for visitors and two tall, empty bookcases.

Ignatius gestured to the chair behind the desk and said, "Please sit down, Mr. Stewart," and when I was seated he sat in one of the visitors' chairs.

He said, "I'm sure I speak for the Governor as well as myself when I say how pleased I am to see you here and know that there is someone to whom I can talk freely. This is your office, and I'll introduce the clerk who will help you, later in the morning. It wasn't discussed when you were with Sir David, but your salary will be at the official rate for a personal assistant to the Governor. You will also receive an allowance to cover all your travel expenses. The villa is available for you to move into as soon as you are ready, and there is a servant to look after your everyday needs." He paused for a moment then said, "If you have no questions at present Mr. Stewart, I'll leave you to collect your thoughts."

"I have no questions at the moment, Ignatius, but I would like to say how pleased I am to be here with you and the Governor."

He smiled, left the office, and I sat and started to collect my scattered thoughts.

As Sir David had said, my first task must be to study all the documentation I could find about current and future plans for the telegraph. Clearly, I must not take anything I was told or read on face value. To be accurate, in the business climate Sir David had described, I would have to double check everything.

SIX

Sir David's Assistant

About an hour later, Ignatius returned to my office and introduced Silas Browning to me. This young man was the person who was to act as my clerk, and I had to accept that he would immediately be in a position to support me or thwart me. In his favour was the fact that he had been chosen by Ignatius, but even so he would not be a party to my thoughts until I was certain that he could be trusted.

I had to start from the assumption that Ignatius could be trusted, as he clearly had Sir David's ear.

Silas was the sort of person who didn't stand out in a crowd. The average, nondescript man! Medium height, medium build, medium complexion, and so on.

He said, "Good morning, Mr. Stewart. I am very pleased to be able to work for the 'Hero of Mussendam.'"

"Who told you about that?" I asked a little sharply.

"Mr. Ignatius," he responded.

"That's in my past so forget about it and think of me as Mr. Stewart," I ordered.

"Yes, sir," he answered plainly, puzzled by my unexpected denial of past exploits. He couldn't know, of course, that discussing my past inevitably brought painful memories to mind that I preferred to leave buried, but I didn't think it was necessary to explain my reasons to him.

I said, "I want you to search the records and bring me any information there is in the Residence about the electric telegraph. I want to see all of it without exception. Do you understand?"

"Yes, sir," he said again. "Please, will you excuse me?" When I inclined my head, he walked quickly to the door and left the office, closing the door behind him.

Ignatius stood up, turned toward the door, then turned back and said, "I hope you are not offended because I told Silas about your exploits."

"Not at all, Ignatius," I responded. "I just do not want to attract attention to myself. The fewer people who know about my past, the better it will be in my opinion."

"I understand, and it's a sensible policy," Ignatius agreed and then left me to return to his duties.

I realised that until Silas returned I could do nothing. I got up, walked to the window, and admired the neatly trimmed lawn and saw the shrubs that formed a green boundary to the Residence. As I walked back to my desk, I noticed that there was a bell pull within reach so I pulled it to see what would happen. Some moments later there was a knock on the door and a rather breathless Silas answered my call, "Come in," and hurried to the desk.

He stood and looked at me without saying anything. I stared at Silas and suddenly realised that he was waiting for an instruction. After all, I had rung the bell, hadn't I, but it was a whim and I hadn't had the vestige of a reason for tugging on the bell pull beyond curiosity.

After a few embarrassing moments of silence, inspiration came to my rescue and I said, "I want to go back to the inn and pack my trunks so that I can move into my villa. How can I get a carriage, Silas?"

"That's easy, Mr. Stewart. Just tell me when you wish to leave and I can arrange for one of our drivers to take you and then bring you back when you have packed."

"In fifteen minutes?" I asked.

"Certainly, Mr. Stewart," he said. "I'll come for you when the carriage is at the entrance." He hurried out of the office.

Punctually, he came for me, and as I left my office he said, "I'll have the first of the papers about the telegraph ready for you to read when you return, Mr. Stewart."

"Thank you, Silas," I said and realised as I said it that he had made a good impression so far.

The coachman drove me to the inn and waited whilst I packed and paid my bill. He then drove me back to the Residence, but partway along the main drive he turned into a side road that led to the Government villas at the back. How he knew which villa to stop at I have no idea, but as he didn't ask me for guidance I assumed that Silas had told him. The driver and a steward carried my three trunks in through a side entrance whilst I sat in semi-regal splendour in the carriage outside.

The driver then took me back to the main entrance to the Residence.

As I walked along the hall, the "gatekeeper" nodded a greeting, which was, I supposed, marginally more welcoming than the way he had treated me the previous day. When I reached my office, I found that someone had been busy during my absence and fixed a nameplate to the door. It was in polished dark wood with neatly formed letters in gold paint that said,

Mr. J. Smiley Stewart
Technical Assistant–Telegraph

I didn't touch it, as I was sure the paint must still be wet, but took several paces back so that I could admire it at a greater distance. It was the first time in my life that I had occupied an office with my name on a plaque outside and it made me feel quite important. The feeling lasted only as long as it took me to walk to my desk, sit down, and select the document that was on the top of the pile Silas had left in the middle of it. I read industriously until about five when I decided it was time to give up for the day and go to my villa.

I was met at the door by my steward.

He was a rotund man on the short side of medium height, with a round, unlined face and jug-handle ears. He had almost blond, close-cropped hair and metal-framed spectacles with large, round lenses. The spectacles were immediately an irritant, as they reflected the light and prevented me seeing his eyes.

As he stepped back to let me enter he said, "My name is Evan Edwards, Mr. Stewart, and I am your steward. If you need anything at all please tell me, as I am responsible for your welfare. May I suggest, sir, that I show you around the villa before you dress for dinner?"

"That's a good idea, Edwards, please lead on."

"Yes, sir," he responded as he turned and led me into the villa.

It was actually too small to be described as a villa, as it was a small, single story building but it was well designed and furnished and perfectly adequate for a bachelor like me. At the end of my guided tour, I washed and dressed for dinner then sat in my living room and relaxed, looking at the green of the grass and shrubs outside the window.

At seven Edwards knocked on the door and said, "Dinner is ready, sir," and I followed him through into the dining room where I found he had laid my place at the end of a table big enough for eight people. I thought the cutlery looked rather lonely placed at one end of a big expanse of polished wood like that but couldn't think of a better arrangement.

Edwards said, "I hope you like the meal I have prepared tonight, sir. I don't know your preferences yet, of course, so I have prepared tomato soup, roast lamb chops, and there is some apple pie to follow if you wish. When it is convenient, please tell me if there is anything that I should not prepare for you."

"I'll do so, Edwards, but after some years onboard ship and in India, I doubt if you will be able to surprise me with anything."

"Shall I serve the soup, sir?" he asked.

"Of course," I responded, and so in an ordered and civilised fashion, the meal was served course by course, and I found it quite delicious and told Edwards so.

Over the next week I attended the office and read through the reams of paper that Silas put on my desk. It seemed as if he had a never-ending source as he supplied another heap of papers as he took away the ones I had just completed.

In essence, the papers dealt with two main developments. The more important, in my view, was the connection of Adelaide in the south of Australia to Darwin in the north. This endeavour was being masterminded by a man called Charles Todd, who had the title of Government Astronomer and Superintendent of Telegraphs for South Australia. The other development was in New Zealand and was being promoted by a man called Julius Vogel, who seemed to be quite an interesting man from the little I could find out about him. He was described in the text I read as a Jew, and I found that a little strange, as it's not normal to label someone a Catholic or a Protestant when the surname is introduced. As a young man, Julius Vogel had given up a secure position in London to try his luck in the Victorian gold fields. He had then moved to New Zealand where he helped start the first daily newspaper in the country and then became involved with politics. At the time he was the administration's treasurer, and he believed that the best way to stimulate the country's flagging economy was for the Government to increase expenditure. He considered that the limited and poor quality road system, less than fifty miles of railway, and only about seven hundred miles of telegraph line in the whole of New Zealand simply restricted settlement to the coastal areas where ships could be used for transport and communication.

I prepared a short report for the Governor and asked Ignatius to arrange for me to see Sir David at his convenience the following morning in order to present it. In the report I had concluded that the works in Australia were in the hands of a very competent man and suggested that I should concentrate my energies on New Zealand where everything was still in its infancy.

Next morning, Silas came to the office just before ten and said, "Sir James would like to see you now, Mr. Stewart."

"Thank you, Silas," I responded as I rose from my chair, picked up my report, and set off on the short walk to the Governor's office. Ignatius knocked on the Governor's door and waited until Sir David called out, "Enter." He opened the door, introduced me, and then closed the door after I had entered.

Sir David said, "Good morning, Mr. Stewart. Is that your report?" When I nodded, he held out his hand for it and said, "I'll read it later. Please give me the essence of it verbally."

"It's a quite a short report, Sir David, as it only summarises the documents that I have read since I joined your staff. I have concluded that there is not much about the installation of the telegraph across Australia to concern you, but perhaps we need more information about the proposed developments in New Zealand. They are being promoted by someone called Julius Vogel."

"I have heard of him," remarked Sir David, who then asked, "Do you have much more to read?"

"I really don't know, Sir David. As fast I as I read through one pile of dusty, old documents, Silas is able to produce another. I'll ask him to make an estimate, but I cannot believe there is very much more."

"Very well, Mr. Stewart; please come back tomorrow at ten. I will have read your report by then and we can discuss the implications."

"Very well, Sir David," I responded and stood up.

I was halfway to the door when Sir David asked, "Are you engaged for dinner tonight, Mr. Stewart?"

"No, Sir David."

"Would you care to join Lady Megan and me for dinner this evening?"

"Of course, Sir David," I said with genuine enthusiasm—not that I could have treated such a question as anything other than a royal request even if I had wanted to do something else.

"Good," he said. "We'll expect you at seven for seven thirty, and you can help us entertain our guest."

"It will be my pleasure, Sir David." This time I was able to leave the room and return to my office. As I picked up the top document of a new batch of papers, I wondered idly who the Governor had as a guest. *Probably some old politician from Whitehall*, I imagined and then buckled down to work.

Later in the morning, when Silas arrived in front of my desk in response to a tug on the bell rope, I said, "As you know, I was with the Governor this morning, and I have a very serious question for you to answer."

"Yes, Mr. Stewart?" he said neutrally.

"Will there soon be an end to your twice daily deliveries of documents for my perusal or are you perhaps mining in a bottomless pit of old files?"

He smiled and said, "I understand your concern, Mr. Stewart. The pit is not bottomless, and I'm sure you will see the end of this task in a day or so."

"Thank you, Silas, that's very good news. So tonight I can look forward to sleeping without having a nightmare about suffocating under a mountain of paper?"

He smiled again and said, "I'm sure that is so, sir."

I went back to my villa at five and was greeted at the door by Edwards, who said before I could utter a word, "Good afternoon, sir. I believe you are dining with Sir David at seven thirty tonight?" Without giving me a chance to respond, he continued with, "Would you like me to get your bath ready, sir?"

I said a rather distracted, "Good afternoon, Edwards. Yes, please, Edwards," as my thoughts were revolving around the fact that Edwards already knew of the invitation before I returned to the villa, and I wondered how he knew and more particularly why he knew. Probably it was completely innocent and had simply been a helpful hint from Sir David's domestics to mine—but servants are often well placed to hear important officials make utterances in private they would never say in public. Servants are in positions of trust and are generally honourable people, but a disgruntled person could cause a great deal of harm by telling tales. I wondered if I was becoming a little paranoid as a result of Sir David's suspicions, but sensitive information leaving the Residence could be as damaging as false information coming into it.

I would have to bear that possibility in mind.

I bathed, shaved, and dressed appropriately for dinner with the Governor. Edwards had everything ready. My clothes had been pressed, creased, or polished to perfection. I couldn't fault Edwards's skill as a steward; I just didn't care for the way his glasses always seem to reflect the light. It shouldn't have irritated me but it did.

Just before seven I left the villa to walk the hundred yards to the main entrance to the Residence and entered the main hall. This time I walked to an alcove located on the right-hand side of the entrance and then passed through a discretely located and unidentified door that led into the Governor's private apartments. As I stepped into a comfortably furnished anteroom, I was met by a uniformed servant who said, "Mr. Stewart?" When I nodded my agreement, he continued, "Please come this way, Mr. Stewart," and he led me across the anteroom and into a comfortably furnished sitting room. He said, indicating a chair, "If you would be kind enough to wait here, sir, the Governor will be along shortly."

"Certainly," I said and settled down into a very comfortable armchair.

About five minutes later, the door opened and, to my surprise, Lady

Megan appeared in the doorway and not her husband, the Governor. As I stood up, she started to walk across the room toward me, and in the silence of the moment I could hear the rustle of her long skirt as it caressed the floor. As she came up to me, she held out both hands, and I reached out and grasped her hands in mine.

Before I could speak, she said, "I am very pleased to see you, Mr. Stewart, and to know that you have joined my husband's staff. He needs honest and courageous men like you around him." She paused momentarily and then went on, "I was very distressed to learn that Joanna had died so tragically, and you have my every sympathy. She was a lovely young woman."

"Thank you, Lady Megan," I said, and I was slightly relieved to find that recollecting the tragedy that had befallen my family and me was becoming a slightly less emotional experience with every repetition. I went on, "Several well meaning and intelligent people have advised me that I have to rely on the belief that God has a reason for his actions even if I cannot understand them, but I have found this concept very difficult to accept. I have also been told that "time is a great healer," and I do notice that it is becoming easier to bear my loss as the months go by."

"I'm very pleased to know that." She paused momentarily before saying, "Mr. Stewart…" She chuckled briefly. "I am so accustomed to knowing you as Mr. Smiley that I have to stop and make sure I use your new name. How is your father, Captain Stewart?"

"He was very well when I left Scotland and working very hard to be the Earl of Strathmilton in deed as well as in title. He's a very competent man, and I'm sure he will be very successful. There was so much I could have done to assist him, but when Joanna died I couldn't cope with life for a long time."

"I can understand that, Mr. Stewart," she said. "What was that you said about an earl?"

Further conversation about my father was prevented by the arrival of the Governor. Shortly after he closed the door and certainly before I had managed to articulate, "Good evening, Sir David," the door opened again, and as one we turned toward it.

Sir David and Lady Megan knew exactly what they would see and were not surprised. I, on the other hand, had been expecting to see an old parliamentarian. I had imagined he would be fat and gouty or thin and desiccated but definitely an old member of Government on a fact-finding mission that would justify his position and salary.

What my startled and incredulous eyes perceived, however, was a dark-haired beauty from Wales I had known many years before as Mary Thomas. That was before she had been forced by her father to marry a local farmer who had died after a riding accident, I recalled. I couldn't immediately recall his name.

I was struck dumb with surprise, and I only vaguely remember Lady Megan saying, "I'm sure you remember my niece, Mr. Stewart." Suddenly, it was Mary's turn to be surprised as she said, "But your name's Jason Smiley," and she suddenly went very pale and collapsed onto the nearest chair. After a few minutes she recovered enough to whisper, "I had a letter saying you had died in Bombay."

"A number of other people received the same letter," I said, "but happily it wasn't true."

Lady Megan and Sir David asked almost in unison, "What's this about a letter?"

I said, "Someone in Bombay who called himself a friend of my father decided it would be a good idea to send his commiserations on my untimely death to relatives and friends in Britain. Unfortunately for him, I hadn't died and his letters had the exact opposite effect. His commiserations caused upset and then anger. Shortly after I arrived back in England, I went to visit my aunt and uncle in Lenton, and when I arrived, I found that the vicarage was in mourning. When she answered the doorbell, the maid thought I was a ghost and fainted on the doorstep, and my aunt wasn't really convinced I was real until she had pinched my arm and heard me swearing. I discovered later that they had received a copy of the letter advertising my death only the day before I got there."

I couldn't help rubbing the spot as I said reflectively, "I had a bruise for more than a week where she pinched me."

Sir David smiled at that.

"Why is your name 'Stewart' and not 'Smiley'? When my aunt and uncle told me Mr. Stewart would be joining us for dinner, I never imagined it could be you. I had such a shock. When I last saw you in Bombay, you were recovering in hospital, and Joanna," her voice broke and her eyes filled with tears as she said, "I am so sorry about Joanna, Mr. Stewart."

My memory worked at the last possible second and I said, "Thank you, Mrs. Lewis. Please go on."

She sniffed delicately and dabbed her eyes with the corner of a miniscule handkerchief and then said, "You may remember that I was accompanied by a young officer from the Guards when I visited you the last few times."

I nodded my agreement and said, "Yes, I remember him, but not well. I have a recollection that one night you talked at some length to Joanna about your marriage. I was only half conscious at the time, so I may have imagined it."

"No, your memory is accurate, Mr. Stewart. Joanna was a very easy person to confide in," and she blushed a little, possibly from the memory of what she might have said, but then went on. "Lieutenant Jarvis was quite good company at first and amused me when I was very sad about Mr. Lewis's death, but he mistook the depth of my friendship and was rather importunate."

"What?" interjected Sir David. "The young cad, someone should teach him a lesson."

She ignored the interruption except to say, "I did!" She went on, "I wrote to his commanding officer and complained about his ungallant behaviour on the day I boarded a ship to return home to Wales." Sir David nodded to signify his agreement to her action. "The letter about your death arrived a few weeks later. It was just after I arrived home. I was devastated by the news. The husband I hadn't loved was dead, and the man I did love was also dead."

It was nice to know that she had loved me once, I thought.

"Shortly after I returned to Barry, I went to see my father and took with me the letter you had sent to Eileen Davies. She had come to see me shortly after I was married and brought the letter with her. She had let me keep it, as it was the only letter I had of yours. There seemed no point in doing anything about it previously. Nothing could alter the fact of my marriage to Mr. Lewis. When I confronted him, my father didn't deny that he had deliberately kept us apart, Mr. Stewart, and made no apology for doing so. I was so angry with him that I stamped out of Porthkerry House in a fury and didn't return until after he had apologised some years later. I had no need for my father's support at the time and still do not, as my late husband left me his farm and that provides me with a good income."

Sir David brought us back to the present by saying, "May I suggest we go in to dinner? You can carry on with your reminiscences whilst we dine."

Naturally, we did as we were requested.

After the soup, Mrs. Lewis said, "Now, Mr. Stewart, why did you change your name?"

"That's easily explained, Mrs. Lewis. I realised after some time had passed that Captain Stewart was an admirable man, and I had been wrong not to accept his family name when it was offered. Fortunately, the captain was prepared to give me a second chance, and I formally adopted the surname Stewart."

"How is Captain Stewart, Mr. Stewart?"

"May I suggest you call me by my Christian name, Mrs. Lewis? You did when you nursed me in Bombay."

"Thank you, Jason, and you should call me Mary."

"I should be honoured to," I said. "As I said to Lady Megan earlier—"

Lady Megan interrupted, "I think it would be a good idea if you start at the beginning, Mr. Stewart. You had only just started to tell me about it when Sir David joined us."

"Yes, Lady Megan; you're correct," I responded.

I gathered my thoughts and said, "Captain Stewart is the second son of the old Earl of Strathmilton. The elder son inherited the estate when his father died, and he imposed a much stricter and more profit-oriented approach to its management. Captain Stewart was opposed to the changes because of the adverse affects on the estate tenants, and after a serious argument with his brother he left the family castle and went to sea. In time he became a respected senior captain, as you know. Two years ago, both the earl and his son died as a result of a fire in the child's bedroom, and Captain Stewart inherited the title and the estate. My father has given up his seagoing command and is trying very hard to be the earl in fact as well as in title. I was helping him and would probably have stayed on the family estate if Joanna had not died. The memories there were too painful, and I came away. More accurately, I suppose, I was in such a poor mental state after Joanna's death that I'm here because my father forced the issue. At the time I was unable to make a decision for myself."

"So you are the son of an earl, Mr. Stewart," said Lady Megan.

"That's true. I will have to go back and learn how to manage a big estate like Strathmilton, as I will become the earl one day, and I would like to follow my father's good example." I added, "If I manage to keep away from angry natives and live long enough to inherit."

"I hope you do, Mr. Stewart. They nearly finished you last time," Sir David said seriously.

"Do you have a title now?" Mary enquired.

"As the elder son of the earl, I do have the honorary title of viscount," I replied quietly, "but I haven't started to use it. It doesn't fit very well with my perception of myself as a working man."

"In many respects I'm very glad you haven't used your title, Mr. Stewart, as the *pomp and circumstance* surrounding your arrival here would have ruined any possibility of you remaining in the background whilst you are on my staff," remarked Sir David as he accepted the main course from one of his stewards.

Conversation for the next twenty minutes or so was limited to enquiries about each others' enjoyment of the meal and requests for the salt or gravy to be passed from one to another.

After the meal, Mary said, "Jason, should I address you as Viscount Strathmilton if you decide to use the title?"

"No," I said. "To you, Mary, I will always be Jason." I then added with a smile, "Others may have to be more formal!"

"Thank you, Jason," she said. "When I write next to Eileen Davies, may I tell her that the young man she roundly berated for his treatment of me is none other than Viscount Strathmilton?"

"Of course, Mary, but I doubt if that will improve her opinion of me."

"There is no need to worry about that, Jason, as she knows that it was my father's doing, not yours." And there the matter rested as Lady Megan started to discuss family matters with Mary.

Whilst the ladies talked, Sir David and I enjoyed a glass of cognac and had a short discussion about the rabbits that had been imported by a grazier in 1859. He had done it to increase the choice of meat for the pot.

"It appeared to be a very good idea," said Sir David, "until it was realised that they bred like," and he stopped and searched his memory for a suitable alternative simile without success and said, "well, like rabbits, and they had no natural enemy to control their numbers. It's becoming a problem of plague proportions." He drank the last of his brandy.

I took the hint and at about ten I said goodbye to my host and hostess and thanked them for a very enjoyable evening.

To Mary I said, "It was an unexpected pleasure to have your company this evening, Mary. I can only hope that good fortune will smile upon me again and allow me to enjoy the pleasure of your company again."

"Thank you, Jason. I, too, hope we can meet again." She held out a dainty hand, and as I gently grasped it, she said, "Good night, Jason."

I said in my turn, "Good night, Mary," then turned and left the Governor's private quarters and the Residence.

Next morning, I went to my office at my usual time. Silas came in, and after he picked up the thick pile of documents I had read during the previous day, he put down three thin volumes.

"Have you reached the bottom of the pit, Silas?" I asked.

"Yes, sir. These are the last of them."

"Good. I hope they are more interesting and informative than the others."

Silas was not encouraging and said, "I doubt it, sir," and left the office as I lowered my head in order to continue with my task.

I went to Ignatius's office just before ten, and as before he took me directly to the Governor. Sir David was sitting at his desk, and as he was reading a very official looking document covered with red seals, he said nothing and simply waved me toward one of the visitors' chairs.

Just as I was about to sit down, Ignatius said quietly, "I hear that you are a Viscount, Mr. Stewart."

"Yes, that's correct, but I don't use the title. Did Sir David tell you?"

Sir David stopped reading and looked over the top of the document at Ignatius, who said, "No. This is the first time I've seen him this morning."

"May I ask who informed you about my title then?"

Ignatius looked rather puzzled by my question but said, "My clerk mentioned it this morning. Why do you ask?"

"Until last evening no one knew I had an honorary title. I mentioned it at dinner only in response to a direct question from Mrs. Lewis. Only Sir David, Lady Megan, and Mrs. Lewis knew about it last night, but by this morning something that was discussed in the Governor's private quarters has become known to the clerks who assist us. Presumably one of the servants is betraying a position of trust."

Sir David, who had been listening to our conversation with increasing signs of anger, put down the document he had been reading and started to reach out and grasped one of the bell pulls as he said vehemently, "I will not put up with such behaviour. They will have to go."

"Excuse me, Sir David," I said quickly. "Please wait a moment."

He let go of the bell pull and said sharply, "What is it, Mr. Stewart?"

"When you spoke to me about my work here, you said you were concerned about the honesty of some of your staff. Clearly that concern is justified, but dismissing the stewards may not cure the problem. The fact that I can call myself Viscount is really of no major significance if it becomes generally known—but you could have been discussing something of political sensitivity that could considerably embarrass the Government or you personally. I would suggest that you do not discuss anything important when there are servants about. However, you could consider airing views on a subject in private that are contrary to your public opinion and see who becomes informed about them. The servants could provide a useful conduit to the dishonest members of your staff."

"I'll consider what you have said, Mr. Stewart, and now I must finish reading this dossier. Please sit down, Mr. Stewart. Thank you, Ignatius."

When he had finished reading, he rang a small silver bell on his desk and Ignatius returned, collected the dossier, and left again.

Sir David looked searchingly at me for some seconds.

He said directly, "Now, Mr. Stewart, I have read your report. I agree with your conclusions and think you should go to New Zealand. Do you know anything about the country?"

"Nothing at all, Sir David," I admitted. "I didn't know it existed until quite recently and have heard nothing about it except that it used to be administered from South Australia."

"I know very little about the country myself," Sir David admitted, "so I should be pleased to have some factual information from a reliable source when you return, but what I believe to be true is this: Many of the world's leading explorers have visited New Zealand. Tasman was in the area in about 1642, Cook in 1769, and a number of others before the beginning of this century. As you probably know, New Zealand is comprised of two islands. The indigenous population are called the Maori and most of them inhabit the North Island. There are many different tribes who co-operate, or fight together depending on circumstances at the time, but they form the majority of the population. The remainder of the people derive mainly from Europe and is the mixed bag of derelicts, honest people, and do-gooders that you would expect in a new colony. The missionaries are there in force. There are farmers and whalers and everything in between. Alcohol has been introduced to the Maori with predictable results and some temperance societies have been established, or so I have been informed. The Crown appointed Mr. James Busby as the British Resident in New Zealand, but he had so little real power that the Maoris call him 'a man of war without guns.' He did manage to persuade thirty-five of the Northern Chiefs to sign the Declaration of Independence, however. That was in '35, and five years later Busby collaborated with Captain Hobson in the preparation of what has become known as the Treaty of Waitangi. Hobson proclaimed British Sovereignty in May 1840. I recommend that you go to the Bay of Islands, where James Busby has his home and office, and after being briefed by him, travel in the country as you see fit and where Busby advises is safe."

"Thank you, Sir David," I said as my brain tried to remember the content of his comments. "I will check the availability of ships going to the Bay of Islands and advise you when I can leave Adelaide."

"Thank you, Mr. Stewart," said the Governor. "That will be all then," he added as he reached for the packet of papers that lay in red, sealed, and ribboned splendour on the top of a heap of voluminous documents piled on the corner of his desk

I stood up and walked from the office wondering what the next weeks would bring.

Over the next several days, I finished reading the papers Silas had brought to me but found nothing that altered the opinion I had given to Sir David in my report. Silas brought me a few reports and notes about New Zealand, but they contained nothing that amplified or amended the Governor's briefing. I discovered that a steamer called *Swift* was due to leave Adelaide for the Bay of Islands in a little more than a week and arranged for a cabin to be reserved for me. I briefed the Governor on my arrangements and suddenly found I had reached the end of one assignment and had a few days free before the next started but didn't have any idea what to do with them. As I left the Governor's office, I mentioned my dilemma to Ignatius.

He thought for a moment and suggested, "Why don't you visit Hahndorf? It's less than twenty miles from Adelaide. I was told that it's a settlement founded by the Lutherans who managed to escape from religious persecution in Prussia about thirty years ago. I haven't been there, so I should be pleased to know your opinion when you return."

"That's a very good idea, Ignatius. Thank you for the suggestion," I said warmly and then returned to my office and started make plans for a short trip.

I wondered if Mrs. Lewis would have any interest in making such a visit and quickly penned a short note to her proposing the idea. I gave the note to Silas to give to the Governor's butler and then returned to a contemplation of what I would try to do in New Zealand when I got there.

Shortly after I returned to my office after the midday meal, Silas brought me an answer from Mrs. Lewis. It didn't answer my query but politely requested my company for afternoon tea at four in the sitting room of the Governor's private quarters if that should be convenient.

Punctually at four I knocked on the entrance door to the Governor's part of the Residence and was immediately shown into the sitting room where Mary sat at a table laid with fine crockery and silver cutlery for two people. There were cakes and small sandwiches, cups and saucers, and cream and sugar in silver containers.

"Thank you for your invitation to tea, Mary. It was a very nice thought. I'm very pleased to see you looking so well after such a bad experience."

"It was a shock, I have to admit, but Mr. Lewis was not the love of my life, so I was able to recover quite quickly. In any case, I have had longer to get over my tragedy than you have, Jason, and I can still see the pain and sadness in your face. Time is a great healer, you know."

"I hope so, Mary. Indeed I hope so very much," I responded.

Mary picked up a little silver bell and rang it with a very gentle movement of her wrist. Within moments there was a knock on the door and a maid brought in a silver teapot and placed it on a table mat just in front of Mary. As the girl straightened up, I realised I was looking at the girl who had been Mary's chaperone in Wales.

My memory worked quickly for once and I was able to say, "Good afternoon Elsie. I hope you are well."

"Very well, thank you, sir," she said almost automatically, then her eyes became big round O's of surprise as she realised that I had not only remembered the face of a servant girl but also her name after so many years.

Mary said, "Thank you, Elsie," and waved her to a seat at the other end of the room.

Mary poured tea and then passed the milk and sugar.

She said, "Please take something to eat, Jason. The sandwiches are very good, and the cakes are quite delicious."

I did as I was asked and she was correct. Between discrete mouthfuls I said, "You told me the truth, Mary. I haven't tasted better."

"Thank you, Jason. I'll tell the cook. He will be very pleased to know."

After a few more mouthfuls and when I had finished my cup of tea, I asked, "Would you like to come to Hahndorf with me, Mary?"

"I would like to very much, Jason, but Lady Megan and I agree that it would not be very discrete of me to make such a journey when we haven't been seen in public together before. Nobody apart from Lady Megan and Sir David knows that we have known each other for many years. I'm pleased you thought of asking me, Jason, but I must decline you invitation."

"Not thoughtful enough, I'm afraid, Mary. I should have realised that such an outing could compromise your reputation and had the good sense not to ask. I'm really very sorry."

"Don't be sorry, Jason. It has given us the chance to spend a little time together that we would not have had otherwise. Isn't that so?"

"Yes indeed," I said. "I hope we will be able to meet again, Mary"

"When you ask, Jason, I'm quite sure you will find me willing to cooperate with your suggestions." She put her cup down and said, "And now, my friend, I must go and see Lady Megan and help her choose a dress to wear to her next soiree."

"Thank you for your invitation this afternoon, Mary. Please extend my best wishes to Lady Megan. When I return from New Zealand, I will contact you immediately, and then I can tell you firsthand about my experiences."

"Will I not see you again before you leave, Jason?"

"I don't think so, Mary. I'm going to Hahndorf in the morning, and when I return I will have to get ready to go to New Zealand."

"Do you think I will have no interest in Hahndorf, Jason?" she said with an edge to her voice as she turned away and then left the room.

For a few minutes I stood there slightly bemused by the strange turn in the conversation then went back to my office unable to understand what I had missed, because clearly I had missed something.

I rang for Silas as soon as I was at my desk. When he came in, I said, "Silas I want you to arrange for a carriage to take me to Hahndorf tomorrow leaving my villa at nine. Please also send the messenger to reserve a room at the Union Hotel for me for two nights."

"Yes, Mr. Stewart, of course," and he left to do as I had instructed.

At five I returned to my villa and instructed Edwards to pack clothes for two days then dined and went to bed. I couldn't sleep for a long time, as I couldn't rid my brain of Mary's sudden departure. Her posture had appeared angry although I could not understand why she should have been; particularly so suddenly. After a poor night I ate a good breakfast and promptly at nine climbed into the carriage. Edwards stowed my luggage and the driver set off along the dusty outback roads toward Hahndorf. In the town we drove directly to the Union Hotel, and when I tried to get a key to the room Silas had been instructed to reserve, I was told to my dismay that there were no rooms vacant.

I said, "I sent a messenger from the Residence yesterday to reserve me a room. My name is Stewart. Did the messenger not arrive?"

"Oh! Yes, sir! A messenger arrived late yesterday and he booked our last available room on behalf of the Residency but not in the name of Stewart."

"Is there another hotel I can go to?" I asked the manager.

"Yes, sir. There's the German Arms Hotel. It's a little farther along the street. Shall I send the porter to see if they have a vacancy?"

"Yes, please," I responded, and then out of simple curiosity I asked, "For whom did the messenger book a room? I was unaware that any one else from the Residence was going to be in Hahndorf tonight."

"Well, we are all a little excited about it, sir. Viscount Strathmilton will be staying tonight. Do you have any idea what time the Viscount is likely to arrive, Mr. Stewart?"

"Yes!" I said. "He has."

"I beg your pardon, sir," said the manager. "I don't understand."

"Oh! Never mind!" I said, "I hope you will not be disappointed, but I am Viscount Strathmilton, but I prefer to travel using my normal sur-name of Stewart." With a little edge of anger creeping into my voice, I said, "Now! Can I have a key to my room?"

"Yes, of course, sir." He banged the striker on the top of a brass bell that stood on the reception desk and when the bellboy came in response to the chime the bell made, he said in a loud voice and to the intense interest of everyone in the foyer, "Take Viscount Strathmilton to his room immediately."

So much for anonymity, I thought, suddenly aware that all the other guests in the foyer had stopped talking and turned toward me.

I turned to the bellboy. "Take me to my room," I ordered. I added, "Immediately, please," and followed him across the foyer whilst trying to ignore the stares.

After taking time to wash and change out of my travelling clothes, I decided to take a look at this small town that Ignatius had recommended. It was a clean, tidy, little place, but I couldn't read the names above the stores, as they were in a script I had never seen before. I stopped and asked two elderly men for guidance about what there was to see in Hahndorf and couldn't understand a word they said in response. They wore the same clothes and had the same colour skin as all the other Australians I had met, but they spoke a totally unfamiliar language. I have met people from many different parts of the world who spoke a different language, but they wore different clothing or had a different colour skin or both. The differences were obvious. Here, everything appeared to be normal until I tried to read or speak. It was quite eerie. I went back to the Union Hotel and happened to see the manager as I entered the foyer.

He said, "You're soon back, Mr. Stewart. Is everything in order?"

"I cannot read the shop signs, and I do not understand a word people say. This is still South Australia, I hope?"

"Yes, sir," he said. "What you have to remember is that this town was founded by people from Prussia only about thirty years ago. They had only their native German language when they arrived, and many of them have not yet learnt any English, particularly the oldest part of the population. Fortunately, I have learnt enough German to be successful here."

"Thank you," I said and went to my room.

As I sat and waited for dinner, I wondered what Mary would have made of the situation. In the circumstances it would have been difficult for us to make a satisfactory tour in a town where we couldn't converse with the locals or read the written signs, and consequently I was more than a little pleased that she had declined to come with me. As a result, I decided to leave Hahndorf first thing after breakfast the following morning and return to the Residence. I thought it would be nice to talk to Mary and describe my limited experiences, as I would have time to see her now since I had decided to leave Hahndorf early. It dawned on me that I would have had time anyway and thought I understood why Mary's mood had suddenly changed for the worse. She must have known there would have been time for us to meet before I sailed south unless I didn't want to—and that must have been the interpretation she placed on my remark. I could almost hear her saying under her breath, "He doesn't want to meet me again. I'm not important enough."

Oh dear! I thought. *Two left feet again.*

When I returned to the Residence more than a day early, I rang for Silas as soon as I reached my office.

When he came in I asked, "Who gave you permission to tell the Union Hotel I am Viscount Strathmilton?"

"I didn't know you are Viscount Strathmilton, sir. The messenger was told to book the room for Mr. Stewart. Was there a problem, sir? Is that why you are back earlier than you planned?"

"No! There was no problem," I said. "But I do wonder who told the messenger if you didn't know?" I mused out loud.

"Should I ask the messenger?" Silas asked, but I said there was no need. It wasn't really so important, and an enquiry might make it seem so.

As Silas turned to leave my office, I said, "Wait a moment please, Silas." I wrote a short note to Mary to tell her I had returned and should be pleased to see her if she could make time. I gave it to Silas to deliver to the Governor's wing and then sat at my desk and wondered what I should do to fill in my time.

I didn't have long to wonder as Silas returned quite quickly with a reply.

Mary wrote simply, "Hello, Jason. You have returned early. Please come now and tell me your news if you can."

As you would expect, I went directly to the private wing and found Mary in the sitting room with the faithful Elsie sitting discretely in the background.

In response to my greeting, Mary said, "Good afternoon, Jason. What happened to cause you to come back so much sooner than you planned? Did something go wrong?"

I described all my experiences and ended my recitation by saying, "It was such an unfamiliar place. It was as if I had travelled to a foreign country and not to a small town in Southern Australia twenty miles from where we are sitting. I thought it looked a nice place, and I'll go back when I know more about the people and their language. Perhaps I can find an interpreter to help me."

"It certainly sounds very interesting, Jason. It's a little piece of Prussia in the south of Australia. When you return from New Zealand, perhaps we can find a way of seeing it together without offending local morals."

"I would like that, Mary. It's nice to share new experiences. Perhaps Lady Megan would like to go as well and be your chaperone at the same time."

"I'll ask her," said Mary with a smile.

Two days later I boarded the *Swift* and set sail for New Zealand.

SEVEN

Aotearoa

I woke to the sound of a sharp *rat-tat* on the cabin door and in the pre-dawn gloom could just make out the dim shape of one of crew in the doorway as he called out, "Captain's complements, Mr. Stewart. It's just past three bells, and if you would like to come to the bridge in about thirty minutes, you should be able to see the coast as dawn breaks."

"Thank you, Edwards," I responded as I swung my legs out of the bunk and then balanced to the easy motion of the *Swift* as it steamed at a reduced speed across the swells that were bearing down on the coast of New Zealand. The *Swift* had not been quite as speedy as I had hoped, but even so we had made a respectable time on our passage from Adelaide to the Bay of Islands, and later in the morning I hoped to step ashore onto New Zealand soil for the first time.

I washed and dressed quite quickly and made my way up the ladders to the bridge where the second officer and the helmsman were on watch with Captain Schmidt standing in the back of the wheelhouse enjoying the morning air.

Captain Schmidt turned to me as I entered the bridge and said cheerfully, "'Morning, Mr. Stewart. You dressed quickly. There's nothing to see yet." He gestured out across the bows.

"It's no matter, Captain. Better to be early than late, I believe," I answered.

"Indeed," he said and relapsed into silence.

I had known Captain Schmidt for a little less than two weeks, but I had been able to establish a reasonable accord with him. I think this was mainly because I had been a sailor at one time and we were able to exchange stories and experiences. He spoke quite good English although German words and phrases found their way into his narrative when he was excited. He had been one of the officers on a whaler but decided that the regular life of a small steamer captain was more suited to his temperament. He gave the impression that he was a very happy man and seemed to be extremely proud of his Maori wife and their two children.

Our friendship was the reason for the invitation I had received to be on the bridge during our approach to the Bay of Islands.

He nudged me in the ribs to attract my attention and passed me his telescope as he gestured out over the bow.

I looked and could just make out a smoky-looking smudge on the horizon that was a shade too substantial to be a cloud. Every five minutes or so I looked out over the bows with the telescope, and as the light improved and the distance shortened, the detail of this new land became more visible.

As we sailed in a westerly direction toward Waitangi, we started to navigate between two headlands. Captain Schmidt pointed out Cape Brett to port with Purerea Peninsula to starboard, but I could make out little detail in the predawn light. There were also several islands ahead on our port side, but I do not remember the names they were given by the captain. I continued to watch the approaching land in the improving light and I was struck by the denseness of the forest that covered most of the visible area. Different greens, of course, but an overwhelming impression of dark green foliage covering and softening a landscape that seemed to have been chopped out of the ground it was so sharp-edged.

After a little while I could make out a headland with a flagpole in a prominent position, just to starboard of our heading, but even with a telescope I was unable to identify the flag, as the wind was blowing it almost directly away from me.

"I can see a flag on the flagpole on the headland but the wind is blowing it away from us," I said to the captain as I gestured toward it. "It looks like the Union Jack, Captain. Can you tell me what it is?"

Captain Schmidt turned away from his examination of the bay and said, "The flagpole marks the place where the Treaty of Waitangi was signed. Possibly you can see the building just behind it."

I assumed it was a question and said, "Yes, I can see it."

"That's where James Busby, the British Resident, lives with his family.

He has his office there," he said, and then, answering my previous question, he added, "You're correct, Mr. Stewart. It's the Union Jack." He saw the look of surprise on my face and said, "It's been the official flag of New Zealand since 1840. Didn't you know?"

"No," I said. "I had no idea which flag was flown here. I assumed that they had their own."

After a pause, during which I examined the approaching building on the headland, the captain looked all around the bay again and then continued with his explanation. "Another flag was flown some years ago. It was one of three designs produced by the Reverend Henry Williams at Busby's request. About twenty-five Maori chiefs from the North Island and some of the settlers together with a number of British and American naval officers were present when the designs were presented to the chiefs. The chiefs voted individually for the different designs, and the one with the majority of votes was accepted as the official design. Although the whole business was initiated as a device to allow ships built in New Zealand to be registered officially, the flag soon became known as the flag of the United Tribes of New Zealand. That flag had St. George's cross on a white background with four white stars separated by a smaller cross of St. George on a blue background in the first quarter. I was told that the stars represented the four main Maori tribes but don't know if that's true or not. It was the official flag for only six years or so, and when the treaty of Waitangi was signed in 1840, it was replaced with the Union Jack, which was a change some of the Maoris were not prepared to accept. One of them, a fiery Maori called Hone Heke, has cut down the signal flag pole in Kororareka once or twice already."

I thought over this nugget of information for a moment as Captain Schmidt scanned the bay with his telescope once more.

"How do you know all that?" I asked curiously.

"It's not so long ago," he answered, "but I have to admit that I was told by someone I knew who was living in the Bay of Islands at the time."

"I don't know anywhere called Kororo…" I spluttered into silence as my tongue tripped over the unfamiliar syllables.

"Kororareka," corrected Captain Schmidt with the familiarity of long use. "You will probably have heard of Russell. It's about five miles from Kororareka and was the Capital for a time."

"Remarkable," I responded and then lapsed into silence as Captain Schmidt started his preparations to anchor. We were quite a long way out from the shore still, but clearly Captain Schmidt intended to err on the side of caution since we had a brisk following wind. From my rather rusty knowledge of the sea and ships I couldn't blame him for his caution, even though it would mean a much longer journey in a small boat when I went ashore.

After the ship was anchored Captain Schmidt turned his attention back to me. "I don't know what you plan, Mr. Stewart, but I'll remain at anchor here until two bells in the afternoon watch," he said. "I'll arrange a boat to take you to Hobson's Beach, which is just below the Resident's home, and when you disembark you will find a path up to the Residence at the northern end."

He paused to stoop over the binnacle to check a bearing on a prominent landmark then said, "You will be treading in historical footsteps, Mr. Stewart, as you will be following the path that Captain Hobson used to get up to the Residence just before the treaty was signed."

"Thank you, Captain," I said again and started to wonder what other historical gems the man knew.

"I'll send the boat back to the beach at eight bells. You can come back onboard and sail with me to Auckland, or I'll send your trunks ashore if you are going to stay here."

"That's very generous of you, Captain." I said, "Thank you for your thoughtfulness."

Captain Schmidt said nothing, but his smile indicated that he had been pleased by my few words of praise, and then he ordered the boat over the side.

A few minutes later I was being rowed toward the shore, and in fifteen I was standing on the golden sand of a beach in the northeast of a country I had heard about for the first time only recently and knew nothing at all about.

And it started to rain.

Not too heavily, but the unbroken grey clouds that drifted by overhead suggested that a long spell of wet weather was imminent, and I knew that it would make up in duration what it lacked in intensity. I was in for a wet walk up to the Residence.

I waved goodbye to the boat crew, turned my back to the sea, and started to walk up the beach as I looked for the first time toward the land.

I stopped moving as my brain registered that the whole of the slope in front of me, from the crest of the beach to the top of the rain-greyed ridge, was a solid carpet of foliage. There was not a single break in the multi-hued sea of green, and with one possible exception I recognised none of the plants I could see. That exception was a plant that I would have called a fern if I had been at home and if it had been knee-high. Here it was tree size and clearly a dominant species from the number of them I could see.

I walked along the beach toward the northern end where the path was supposed to be located and was starting to believe that I had been mis-informed when a gap in the foliage became discernable through the rain and mist. The track led up the slope and through the trees, so I turned onto it and started to climb. As I struggled up the sodden, slippery slope, I tried not to think about the discomfort caused by clothing that was rapidly absorbing large quantities of cold water, nor the increasingly noisy breathing as my out-of-condition body panted up the slope. I had to get to the top. I had no option if I was to meet the Resident, but in the back of my mind I did wish that he had chosen somewhere closer to the sea to set up his home and office. Suddenly, I sensed the slope lessening and very soon afterwards the foliage started to retreat as I entered the open, flatter area I had seen from the ship. In the distance, the façade of James Busby's house was visible.

It was rather disappointing.

The sole representative of British Government and essentially the ruler of the country, at least on paper, lived in a small, single story, wooden house with a porch and one chimney, so presumably only one fireplace. There was also no one about. There should have been a guard or two in evidence, but I could neither see nor hear a single person.

And the hair on the back of my neck started to prickle. I hurriedly looked back over my shoulder but could see no one behind me—but the knowledge I was alone didn't stop the hair on my neck prickling continuously.

I walked across the open area to the house, stepped up onto the veranda, and knocked on what I supposed to be the front door. No answer. I walked around the small house in the rain—in a silence broken only by my footsteps and the noise of rainwater from the roof shingles splashing in the puddles beside the path.

I saw no sign of life inside or outside.

As I finished my circumnavigation of the house, I realised that it would not be possible to have the meeting with James Busby I had planned in accordance with Sir David's suggestion, and my only course of action now was to return to the *Swift*.

I set off across the grass toward the path down to the beach and the rain continued to saturate my clothing.

The hairs on the back of my neck prickled with the feeling that many hostile eyes were watching my every step, but even though I saw and heard nothing, I decided to stand at the water's edge in the rain when I reached the beach and examine the forest edge rather than stand in the shelter of the trees that lined the crest of the beach.

I continued my careful observation of the edge of the forest and didn't know the *Swift's* boat was approaching until I heard its bows crunch into the sand just behind me.

I turned, waded into the shallows, pushed the bows off the sand, and as I climbed into the boat I heard the bowman's fearful voice say, "Look at that!"

As I turned to look, I heard the bosun's voice ordering urgently, "Altogether now. Back your oars. Row." I saw what he and the bowman had seen seconds before. The edge of the forest was alive with dark-skinned men with spears and clubs, but we were soon far enough from the beach to allow the crew to turn the boat, and we headed out to the safety of the *Swift*.

As soon as I was onboard, I went up to the bridge to speak to Captain Schmidt. I needed some local advice now that the Resident was inaccessible, and it was possible that the captain could suggest someone I could consult.

Captain Schmidt said with a chuckle, "I saw you had a group of local people to see you off, Mr. Stewart. Did they threaten you?"

"No," I answered. "I sensed someone was watching me but saw and heard nothing. They suddenly came out of the trees as I was getting on to the boat but were not threatening in any way that I noticed."

"Did you meet Mr. Busby?"

"No. The house was empty and locked up."

"What will you do now?" Captain Schmidt asked. "You can stay onboard and sail over to Kororareka and then Auckland, if you wish."

"Thank you, Captain Schmidt," I responded gratefully. "I should be happy to accept your offer, and perhaps you would let me impose on your generosity a little further and ask you for advice about whom I should try to meet now that Mr. Busby is not available."

"When we have anchored off Kororareka tonight, perhaps you can come ashore with me and we can have dinner together. You can tell me what you need to know and I'll try to advise you. Now, if you will excuse me, I must return to my duties."

"Of course, Captain," I said and left the bridge.

As arranged, I met Captain Schmidt at the gangway and we were rowed to the jetty at Kororareka, where we disembarked and walked up to a hotel on the waterfront called the Duke of Marlborough. We ate a good dinner, and I had several hours of instructive conversation with several local people.

SS Swift
Anchored off Kororareka
Your Excellency,

I have attached for your attention a report describing my initial experiences in New Zealand. I will relate what I have heard and hope I do not bore you with a repetition of information you already possess.

I hope you are in good health and request that you extend my felicitations to Lady Megan and Mrs. Lewis.

I will make use of the local postal service to send this report to you when I can go ashore later this morning.

Your obedient servant, sir,

Jason Smiley Stewart

NEW ZEALAND
Report No. 1
for
Sir David Tallboy

In accordance with your instructions, your Excellency, I sailed to Aotearoa—New Zealand—on the SS Swift with Captain Schmidt in command. After a better than expected passage, Captain Schmidt anchored off Waitangi and allowed me to use one of the ship's boats to go to the shore where I landed on Hobson's beach, which is just below the Residence. I climbed up to the top of the bluff and found the house and surrounding area unoccupied. I returned to the beach and just as I embarked on the ship's boat that had been sent by Captain Schmidt to collect me, a big group of Maori warriors armed with spears and clubs emerged from the bush.

They did not threaten us but might have done so if we had not immediately rowed away. We would have fared badly if they had attacked, as we were unarmed and out-numbered about five to one.

I returned onboard the Swift and arranged to stay on the ship while she was sailed to Kororareka. At Kororareka I went with Captain Schmidt to the hotel known as the Duke of Marlborough, which is on the waterfront, and there I had the opportunity to discuss local affairs with the captain and several local people who happened to be in the hotel at the same time. What I learnt from my conversations is described in the following pages.

I was told that James Busby is away at present. He has gone to America with a ship full of Kauri gum. His wife and children have gone to Sydney for safety, as there is a war going on between some of the northern tribes, and the Residence is not considered to be a safe place to live.

When I related what I had experienced earlier in the day, one of my companions looked very serious and said that I was very lucky not to have been attacked.

The other said that it was quite common for the Maori to eat their dead opponents. He seemed quite amused by the concept, but I was unable to find anything remotely humorous in the prospect of being a cannibal's luncheon.

Kororareka was a small Maori village at the turn of this century. After whaling ships started to moor here to replenish food and water, Europeans began to settle, but in the most part these people were deserters from ships and ex-convicts from New South Wales; simply the riff-raff of society. After about forty years, Kororareka was the biggest European settlement in New Zealand and lawless, if one ignores gun law, despite the best efforts of the missionaries. To this day it remains a hotchpotch of Maori and European architecture and culture and is crowded with shops selling liquor and the services of local women. As a sailor, I have visited some very squalid and disreputable harbour areas, but this town has become so dissolute it has earned the sobriquet "The hellhole of the Pacific."

I can assure you, Sir David, that the title is richly deserved.

Although the Treaty of Waitangi has been accepted by a large percentage of the Maori population, there are still many who are suspicious of our long-term intentions. One such is a man called Hone Heke, who is a nephew of one of the chiefs who signed the treaty. Up to now Hone Heke has demonstrated his displeasure by cutting down the ship signalling mast at Kororareka three times. The first was in 1841, when the Government imposed customs duty on visiting ships thereby reducing the number of ships visiting the port and also Hone Heke's income. When the Government cancelled the customs duty, Hone Heke offered to erect a new mast. The second occasion was in January 1845, when he had been encouraged by the American consular agent to emulate the American War of Independence. The Governor then chose to replace the mast, guard it with Maoris loyal to the crown, and put a bounty on Hone Heke's head. It was an irresistible challenge, and ten days later Hone Heke marched through the guards and chopped the mast down again. I have to report that the mast has again been erected, but this time the base is sheathed in iron and a blockhouse has been built all around it.

As you undoubtedly know, Your Excellency, the Capital is now in Auckland, but you may not be aware that the remaining buildings in Russell, including what was known as Government House, have been burnt down. Accidentally, I believe.

I enquired but to date no one has attempted to develop a telegraph system here. From what I was told, I imagine the centres of population are too small, too far apart, and as they are generally coastal settlements, transport by sea is the preferred method of communication. There is a post office here in Kororareka, but I have no details of postal arrangements as yet and will try to include more information in my next report, which I expect to write from Auckland.

On a more parochial note, I should advise you that the local settlers have ignored the missionaries and built their own church with Charles Darwin amongst the benefactors. It is known as Christ Church and was completed in about 1835. I look forward to a tranquil hour there when I have a chance to visit it.
  Your obedient servant,
  Signed: Jason Smiley Stewart

After sealing my letter and report in an envelope, I went up to the bridge to arrange with Captain Schmidt for a boat to take me ashore. This was soon organised, and the captain accompanied me to the head of the gangway.

He said, "As you know, Mr. Stewart, I expect to be at anchor here for several more days before I sail for Auckland. If you wish to see something of the town and surrounding country, you may find it more convenient to take a room in the Duke of Marlborough instead of spending a good deal of your time in a small boat."

"Thank you, Captain," I said. "That's a very good idea, and I expect you will have plenty of work for the boat crew to do when they are not acting as my personal transport."

"I cannot deny the truth of that, Mr. Stewart," Captain Schmidt responded with a smile.

"If the boat crew can wait for me, I'll pack a small bag and you can send it over if I can get a room."

"The boat can certainly wait, Mr. Stewart," responded Captain Schmidt. "May I suggest that you take your bag with you? The coxswain can accompany you to the hotel, and if you decide to take a room you can arrange with him when you wish to be picked up again."

"That's a very good suggestion, Captain. Thank you," I said.

And so about an hour later and after posting my report to Sir David Tallboy at the local post office, I was safely ensconced in a comfortable little room overlooking the Bay of Islands and the Pacific Ocean.

After lunch I walked along the beach and then up to Christ Church, where I sat in one of the box pews for a reflective and contemplative hour or so. I was a little relieved to recognise that the pain of Joanna's death was becoming less debilitating and found also that I now believed a little more in the adage "time is a great healer."

My offhand remark to Mary Lewis about managing the estate in Scotland when my father retired came back to mind. I hadn't given it any thought previously, but clearly I would have to plan for the eventuality.

When I left the church I noticed a small plaque in the porch describing how Captain Hobson had used the church in its alternate role of a public hall to read the Crown Proclamation, which declared New Zealand a dependency of New South Wales and his commission as the first Lieutenant Governor.

In the late afternoon I walked back to the Duke of Marlborough, ate a healthy dinner, and retired to bed with the intention of arising early and exploring as much of my surroundings as possible.

I have kept a diary since I was appointed an officer cadet on Gold Star Line more years ago than I care to remember, and as the reader has a right to expect, I consult it extensively as I prepare these memoirs. Because of the importance of the day I decided to quote the entry for 11 March completely rather than make a summary of it, as is my usual practice. I wrote up my diary on passage from Kororareka to Auckland but had to rewrite this part after the *Nimrod* sank.

11 March
Duke of Marlborough Hotel
Kororareka

I was disturbed very early this morning by a cracking noise that I initially thought was someone rattling on a shutter, but as I regained consciousness I rapidly identified the noise as gunfire. I dressed as quickly as I could in the predawn gloom and went downstairs to try to find out what was happening. The hotel servants I discovered on the ground floor were in a state of confused panic, and as they were totally unable to satisfy my thirst for information, I decided to go and look for myself.

In a few moments I was standing outside the hotel. I could hear guns firing somewhere to the east of me and more distinctly, and therefore closer, also from a westerly direction. I was in two minds about what to do next as memories of the pain and suffering I experienced the last time I was wounded flooded through my mind together with the discomforting thought that I would not have Joanna to nurse me through it if I was wounded again. I wanted to distance myself from the danger as quickly as possible, but at the same time the professional man in me wanted to know more about the conflicts in order to report facts to Sir David and not conjecture or hearsay.

After a few minutes of mental anguish, as I seesawed between duty and the infinitely preferable escape to safety, I decided to walk at least a little way toward the nearer conflict to see if I could ascertain what was happening.

I hadn't gone very far before I realised that I must be walking toward the area where the signalling mast was located. The gunfire wasn't lessening, and my fear of injury increased with every step I took toward the fight. It wasn't very long before I heard people running toward me in the half light of dawn, and I quickly stepped off the road into the concealment of the bushes beside the track so that I could see who was approaching and remain hidden if they looked at all threatening. After a few tense minutes, during which I seemed to stop breathing and my pulse rose alarmingly, I could heard them calling to each other in English and hoped that that was a good sign.

I stepped out of concealment onto the track and so frightened the leader of the group that he fired his pistol at me, but fortunately he didn't aim accurately and the bullet hummed passed my left ear. It was a reflex to duck, but I was far too late and my knees almost gave way with fear as the leader ran on past me trying to reload his pistol as he went. I managed to stop one of the other Europeans who were hurrying after their leader in a direction opposite to mine and away from the conflict.

"What's happening?" I called in a much calmer voice than I expected to utter. I was quite proud of my appearance of sangfroid, counterfeit although it was.

"It's that Hone Heke," the man panted. "He's chopping the mast down again." He pushed past me and started to hurry away toward the centre of town then, when he realised I wasn't following him, he stopped and called back, "They're coming this way. Run! They'll kill you if they catch you!"

I didn't run, of course, although in my fearful state I wanted to quite desperately. But in the circumstances, and as I knew now what was happening at the west end of Kororareka, I did think it was prudent to return to the centre of town to try to obtain more factual information about the situation at the east end. I realised as soon as I got there that I was going to be unsuccessful, as I only found panic and confusion wherever I looked. People were calling to each other. They were screaming and jumping at shadows and rushing about in the dawn light like small groups of leaderless sheep.

The gunfire on the eastern side of the town was increasing, and I overheard someone telling his companion that Kawiti's men had attacked the Royal Navy signal gun at Matauwhi.

There was a loud explosion from the direction of Polacks stockade, and the settlers started to scurry from the town toward the jetty so that they could get to the safety of the ships in the bay. As the settlers moved out, the Maoris moved in and started to plunder and set fire to the buildings on the western outskirts.

I looked at the people heading for the jetty and safety with envy.

I wanted to keep my skin whole if I could, but I couldn't find out who was attacking what without walking in the opposite direction. I set off along the beach, and before reaching Pompallier I headed for Christ Church with the intention of changing direction to the eastward again so that I could get closer to the increasing sounds of gunfire.

Suddenly, I was in the middle of the battle. It had decided to come to me. There were marines and sailors hazed in gun smoke in front of me in the churchyard and seen dimly through the smoke from burning buildings, the dark skins of the Maori attackers behind me when I risked a look over my shoulder. Both sides were firing, and as the bullets whizzed past, my first reaction was to find a nice deep hole to hide in but I couldn't see one. For the next few seconds I lead a charmed life because I decided that my only option was to join the sailors and without further consideration made an undignified run for the imagined safety of the wall surrounding the churchyard.

When I started to pick myself up from the grass after diving over the wall, one of the sailors pushed a gun in to my hands and said, "Stupid sod! Lucky we didn't shoot you! I hope you can use this."

Gasping for breath after a hard bump on the turf, I managed to say, "Watch me," and realised that all my fear had evaporated at the instant of joining battle. I loaded, aimed, and fired as if I had last handled a gun the day before and not many years previously.

We loaded and fired, loaded and fired, and each time

I looked over the wall to find someone to aim at, I feared it would be my last move in this life. I was just about to aim again when a razor sharp sliver of stone from the top of the wall sliced across my scalp. The ricocheting bullet that had just given me another scar hit my naval companion in the shoulder with a thud, and as I clutched my throbbing, bleeding head, he collapsed with a shout of pain and his rifle thudded onto the turf. I wondered how many more men we could loose before our situation became indefensible. Suddenly, the Maoris gunfire lessened. Then it died away altogether, and as we peered cautiously over the wall, we realised that for the time being we were safe from attack. The Maoris were moving away.

One of the Navy personnel started to rally his men together, and they checked and reloaded their weapons. Then they picked up their dead comrades and laid them out beside the church. I noticed that quite a few of them were shedding tears but whether of sorrow for the dead or relief that it was over was impossible to tell. I imagine that it was probably a mixture of both.

Perhaps when one has been in command of men, one wears a label that is invisible to all except those who need a leader, and it certainly appeared to be so that day. Automatically, it seemed the men followed me when I decided it was time to head for the jetty. They picked up, or otherwise supported the wounded and followed me when I walked out of the churchyard without a word being said by anyone. I cannot speak for my companions, of course, but I imagine that they were as bone weary as I was. I was finding it difficult to put one foot in front of the other no matter how hard I tried to set an example.

At that moment, we were a spent force.

A ragged, untidy group of war-weary men.

As we walked along, we were all examining the countryside around us, as we didn't want to be ambushed, but we had used all our reserves of energy and could do no more than be watchful and hope nothing occurred.

Added to my physical exhaustion was the realisation that I was becoming very, very hungry and thirsty. A feeling that was accentuated by the thought that I had missed breakfast and a meal at midday seemed extremely unlikely.

We shuffled slowly along the track and the uneven sound of our footsteps was punctuated by the groans and gasps of pain emitted by the wounded as they moved. We saw no one for some time, and I was beginning to hope that the Maoris had given up their attacks when I heard a scream of fear and anger from the side of the track just ahead. Whatever was amiss was obscured from my view by some bushes on the left-hand side of the track.

I hurried forward, not knowing or caring if the sailors were keeping up, and as I rounded the end of the bushes I saw a young woman struggling with two big, brawny Maoris.

I shouted and charged toward the group with all the strength and energy I could generate, and as one of the Maoris loosened his grip in surprise at my voice, the girl tore her right hand free and reached up to the big bun of black hair at the back of her head. Something flashed in the light and as she stabbed at the man who was in front of her, I realised she had pulled a bodkin out of her hair. He reeled back holding a hand to his fiercely tattooed and bleeding face, but the other man simply held on tight. I was close enough to take an active part in the young woman's defence, and as I didn't dare to shoot in case I hit the girl, I reversed the rifle and took a great delight in hitting the man over the head as hard as I could. He dropped to the ground without a sound, as the rifle butt parted company with the breech and his companion, seeing how many of us had appeared, took to his heels and ran with a few poorly aimed bullets from the sailors flying around his ears.

I said to the girl, "Are you alone here?"

"No," was the response. "My mother and younger sister are in the house over there." She pointed. It was in a hollow and I could just see the roof.

"Are any Maoris there?" I asked.

"No," she said. "At least there were none when I came to look for help."

"We're going to the jetty. You had better get your mother and sister and come with us. We'll come to the house with you in case your two Maoris were not alone."

I took a rifle from one of the walking wounded, checked that it was loaded, and walked slowly and carefully through the bush until I was close to the edge and could see the house clearly.

She was wrong.

There were four of them standing in a group near the front door talking and gesticulating in our direction. I knew that they must have heard our guns, but they hadn't decided what to do about it. We crawled forward to the edge of the hollow. The front door was closed, but I couldn't be sure there were no more Maoris in the house, and I didn't want to initiate an attack on the ones in the garden in case it precipitated an attack on the mother and sister.

As I watched, I saw a movement behind a window in the attic.

I nudged the girl, pointed to the window, and asked, "Is that your mother?"

"Yes," she said.

"Do you think she is free to move about? No Maoris in the house?"

"Yes."

The window slowly opened. We heard the creak, but I think the men in the garden were arguing to loudly to notice. The end of a gun barrel appeared, and I said quietly to the sailor lying beside me, "Don't shoot until her mother fires. Pass it down the line."

"Aye, sir," he said.

After what seemed to be an age, there was an enormous explosion from the house and dense black smoke started to billow from the attic window. I couldn't see the gun anymore, and I had to hold the girl down to stop her running into our field of fire. She was sobbing and crying out, "She's used too much powder again. I keep telling her to be more careful."

Whilst this was going on, my companions dispatched the four attackers in the front garden and then the three others who came running from the back of the house.

In the ensuing silence we all rushed to the house where we met in the doorway a smoke-blackened lady and a very tearful little girl. As quickly as we could, we marshalled everyone together and set off for the jetty and it wasn't many minutes later that we saw smoke rising from the hollow where the house lay. The Maoris had returned for vengeance.

As we walked onto the jetty, the girl took my hand and said, "I can only thank you for saving us." She shuddered as the enormity of the tragedy we had averted registered for the fist time. "What's your name?"

"Jason Smiley Stewart, Miss," I responded with a smile. "I hope your life is calmer from now on."

"I too," she said. "Thank you again."

With that she was gone, simply swallowed up in a crowd of well-wishers together with her mother and sister.

I walked along the jetty and managed to get onto a boat together with a number of local people who were being evacuated and was able to persuade the boatman to drop me at the Swift as we passed by.

When I reached the bridge, Captain Schmidt took one look at my face and said, "I see you have been too close to the fighting, Mr. Stewart,"

"It was a rock splinter from a ricochet and bled a good deal," I said. "It looks worse than it is, Captain." My head throbbed as if it was being beaten with hammers.

I told Captain Schmidt what I had observed or had been told, and then we watched the final stages of the looting and burning of Kororareka from the bridge.

Later in the day, I recorded in my journal.

Kororareka no longer exists as a township.

Apart from the church and the Mission houses, everything else has been reduced to smoking debris. The settlers are all onboard the various ships that are in the bay, and the Maoris have gone back to their villages.

There are many rumours about the number of people who died and how many Maoris were involved in the attacks but no definite information except that two Marines and four sailors from the Navy were lost in the fighting at Christ Church. It is incredible to think that yesterday I sat in peaceful solitude in Christ Church and today it has been the site of a battle between two very different cultures that has lead to the deaths of people on both sides.

We will sail for Auckland with our small group of mainly female evacuees in a few hours' time.

I talked briefly to one of the evacuees earlier. Her name is Hannah King Lethbridge. She was born in 1816 and thinks she may be the first white woman to be born in New Zealand. Unlike many, her first reaction to the tragedy that has befallen Kororareka is not to abandon the country.

The next day I penned the following report to Sir David Tallboy in Adelaide.

SS Swift
Anchored off Kororareka
12 March
Your Excellency,

Against my expectations, I write to you from the anchorage off Kororareka and not from Auckland, as I had planned.

Kororareka was attacked by the Maori yesterday morning and today is a smoking ruin with only the church and Mission houses still standing. The local population was evacuated onto ships lying in the anchorage and all, including SS Swift, will sail for Auckland during the day to deliver the evacuees to the authorities there. The total number of casualties is not yet known, but we do know that two marines and four sailors from HMS Hazard were killed in the fighting in the churchyard. As the post office was one of the buildings destroyed in the fire, I have included a copy of my first report in case the original was consumed in the fire.

Your obedient servant,
Signed: Jason Smiley Stewart

EIGHT

Onward

The arrival of a small fleet of ships in the anchorage caused some surprise amongst the inhabitants of Auckland who saw the event, but it was nothing to the wave of consternation and disbelief followed by panic that swept the town when the reason for our arrival became known.

It was inconceivable, they thought, that Kororareka had been destroyed by the Maori with an estimated loss in excess of fifty thousand pounds.

But it was true, and as the reality of the situation was accepted, many former colonists sold land and property for whatever they could get for it and sailed for home and safety on the first ship on which they could get a berth.

Following the panic, justifications for the debacle circulated freely and these included gross exaggerations of the number of Maori involved, missionary treachery, or an act of divine providence. Some saw it as an up-to-date version of Sodom and Gomorrah given the excesses for which Kororareka was infamous.

I had no involvement in the rumourmongering and apart from giving the authorities a factual account of the day as I remembered it, I tried to concentrate on the duty that had brought me to the country in the first place.

I said goodbye to Captain Schmidt and the officers of the *SS Swift*, posted my reports to Sir David, and after finding myself somewhere to stay, started to consider what I could do to further the search I had been sent on.

My thoughts returned to the letter I had posted. Perhaps the Government officials in the post office would know something about plans for the telegraph. It was a competitive form of communication to be sure, but it was not inconceivable that the post office would cater for different segments of society by providing different services.

I walked back to the post office. It was a muddy and disagreeable activity after the heavy rain of the past day, as there were no metalled roads in the Capital and the tracks were just that. Tracks! The post office consisted of two rooms in the Customs House, and when I arrived there were two men working on a pile of letters.

"My name is Stewart," I announced when one of the men looked up and noticed me. "Jason Smiley Stewart. May I know who is in charge here?"

He looked carefully at me, as if seeking some sign that he had seen me before, and then realising he didn't know me gestured at his companion and said, "Mr. William Turner is the chief clerk and in charge of the post office and I am his assistant. My name is Corbett. William Corbett."

"Thank you, Mr. Corbett," I replied and then turned my attention to Mr. Turner and said, "I should be grateful if you would grant me a few minutes of your time, Mr. Turner. I would like to ask you a question that you may be able to answer from your local knowledge and your position as an official of the post office."

"I'll certainly listen to your question and answer you if I am able," he said cooperatively.

"Thank you, Mr. Turner. I am interested in the electric telegraph and wondered if you know of any plans to build a telegraph here. Perhaps a telegraph has already been constructed?" I added hopefully.

He straightened his back, stretched, and then scratched his head with the sharpened end of a pencil, leaving a long, black mark on his scalp.

He said solemnly, as befits the official representative of a Government department, "There are about four thousand people living in Auckland at present. The south side of the town is protected by the settlements there, but I have heard some talk about establishing a telegraph to warn of a Maori attack on Auckland from the west. I haven't heard if anything has been constructed."

"That's very interesting," I said enthusiastically. "Do you have any idea who might be in charge of such a venture?" I enquired, already starting to compose a positive report to Sir David in my mind.

"No idea, Mr. Stewart, but probably the Navy or the Army. It won't be of any use if the weather's bad," he commented gloomily.

My embryo report evaporated. Bad weather! I had never heard of the telegraph being affected by bad weather before and said, "What did you mean when you say 'being affected by bad weather'?"

"If the weather's bad," he said, "raining heavily or misty for example, you cannot see the balls."

"Did you say 'balls'?" I asked with the pitch of my voice rising with incredulity.

Then I suddenly realised that I wasn't conversing with a madman. He was talking about a visual telegraph.

Napoleon had used them extensively I had read somewhere. The British Admiralty had a string of semaphore stations between London and Portsmouth until a few years previously, and it was claimed they could transmit a message seventy miles in fifteen minutes. Provided the weather was good. If it was bad, the system was worse than useless. There was the classic example of a message that was sent to London about a battle during the Peninsular War. Two words were received, "Wellington defeated," and then fog prevented further transmission.

London sank into the depths of despondency until next day when the fog lifted and the full message was received, "Wellington defeated the French at Salamanca."

I said into the confused silence my previous utterance had caused, "I quite understand what you mean, Mr. Turner, but I was enquiring about the electric telegraph. Do you know if there has been any discussion about installing such a system?"

"No. Nothing that I am aware of," he responded. "You should realise, Mr. Stewart, that there are estimated to be about one hundred and twenty thousand Maoris and about fifteen thousand settlers living in this country. The Maoris have no need of the electric telegraph, and the settlements the Paheka live in are generally too far apart for such a system to be financially worthwhile. At least that's my opinion based on the difficulties I have to get the mail for the settlements delivered by hand."

"Can you recommend someone in Government with whom I could speak?" I asked.

"Probably you should go to the top and see Governor Grey, but you'll probably have to go to New Munster to see him, as he seems to spend most of his time there."

"New Munster?" I asked.

"Yes," he said. "The 1846 Constitution named the northern part of the colony New Ulster and the southern part, which is centred on Wellington, was named New Munster. Now if you will excuse me, Mr. Stewart, I must return to my duties."

"Of course," I said. "I must thank you for your devoting so much time to a stranger and for the information you have given me. Good day, Mr. Turner."

I trudged back to my hotel along the muddy track wondering whether I should simply follow Turner's advice and sail to Wellington or stay on in Auckland in the hope that something useful might turn up. I realised that if Governor Grey was in Wellington, then it was a safe bet that most if not all the influential men in his administration would be there too. Alternatively, and I had to admit that the alternative was quite attractive, I could just get on the first ship heading for Adelaide and tell Sir David that there was no point in proceeding with my search, as it seemed that nothing short of a war would precipitate the need for speedy communication by telegraph. And in that case, since the Army would undoubtedly organise the endeavour, there would be little scope for private enterprise. By the time I reached my small hotel, I had decided to tell Sir David I would go to Wellington but also advise him of my intention to return to Adelaide if there was no positive news in the Capital of New Munster.

Before I entered the hotel, I changed direction and walked down to the port area to see when I could sail south.

Next day at about midmorning, I sent my bags to the jetty and then walked over to the post office to send my latest report to Sir David. Turner was away somewhere so Corbett took the package, some of my money, and assured me that the package would be on the next ship to Australia—not that he was able to forecast when that would be. Clearly improving the speed of communications between the colony and the outside world was not yet a priority.

I walked to the jetty and waited in the rain for the boat from the steamer *Nelson*, which was to take me to Wellington.

When eventually I was able to board the *SS Nelson*, I was soaked to the skin and not in the best of humour. The consistently grey, rain-soaked days and the apparent futility of the task upon which I was engaged conspired together to make my hold on my temper rather precarious. The trigger that finally fired my exasperation was provided by a small, thin, unpretentious, pallid-faced cabin boy who managed to drop one of my bags. When he attempted to pick it up by one handle, it opened, and he managed to strew the contents, including all my undergarments, across the soaking wet iron decks. This was bad enough, but he managed to do it in front of three young lady passengers who had just boarded from another of the ship's boats. The gasps of horror and bright red blushes of a bevy of shocked virgins confronted by a man's unmentionables will live with me until the day I die—as will the embarrassing thought that I would have to share the dining room with the same young ladies for the next week. My roar of fury brought the captain from one end of the ship and the mate from the other, and between them they quickly managed to usher the ladies off the deck and down to their cabin. Beetroot red in face the boy picked my soggy, rust-stained items of clothing from the main deck and scuttled below. Someone else picked up the bag, closed it, and ushered me to the companionway with the almost empty case tucked under one brawny arm and the other bag dangling from his hand.

In my cabin he waited patiently for me to run out of breath and stop swearing, then said, "Worse things can happen at sea, Mr. Stewart. My name is Jones, and I'm the second officer. On Captain Martin's behalf, may I welcome you aboard, sir?"

"Thank you, Mr. Jones," I responded. "Indeed. Many worse things happen at sea, as you say. He could have dropped the case over the side for example. I'm sure your young ladies would have preferred that. Who are they anyway?"

"They're the daughters of a missionary who's working with the Maori outside Wellington somewhere."

"They seem to have lived very sheltered existences," I remarked as I remembered the incident on deck. "Would you send that boy to me, please? I want to find out what he is doing with my clothes, as I'm soaked to the skin and need to change. It looked as if all my underclothes were spread on the deck."

"His name is Jack Wylie, Mr. Stewart. I'll send him to you directly. I'm sorry your welcome aboard was so unceremonious."

"Thank you, Mr. Jones," I said as he left the cabin and closed the door, but I could already feel the corners of my mouth twitch as I started to see the funny side of what had happened.

Jack Wylie arrived with many apologies and the clothes that had not fallen onto the deck and rushed off immediately to ensure that the remainder were laundered as quickly as possible. I felt better after I had given myself a brisk towelling and put on dry clothes, so my comments to Jack Wylie about his clumsiness when he returned lacked the edge that they would have had fifteen minutes earlier. As I threatened him with keelhauling and Davy Jones's locker, I was reminded of a similar incident of clumsiness when I had been the perpetrator and my father had issued a similar warning. I hoped his life would be as interesting as mine had been.

But without the tragedy!

We sailed in the late afternoon, and I stood on deck in the lea of the bridge and watched Auckland disappear from view as we sailed out into the Hauraki Gulf and then turned toward the east to pass between the north end of Coramandel and Great Barrier Island.

Later, as the ship's heading turned more toward the south, the ship started to roll gently to the Pacific swells, and I went down to my cabin and then later to the small dining saloon for dinner.

Only the three young ladies were there when I arrived, and their conversation died as I let the saloon door swing closed behind me. Jack Wylie appeared from a side cabin in an immaculate steward's outfit and started to usher me to a table.

"Wait a moment, Jack," I said quietly, and I walked across the saloon to the table at which the three young ladies were sitting.

"Excuse me," I said politely, "as we didn't have any opportunity for introductions earlier and we will be together on the ship for at least a week, may I introduce myself? My name is Stewart."

The elder of the ladies looked at me for a moment as if deciding whether she should acknowledge my existence or not and then, having decided it would be safe to talk with me, said, "Good evening, Mr. Stewart. My name is Ball, Miss Lucinda Ball, and these young ladies," and she waved a hand at her two younger companions, "are my twin sisters, Margaret and Eliza."

"Good evening, ladies. I am pleased to make your acquaintance. I hope you have a pleasant voyage." After saying, "Please excuse me," I followed Jack Wylie to my table. The ladies left the dining saloon whilst I was still eating, and after dinner I went on deck for a time and then went to my cabin.

Next morning, after an early and solitary breakfast, I went on deck in the hope that I would be able to enjoy a little exercise without being soaked by rain. It didn't rain, but the showers of salt spray blown by the wind across the deck each time the bows ploughed through an oncoming wave soon drove me into the shelter of the bridge. As I stood there, Second Officer Jones came on deck.

"Good morning, Mr. Stewart," he said in greeting. "It's a very pleasant morning."

"Good morning, Mr. Jones. It is certainly very bracing," I responded. "Would it be possible for me to come to the bridge and look at the chart?"

"Of course," he responded. "Are you familiar with marine charts, Mr. Stewart?"

"I was the third officer on a ship that sailed regularly from Liverpool to Bombay and back," I responded by way of explanation.

"Really?" he said. "In that case, please come up to the bridge and I'll get the chart out for you."

I followed him up the bridge ladder, greeted the mate who was just going off watch, then spent a very happy half an hour looking at the chart with Mr. Jones ready and willing to point out important features. After a time, I thanked Second Officer Jones for his courtesy and left the bridge so that he could concentrate on his watchkeeping duties. I resumed my position by the rail in the lea of the bridge structure and watched the distant coastline of the Bay of Plenty sliding past in the haze away out to starboard.

The elder Miss Ball came on deck and walked up and down between the bridge and the forecastle with the practised gait of a sailor. She was an attractive young woman although very demurely dressed in the sombre colours one would expect the daughter of a missionary to wear. Some of her hair had escaped from under the edge of her bonnet, and I could see that it was light brown and shining from vigorous brushing. She had regular white teeth and brown eyes. I remembered that I had noted the previous evening what a lovely, healthy complexion she had, and this morning how her exercise had given her cheeks a touch of pink. *If she's a good housekeeper, she'll make someone a very good wife*, was the thought that crossed my mind.

"It's a pleasant morning, Mr. Stewart," she said when she stopped walking and came to stand by me on the lea side.

"It certainly is," I responded.

"May I ask you a question?" I asked after we had stood in silence for several minutes.

"Of course," she replied.

"Do you live in Auckland?"

"No," was the simple response.

"When you came onboard yesterday, I assumed that you are living in New Zealand and simply travelling with your two sisters from Auckland to Wellington, as that's the easiest way to make the journey. That is what I am doing, after all. Clearly, my assumption was incorrect."

"That is correct, Mr. Stewart," she said without elaboration, and I wondered if I should pursue the conversion.

"May I assume you live in Wellington, Miss Ball?"

"You may not, Mr. Stewart."

Again there was the less than helpful answer, but it was said in a way that invited further conversation and not the rejection of it.

"I imagine that you are English, Miss Ball?"

"Your imagination is correct, Mr. Stewart."

I thought about what she had told me and realised that there was only one set of circumstances that fitted what I knew.

I said, "I believe, Miss Ball, that you and your sisters sailed from

England but could only get a ship as far as Auckland and then changed to this ship for the journey south. How long was the passage to Auckland?"

She said, "Nearly one hundred and fifty days." She then cried, "Oh!" as she realised that I had guessed the beginning of her story.

"Are you going to take another ship to Christchurch, Miss Ball?" I asked.

"No."

"I don't know South Island at all. Perhaps you can tell me where you will live?"

"No. I cannot," she said, and I saw the corners of her mouth twitch up in the beginning of a smile.

I thought about that. *Did she mean she is not allowed to or cannot because she hasn't an address in South Island,* I wondered and then remembered Second Officer Jones telling me that their father had a Mission outside Wellington.

"How far outside Wellington is the Mission?" I asked suddenly.

"About ten miles," she answered without thinking and then said, "Bother." The smile disappeared when she recognised that the guessing game was over for the time being.

"What about you, Mr. Stewart? Are you going to Wellington to meet your family?"

"No," I said, knowing that I would have said more in other circumstances but deliberately stretching the conversation out as she had done. There are so many empty hours to fill when one is a passenger on a ship that a diversion of any kind can be welcome.

She looked at me for a moment, considering what she could deduce from my appearance, and then said, "You have a very sad expression sometimes, Mr. Stewart. Perhaps you are here to forget a lady?"

She had been remarkably and uncomfortably accurate, and I said, "In a way, Miss Ball. My wife died recently giving birth to our son. I'm trying to forget the pain, not the person."

She was full of contrition and said, "I'm very sorry to learn of your misfortune, Mr. Stewart. Perhaps I should leave you?"

"No," I said. "Please stay, if you will," realising that it would be good for me to talk to a stranger. "Ask me another question if you would like to."

She was silent for quite a time as she decided what she could ask without rubbing more salt in my wounds; then; having decided on a safe topic; she asked, "Are you emigrating to New Zealand; Mr. Stewart?"

"No," I responded without elaboration.

"A lot of young men do," she said. "Perhaps you are an explorer?"

"No," I responded.

"Then you must be a businessman," she said triumphantly.

"No," I responded, then elaborated a little by adding, "I wouldn't consider myself a businessman."

She studied me closely as she considered the little she had learnt about me, then said, "You seem to be comfortable onboard, Mr. Stewart; are you a sailor?"

"Not any more."

"Why did you leave the sea?"

"I was asked to," I said and once again had to suppress my natural inclination to elaborate in order to prolong our meeting.

She considered that and then asked, "Did you do something wrong?"

"No."

She changed the line of her enquiry and asked, "Is your father a sailor too?"

"Not any more. He has retired from the sea," I replied, being a little more expansive than I had intended.

"So he lives on a huge estate and is lord of all he surveys?" she said in jest.

"Yes," I said and began to enjoy myself as I saw her puzzled expression.

"Literally?" she queried.

"Yes," I said again.

"So you are the son of a lord."

"Yes."

"But you said your name is Stewart."

"Yes," I said and started to feel uncomfortable about the deliberate procrastination.

"Are you Lord Stewart?" she asked.

"No," and I decided it was time to end the game. "My name is Jason Smiley Stewart. My father is a Stewart, but he is also Earl Strathmilton. My title is Viscount Strathmilton, but I don't use it as a matter of course. Stewart is the name I normally use."

We stood for a few moments in silence, and then I noticed a conical island ahead and to starboard of our route and asked, "Have you ever seen a volcano, Miss Ball?"

"No," she said.

"Well, if you look toward the bows you will see one. It's called White Island and is quite active, as you can see from the steam and smoke belching out of the top of the cone."

"How do you know what it's called, Mr. Stewart?"

"I looked on the chart with Second Officer Evans earlier this morning."

"That is amazing! I must go and get my sisters at once," she said and rushed away.

The three sisters were soon up on deck and went immediately to the rail to look at the volcano. There was much pointing and a great deal of excited chatter, and then it was time for lunch and the afternoon drifted by. In the evening it was possible to see the orangey-red glow of lava reflecting on the undersides of the clouds of steam, but I could neither hear nor smell any of the volcanic activity.

Over the next few days, Miss Ball and I exchanged amicable greetings when our paths crossed, but there was never an opportunity to talk privately again, and then we were within sight of Wellington. And after that the ladies were so engrossed with preparations for seeing their parents again that I only saw them from a distance. Then we anchored and they were rowed to the shore where a carriage waited to whisk them away.

As I had been unable to arrange for accommodation in Wellington before leaving Auckland, I asked Captain Martin if I could retain my cabin for a few extra days in order to look around for a hotel.

He said, "We will be at anchor here for at least two days discharging and then loading cargo. I have no objection if you use my ship as your base, but as it's the only time my engineer can make repairs to the engine and auxiliary equipment you may be without some of the facilities you are accustomed to use."

"That's quite acceptable, Captain, and I thank you for your cooperation," I agreed.

I went into Wellington the next morning and directly to the Government offices. I explained that I wished to see the Governor and ask about any plans he had to develop the electric telegraph in the colony.

"The Governor is not here," I was told, "but even if he was, I doubt if he would see you personally. His secretary would probably direct you to the Postmaster General, as he is the most likely person to know the answer to your question."

I thanked the official for his help and following his directions walked to the post office building and, after a number of fruitless enquiries, found myself in the office of Mr. George Eliot, the secretary to the post office. He listened politely to my request for information but shook his head.

"We have no plans for telegraph construction here," he said. "But I have heard that the Canterbury Province intends to build a telegraph line from Christchurch to Lyttelton. If you go there, you should ask for Mr. Sheath. He will know if anyone does, as he worked for a telegraph company in England before immigrating to New Zealand. Now if you will excuse me, Mr. Stewart, I must return to my duties."

Thus dismissed, I had no option but to say, "Thank you for your time, Mr Eliot," and leave his office as quickly as practical.

I went back to the harbour, and as I sat in the back of the boat taking me out to the *Nelson*, I had time to think back over the past months of fruitless journeying. I realised that the first tangible news I had received about plans for the development of an electric telegraph directed me to the southernmost of the two islands, and I wondered if the Maori uprisings in the North Island were having a negative affect on settlement and development there. Nothing I had been told confirmed what I was thinking, but it certainly seemed a reasonable conclusion. Also, I had been told that the Governor spent a lot of his time in Wellington and wondered if the Capital would move from Auckland to Wellington. It made geographic sense to have the seat of Government in the middle of the country and would remove it from the risk of attack from the Maoris at the same time.

When I returned onboard, I sought out Captain Martin.

"Good afternoon, Captain," I said when I found him. "Do you know of any steamers going to Christchurch in the near future?"

"Your luck is in, Mr. Stewart. I have just received orders to take a cargo to Christchurch and load something there for Sydney. We'll sail in the morning, and I should be pleased to offer you passage. May I ask why you have changed your plans?"

"I should be pleased to accept your offer, Captain, and I'm going to Christchurch simply because the only development of the electric telegraph I have heard about seems to be taking place near there. If I find nothing, I'll give up the search and return to Australia. I have already spent more months on this expedition than I expected when I agreed to make the investigation, and most of it has been on a ship sailing from one place to another."

"This came for you earlier," Captain Martin said as he handed me a letter. "The man who brought it was from the Mission Station and caused a deal of confusion asking for Viscount Strathmilton. The mate told the messenger we had no one of that name onboard, but he insisted that Miss Ball had sent the letter and Viscount Strathmilton must be on the ship and went on and on in the same vein. Anyway, to cut a long story short, the mate looked at the letter, saw your name on it, and accepted it on your behalf. I hope he acted correctly."

"The mate acted quite correctly, Captain. I don't use my title ordinarily, but I am Viscount Strathmilton. Please thank the mate for me. If you will excuse me, Captain, I'll go to my cabin and see what this is about." I brandished the envelope as I left the captain's cabin.

The letter was from Miss Lucinda Ball. In an admirably neat script she wrote,

Dear Mr. Stewart,

I must apologise for leaving the ship without being courteous enough to say goodbye. I do so now and send my every good wish for your future happiness and success.

I sat down at the desk in my cabin and in a less admirable hand wrote,

Dear Miss Ball,

I was very pleased to receive your note. No apology is necessary, as I know how time rushes past when one is trying to get ready for disembarkation, but I do appreciate your courtesy in sending it. I am just about to sail to Christchurch with Captain Martin, but when I return I should be pleased to have the opportunity to renew our acquaintanceship before I return to Australia. I will write to you and request an appointment when I return.

I sealed the note and gave it to the captain and requested that it be sent ashore at his convenience.

I expected it to be sent with the pilot after we had sailed and consequently was very surprised when Jack Wylie handed me another letter at breakfast. I opened it and found that Miss Ball had not only received my letter but had answered it. She wrote,

Dear Mr. Stewart,

I'm sorry to learn that you are leaving Wellington so soon and wish you well. I, too, should be pleased to renew our acquaintanceship, and consequently, I look forward to receiving a note from you when you return to Wellington.

How nice, I thought. *I have some intelligent and attractive company to look forward to.* I ate my breakfast in a more cheerful frame of mind than I had for a very long time, and the *SS Nelson* sailed whilst I dined.

Captain Martin took the ship out of the harbour into the Cook Strait and then turned in an easterly direction. My next voyage had begun, and I hoped it would be the last before I turned for home.

======

"Did you know that the original planners of Christchurch wanted a city built around a cathedral and a college?" asked Captain Martin at breakfast the following day.

"No, Captain," I had to admit. "I didn't know that. In fact, I know nothing about Christchurch at all except it's located on the east coast of the South Island."

"I see," said Captain Martin. He went on, "Christchurch was conceived by the Canterbury Association, and they dreamed of a city built around a cathedral and a college. As their model, they took Christ Church in Oxford. In 1850, the first settlers landed at Port Cooper, Lyttelton to you, Mr. Stewart, and founded Canterbury on the plain, which was located about nine miles to the north of Port Cooper on the opposite side of a very rugged range of hills. Over the years they have tried to realise their dream of a cathedral, and the foundation stone was laid with great celebration by Bishop Harper in 1864. The foundations are visible in the centre of the town, but there is no work going on at the moment, as they do not have money for it."

Captain Martin added philosophically, "It's a pity really but cathedrals always seem to take centuries to complete."

I thanked Captain Martin for his brief description and not for the first time marvelled at the local knowledge some of the sea captains possessed.

The voyage was quite short and completed without any incident worth recording, but as I walked up into the port area of Lyttelton after disembarking from the *Nelson*, I saw a heap of poles. I couldn't believe my eyes when I examined them closely, as I hadn't seen anything like it since before I left England. They were wrought-iron poles for a telegraph line.

I couldn't have been happier if I had struck gold.

I managed to get a ride on a cart going to Christchurch. When I reached the town, I took my bags to an establishment known as the Commercial Hotel and arranged a room for the next three nights with an option to extend the hire if I planned to stay longer.

Next morning, I went in search of Mr. Albert Sheath.

I found him with surprisingly little difficulty but what he told me after I had enquired about the telegraph line was not very encouraging.

He said, "I can describe our situation in a single word, Mr. Stewart: Unsatisfactory! We need to establish a telegraph line to our port and we have not. All the materials for an electric telegraph between Canterbury and Lyttelton were sent out by Canterbury's London agent some time ago. We have the posts, batteries, cable, and insulators and so on stored here, but so far we do not have permission to erect the line. The Provincial Council has to allocate money for the work but hasn't done so, and I do not know when they might. It's my opinion that the establishment of a telegraph line between Christchurch and Lyttelton could be the first step in the construction of a telegraph system that stretches throughout the province of Canterbury and may, in time, give birth to a system that stretches throughout the South Island. But nothing is happening at present."

"Being prevented from doing what you know should be done must be very frustrating for you, Mr. Sheath," I said in commiseration.

"It is, Mr. Stewart, and the editor of the *Times*, which is our local newspaper, frequently comments upon the lack of progress but without affect. However, the interest of the editor is not entirely altruistic," he added dryly.

"Why is that?" I asked.

"The line we are discussing is of little practical value to the paper, but they are looking to the future. When there is a network of telegraph lines, the newspapers will be able to learn about foreign events very quickly, and the newspaper that has the most up-to-date information expects to sell more copies than its rivals. A submarine telegraph cable laid across the Cook Straits and another laid across the Tasman to Australia are quite practical propositions, and they are being discussed, but the political climate does not support such developments at present."

"That's a great pity, Mr. Sheath, as the benefits the telegraph can bring are widely understood in other parts of the world."

"The advantages are well known, Mr. Stewart, but the colony of New Zealand has not developed enough for the political leaders to seek them. The cables will be laid but not in the near future. You may not be aware of it, but I can assure you that there is enough expertise here to guide the effort, and we can very easily call on the help of telegraph specialists at home if we have any particular problems."

Mr. Sheath's statement effectively answered the question I was about to ask and meant that Sir David's desire to be involved in the development of the New Zealand telegraph from the very beginning was doomed to failure. I could only say thank you for the information that had so freely been imparted and take my leave of a very knowledgeable and courteous man.

Later in the day, I sat on the edge of my bed and reviewed the past months. If a failure didn't count as an achievement, then my efforts had realised nothing. I certainly hadn't been able to find the information that Sir David desired, and there really was no point in continuing my search now that I had spoken with Albert Sheath. He was too knowledgeable about the telegraph for his opinions to be ignored. I would have to send a report to Sir David explaining my lack of success, but whether I sent it from Christchurch or Wellington or simply took it with me was the next issue to be resolved. I decided on the basis of personal rather than business preferences. I would go to Wellington for a few days and try to arrange a meeting with Miss Ball and write my report whilst I waited for an appointment. A few hours with an intelligent young woman would make a welcome interlude after months of male company, and a little relaxation could be beneficial before facing Sir David Tallboy.

I sent a note to Captain Martin requesting a passage back to Wellington and had a reply by return that simply said, *I plan to sail before eight bells in the morning, so please come aboard this evening if you want a passage.*

I packed then hired a cart to take my bags down to the harbour. I walked behind the cart to the harbour where I hired a boat to take me out to the *Nelson*. Once onboard, I went to find Captain Martin to confirm my presence.

He said, "There was someone looking for you earlier, Mr. Stewart. Did you see him?"

"No," I said. "Who was it?"

"He said he was a friend of yours but wouldn't give a name. An uncouth man in my opinion. and I don't believe he was someone you would call a friend, Mr. Stewart. He was tall and broad shouldered with a thick, black beard covering most of his face, a snub nose, and small, bright blue eyes. He didn't take off his hat so I couldn't see his hair. When I told him you were sleeping ashore, he just turned on his heel and climbed down into his boat without another word. It wasn't so long ago, so I'm surprised you didn't see him on the quayside."

"No," I said. "I noticed no one, uncouth or otherwise. It's a mystery that will have to remain unresolved, as you will sail early tomorrow, and I have no intention of seeking him out tonight." Then I added, "As far as I know, Captain, there is no one in this hemisphere who could claim to be a friend, and if there was someone here who knew me that well, I am quite sure that person would have no qualms about advertising their identity."

"I see," he said. "Excuse me for a moment, Mr. Stewart." He turned away to order the anchor to be raised.

When he returned to my side a few minutes later, Captain Martin asked conversationally, "Did you know they've found gold in the Lindis River?"

"No," I said, "but in any event, I've no idea where the Lindis River is located?"

"Inland from Dunedin, I believe," he responded. "My joints are too stiff for mining, Mr. Stewart, but a young man like you could make a fortune provided you have some luck."

"I'm too busy at present to contemplate gold mining, Captain, and in any case, I know nothing about mining for gold or anything else for that matter," I said firmly, although the thought of making a fortune was very attractive. "I have to complete the task I was given before I am a free agent again. But it would be nice to return home with a fortune," I added wistfully.

Not that I have anyone to spend it on, I thought sadly.

There the matter rested and early next day we sailed for Wellington, and my mystery visitor remained just that, although Sir David's warning about the risks associated with my enquiries came back to mind. It also occurred to me that I had nothing to defend myself with if I should be attacked, and I was grievously out of practice anyway. The almost daily weapon drills on the *SS Earl Canning* were a long time in the past.

Needless to say, I slept very badly that night as I woke quite unnecessarily to every strange noise.

Next morning, I decided to take Captain Martin into my confidence. He listened without comment whilst I described the task I had been set by Sir David and my concern that the agent of one of Sir David's opponents had managed to catch up with me.

He said, "You don't need a weapon whilst you are onboard, but you do have a few days to practice. I can lend you a handgun, and we have plenty of powder and shot if you want to have some target practice. You can buy a good handgun at Black's, the gunsmith in Wellington."

"Thank you, Captain," I said. "I'll follow your advice, but I would like to practice with a knife as well. If the man you describe is a danger to me, then he is likely to try an ambush, and a knife might be a better defensive weapon than a pistol. In any case, I think it's easier to carry a knife than a pistol."

"I'll speak to the bosun and see what we can arrange for you, Mr. Stewart," Captain Martin said with a half-concealed smile I didn't like one little bit.

Several hours later, the bosun came to my cabin.

"Captain Martin says you would like to practice fighting with a knife, Mr. Stewart."

"That's correct, bosun" I responded.

"Have you used a knife before?" he asked.

"Yes, but not for some years."

"If you follow me up to the foredeck, Mr. Stewart, I'll see what you can remember."

The bosun looked much too relaxed and cheerful for my peace of mind, but I followed him up on deck; not that I had an option if I wanted to practice with a knife. He produced a pair of knives from scabbards attached to the back of his belt and held them out handle first so that I could choose one of them.

He said, "Are you ready, Mr. Stewart?"

When I said, "Yes," he dropped into a fighter's crouch and started to circle me. He made a few stabbing gestures, and as I easily avoided them, I started to feel a trifle complacent. He stopped moving to the right for a moment then suddenly stepped to the left and I followed. As my brain recognised the movement as a feint, there was a sudden blur of activity and he was standing behind me with the flat of his blade against my throat.

"That's not very good, Mr. Stewart. We'll try again."

And we did. Time and time again. But the old skills started to return, and I was able to feel that with a little more practice I would be able to give a good account of myself if the need arose. The next few days of my voyage to Wellington passed quickly, as I practised intensively with a knife when the bosun could spare time from his shipboard duties. I practiced with a handgun by firing at bits of wood thrown off the bow by a crewman when the bosun was unavailable. Slowly but steadily, my rusty expertise was polished to an acceptable degree.

In Wellington, I had to go ashore as soon as we arrived in the anchorage, as Captain Martin and the Nelson were proceeding north to Auckland when they had picked up the mail.

My first priority was to find somewhere to stay, and I was lucky to find an inn near the waterfront with a room to let. It was clean, but only furnished with a bed and a cupboard until I persuaded the owner to loan me a small table and a chair so that I would have somewhere to write my report. In fact, my first action was to write a short note to Miss Ball to announce my return and express my willingness to call at her convenience.

Convention suggested that I should have written to her father, but as she had said I could write to her directly, I took her at her word.

When the note had been sent to the Mission, I settled down to write my final report to Sir David. It took many hours of head-scratching as I wrote and erased and wrote again, but eventually I found that I had prepared a reasonable final draft. There were only a few sheets of paper, and these slipped easily into a concealed recess in the bottom of one of my bags.

I went down to the taproom to find out what I could get to eat. The owner offered cheese and pickles with a slice of cold roast beef. It was "Hobson's Choice."

I said, "I'll take the beef, cheese, and pickles, and I'd like a pot of beer to wash it down with, please."

The owner asked, "Would you like to have a *stone fence* instead of a beer?"

"I've never heard of a drink called a *stone fence*," I said. "What is it?"

"It's a mixture of brandy and ginger beer. It's very popular with the colonists," he told me with a grin.

The thought of something as strong as a *stone fence* didn't appeal, and I said, "Thank you for the suggestion, but I would rather have a beer tonight."

"Certainly, Mr. Stewart," he responded.

I was about to turn away in order to sit down in a corner away from the drinkers when the bar owner said, "Someone was asking after you earlier, Mr. Stewart; a big man with a bushy, black beard. He didn't give his name—but when I told him you were here, he said something like, 'Good! I've caught up with him at last,' as he turned away from the bar' and then he hurried outside without another word. I hope it was in order for me to say you were here' Mr. Stewart?" he added.

"Yes' of course," I said brightly whilst trying to conceal a sudden shiver of disquiet. "I have no idea who he is, nor why he should be following me but I expect I'll find out in time."

I walked over to the seat I had chosen and sat down to wait for my meal to arrive. I didn't really feel as confident as I had sounded and became less so when I realised that I had forgotten to purchase a gun. I still had the knife the bosun had presented to me after we had finished practicing, but rather stupidly I had left it in my room. I jumped to my feet, hurried toward the door, and almost collided with the tray containing my meal that was being carried in by one of the helpers.

I indicated where I was sitting and called, "Back in a moment," and noisily headed up the stairs two at a time. There was someone near the landing at the head of the staircase when I started to climb up, but whoever it was hurried away, leaving only a vaguely disquieting impression of a big man dressed in black. I collected my knife from my room and was comforted by the feel of it in its scabbard, just behind my right hip and under the tail of my coat. I went back downstairs, ate my meal, drank my beer, and then decided the day had been long enough to justify an early night.

As I headed for the door, one of the men near the bar said quietly, "That black-bearded man who was asking for you—do you know him?"

"No. I've never met him," I answered.

"He was in here looking for you several weeks ago. He's a bad one. His name is Silas Gravenor or something similar. Just come out of prison for robbery and attempted murder, so you'd best watch your back if he's interested in you."

"Thank you for the advice," I said gratefully.

"It's nothing," he said. "Do you have a gun?"

"No. I intended to buy one today but didn't have time. I have a knife and know how to use it, so I am not entirely defenceless. I intend to go to Black's in the morning."

"Did you come from Christchurch today?" he asked, changing the subject abruptly.

"Yes," I said. "Why?"

"Rumour says they've found gold down south. Do you know where?"

"I was told the strike is on the Lindis River, but I have no idea where that is."

"I do," he said with glee. "Were there many gold miners about?"

"Not as far as I know," I answered, and then, because my curiosity had been aroused, I asked, "Why do you want to know?"

"If I can get there quickly before word gets out, I might strike it rich."

"Are you a gold miner?"

"Not yet, but I'm going to try my hand at it. I know what to do, and as I'm not having any luck here, I have nothing to lose by going. I just need to get enough money for the boat and transport to Lindis River."

"How much is that?" I asked.

It was not a great deal of money, and I felt that his unsolicited advice deserved a complementary gesture. I took out my wallet, counted out the required amount, and handed it to him.

"I'll loan you the money," I said. "If you strike it rich, you can repay me, and if you don't, it's a thank you for your advice."

"Thank you," he said seriously. "That's very generous of you. My name is Marshall, Jamie Marshall, and I very much hope your generosity will be repaid in full. May I know your name, sir?"

"I'm Jason Smiley Stewart, and I hope you are successful as well, Mr. Marshall," I said as I shook his outstretched hand. "You never know, I might just come to find you when I have finished my present task, then we can make a fortune together. After you have taught me gold mining, that is. Good night to you."

"Good night, Mr. Stewart. Remember to bolt your door and keep your knife handy."

"I will," I said as I left the room and climbed the stairs to my room in the light from a flickering oil lamp that was hanging from a hook above the landing.

I unlocked the door and pushed it open.

For some reason I don't understand to this day, I hesitated as I entered the room, and that slight pause in my movement probably saved me from serious injury or worse as a bludgeon whistled past my face, and involuntarily I took a pace back. There was a shout of anger from behind the door, and whoever was there must have thrown his entire weight against it. It was a heavy door, and in the gloom I didn't see it as it swung back violently toward me and crunched into the side of my face before hitting me in the chest. I was knocked out into the corridor where I hit my head on the floor with a thud and a burst of pain and sprawled semi-conscious on the boards.

NINE

Running

I felt a big hand grab my coat and lift my head and shoulders off the plank floor. I was then dragged across the landing and into my room, where my assailant dropped me. My head hit the floor with a dull thud and a burst of pain. I don't know if I was unconscious for long, but as soon as I showed some signs of life, I was picked up and pushed into the chair by the table. In the light from a small lamp I saw the thick, black beard and piggy blue eyes of my assailant just a few inches from my face and knew it could only be Silas Gravenor.

"Where is it?" he growled, and the stench of his bad breath wrinkled my nostrils.

"Where is what?" I managed to ask through the throbbing pain in my head.

"The report for Tallboy," he said, and he hit the side of my head with his bludgeon. Presumably, he intended to wake up my brain although the opposite affect was achieved.

A little later, I started to wake up again and soon realised that I was now gagged, tied to the chair, and Gravenor was ransacking my bags. I realised that I was in a quite desperate situation.

He didn't find anything and strode across the room to the chair.

He shook me, took out the gag, and said angrily, "What have you done with the report to Tallboy?"

"Why do you want my report to Governor Tallboy?" I asked. "I have written several reports, which have all been mailed to His Excellency already."

"John Darcy has intercepted those," he said, smugly confident as he towered over my bound and seated form.

As he said it, I realised that one of the clerks in Sir David's office must have been diverting my reports to Darcy, and I felt real fear strike my stomach, as I recognised that the disclosure made my situation far, far worse. Gravenor only had to find my final report and eliminate it together with its author, and Darcy's problems were solved in one move.

I had no idea how I could prevent it happening, and my thought processes were seriously hampered by my throbbing head and a pain in my side. Play for time was the only solution I could think of.

He had raised his bludgeon to head height in preparation for administering another wake-up clout on my temple when I said hurriedly, "How do you know I haven't posted it already?"

"That's not possible," he said. "I've watched you all day." I thought I detected a shadow of doubt flash across his eyes in the poor light.

I capitalised on his uncertainty.

"The *Nelson* only called here to pick up the mail," I said, taking a chance and assuming Gravenor's knowledge was limited. "My last report was written during the voyage here and given to Captain Martin so that he could post it in Auckland."

The expression of uncertainty was much more pronounced now.

"You can't, can you?" I said in a voice that sounded much calmer than I felt, as I'm sure he would have seen my arms and legs shaking with fear if the light had been better. I moved in my seat and the pain in my side increased. As I moved back, I realised that it was the hilt of my knife being forced into my ribs by the pressure of the scabbard point on the chair. At that moment I couldn't see how it could help me, but at least I was still in possession of a knife that was razor sharp and long enough to kill a man.

Thinking was not one of Gravenor's attributes. He was quite obviously a man who was hired because he would follow his orders blindly, without question. I was certain that he had been told to find the report and then kill me, and as he couldn't find the report where he expected it to be, he didn't know what to do next. He pushed the gag back into my mouth and moved away from where I was seated. He flopped down heavily on the edge of my bed with a screech of tortured springs and sat with his chin cupped in one hand as he tried to decide what to do. Whilst he sat half turned away from me, I prayed to anyone who was listening to distract him from my wriggling as I tried to reach my knife. I don't know why I wanted to get my knife. I had no idea if I would be able to use it, but if the chance came I thought that the element of surprise a sharp weapon gave me could be invaluable. He had tied my wrists together behind the back of the chair. By pushing back and twisting my arms to the right, I found I could easily touch the hilt of my knife through a gap between the side and back of the chair. There was just enough slack in the bindings for me to rotate my right wrist, pull up the tail of my coat, and grasp the knife hilt. By leaning forward very slowly and carefully to prevent the chair from creaking and twisting to my left at the same time, I slowly and carefully withdrew the knife from under my coat.

Gravenor was still sitting and staring at the opposite wall seeking inspiration. I didn't think he could see me clearly in the poor light, but I was amazed that he hadn't detected my movements, as the noises emitted by my chair as I moved seemed deafeningly loud to my ears.

Very slowly and carefully, I manipulated the knife between my fingers until it was firmly in my right hand but now point up, as I hoped to cut the binding at my wrist. I moved my right hand slowly upwards until I could feel the steel blade cool against my wrist and tried to visualise the position of the bindings relative to the knife and my wrist. I slowly slid the blade down the inside of my wrist until I felt resistance. With a silent prayer that it was the binding and not my body, I started to work the knife to and fro. There was no instant burst of pain, so I continued sawing, and very quickly the razor-sharp blade severed the binding and my hands were free. I bent forward and sliced through the binding that held my ankles to the front legs of the chair. As I straightened up, I saw Gravenor's black silhouette rushing across the room toward me like the angel of doom and thought my last moment had come.

Without any thought and responding to a panic reflex, I flicked the knife in Gravenor's direction as I threw myself sideways off the chair in an effort to avoid his assault. I hit the floor and scrambled toward the door as quickly as I could crawl.

Gravenor, who was unable to stop his wild charge, collided with the chair and smashed it into firewood as he tripped over it and dived head-long into the wall with a sickening thud. He fell to the floor, and the impact of his inert body on the boards shook every beam in the building. The noise should have woken everyone in the hotel but didn't appear to.

He lay unconscious and face down.

I pulled the gag out of my mouth, opened the door, and shouted, "Help!" After a few moments, I shouted again but this time more strongly and a voice responded faintly in the distance. I picked up the lamp and started to look for my knife and something that I could use to tie up Gravenor.

A voice on the landing outside called, "Who wants help, then?"

"I do," I shouted, and a moment later fat, puffing Jack Tyler appeared in my room and I noticed he was wearing only one boot and still trying to fasten his trousers. I was pleased to see that he'd obviously answered my call for help with great alacrity.

"I need some rope to tie up Silas Gravenor."

"What's he doing in your room, Mr. Stewart?" he asked.

"Trying to murder me," I said bluntly. "Now, Mr. Tyler, do you have some rope, or shall I rip up one of your sheets?" and I grabbed one of the bed sheets to show I was in earnest.

"I'll get some rope," he said quickly

"Well, be quick about it. I want to tie him up before he comes round."

"What did you hit him with?" Jack Tyler asked, and his admiration for someone my size knocking down someone as big as Silas Gravenor was apparent in his voice.

"I'm sorry to disappoint you," I said, "but he was chasing me, tripped over that chair," and I pointed at the debris, "then dived into the wall head first. I'm surprised he didn't go through it."

I looked at the still inert form on the floor and said, "With luck he's broken his neck and won't bother anyone again," but he groaned just as I finished saying it.

Tyler disappeared and quickly returned with a length of rope, which we used to tie up Gravenor. We found my knife in the process. Gravenor had been lucky, as the blade had passed between his arm and ribs and stuck in the coat. I hadn't found the knife before, as he was lying on top of it, and realised as I picked it up that if it had been a few inches to the left, Gravenor could have forced the blade into his heart when he fell on it.

And that would have saved everyone a great deal of trouble, I thought.

With Gravenor immobilised on the floor, Tyler picked up the lantern and was about to inspect the room when the light shone on my face. "Lord, Mr. Stewart," and he pointed to Gravenor as he asked, "did he do that to your face? It's covered with blood."

"He hit me with the door and then several times with a bludgeon," I responded as I started to examine the damage to my face and head in the mirror. There were some quite bad cuts, and obviously I was going to have some bright blue and yellow bruises, but the injuries could have been much worse.

From the way they feel, I thought, t*hey should look far worse than they do.*

Tyler woke one of the servants and sent him to call the constable, but when that worthy eventually arrived, we found he had come on his own. Consequently, Tyler, the servant, and I had to help the constable carry Gravenor's bound body down the stairs and into the street, where we dumped him unceremoniously in the back of the cart the constable had driven to the inn.

When we were back in my room, I told the constable what had happened and said that I wanted Gravenor to be charged with attempted robbery and attempted murder at the very least. The constable went back to his duties and Tyler to his bed whilst I did my best to wash off the dried blood without reopening the cuts.

Whilst I doctored myself, I gave some thought to what I had learnt from Gravenor during the evening.

If he had told the truth, then Sir David would not have received any of my reports and must be wondering what in the world I was doing and, more particularly, where I was. There was no point in sending my last report by mail, as it would be diverted like the others, and it dawned on me that I had only one course of action open to me. I would have to return to Adelaide as quickly and secretly as possible in order to talk to Sir David before Darcy knew what was happening.

And as I didn't know how big a network Darcy commanded, it was going to be a difficult and dangerous task.

I bolted my door and lay on the bed but was too shaken by the events of the past few hours to relax enough to sleep. My face hurt too much for sleep in any case. At dawn I got up and walked to the harbour to find out if any ships were sailing north in the next few days. I needed to get to Adelaide before the news of my encounter with Gravenor became common knowledge, and that meant getting on the fastest steam-driven ship leaving the port and not necessarily the first ship to pull up her anchor and sail out of the bay. At the harbourmaster's office, the state of my face raised eyebrows but fortunately no questions, as it was clear I had been in a fight. I was sorry to discover that they had no specific information about vessel departures in the immediate future, and I returned despondently to the inn.

I was tired and hungry, and my face hurt like fury, but I sat in the tap room and had one of Tyler's helpers find me something to eat and drink. Unfortunately, I was so conscious of the surreptitious glances directed at my bruised face by the other occupants of the bar that I escaped to my room long before I had eaten my fill. I bolted the door and lay down to consider my situation once more but fell into a sleep of exhaustion that was interrupted by the snores caused by my damaged nose when I lay on my back and pain in my face if I lay on my side. I was woken from my erratic slumber by someone knocking on my door. I climbed stiffly from my bed and walked like a very old man to the door.

I called, "Who's there?"

"Tyler," was the response, and I unbolted and opened the door.

He looked at my face and said, "That looks very painful, Mr. Stewart."

"It is," I responded without elaboration, as every movement of my jaw sent stabs of pain through my face.

"Beautiful colouring," he said with a grin.

I looked in the mirror and smiled carefully. My face was already a swollen riot of yellow and dark blue.

"What is it, Mr. Tyler?" I asked.

"I have a letter for you, and the harbourmaster says there will be a steamer calling for mails tomorrow afternoon and then sailing for Auckland and Sydney, if you are interested."

"Thank you, Mr. Tyler. Please send someone to the harbourmaster and tell him that I would like a berth on that ship if at all possible. Thank you for bringing the letter."

"Not at all, Mr. Stewart," he responded. He looked at my face in a considering way and said, "Will you come down for a meal later, Mr. Stewart?"

"I expect so," I said. "Like me, the world has to get used to new face."

He laughed and left me to my lonely afternoon, or was it now evening? I had lost track of time.

I opened the envelope and took out the letter. It had been folded very neatly into a small square, and when I had managed to unfold it without ripping it, I found it had been signed by the Reverend Ball. *It's a good job he's not a canon*, I thought rather irreverently and wondered at the same time which one of the many religious sects he represented.

I had been sent a very short letter.

> *My daughter has shown me the letter you sent to her requesting a meeting and has explained that you became acquainted on the passage from Auckland to Wellington. She has expressed a desire to learn what you have discovered on your journey to the South Island, and whilst I have no objection to such a meeting, I have instructed my wife to ensure that Miss Lucinda is properly chaperoned whilst you are together.*

Stupid man, I thought. *Young ladies are always chaperoned when they meet a man, so why make a point of telling me the obvious. In any case, I anticipated conversation, not seduction.*

Reverend Ball went on,

> *I have no objection if you call on my daughter on Wednesday next, at eleven in the morning.*

When I would no longer be residing in Wellington, I realised.

I wrote back to the reverend and informed him that I would be unable to keep the appointment, as business considerations required me to leave almost immediately. I concluded by asking him to extend my apologies to Miss Lucinda for failing to honour the appointment and expressed my hope that she would enjoy a long and happy life. A little wickedly, I signed the letter Strathmilton, suspecting that Miss Lucinda would enjoy telling here father the little she knew about me.

I went downstairs and asked Tyler to send my note to the Mission house and then sat quietly in a corner to have my first proper meal since the previous evening. It was not an enjoyable experience, as my face was stiff and ached every time I chewed. And I had to chew a great deal, as the mutton was not as tender as it could have been.

Jamie Marshall came in. After looking around the room, he came immediately to my corner seat and sat down in the chair I indicated.

He said excitedly as soon as he was seated, "I have a passage to Christchurch thanks to you, Mr. Stewart. I sail first thing in the morning." He then noticed my face and after close inspection added, "I heard that you had captured Gravenor, Mr. Stewart. Congratulations! He gave you some trouble by the look of it."

"Nothing's broken fortunately, Jamie," I replied, then, changing the subject, I said, "I hope you are successful with your gold mining. How will you do it?"

"It's panning, not mining," he said. "I don't plan to dig a mine single handed. I'll find a likely spot on a bend in the river where the water is running slowly, and hopefully it will be a place where no one has prospected before and there I'll set up my camp. The process of panning is quite simple and relies on the fact that gold is heavier than sand and sinks to the bottom. I have a shallow, round, metal pan about fifteen inches across. I put some shovelfuls of the sand and gravel from the riverbed in the pan and then hold the pan under the water and move it round to wash out the light material. I take out any large pieces of gravel and continue swirling water through the sand. If I'm lucky, I'll find some grains of gold amongst the sand. Then I'll start again."

"It sounds a very wet and tiring process," I said.

"It is both, but if I'm lucky I'll find enough gold to be able to set up a sluice and employ a few men to help with the work. I'll return your stake when that happens."

"No," I said. "You can keep the stake and make me a partner," and we both laughed.

"If only that could happen, Mr. Stewart," he responded, still chuckling.

We stood up, shook hands, and Jamie Marshall went to seek his fortune whilst I went to my room. Just to be on the safe side, I asked Tyler to come with me in case Gravenor had a partner, but there was no one there, and after bolting the door I went to bed and slept until dawn.

Next morning, after a quick breakfast I arranged for Gravenor to be kept incommunicado for the next three months, as I didn't want him sending a message to alert Darcy to my continuing existence, and then packed into one of my bags the few items I had been using. In the taproom I paid my bill and said, "Goodbye," to Jack Tyler.

"Will you come back again?" he asked.

"I have no idea," I answered. "There is really nothing here for me to come back for so probably not. I wish you well, Mr. Tyler."

"And I wish you well and a safe voyage, Mr. Stewart," he said as I shook him by the hand and turned to leave.

Jack Tyler's helper picked up my bags and headed for the door, and I followed behind. In the doorway I nearly collided with a man coming in. I couldn't see him clearly, as the light was behind him, but was startled by the pattern of marks on his dark skin. I stepped back to let him enter and realised that I was face to face with a fully tattooed Maori dressed in western clothes.

He said, "I'm from the Mission."

He looked around the taproom with an expression of distaste written all over his face. I noticed that he was clearly trying very hard not to get too close to any of the tables and chairs in case something touched and soiled his clothes. I wondered if he had joined a temperance society as well as becoming a Christian missionary.

Tyler said, "How can I help you?"

"I look for Mr. Stewart," he said in understandable but strangely accented English. "I am Joseph Mathew from the Mission."

"I'm Stewart," I said. "Why are you looking for me?"

His eyes widened as he looked at my bruises, but he didn't comment about my appearance. Instead he said, "Miss Ball is outside on the cart and would like to see you."

"Really?" I gasped in amazement and immediately headed for the door and strode quickly to the cart.

"Miss Ball!" I cried out as I approached. "What a pleasant surprise."

She looked up at the sound of my voice, glanced in my direction, and said, "Mr. Stewart, I…" She paused as she inspected my bruises. "My word, Mr. Stewart, whatever has happened to your face? You look as if you have been in a fight."

"I was," I said without elaboration, wondering if she would indulge in the guessing game again, but she was too businesslike for that on this day.

"Are you going to the harbour?" she asked.

"Yes. The boy from the inn has taken my bags there already."

"If you climb up, Joseph can drive us to the harbour and we can talk on the way."

"I should be delighted to," I responded with a smile of pleasure that turned into a grimace as the bruises reacted to the movement. I climbed up as she had requested, then asked, "How did you know I was leaving?"

"Your letter to my father was delivered last evening, and he told me about your departure at dinner. I persuaded him to let me come to say goodbye, and he arranged for Joseph to come with me." She turned her companion and said, "Please drive us to the harbour, Joseph."

"Yes, Miss Ball," he responded and shook the reins to get the pony moving.

She turned her attention to me again and, after a closer inspection of my face, said, "What happened?"

"There was a man in my room when I returned from dinner the night before last. He was trying to steal my report to the governor and knocked me down when I disturbed him. I was tied up for a time but managed to get free, then he tripped over a chair and knocked himself out trying to catch me again. I didn't realise how valuable my report had become until Gravenor—" I stopped talking when she said, "Silas Gravenor?" When I confirmed the name she went quite pale.

"But Silas Gravenor is a huge man," she gasped, "and everyone believes he's a murderer. Where is he now?"

"In prison charged with attempted murder and attempted robbery."

"You were very lucky not to be killed, Mr. Stewart. I'm very pleased you are here and only sore and bruised."

"Thank you, Miss Ball," I said. "As I am."

"Why is your report so important?" she asked next.

"Someone is trying to make a big profit by persuading the governor to spend a lot of money to buy equipment for a development, which my report proves is not going to take place. I'm leaving as soon as I can and hope to get to Adelaide before news of Gravenor's capture is known there. If I'm not quick enough, then they will try to catch and kill me before my report can be delivered. Some men will do anything for money, and Gravenor is one of them."

By this time we had reached the building where Captain Prendergast, the harbourmaster, worked from, and Joseph jumped down to help Miss Ball alight whilst I climbed down from the other side of the cart.

The harbourmaster heard us arrive and came bustling out of the building to greet us.

"Mr. Stewart?" he asked.

"Yes," I answered.

"Your bags are here, sir, and the boat from the *Nimrod* left the ship's gangway a few minutes ago. I understood you were travelling alone, sir, and didn't know your wife would be travelling with you."

Miss Ball went quite pink when she heard herself described as my wife and pinker still when I said, "I'm sorry, Captain, but this lovely young lady is not my wife and will not be travelling with me today."

"I beg your pardon, Miss," Captain Prendergast said, and I noted that he was more than a little embarrassed by his gaffe. "Mr. Stewart," he asked, "would you and the young lady like to sit in my office until the boat comes, or would you prefer to walk along the shore?"

I glanced at Miss Ball, and she indicated with a tilt of her head that a walk along the shore was more to her liking. Joseph stayed by the cart and was soon in an animated, arm-waving conversation with Captain Prendergast.

Miss Ball said, "I'm truly sorry that you have to leave so soon, Mr. Stewart. I was really looking forward to talking with you."

I said truthfully, "I was looking forward to some intelligent conversation with an attractive young lady, if I may be so bold as to say so, Miss Ball?"

She coloured again but said calmly enough, "It's kind of you to say so, Mr. Stewart. When will you come back to Wellington, if I may ask?"

"In all honesty, I have to say I don't know," but as I said it, I knew that I would like to return and get to know Miss Ball better if the opportunity presented itself.

Miss Ball was clearly of the same mind, as she reached into her little bag and took out a miniature of herself. She offered it to me and said, "I hope you will accept this miniature as a reminder of a friendship that didn't have a chance to do more than begin."

I didn't know what to say and was saved from uttering more than, "Thank you, Miss Ball, I'll cherish it," by the shouts of Joseph and Captain Prendergast that made us hurry back along the beach to the landing.

I said, "It was very good of you to come to see me sail, Miss Ball." I gently grasped and shook her hand.

"I wish you a safe journey, Mr. Stewart, and hope you will return soon."

I climbed down into the boat where Captain Prendergast was already sitting, and as soon as I was aboard the boat crew shipped their oars and started to row out into the anchorage.

Miss Ball stood and watched for a little while and then climbed onto the cart and was driven out of sight by the faithful Joseph.

For the first time in a long, long time I felt a little sad to be leaving somewhere.

Once onboard, Captain Prendergast and I made our way to the bridge so that I could be introduced.

Captain Giles of the steamer *Nimrod* took one look at my face and said loudly to the harbourmaster even before we had been introduced, "I assume this gentleman is Mr. Stewart. He looks as though he has been in a fight. Is he free to leave Wellington?"

"Yes, Captain. He captured a wanted criminal yesterday, which is why he is so badly bruised. The man in question is in prison awaiting trial for attempted murder."

"Who was he attempting to murder?" Captain Giles asked.

"Me," I intervened, "because I stopped him stealing something from me."

"I see," said Captain Giles. "In that case, Mr. Stewart, may I welcome you aboard and at the same time request that you do not frighten my passengers by appearing in the dining room until you are less..." and he racked his memory for a suitable word and decided upon the least offensive adjective he could call to mind, "colourful."

"I am perfectly happy with that arrangement, Captain, and will stay in my cabin during the day. I would like permission to be on deck after dark, and perhaps I could spend some time on the bridge with the officer of the watch?"

"Mr. Stewart," he responded, "I cannot order you as a fare-paying passenger to stay in your cabin all day, but I would appreciate your cooperation for the benefit of my other passengers. I'm quite sure that the ladies have never seen bruising such as yours."

"Perhaps, Captain, you are depriving your lady passengers of a topic of conversation that would keep them occupied for the whole voyage," I said jokingly.

He laughed and said, "Perhaps so. I'm sure we will get on famously, Mr. Stewart. Please let me know when you wish to go to the bridge, and I'll inform the watch officer."

"Thank you, Captain. Perhaps someone can guide me to my cabin?" To Captain Prendergast, I said, "Thank you for your assistance, Captain; perhaps we will meet again one day."

"Perhaps we will, Mr. Stewart, but I hope it will be in happier circumstances. Goodbye." With that he turned and went down to the boat and was rowed ashore.

I watched until the boat returned and had been hoisted up in its davits, and then, as Captain Giles set sail, I went to my cabin secure in the knowledge that no one had left Wellington before or with me, so for the time being my life was not at risk. The voyage up the coast to Auckland passed without incident, although the seas were quite rough from a storm that had affected the area in the previous week. I spent the first few days in my cabin and was glad to have peace and solitude in order to recover from the attack and to finish my final report. I added a few paragraphs to include what I had learnt from Gravenor and then it was done. All that I had to do now was to deliver the report to Sir David, but how I was to do that and keep a whole skin was a problem I had yet to puzzle out.

I spent a good deal of my time on the bridge, and it was not long before my familiarity with the life of a seaman brought the inevitable questions and discussion of my life as a third officer.

In Auckland I had no need to go ashore and chose not to. Instinctively, I felt that the fewer people who knew where I was the better. I considered a disguise, but my red hair was difficult to conceal effectively, and I decided in the end that arriving in Sydney by boat as Mr. John Brown, for example, might be as effective a way of concealing my location as any. Once the *Nimrod* had sailed again, there would be no one who could connect Jason Stewart with John Brown unless I met someone I knew.

And that was a very unlikely event.

We set sail from Auckland in a northerly direction up the Hauraki Gulf after less than a day in the harbour. A few passengers left the ship and a few new ones arrived. I was quite confident that none of the disembarking passengers had seen me, and unless one of the crew had gossiped, my presence onboard was still only known to a few of the ship's company.

We had just sailed past the entrance to the Bay of Islands I remember, and I was standing on the wing of the bridge enjoying the evening air when there was a *thud thud* noise at the stern, then some violent metallic crashes and bangs from the engine room beneath my feet, and the steady beat of the engine died.

Suddenly, the noise of the sea seemed very loud and threatening.

Captain Giles was on the bridge before the way was off the ship. He was closely followed by the chief engineer, who walked up to the captain, saluted, and said, "Sir, I have to report that most of the bolts in the coupling between the engine and propeller shaft have sheared. The propeller must have hit something. A tree trunk in the sea is a possibility. I can see no distortion in the shaft, and we have spare bolts so I have set a gang to work to replace the broken bolts in the coupling. However, we need to put someone over the side to check the propeller for damage before we try to run the engine again."

Captain Giles was suddenly in a very dangerous situation.

It was dark, and the wind and sea were steadily pushing the ship westwards toward a very rugged and dangerous shore. The ship had started to roll in the beam sea to an extent that was extremely uncomfortable for all on board and if any of the cargo shifted it could rapidly become a threat to the ship's stability.

Captain Giles turned to the first mate and said, "It's too deep to use the anchor, but we must try to get the bows round and stop the rolling. This is what I want you to do. Get the bosun and some good hands and pull our tow line out of the cable locker. Flake it in the deck in bights about twenty feet long and then lash them together into a bundle. Fix a bridle to the bundle about five feet in from each end. Fasten the bridle to our longest mooring line and stream it over the bows to act as a drogue and keep us head to sea. Lower the anchor when the drogue has been streamed."

"Aye, sir," he said, and the mate rushed off the bridge and clattered down the ladder to the main deck shouting for the bosun as he went.

Captain Giles turned next to the chief engineer, who had been standing patiently waiting for the captain to return his attention to the problems in the engine room.

"Now, Chief," he said, "repair the main shaft coupling as quickly as you can. If I can put a man in the water and inspect the propeller I will, but it's dark and with this sea running it might be impossible." He stopped and thought for a moment, then said, "I may be forced to use the engine without an inspection to avoid going aground."

"I understand, sir," he said. "I'll get back and make sure the shaft is repaired as quickly as possible."

On the foredeck the mate, bosun, and a few hands worked with commendable speed to prepare the drogue described by the captain as the ship rolled violently from side to side. After a quick consultation between the bosun and the mate, the captain agreed that it would be a good idea to lash some lengths of chain to the rope bundle to make it less buoyant, and in about fifteen minutes it was ready. At a nod from Captain Giles, the mate's party deployed it over the bow and the end of the mooring line was made fast to the bits on the port side of the bow. After a few minutes, the extra drag started to have an effect and the ship started to swing up into wind and sea. We were still drifting down toward the shore at an alarming rate, but at least the violent rolling had been replaced by less exaggerated and more tolerable pitching. The anchor was lowered to the maximum extent possible but did not touch bottom.

The mate came back along the main deck, and when he was immediately below the bridge he exchanged a few loud-voiced sentences with the captain, who was leaning over the bridge rail.

The mate said, "Aye, sir," and led the bosun and his group of sailors aft to the stern to see if an inspection of the propeller was possible.

The winch man in the bows shouted up to the bridge, "Captain, sir. Anchor's touching bottom."

In order to know when the anchor started to hold, Captain Giles ordered the second mate into the bows to check what the winch man was reporting.

"Is there anything I can do, Captain?" I asked.

Captain Giles looked at me in surprise, as he had forgotten I was on the bridge, and then said, "Yes, Mr. Stewart. Please go aft to the mate and ask him with my compliments what progress he has made with his inspection of the propeller."

"Aye, Captain," I responded and went aft as quickly as I could.

I arrived at the stern just in time to see the mate leaning over the rail as the head of one of the crewmen disappeared over the side of the ship sitting on a hastily rigged bosun's chair.

When the mate stood back from the rail, I went to him and said, "Captain's compliments, Mr. Mate, but he would like to know if you have had time to make any progress."

"Have you been press-ganged into the crew Mr. Stewart?" he asked with a laugh. Then more seriously he said, "I have just sent a man down with a lantern to see what he can see. I hope that when the bows pitch down after a wave passes and the stern comes up it will be sufficient to see the top of the propeller. If we can see it and the blades are undamaged, the chief engineer will have to find a way to rotate the propeller so we can inspect the rest of it. Wait a minute, Mr. Stewart; they're just pulling him up."

We went to the rail and watched as a very wet and bleeding crewman was being helped back onboard by the bosun and a few men.

He said to the mate, "You were correct, sir. When the bows drop, the stern is high enough out of the water to see the top of the propeller. One blade appeared to be missing, and the next one was bent and touching the hull. That was all I saw before the stern dropped again and I went underwater and put out the lantern. The barnacles are very sharp," he said unemotionally as he surveyed the bleeding scratches on his arms and legs, although I was certain that they must have been stinging like fury from the saltwater.

Suddenly, we heard a faint, dull booming sound from the darkness.

The mate and I exchanged glances of concern and then rushed to the stern rail where we stood and listened with all our concentration. The booming noise repeated itself at regular intervals like a far-distant bass drum slowly beating time, and after less than a minute the mate and I exchanged glances of extreme anxiety.

I said, "That sounds to me like waves breaking on the shore."

The mate replied with real concern in his voice, "To me it sounds like big waves breaking against a cliff, but whichever it is…" and his voice tailed off as he contemplated the disaster that awaited us. He turned to the bosun and ordered, "Standby here and await orders. I'm going to the bridge. Come along, Mr. Stewart."

He turned, strode along the deck, and ran up the ladder to the bridge. The second mate and the engineer arrived almost simultaneously, and we stood in a loose group in front of the captain.

He surveyed our faces for a few seconds and then asked, "Well, Chief, is the repair complete?"

"Aye, sir," he responded. "We can use the engine as soon as we know the propeller is sound."

Captain Giles looked questioningly at the first mate, who said sombrely, "I'm sorry, Captain, but one blade is bent and touching the hull plates. The next blade appears to have broken off. What is worse, we," and he indicated me with a gesture, "believe we can hear the sea breaking against cliffs."

"The anchor is still not holding second?" Captain Giles asked, but it was almost a statement not a question.

"That's correct, sir," the second officer said. "It seems to catch and then break free. It was dragging across the bottom when I came up to the bridge to report."

The captain turned away from us and walked to the rail where he stood in silence as he grappled with the problems that he had to face. Even in the poor light on the bridge I could see the white-knuckled grip he had on the rail. He straightened his back and turned toward us, and once again I recognised how quickly a calm and peaceful night at sea can become a potential disaster.

He said, "Gentleman, our situation could only be worse if we were in a severe storm. We have lost our engine, the anchor is dragging, and we are drifting down onto an exposed and rocky coast. My first duty now is to save life, and I propose to put all the passengers and crew into the two big lifeboats and only keep a small volunteer crew onboard with me. You will be in charge of one boat, Mr. Mate, and in overall command, with the second officer in command of the second boat. You are to row seaward until dawn. If it is safe to come back onboard I'll signal, but if the ship has gone aground, make sure you get all the passengers and crew to safety in Kororareka. Make sure there is adequate food and water in each boat. Where's the bosun?"

"In the stern waiting for orders," the mate responded.

"Send him to me," ordered Captain Giles.

"Aye, sir," responded the mate, and he strode to the rear of the bridge and shouted down to the bosun.

"I'll stay onboard, Captain," I interrupted. "I know that I'm not part of your crew, but I can be useful, and your officers have to look after your passengers and the rest of the men."

"Sir," said the first mate, "if anyone should stay to assist you it should be me. Mr. Smiley is a passenger and should go in one of the boats with the other passengers."

"Mr. Judd," I said to the first mate, "you told me last evening that you are married and have two children. I think you have a duty to your family as well as responsibility for the safety of the passengers. I have no family to consider, and whilst I am not as experienced a sea officer as you, I do believe I can assist your captain over the few next hours."

Captain Giles looked at us each in turn for a moment, then said quietly, "Thank you, Mr. Judd, but my order stands. I want you to ensure the safety of our passengers. Mr. Stewart can stay onboard if he wishes, but what anyone will be able to do except pray I don't know. Please carry on, Mr. Mate."

"Aye, sir," was the glum response from the mate as he saluted, turned, and left the bridge.

When the bosun arrived, the captain ordered him to identify four volunteers from the crew to stay onboard and then to help the mate and second officer organise the orderly transfer of the passengers and remainder of the crew into the boats.

When all were embarked, Mr. Judd gave a final salute to his captain, shouted an order to the second mate, and the two boats cast off the falls and rowed away from the ship's side toward the open sea. It was suddenly very quiet onboard, and the gap between the lifeboats and the *Nimrod* rapidly widened and the boats soon disappeared into the dark predawn hours.

As the ship continued its slow and inexorable stern-first drift toward the shore, the bosun ordered his few remaining hands to launch the jolly boat and pull it around to the bow where it was moored and a rope ladder rigged for access but rolled up and tied to the rail. The oars, food, and water were checked, and then they had nothing to do except wait for the ship to ground as the anchor continued to drag across the seabed.

"I don't understand why the anchor fails to bite," I remarked to Captain Giles as we stood side by side at the bridge rail.

"I assumed earlier that the water was too deep for the flukes to dig in, but now I can only imagine that it was fouled after it was let go," he answered.

"We have a few hours before we ground, so we could pull up the anchor with the steam winch, free it if it's fouled, and then let it go again," I suggested. "We have nothing to lose now except that we will drift a little more quickly without the drag of the anchor and chain across the seabed."

Captain Giles looked at me for a moment.

"Hell and damnation," he shouted as he struck his forehead with the heel of his hand. "I should have thought of that." He shouted down to the bosun, "Send someone forward and start pulling the anchor up! Then come to the bridge!"

The bosun looked up, opened his mouth as if he was about to ask the captain to repeat the order. but changed his mind and said, "Aye, sir," and gave the necessary orders. Very soon we could hear the healthy hiss of steam and the *clank clank* noise of the chain passing through the winch and the clatter as the chain fed down through the hawser hole into the chain locker.

The bosun arrived on the bridge quite quickly, and Captain Giles said, "The anchor should have held us by now but continues to drag, and I think it could be fouled. As soon as it's above the surface, clear it and lower it again as quickly as possible, as the ship is drifting faster now, we don't have the drag from the anchor and chain."

"Aye, sir," the bosun said smartly and hurried quickly down off the bridge and was soon seen in the bows looking down into the water.

Captain Giles was right. We were drifting faster now that the anchor was off the seabed, but the wind was blowing off the land, which helped reduce the effect of the waves a little. It was also clear from the increasing steepness of the waves that we were approaching the shore quite quickly as well. The muffled distant drumbeat of breaking waves we had heard earlier was now a continuous and much louder background noise, and I realised that if we failed to anchor we would soon be aground in the surf with a very slim chance of survival if the ship started to break up. We were very lucky that there wasn't a gale blowing, as we would have no chance at all, but at least the sky was becoming lighter in the east.

It would be a blessing to have daylight and see what was happening.

I heard a shout from forward and looked down from the bridge in time to see the bosun gesturing over the bows. The winch stopped, started, then stopped again, and the winch man screwed down the brake and hurried across the deck to join the bosun. Captain Giles and I almost ran to the bridge ladder, then along the main deck and up into the bow where we joined the bosun and his men and looked down in amazement.

Somehow, and we didn't stop to speculate how it had happened, the anchor chain had wrapped itself around one of the flukes on the anchor so that it was dragged backwards across the seabed and it needed to be cleared as quickly as possible if we were to have any chance of stopping the inexorable drift toward the beach. Captain Giles issued a few succinct commands and very quickly the bosun and his men had put the eye of a mooring rope over a bollard and fed a bight of cable out through the fairlead. They tried to pass it under the anchor but the line was just too far forward.

Captain Giles ordered, "Pull it up. Put a heaving line on it and pull it aft."

As the bosun said, "Aye, sir," I said, "Wait!" I kicked off my shoes, threw my coat onto the deck, climbed over the rail, and then down the cold, wet anchor chain to stand on the stock of the anchor. I grasped the chain with one hand and the mooring rope with the other, and as I passed the bight of rope under the anchor, the bosun pulled up the slack. I climbed back up the anchor chain and was helped over the rail onto the heaving deck by a beaming Captain Giles.

He said, "Very well done, Mr. Stewart."

As I responded with, "Thank you, Captain," the bosun put two turns of rope around the barrel of the winch and started pulling the rope up with it. As soon as he had taken the weight of the anchor from the chain, he stopped pulling. One of the seamen leaned over the rail, gave the chain two hearty bangs with a sledgehammer where it was trapped under the fluke, and the chain dropped free. The anchor was lowered until its weight was once again taken by the chain.

As soon as the mooring line was freed, the captain ordered, "Drop anchor."

The bosun knocked the stopper off the chain and it ran out with a satisfactory clatter through the hawser hole and then the noise just as suddenly stopped as the anchor came to rest on the seabed. A few more fathoms of chain clanked slowly over the side—then silence again apart from the noise of the sea and the surf behind us.

Captain Giles said, "Make fast," and the bosun secured the chain.

All we could do now was to wait and, for those who had faith also, to pray.

The ship continued to drift back toward the shore and a few hundred yards distant we could clearly see in the dawn light the line of surf where the waves were breaking but even more menacing were the almost vertical cliffs that rose from the narrow strip of sand we could see beyond the breaking waves.

We could see that the waves were getting steeper as we approached the shore, and it was obvious that we must abandon the ship, as it would be soon too rough to use the small boat that was plunging and rearing and slamming against the bow plating.

Captain Giles called, "Bosun! Get your men together; we will abandon ship."

"Aye, sir," he responded, and he dropped a rope ladder down into the boat and ordered the first man over the side.

It looked a very precarious descent, as the rope ladder was sometimes vertical and sometimes sagging out over the sea as the boat danced about in a random movement dictated by the passing waves.

He was not halfway down when we sensed a change in the ship's motion.

"Anchor's holding, Captain," said the bosun quietly, as if he didn't really believe it.

Moments later he said in a very disconsolate tone, "Dragging, Captain."

"Anchor's holding again, Captain," the bosun said in a normal and more cheerful voice that was belied by his clearly visible crossed fingers.

We all stood in the bows and at least metaphorically held our collective breath hoping that the anchor would continue to hold. We were so close in now that I thought I could feel the ship touching bottom when the stern dropped into a trough between the bigger waves. It was a sudden slight sensation of solidity that a ship should not transmit and was very disturbing. I hoped we were nearer to low water than full tide.

After a period of minutes that passed as slowly as hours, Captain Giles told the bosun to recall the man from our small boat.

He continued, "The anchor appears to be holding for the time being, bosun, so I want you set an anchor watch. An experienced hand, if you please. If the anchor slips again, he must call us all immediately. Do you understand?"

"Aye, sir," the bosun responded.

The captain continued, "Send one man to stoke the boiler so we have steam for the winch if we need it and get breakfast for yourself and the rest of your men. Relieve the man on watch as soon as you can."

"Aye, sir," he responded.

Captain Giles and I went aft to the officer's mess where we gathered whatever we could find for a meal. As we munched, Captain Giles reviewed his situation.

He said, "The anchor appears to be holding, but it's low tide now so another four or five fathoms of chain will need to be released to keep the anchor on the bottom as the tide rises. The wind is not too strong and sea not too rough. The weather appears to be stable, so in the short term the ship is probably safe. We cannot repair the propeller so the ship will inevitably go aground if we cannot be towed off."

He stopped and sat in silent thought for a time, then said, "Everything will depend upon the news the first mate can get in the morning, Mr. Stewart. If there isn't a ship in Kororareka that can help us, then we will have to abandon the *Nimrod* and save the remaining crew."

I could only sit and nod my head in silent agreement.

We went back to the bridge, and it wasn't long before the ship's boats appeared and hove to seaward of the bows. The captain shouted his instructions to the mate through a megaphone and then watched as the boats rowed out to sea and then turned parallel to the shore to head south for Kororareka.

We waited. We sat or leant on the rail or paced up and down, depending on our individual temperaments, as there was nothing to do but watch and wait.

I am not very good at keeping still, so I spent some time looking around a class of ship with which I was not familiar. Essentially, it was a new design of cargo ship with accommodation for a relatively small number of passengers in cabins under the bridge. It had been equipped with a king post and a pair of thirty-foot-long cargo booms between the holds both in the fore and aft parts of the ship to aid loading and unloading into barges or small boats lying alongside. At the foot of each king post was a four-barrel steam winch.

I stared up at the king post between Number 1 and 2 holds and thought back to the *Earl Canning* and the sails she could carry on her masts when Captain Stewart didn't want to use the steam engine. It was an old-fashioned notion, but having two forms of propulsion on a ship seemed to be a very good idea when our present situation was considered.

"Wishing for wings, Mr. Stewart?" I jumped slightly as the bosun's unexpected voice behind me broke into my thoughts.

"No, bosun," I answered. "Sails."

"Can't help you there, sir," he said. "No sails onboard; only spare hatch covers."

"Really?" I said as the beginnings of an idea took root in my mind. "How many spare covers do you have and how big are they?" I asked.

"There are six," he answered. "They are all twenty feet long by fifteen feet wide and very good quality canvas."

"Thank you, bosun," I said and left a rather puzzled man behind me as I turned away and went back toward the bridge to speak to Captain Giles.

"I saw that you were interested in our cargo equipment, Mr. Stewart," he said.

"Aye, sir," I said automatically, and Captain Giles grinned at my unconscious use of the naval response. "We didn't have a refinement like that on *Earl Canning*. She carried sails as well as an engine so we used the main yard if we needed to work over the side."

"I know the class of ship you refer to, Mr. Stewart."

"Captain," I said, "I have the germ of an idea that may help get the ship out of immediate danger. May I explain?"

Captain Giles was immediately interested and his enthusiastic, "Yes, tell me," had me reaching immediately for pencil and paper in order to sketch the idea that had come into my mind.

As I sketched, I said, "The bosun said he has some spare canvas hatch covers. I think we can stitch them together to make two rudimentary sails. The king posts would be the masts and the loading booms would be used to support the foot and head of the canvas. We cannot rig the sails during the day, as we would be blown straight onto the beach, but during the night there is a period of calm before the offshore wind starts blowing. We would need to have everything ready so that we can rig the sails in the calm period, and if the offshore wind is strong enough and the sail area big enough, we might be able to move the ship farther offshore."

"It's a good idea," Mr. Stewart, "and if it doesn't work, nothing is lost except some canvas and labour."

He leant over the bridge rail and ordered one of the sailors to tell the bosun to report to the bridge.

When the bosun came up to the bridge, Captain Giles took my sketch and explained what I had suggested. The bosun scratched his head as he studied the sketch and clearly supported the concept as his practical comments improved on the ideas I had proposed. Within fifteen minutes he had assembled his few men on the foredeck and five minutes later they were hard at work sewing the hatch covers together with two-inch cordage.

The mate returned with both boats and the remaining crew late in the morning, and when he came onto the bridge, his news was not good.

"I'm sorry, Captain," he said. "There are no steamships in Kororareka at present and none expected in the near future, so we cannot expect to tow the ship out of danger. There was a schooner in port and I have arranged for our passengers to sail to Sydney on her. She sailed just before I left. I imagine there is nothing we can do now except to abandon the ship."

"It may come to that, Mr. Mate, but tonight we are going to try to sail her into deeper water." He handed the first mate my sketch.

He looked at it for a moment then laughed.

"Is this some kind of a joke, Captain?" he asked. "It must be a joke, as it will never work," he scoffed.

"It might work and it might save my ship. This is what I intend to do, and if it doesn't achieve the desired result then…" and his voiced tailed off as he considered the other alternatives.

After a few moments, he returned to the matter in hand and said to the mate, "I want the sails and rigging prepared for hoisting before sunset. As soon as the offshore wind starts, set the aftersail on the port side and the other to starboard, as I don't want the aftersail blanketing the forward one. Ensure that there is a good man on the anchor winch. He is only to pull in slack chain if the sails produce enough thrust and the ship gets underway. He is not to pull the ship forward against the anchor. Is that clear?"

The mate was a good officer, and although he didn't agree with the orders he had received, he simply said, "Aye, sir," saluted, and left the bridge to join the bosun on the foredeck.

The bosun and mate consulted each other frequently and gesticulated often as they solved one problem after another in their effort to meet the captain's deadline. There was no manual to guide them. They had to rely on experience and imagination to make the best use of the materials and equipment available. Some of the crew laboured with canvas and rope to make useable sails from canvas hatch covers whilst others set up rigging to control the lower boom of each sail. The engine room men operated the cargo winches and made adjustments where necessary. As the sun set, the captain went down from the bridge to inspect progress, and as the last gusts of the onshore wind whispered past, he turned to the mate.

"I don't want the sail catching any of the last gusts of onshore wind so make sure the sail remains fore-and-aft as you hoist it. Please carry on, Mr. Mate."

"Aye, sir," he responded. Slowly and systematically, he gave the orders necessary to hoist our rather strange sails.

I hadn't been involved with the work since Captain Giles had adopted my idea, and I was impressed with the results achieved by the first mate and the crew. They had taken the time to lash the foot of the makeshift sail to the bottom boom with short lengths of rope at regular intervals, and as the head of the sail was hoisted up the king post with a rope passing through a block at the top of the post, one of the crew passed short lengths of rope through eyelets in the luff then around the king post. Each loop was tied off with a reef knot. The middle and outer corner of the sail were supported with a bridle fastened to the end of the cargo hoist wire of the second cargo boom. A length of stout timber was lashed to the bottom ends of the bridle to keep the sail spread. As soon as this sail was up, the crew moved forward and erected the sail on the forward king post in the same fashion.

Then we waited with varying degrees of impatience for the offshore wind to start to blow. The hackneyed old adage of "time passing by on leaden feet" was never as true as it was that night.

After several hours, we felt the first soft touches of the offshore breeze, but it seemed as if it would never strengthen to anything beyond the gentlest zephyr.

"The offshore wind has set in so there is no danger of us being blown onshore now," the captain said. He ordered, "Set the forward sail to starboard and the aftersail to port, Mr. Mate."

"Aye, sir," was the prompt response, and very soon both our homemade sails were swung out to catch the wind but it wasn't strong enough to even make the canvas flap.

Another thirty minutes passed without change and then suddenly the offshore wind decided to blow in earnest. The aftersail filled, the bottom boom swung out, and the block and tackle that made up the main sheet sprang of the deck with a twang as it suddenly tightened. There was a screech of anguish, and we dimly saw one of the crew writhing in agony on the deck holding his crotch.

The bosun shouted up to the captain, "He'll be all right, sir. The idiot was standing astride the main sheet when the sail filled. It gave him a nasty clout."

The captain muttered something like, "Stupid man. He won't do that again, I'll wager," as someone dragged the moaning sailor to one side.

The forward sail had also filled but there didn't appear to be enough wind to move the ship; not that we had a fixed point of reference to judge movement by.

Without speaking we waited and the sails filled and flapped, filled and flapped, but the ship didn't move as far as anyone could judge. Time was starting to run out, as the offshore wind would not last for many more hours, and the captain, whilst concealing his feelings behind a carefully composed face, had his fingers firmly crossed behind his back.

The first mate was standing behind his captain and trying unsuccessfully to conceal the smug "I told you so" expression on his face when the silence was shattered by the anchor winch as it started to turn. A few links clanked into the chain locker, then there was a deep, long silence again and everyone held his breath once more. The wind was continuing to fill the sails only fitfully, but after a few more minutes the winch broke the silence again and a few more links came onboard. It seemed that the wind was only just strong enough to move the ship a few yards at a time, and I think we all wished or prayed for the wind to strengthen. I noticed that the forward sail seemed to catch more of the wind than the aftersail, but I could imagine no reason for this phenomenon. Suddenly, I realised that the wind had become a little steadier and the sails had stopped flapping every few minutes.

Almost simultaneously the anchor winch started to work again then stopped and after a very short interval started again and continued to pull in the anchor chain as the helmsman called out, "Captain, sir. I have steerageway."

"Maintain this course," Captain Giles ordered.

"Aye, sir," answered the helmsman quickly.

As the ship progressed slowly seaward away from the cliffs, the breeze became stronger, and the reason for the phenomenon I had noted earlier became apparent. The cliffs had been shielding us from the full strength of the offshore wind and the aftersail had been most affected.

As the anchor was pulled up and secured, the crew cheered and the ship slowly accelerated as the full force of the breeze filled our homemade sails.

"Well, Mr. Stewart," said Captain Giles as he gave me a congratulatory thump on the back, "your scheme has worked, I'm pleased to say. Even my first mate is convinced. Isn't that so, Mr. Judd?"

"Aye, sir," he said. "I didn't think the idea had a snowball's chance, but I'm pleased I've been proved wrong."

"Now," said Captain Giles, "we have steerageway and can expect the breeze to last a few more hours. The nearest harbour where we can moor and make repairs in safety is Kororareka, which means altering course toward the south. Reset the forward sail to port, Mr. Judd."

"Aye, sir," he responded and left the bridge.

It was an easy order to give but an extremely difficult order to execute, as the first mate soon found. The sail was drawing well, and it was impossible to pull the boom in using the main sheet. It wasn't possible to turn the ship into wind to take the pressure off the sail and the only other option was to lower it and then reset it on the other side of the ship. Lowering the sail was another of those easy to formulate and difficult to execute solutions to a problem. The outer part of the sail supported from the cargo boom could be lowered, but the head of the sail would not come down as the rope ties were gripping the king post too tightly under the pressure of the wind. After many attempts to lower the sail under its own weight had failed, the bosun sent one of the sailors up to the top of the king post using the sail ties as a rudimentary rope ladder. He attached a rope to the head of the sail and then one by one undid the rope ties as he climbed back down to the deck. Once the sail was down, it was a simple matter to swing the boom over to the port side of the ship and raise the sail again. As soon as both sails were drawing again, Captain Giles started to change the ship's course toward the south a few degrees at a time, and each time he made the alteration, the main sheets were pulled in so that the sails remained square to the wind. I noticed that the ship was listing slightly under the wind pressure on the sails, which was to be expected. It wasn't an alarming angle but meant that we now walked on a deck that was sloping to one side as well as pitching and rolling to the passing seas.

It wasn't long before daylight came and the offshore wind, which had been lessening in strength for more than an hour, suddenly died away altogether. Captain Giles used the last of the ship's momentum to alter course again, and when we coasted to a halt and lay dead in the water, the ship's head was pointing almost due south. Captain Giles ordered the mate to set both sails to starboard.

As the morning hours passed and the temperature started to climb in step with the sun's rise in the sky, the onshore wind started to develop and after some minutes of useless and noisy flapping, the wind strength increased a little more and both sails started to draw. As soon as the ship had settled onto a course that paralleled the coast, Captain Giles went to his cabin for a meal and a rest, leaving the second officer on watch as the first mate was down in the officers' mess getting something to eat. I had breakfasted earlier, and as I didn't feel in the slightest bit sleepy, even though I had been up all night, I decided to remain on the bridge. There was a steady breeze from the east that I estimated was about Force 4 on the Beaufort scale, and the ship was rolling gently in time to the swell. The ship had again developed a slight list from the pressure of the wind in our rudimentary sails but was making steady but unspectacular progress toward Kororareka.

I stood in the sun on the port side of the bridge, swaying to the movement of the ship and enjoying a beautiful day after the near disaster of two days before. The sky was blue, and only a few miles away the many shades of green in the densely forested coast slipped slowly past. I knew that I should consider what to do about my assignment when we reached Kororareka later in the day, but I consciously postponed the mental effort in order to enjoy the beauty of this sunny morning.

How long my reverie lasted I have no idea, but I came back to consciousness with the gabble of confused shouting and the whistle of strong wind sounding in my ears. The list of the ship was rapidly increasing, and I had to grab hold of the bridge rail to stop myself sliding down a deck that was becoming steeper by the second. Instinctively, I knew we were about to capsize and scrambled over the rail as it became horizontal and stood momentarily on the side of the ship. I looked down just in time to see the panic stricken, wide-eyed face of the second officer disappear below the sea then turned and started to scramble up the side of the ship as it rolled toward me. I grabbed hold of the bilge keel and paused for a moment before I continued scrambling over the rusty, barnacle encrusted iron plates until I reached the keel. Here I stopped and held on with all my strength as the ship rolled past the vertical and then came back to float inverted on an even keel for a few seconds before sinking, taking me down into the depths with it.

TEN

Rescued

As the ship sank beneath me and I found myself immersed in violently turbulent water, I started to fight the suction that was trying to drag me to my death with all the energy and determination at my disposal.

I was almost at the end of my endurance and the urge to open my mouth and gulp for air was almost uncontrollable even though I knew it would kill me and then my head broke surface again. I coughed and gasped as I took several deep gulps of the best air I have ever tasted. From unknown, hidden reserves, I managed to dredge up enough energy to tread water and keep myself afloat until I had stopped panting, and then I carefully looked around my visible horizon from the crest of a succession of waves.

I was devastated to realise that no one else had escaped when the ship capsized and there was nothing left of the *Nimrod* except for some wooden debris bobbing serenely a few yards away. I swam to the largest piece of wreckage I could see, and when I pulled my upper body on to it, I took some comfort from the fact that I could rest at least momentarily from my constant attempt to stay above the surface.

I rested my face on my folded arms and closed my eyes to blot out the reality of the moment and the struggle to stay alive that must follow.

Why have I survived? I thought to myself. *Haven't I suffered enough following Joanna's death and Gravenor's attack? The agony of drowning with the ship would have been quite short, but now I have a long drawn-out struggle to stay alive until I'm too exhausted to fight anymore and drown anyway. Why does God want me to stay alive longer? Surely there must be a better purpose than simple suffering.*

A wave slapped my face and filled my mouth with water. I coughed and spluttered as I opened my eyes to the reality of my situation and then couldn't stop myself wondering what had happened. One minute I was happily enjoying a warm and relaxing daydream and the next moment I was fighting for my life.

I thought back over my last few minutes on the bridge and realised that the second officer had probably not noticed that a squall was bearing down on the ship. Even if he had seen it coming, he was too young to have served on a sailing ship and could have had no idea how devastating a strong wind could be on a steamer that was never designed to carry sails. The wind must have blown the ship over onto her beam ends, and once she was on her side, the effect of seawater flooding in through openings in the deck coupled with the inevitable movement of cargo in the holds would have quickly conspired to roll her right over.

I recognised that it was only conjecture and whatever had taken place had occurred very quickly and without a sound once the initial cries of alarm had been silenced beneath the sea, except for the chilling sounds of a ship dying, and I knew I would never forget them!

It was only luck that had placed me on the port wing of the bridge and allowed me a chance to escape. The other crew members, including the second officer, had all been on the starboard side of the ship and it had rolled over on top of them, and every member of the crew from the captain to the cabin boy who had been inside the hull of the ship had died in that tragic few moments.

If God intended me to survive, I had to get to the shore, and I wouldn't do that if I simply lay on my piece of wreckage and waited for help to arrive.

I raised myself as high as I could as my raft reached the top of the next wave so that I could try to see where the land lay. I turned my head from side to side but could see nothing. I wriggled around on my raft so that I could look in the opposite direction when the next wave passed under me. I could still see nothing of the land that I had been able to see so clearly from the bridge of the ship only half an hour earlier.

I wasn't particularly dismayed, as I knew from the position of the sun the direction in which to paddle to reach the coast, but it would have been encouraging to have had something tangible for which to aim.

I wriggled about on my piece of debris and managed to remove my shoes and then my trousers so that I could move my legs more freely. I rolled them into a bundle that I placed in front of me. I manoeuvred my piece of board until it pointed in the correct direction and started to slowly kick my feet to push me forward over the waves. I stopped after a time and was quite disheartened at my apparent lack of progress until I looked back and realised that I had left all the other floating debris quite a long way behind.

Unfortunately, land was still invisible and a very, very long way in front.

It was very hot in the sun, so I took my trousers from the bundle and draped them over my head and shoulders to give a little shade. I couldn't decide what to do about my shoes and eventually did nothing and watched listlessly as the next small wave that washed over my raft sent them floating out of reach. They rapidly filled with seawater and sank into the depths.

Gone to Davy Jones's locker, I thought.

I started to kick again and as I did so, I felt the tiredness in my legs and the first real pangs of thirst. They were ominous signs, and whilst I was confident about my mental resolve, I wondered for the first time if I would be physically able to survive.

I rested for a time then tried to use my hands as paddles, but the piece of wreckage was just too wide for me to use my arms effectively, and I had to urge my tired legs into action again.

My thirst was becoming very strong, and I remembered the last time I had been so dry. *If only an Arab would appear with a goatskin bag of water,* I thought. I wouldn't complain no matter how foul it tasted if it reduced the agony of a dry mouth and throat.

I rested again and couldn't resist the temptation to close my eyes against the glare. I must have been asleep from exhaustion in seconds and woke moments later as I struggled back to the surface coughing and spluttering after slipping off the raft into the water. I managed to find the strength somewhere and, still gasping for breath, swam desperately after my piece of wreckage and pulled my upper body on to it again when I caught up with it.

I was not only very tired and thirsty but also very frightened, as I knew that the next time I slipped off this small piece of wreckage would probably be the last thing I did in this world.

The thought stiffened my resolve for a time but did nothing to alleviate my fatigue or the increasing agony of a raging thirst that was made less bearable by the fact that ninety percent of my body was immersed in water. I wondered if it was true that I would meet Joanna in the next life if I died. *Probably not*, I thought. She will be in heaven and I would be consigned to hell in all probability. *Could I feel worse in hell than I do now?* was the next thought that crossed my mind. I couldn't find the energy to formulate an answer.

I heard something but couldn't identify it and sank back into my jumbled thoughts. The noise came again and it sounded like a man calling from somewhere behind me.

Perhaps I should turn around and look, I thought but couldn't find the energy necessary for such a manoeuvre. *It's only a figment of your imagination.* I said to myself to justify my lack of action.

There was a splashing noise beside me, some more muffled shouting. then I was dragged out of the water by my arms and put down none to gently on a hard surface with ribs that dug into my back. Water splashed over my head and ran with delicious coolness down my parched throat. I opened my salt-encrusted eyelids with difficulty and stared into a sun-tanned but obviously European face. He opened his mouth and said something in a language that was totally incomprehensible to me. It sounded vaguely familiar, but it was beyond my powers to identify it at that moment. He gave me a water bottle and my trousers before turning away and issuing some orders that had the boat turning around in its own length before heading for some distant sails.

I sat in the bottom of the boat and divided my time between drinking water and putting on my trousers without impeding the stroke of the two sailors who sat and rowed skilfully beside me.

As we came closer to the ship, I could see that she carried square sails on all three masts and from the number of gun ports I counted in the wide, white-painted strake along the side she was also very well armed, and I imagined she was probably a frigate. There was a flag with horizontal bands of red, white, and red and some sort of central medallion flying at the stern, but I couldn't identify it. As soon as the boat was alongside the ship, a line was lowered and one of the boat crew passed a sling around my chest and under my arms. There was a sharp word of command, and I was hauled off my feet and up the ship's side before I knew what was happening. I was lowered to the deck where I landed with all the grace of a badly stuffed, soaking wet sack and collapsed.

A sailor reached out a hand and helped me to my feet, and I stood on shaking legs as seawater drained onto the immaculately clean deck from my sodden clothing. He removed the sling and supported me for a moment or two, but when he saw I was able to stand unaided, he pointed aft and said something, which was again incomprehensible. I didn't bother to say anything in return but did as I was bidden and walked barefoot and dripping in the direction indicated. Halfway along the deck I saw a group of men dressed in uniform and assumed they were some of the ship's officers.

When I reached them, I halted and the senior of the officers said in a polite and cultured tone, "Sprechen sie Deutsch?"

"I'm sorry," I said. "I don't understand what you said, but I would like to thank you for rescuing me."

"You speak English?" he asked but it was more a statement than a question.

"Yes, sir," I answered, and I remembered my visit to Hahndorf. The similarity in the language spoken by the old people in Hahndorf and that of the officer was unmistakeable. He was speaking German.

"I am Fregattenkapitän Pueckh of His Imperial Majesty's frigate SMS *Novara*. May I know whom I am addressing?"

"My name is Stewart, Captain," I said politely and immediately regretted that I had not seized the opportunity to escape my previous identity and the people I knew would be looking for me. "Jason Smiley Stewart." I went on, "I would like to thank you and your crew for rescuing me from certain death. I do not believe I could have stayed on that piece of driftwood for many more minutes."

"Perhaps when you have had a little time to refresh yourself, you will explain why you were swimming alone in the Pacific Ocean ten miles from land."

"At your convenience, Captain, I should be pleased to explain everything that led up to my rescue, but if you will permit me to borrow some dry clothes first I would appreciate your kindness."

"Clothes and something to eat and drink as well, I think," Captain Pueckh said then called out something in German and one of the other officers saluted and stepped forward. He was given some detailed instructions, saluted as he responded, and then stepped smartly toward me.

"I am Fregattenleutnant Pirker," he said in good but slightly accented English. "If you will follow me, Mr. Stewart." He turned and led me to a companionway and then down into the ship. One deck down he opened a cabin door and gestured for me to enter, which I did.

"Please wait in here a moment, Mr. Stewart," my guide said and closed the cabin door behind me.

Within a very few minutes he returned to the cabin and following close behind him was a mess boy carrying a tray on which were placed a bottle and two glasses. The mess boy put the tray down on the table, took the stopper out of the bottle, poured a generous measure of a dark brown liquid into each glass, then stepped to one side.

Fregattenleutnant Pirker passed me a glass, took one himself, and said, "A small drink to warm you, Mr. Stewart, and to celebrate your rescue." As he raised the glass in salute, he added, "Prost!"

Without thought I uttered what seemed to be the appropriate response to the lieutenant's gesture.

"Your health, sir," I said and hoped that it was apposite.

After my first sips, I said appreciatively, "That's very good. What is it?"

He smiled and said, "It's similar to the rum your Navy uses and it's made at a small distillery near to my home in the city of Klagenfurt."

When we finished our drinks, Fregattenleutnant Pirker spoke to the mess boy, who replaced the bottle and glasses on the tray and carried it from the cabin.

"If you wait here a moment, Mr. Stewart, I'll send a steward with towels and some food," he said, and he turned and left the cabin.

Moments later the door opened again and a steward appeared. In one hand he had a plate of dark bread, cheese, and what looked like ham, and in the other a large glass of water. Over his shoulder he carried a towel. He put down the food and gestured to me to take off my wet clothes as he gave me the towel to dry myself. As he stooped to pick them up, I remembered that my wallet had been in my trouser pocket when the ship sank and took my trousers back. The wallet was still there, and I took it out and put the soggy lump on the table beside the plate. The steward left the cabin with my clothes and closed the door behind him

As I stood there draped in a towel, the full magnitude of the disaster I had suffered dawned on me. I had nothing except the clothes I had worn when I came onboard and a saturated wallet.

I had almost no money and didn't know how I could get more without revealing my name and whereabouts, added to which I knew no one in New Zealand well enough to expect them to support me whilst I arranged to have money forwarded to me. At the same time I had to try to conceal my identity in order to reach Adelaide in one piece and report to the Governor, and how I could achieve that feat I couldn't even begin to imagine. That last thought reminded me that all my reports and my diary were at the bottom of the Pacific in my cabin on the *Nimrod*, which meant that I would have to try to rewrite them from memory if I was ever fortunate enough to return to my office.

I sat at the table draped in my towel and mechanically ate the food that had been brought for me as I mulled over the various problems that beset me. The realisation that there was absolutely nothing I could do at present gave me temporary peace of mind, and when the steward brought me some clothes I was able to give him a cheerful smile as I dressed again. I checked the contents of my wallet or, more accurately, I cleaned out the sodden paper and then counted the gold coins I had stored there as a reserve. It wasn't much, but I was not entirely destitute and could pay for a few nights' lodging if I was frugal.

Some time later Fregattenleutnant Pirker came back into the cabin after knocking politely on the door.

After quietly closing the cabin door, he said, "Have you had enough to eat, Mr. Stewart?"

"Yes, thank you," I responded. "Which country are you from, please? I saw the ensign on the stern just before I came aboard but didn't recognise it."

"It's the flag of the Austro-Hungarian Empire," he said with great pride evident in his voice.

"I thought your country was landlocked and didn't have any deep-sea ships," I said.

"In the past that was true," he said, "but in recent years the Austro-Hungarian Empire has built up a big Navy, and one of our major ports is Trieste. That's where we sailed from two years ago."

My interest was aroused, and I couldn't help asking, "If it's not a secret, could you tell me what has taken a well-found ship like the *SMS Novara* two years to get from Trieste to New Zealand?"

"We are sailing around the world on a scientific expedition. It's the most ambitious enterprise the Austro-Hungarian Navy has undertaken," he said proudly. "It's supported by the founder of the Austro-Hungarian Navy, Erzherzog Ferdinand Max. He's the brother of Franz Joseph, the Kaiser."

"Kaiser?" I asked interrogatively.

"That means emperor in English," he said. "Kaiser Franz Joseph of the Hapsburgs is the emperor of the Austro-Hungarian Empire. Haven't you heard of it?"

"No," I said. "I don't think I have, but in England we seem to spend all our time and energy fighting the French so we don't have much time for the rest of Europe."

He looked a little surprised at my flippant remark but didn't offer a comment. Instead he said, "If you will follow me, Mr. Stewart, I'll take you to my captain." He turned and led the way out of the cabin.

I followed him as he led me toward the stern of the frigate and halted in front of the armed guard standing outside the door that I assumed lead to the captain's quarters. After a short exchange between the fregatenleutnant and the guard, the door was opened and I was led into the stern cabin where three people were awaiting our arrival. I didn't expect it, but they all stood as we entered, and Fregattenkapitan Pueckh introduced me. in turn. to Commodore Bernhard von Woellersdorf–Urbair and Dr. Karl von Scherzer. If I remember correctly, the commodore was the scientific leader of the expedition and Herr Scherzer was a specialist on countries and ethnology.

Fregattenleutnant Pirker left me standing in the middle of the room and walked to one side with his captain where he had a short, low-voiced discussion with him, then saluted and left the cabin.

I was ushered to a seat at a big desk near the stern windows and was given a glass of port wine.

Fregattenkapitan Pueckh raised his own glass and said, "I wish you continuing good health, Mr. Stewart."

"Thank you, sir," I responded. "I must again thank you for rescuing me."

"My task was quite simple, Mr. Stewart. I only had to send a boat. Responsibility for sighting you rests with one of our scientists. He is only really happy when he has a telescope and the freedom from regular duties to scan the surrounding seas for marine life. He thought he had found a new species when he spotted a strange-looking object splashing about on the horizon. When we were closer and could see it was only a man on a raft, he was very displeased, as he had already started to define a suitable Latin name for his discovery. I'm afraid you are a grave disappointment to the scientist who spotted you, Mr. Stewart. Now, please tell us in detail how you came to be swimming in the Pacific."

I saw no reason why I should involve the captain in the events related to my enquiries for Sir David and commenced my narrative by saying, "I joined *Nimrod* in Wellington as a passenger bound for Sydney." I went on to describe all the events that had taken place up to the time I was fished from the water at the end of my strength.

There was silence for a half a minute or so after I had finished relating my tale.

Then the commodore, who had been taking copious notes during my explanation, asked, "Herr Stewart, whose idea was it to put temporary sails on the *Nimrod?*"

"Mine, sir," I said. "Although I think now it would have been better if I hadn't had the idea. The ship would have been lost eventually by going aground, but many good men would still be alive today if I hadn't suggested it."

"Do you know what happened to cause the *Nimrod* to capsize?" asked Herr Scherzer.

"No," I said, "but I assume that there was a squall and it wasn't possible to reduce sail quickly enough to prevent the ship being blown over onto her beam ends. The sea would have done the rest very quickly. *Nimrod* wasn't designed to carry sail and had already shown a tendency to list in a slight breeze, so she would have rolled over quite quickly in a squall. As you know, even a well found sailing ship can be blown down if the crew do not reduce sail quickly enough."

"You were on the *Nimrod* as a passenger, Mr. Stewart, but you saw a possibility for getting the ship underway again that an experienced captain did not see. Perhaps you have some knowledge of the sea and ships?"

"Yes, Commodore. I was a cadet and then third officer on a ship called *Earl Canning*. She had an engine but also sails on all three masts, so I learnt a great deal about using sails or steam as circumstances dictated. The lessons have not been forgotten."

"Why did you give up the sea?" Fregattenkapitan Pueckh asked.

"The governor of Bombay needed someone to help the manager of the telegraph company, and my captain was persuaded to release me. I went ashore and became involved with telegraph work and haven't been to sea as a sailor since."

There was another short silence, which Fregattenkapitan Pueckh broke by saying, "You have been extremely fortunate, Mr. Stewart. You were able to save yourself when the *Nimrod* capsized and then extremely lucky to find a piece of wreckage to keep you afloat until a curious scientist spotted you. Until we reach Auckland in a few days' time, you will be my guest, and in Auckland I will report the loss of the *Nimrod* to the authorities."

"Thank you, Captain," was all I could say.

"Fregattenleutnant Pirker is waiting for you. He will show you around my ship and introduce you to some of the officers and scientists."

It was a politely phrased dismissal and I said, "Thank you, Captain. Good day gentlemen." I turned and left the cabin.

As I had been informed by the captain, Fregattenleutnant Pirker was waiting for me in the anteroom outside the captain's cabin, and he lost no time taking me to the officers' mess, where I was introduced to some of the officers who were not on watch. When I had finished answering their questions about the loss of the *Nimrod*, I was able to ask some questions of my own about the scientific expedition upon which the *SMS Novara* was engaged.

I believe I'm correct when I say that the voyage had lasted for almost two years by that time and amongst other port cities they had visited were Rio de Janeiro, Cape Town, Ceylon, Singapore, Manila, Hong Kong, and Sydney. It was a circumnavigation of the world and a feat that the crew could be justifiably proud of, but the scientists onboard had acquired a mass of unique scientific information of which they were very proud as well.

I can only remember the name of one of the scientists, and that was because I met him again on my return to Auckland some months later; his name was Ferdinand von Hochstetter.

The *SMS Novara* arrived in Auckland on 22 December, and the ship's company were welcomed with a display of war dances and speeches from local tribal leaders. The scientists then set about collecting physical data from the bodies of the Maoris for the study of comparative anatomy.

I said goodbye and thank you to Fregattenkapitan Pueckh just before his ceremonial departure from the ship to make his courtesy visit to the authorities in Auckland and to report the loss of the *Nimrod*.

I left the ship unceremoniously about an hour later wearing my own shirt and trousers and a pair of rather worn shoes donated by one of the scientists. I had no plan except to find out how I could have money transferred to Auckland and how to get to Australia as soon as possible, so I started to walk toward the settlement, as this was the only place I was likely to find answers.

As I trudged through the ever-present mud, I noticed two people walking toward me.

I could see that they were having an argument as one of the men, the short, thin one, was waving his arms about and almost dancing from foot to foot in vexation. The other, a slightly taller but much broader man, was not persuaded by whatever argument was being presented to him, as he kept waving his hand at his companion as if he was trying to rid himself of a particularly irritating fly. As they came closer, I started to hear occasional disjointed words but could make no sense of them.

Just before I passed them, matters obviously came to a breaking point, as the short, thin man shouted, "If you won't pay me more, Captain, then I won't sail with you." He turned about and stamped away through the mud back toward Auckland.

As he reached me, I said conversationally, "I see you are having crew troubles, Captain."

Under normal circumstances, I think he would have ignored a comment from a stranger, but he said, "Of the worst kind. The mate is in the Mission infirmary with a broken leg. The second," and he pointed over his shoulder at the retreating figure, "is due for leave, and as he's taken up with a Maori girl from a local village, he wants to take his holiday here. I have a cargo loaded and should have sailed this morning but Jenkins—"again he pointed at the retreating figure, "didn't come back on time. I had to go to the girl's village to get him, and it was very difficult to get him to leave in the first place. Then on the way back he started asking for more money for the trip and I refused him, as he is still under contract with my owners. You saw what happened?"

"Yes indeed, Captain. Where are you bound?" I asked casually.

His unexpected reply, "Adelaide," sent a jolt of excitement through my brain.

"Perhaps I can help you, Captain," I said as casually as I could.

"How can you help?" he said derisively then added with a degree of rudeness to which I couldn't take exception in the circumstances, "Are you able to conjure up a first mate who can sail in the next hour? You don't look like a fairy godmother to me." He started to push past me.

I laughed and said, "I don't feel like a fairy godmother, Captain, but we may be able to help each other. I have very little money left and need to get to Adelaide. I'm not a first mate, but for about ten years I was a cadet and then the third officer on a ship sailing from Liverpool to Bombay, so I have done my share of watch keeping. If you will take me on, I should be happy to work my passage." He was openly sceptical about my claim at first, but after a good deal of discussion, during which he probed my expertise, he warmed to the idea and eventually agreed. He said he would sign me on as acting first mate and, as he was one officer short, we would take watch and watch about.

Captain Miller, for that was his name, and I shook hands, and half an hour later we sailed for Adelaide. As Fregattenkapitan Pueckh had said, "You have been extremely fortunate, Mr. Stewart."

I was in some things but not with Joanna, I thought sadly.

I realised that I had forgotten to make my report about the *Nimrod*, but it would have to wait until I reached Adelaide now.

Later that day I was on watch when Captain Miller returned to the bridge. He looked around the horizon then said, "I'm going to my cabin for a few hours. Send someone to call me at three bells in the first watch. I have to make a course change at four bells."

"Aye, sir," I said automatically.

"You sound as if you have never left the sea, Mr. Stewart," he said.

"I was a little rusty to start with, but I feel the same now," I responded.

"Good night, Mr. Stewart" he said.

"Good night, Captain," I responded and returned to my duties as officer of the watch.

A week later we sailed into Adelaide. Both Captain Miller and I were very tired after sharing the watches between us, but I was buoyed up by the knowledge that I had returned to the life of a sailor without a hiccup. It was a tribute to the tuition I had received under my father's guidance all those years ago.

Suddenly, I missed the guiding presence of my sole-surviving parent and felt the warmth of tears prickling the back of my eyes.

I accepted Captain Miller's very generous offer of half pay after we had agreed initially that I would work my passage, and I declined Captain Miller's request that I continue sailing with him.

I said, "Goodbye, Captain. Thank you for taking me on trust in Auckland. I wish you safe voyages." I shook his hand with enthusiasm then disembarked.

It was late afternoon, and it seemed probable that I had managed to reach Adelaide without any of my enemies being aware that I had even left New Zealand. All I had to do now was to enter the Residence and see Sir David before anyone knew I was there.

How I could achieve that was something I still had to work out.

I went to a small hotel where I was certain I wouldn't be recognised and booked a room for the night. I paid in advance and the proprietor didn't present a register for me to sign and wasn't interested in my name. I had something to eat then lay on my bed wondering how best to proceed. Lying down was nearly a disastrous error, as I only just managed to stop myself going to sleep, and I was so tired I would have slept until morning if not longer. I sat in the chair and seconds later just managed to stop myself falling on the floor as I went to sleep again. All I could do was to get out of the room and hope the fresh air revived me enough to let my brain work again. In the street I turned and started to walk in the direction of the Residence, and as I walked, I pondered what to do.

The only solution that presented itself to my tired brain was simple but ludicrous. I only needed to break into my own office in the Residence and wait for Silas Browning to arrive, then he could go to Sir David on my behalf. After that, all my troubles would be over.

Inshallah, I thought.

I had walked about halfway to the Residence by this time, and I used the remainder of the walk to try to remember the layout of the building and the exact location of my office and, most importantly, whether there were any guards around the building. I hadn't seen any and hadn't heard guards mentioned by anyone when I worked in the Residence, so it was probably safe to assume there were none. Nevertheless, common sense dictated that I should proceed as if there was an armed guard hiding behind every bush.

Before I reached the entrance to the drive, I left the road and started to pick my way slowly and carefully in the starlight through the bush and scrub parallel to the boundary of the Residence. At the back of the Residence, I skirted around the outside of the villas and was relieved to find that there were no late night revellers about. When I was opposite my office window, I started to move toward the Residence using the bushes for cover and suddenly came to a standstill.

I had forgotten totally about the enormous expanse of well-kept lawn that surrounded the building.

In the light from the stars I knew it would be impossible to cross that open expanse of green without being as conspicuous as a red ball on a billiard table, so I retreated a few steps and lay down behind a large bush whilst I contemplated what to do.

After a long wait, during which I heard nothing and saw no sign of movement, I decided that it wouldn't be sensible to delay further and moved forward to the edge of the lawn. I looked around again and was just about to set off across the flat, empty area when a window on the upper floor squeaked and I watched with horror as it started to open. With a palpitating heart I recoiled back into the shelter of my bush and watched with considerable concern as an unmistakeably Army-helmeted head appeared in the opening. The helmeted head turned slowly from side to side as it slowly scanned the lawn and then withdrew. Unfortunately, the window remained open.

From the shelter of my bush I sat and contemplated my options until I realised that a million black ants were using my outstretched trouser legs as part of their route to and from somewhere. It was very difficult to jump to my feet under a bush in the middle of the night and brush of all the ants without making a noise, but I must have achieved it, as the Army head didn't reappear.

I didn't have many options really.

I could simply walk around to the front door, give myself up, and hope my gaoler would permit me to send a message to Ignatius or Silas in the morning. I could try to find where Ignatius or Silas lived—but wandering around the villas peering at names on gates was likely to attract the attention of a watchdog, servant, or wakeful occupier and bring me unwelcome company. I considered simply waiting until the office opened and walking up to the front door, as I had every right to do, but rejected this option as the clerk at the entrance could well be one of John Darcy's people and have me arrested and that wouldn't help my cause in the slightest. A very simple option was to run across the grass to the building. If I took this course, I would have to hope that there was no one looking when I made the attempt.

I decided on positive action.

I took off my shoes and crawled to the edge of the bushes. I looked carefully up at the open window but could see no movement and hear no sound. Without further delay I picked up my shoes, ran across the grass as quickly as I could manage, and stood flat against the wall trying to pant quietly.

The window above me squeaked farther open, and I could sense the guard looking out but managed to retrain my instinct to look up in case he noticed the movement or my pale face reflecting the starlight. After an interminably long wait, a voice above called, "Ain't nout there, Sarge." I heard more faintly from inside the room, "Couldabin a 'roo," then silence.

I realised that if I stayed close to the wall, I couldn't be seen by the watchers above unless they looked directly down, and as I thought that was unlikely, I walked openly along the edge of the lawn until I was standing outside the window of my office. It took only a few seconds to slide my knife into the joint between the window and the frame and ease the catch open. Moments later I climbed through the window and into my office. I closed the window, turned, and looked around the office in the poor light and was pleased to see that it was just as I had left it.

Now what? I thought. *I've returned to the Residence undetected but somehow I must speak to Sir David before news of my arrival slips out.*

I sat at my desk for a few minutes then got up and walked over to the door and locked it simply as a precaution, as it was far too early for anyone to be wandering about in the corridors. I returned to my desk and, after a little thought, took a sheet of writing paper and a pen from the drawer and wrote a short note to Silas Browning.

> *Dear Silas,*
>
> *Please do not draw attention to this message by word or gesture. I have returned in secret, as my life is in danger. Without mentioning this request to anyone, please come to my office as quickly as you can and knock twice on the door.*
>
> *Jason Smiley Stewart*

When I had finished my note, I took off my shoes and then unlocked my office door. Very slowly and gently I pulled the door open and peered surreptitiously into the corridor. There was no one about and not a sound to be heard. In my stocking feet I crept along the corridor to the clerk's room, opened the door very carefully, and slipped inside, closing it equally carefully behind me. There was just enough starlight percolating into the room through a window to allow me to locate the desk Silas used. I pulled out his chair, put the note on the seat, and then carefully slid the chair back into place under the desktop. I hoped Silas would be the first person to use his desk and consequently see the note when he pulled out the chair to sit down.

It was the best I could do.

I crept back across the room and was about to open the door into the corridor when I heard heavy footsteps approaching. I released the handle and had just flattened myself against the wall where I would be hidden if the door opened when I heard the footsteps halt outside. The doorknob turned and the light from a lantern shone into the room. Whoever had opened the door didn't enter the room, and after a few seconds the door was closed again and the footsteps moved along the corridor and stopped at the next door. I opened the door of the clerk's office a crack so that I could listen more easily to the progress of the watchman as he continued along the corridor opening and closing each door in turn. When I heard the heavy footsteps on the stairs to the next floor, I opened the door fully, stepped furtively into the corridor, and hurried back to my office, where I opened and closed the door as quickly and quietly as I could. I took a deep breath as I locked the door and realised that I had almost stopped breathing because I was so apprehensive about being caught.

I sat down at my desk then leant forward, cushioned my head on my hands, and started to drift off to sleep.

Suddenly, the thought crossed my mind that I had been extremely fortunate the guard had not entered the room after opening the door to the clerk's office. When I worked in the building, I hadn't appreciated that the doors were left unlocked at night so that the guard could check the offices periodically. I had just locked mine, and I started to smile as I imagined the rumpus there would be when he made his next check and found a door locked that had not been locked an hour before.

The smile froze on my face as I leapt from the chair and almost upended it in my haste to get to the door and unlock it again. That was the end of any thought of sleep, and I spent the remaining hours of the night sitting on the floor where the door would conceal me if it was opened again. As it happened, the guard didn't return, and when I heard the first office workers arrive, I relocked the door, returned to my seat behind the desk, and waited impatiently for Silas to arrive.

My watch had not survived its immersion in the Pacific, and I had not had the opportunity to purchase a replacement. Consequently, I had to estimate the passage of time from the noises of the morning routine percolating through my door and the movement of the shadows cast by the sun.

After what seemed like the passage of the whole morning, I heard a noise outside followed by two tentative knocks on the door.

I rushed across the office, unlocked, and opened the door and almost dragged poor Silas into the office so that I could close and lock the door again. Silas stood there white-faced and rubbing his arm where I had grabbed hold of it.

"Is it really you?" he asked.

That's a rather stupid question, I thought.

"Of course it's me. Who did you expect?" I said acidly.

"I don't know," he responded. "You have been gone so long and, as there has been no word, we were beginning to think you had died somewhere. What has been happening, Mr. Stewart?"

"I don't have the time to give you an individual explanation at the moment, Silas. I have important information for Sir David, but I must give it to him before anyone knows I have returned to Adelaide, as my life will be in danger otherwise. Please go to Sir David with my apologies for the unseemly request and persuade him to come here."

"I doubt if he will see you this morning, as he is to meet with Mr. Darcy very shortly."

I felt my face go pale as I realised how close to abject failure I was at that moment and said, "Silas you must make Sir David understand that the information I have is very important and concerns Mr. Darcy intimately."

"I'll do my best, Mr. Stewart," he said and left the office with a very apprehensive expression on his face.

About fifteen minutes later, there was a peremptory double knock on the door, and when I opened it Sir David marched in followed at a discrete distance by Ignatius and Silas.

Sir David Tallboy, the governor, was exceedingly cross, and he marched across the office and dumped his bulk into my chair with such ferocity that it groaned. His red faced, flinty-eyed appearance were good physical indicators of his mood, but his first few words left no doubt what he felt at that moment.

"Well, Stewart, we thought you were probably dead, but you have decided to return like a thief in the night and dressed like a beggar. Then you have the temerity to request me, the governor, to leave my office and come to you because you believe your miserable life is in danger. I have paid you a generous salary to make an investigation and not one word have I heard from you since you left here months ago. On the assumption that you might be still alive, I was about to sign an order for your arrest, and if you cannot explain yourself satisfactorily, I might still have you arrested and sent back to England in a ship's gaol. I will give you fifteen minutes of my time, as I have a meeting in half an hour. Ignatius, you will take notes." Ignatius nodded his head in assent.

"Sir David," I said, "you have known me for a number of years, and you have never had occasion to doubt my veracity. I ask you to listen carefully to what I say, knowing that I can gain nothing from a deception."

Sir David inclined his head and I took that as a signal to go on.

I said, "You are correct to say that you have not received a report from me whilst I have been away." Sir David opened his mouth to say something, but I didn't give way and said, "I have written regular reports, and I know that each one has been intercepted by someone who is paid by John Darcy. I know this because a man called Gravenor, who was hired by John Darcy, told me. Gravenor was supposed to collect my final report and then kill me but failed on both counts and is now in prison in Wellington awaiting trial. I arrived here like a thief in the night, as you described it, as I don't know if Darcy is aware that Gravenor failed. If he is aware that I'm still alive, then I'm a danger to his schemes to persuade you to authorise the purchase of telegraph equipment and will probably try again to eliminate me.

"In my opinion there is no reason for the Government to spend large sums of money on the manufacture of telegraph equipment for use in New Zealand at present. There are small, isolated settlements on both islands, and because of the terrain, most intersettlement communication is by sea. In the North Island there is no telegraphic development, and until the trouble with the Maori has been resolved, there is unlikely to be enough additional settlement to generate a demand for telegraphic communication. In the South Island a start has been made on a telegraph link between Christchurch and Littleton, but that is lead by a competent man who will not need outside help.

"If you can give me a little time, Your Excellency, I can write my reports again from memory."

"Didn't you keep copies?" Sir David asked incredulously.

"Of course I wrote copy reports," I said with some asperity, "but they are at the bottom of the Pacific in my cabin on the *Nimrod*, together with all my clothes."

"What happened to the *Nimrod*?" he asked.

"She capsized and sank, taking all the crew with her. I was lucky to be on the port side of the bridge and able to get off the ship as she sank and even more fortunate to be picked up by an Austrian frigate called the *SMS Novara*."

"I see," said the Governor; after a pause, he added, "I see I have misjudged you, Mr. Stewart. Clearly you have been adventuring again. Wouldn't you agree, Ignatius?"

"Indeed, Sir David," said Ignatius with a grin at me as he remembered some of my past exploits.

"Now," said Sir David as he resumed his role as governor, "we have no proof of any wrongdoing by John Darcy at present, but I cannot go ahead and meet him this morning, as he will expect me to sign the order for the equipment. I can feel a diplomatic ailment coming on, so I will go back to my quarters. Please cancel the meeting with Darcy, Ignatius, with as many apologies as you can stomach. Browning," Silas jumped to his feet in eager anticipation of an instruction from the Governor, "you will do your diplomatic best to find out which of the clerks is close to Darcy and could have intercepted Mr. Stewart's reports. I expect they are stored in a cupboard somewhere. If we can find them, it will save Mr. Stewart a great deal of writing, for which he will be eternally grateful."

"Indeed, Sir David," I said as I stifled a huge yawn.

"I think we can assume that no one knows about your safe return apart from the four of us, Mr. Stewart. But what we can do to ensure your continuing safety I do not know at present. Please stay in this room with the door locked whilst we consider the situation."

"Yes, sir," I said and locked the door after they filed out.

ELEVEN

A Close Encounter

As I hadn't eaten since early the previous evening, I was very hungry and also extremely thirsty, but it was much longer since I had last slept, and very soon after I sat down and put my feet up on the desk I fell into an exhausted sleep.

I don't think I had slept for long before I was woken by a double knock on the door, and in the first moments of returning consciousness I had no idea where I was.

I looked around, recognised my office, pulled my feet down from the desk, and hobbled stiffly to the door feeling like an old man. I didn't think it could be possible but I was even more thirsty and hungry than I had been before I managed to sleep. I unlocked the door, opened it a crack, and when I saw Ignatius standing outside I opened it partially then stood to one side so that he could enter. He hurried in, pushed the door shut, and locked it again.

I was just about to utter a reproachful comment about letting a friend starve to death when he said, "I'm sorry, Mr. Stewart, and I realise that you must be dreadfully hungry and thirsty, but ensuring your safety has to be our first priority and then we can get you food and drink."

"I see," I said, "and how do you propose to ensure my safety?"

He ignored the question and the testy note with which it was delivered and said, "In a few minutes, Silas will knock on the door to warn me that the corridor will soon be empty. When he knocks again, we must go into the next office as quickly as possible."

"That's Douglas's office. Won't he object if we just march in?" I asked.

"The Governor has just sent him on leave for a week," Ignatius said, but his words didn't explain anything.

There was a knock on the door and Ignatius unlocked it and said, "Be ready, Mr. Stewart."

"Why should I move to the next office?" I asked. "It's no safer than this one."

"There's no time for explanations at the moment. Just do as I ask."

There was a second knock, and Ignatius immediately opened the door, grabbed my arm, and with a tetchy, "Do come along," pulled me into the corridor, and pushed me into the next door office. Silas quickly closed and locked the door.

"No one saw us," he said to Ignatius.

"Would you please explain what you're doing?" I asked angrily, fatigue, hunger, and thirst conspiring together to make me short-tempered.

"It's quite simple really, Mr. Stewart. You need somewhere to stay for a few days where you will not be visited. Like most people, you probably do not know it exists, but at the back of the Residence there is a clinic. It's very small, as it has only a room for a doctor and another room with two beds for temporary patients. There is a small waiting room in between."

Ignatius obviously saw me draw breath to interrupt and held up his hand to stop me.

"Please let me continue." He paused and waited for my nod of assent before resuming his explanation. "In a little while, two men will arrive with a stretcher, which they will pass to Silas and then wait outside. You will lie down on it. We will cover you with a blanket up to your chin and put a hat over your head to hide your red hair. The stretcher bearers will then come in and carry you out of Mr. Douglas's office in full view of anyone who is passing. They will carry you coughing and sneezing to the clinic and leave you there. Anyone who asks will be told that we think poor Mr. Douglas is suffering from the plague, and there will be a note to that effect on the entrance door to the clinic. Mr. Douglas has already left the Residence without saying goodbye to anyone and will not return for a week. As we will carry you out of his office, no one should realise that you have taken his place. Consequently, we should be able to complete our enquiries into John Darcy without anyone discovering that you're here."

"Now, I understand why you wanted me to move from my office, but what about meals?" I asked. "The first time a servant brings me a meal I will be discovered, and that's not much help."

Silas laughed and said, "With a plague notice on your door, we will have to persuade a servant to leave a tray of food on a table outside your door. I'm quite sure he will retreat as soon as he puts the tray down. You must take the food into your room as soon as the servant has gone away, and when you have finished you should put the tray back on the table and return to your room. As I said, with a plague notice on the door no one will want to get too close to you."

"That's very clever," I remarked. "Was it your idea, Ignatius?"

"No. Actually it was the Governor who instructed us after talking with Lady Megan," Ignatius answered diplomatically.

And so it turned out. The stretcher was handed in to Silas. I lay down and was covered over. The stretcher bearers came in, picked me up, and carried me along the corridor. As we progressed, I could hear Silas saying in a worried voice to people we were passing, "Better keep back. Poor Mr. Douglas may have the plague." I added a few coughs to the performance, and it seemed no time at all before I was dumped unceremoniously in the entrance to the clinic between the doctor's room and the sickroom and the bearers left as quickly as they could.

There was no one about, so I jumped off the stretcher and, with Ignatius and Silas close behind, ran into the room where the beds were located and Silas closed the door behind us.

As soon as we were safe from inquisitive eyes, Ignatius and Silas started to laugh. To some extent it was a release of tension, knowing that the plan had worked, but it was coupled with shared recollections of the expressions on peoples' faces when they were suddenly confronted with a victim of the plague.

I looked around the room that would be my home for a few days. At least I hoped it would be only a few days. There were two beds, a writing table and chair, and nothing else.

Ignatius said, "I'll bring some paper and a pen later so that you can start writing your reports again when you have eaten and rested."

"Thank you, Ignatius," I said, and then turned to Silas to ask, "Have you had any success with your search for Darcy's clerk?"

"There hasn't been time to do much yet, but there can be few people with access to official mail and the position to divert it from its intended destination."

"Thank you, Silas. I wish you an early success with your search, and I thank both you gentlemen for your resourcefulness this morning." I added, "Without it, I would be facing some danger, I think."

Ignatius said, "I'll see that food is brought as soon as possible Mr. Stewart." With that, they both left me to enjoy the Spartan comforts of my tiny hospital room.

A little later I heard a tray being deposited on the table outside my room and the sound of footsteps fading rapidly into the distance. Although I was desperate for food and even more so for water, I managed to wait a little while to see if there were any other noises outside. I heard nothing, and when I thought it was safe to do so, I put the hat on and soundlessly cracked the door open just enough to see outside. I was astounded and very alarmed to see someone watching the door.

Was he a friend posted by Ignatius or an enemy watching on behalf of John Darcy? I had to assume he was an enemy, so I stayed one side of the door and the food stayed on the other. My stomach rumbled, my throat seemed to become drier by the second, and I started to curse the continuing absence of Silas and Ignatius, who could at least bring the food in, even if they could not get rid of the watcher.

I sat on the edge of a bed.

I stood up and walked backwards and forwards. Three paces toward the door and three paces back between the beds and the writing table. Whenever hunger overcame caution, I gently cracked open the door and peered out, but the watcher was still in place and I closed the door again.

A very, very long time later, or so it seemed to my rumbling stomach, I heard a knock on the door and a familiar voice said, "Ignatius here. Open the door please."

I unlocked the door again and stood to one side so that I couldn't be seen when Ignatius opened it.

I called quietly, "Please bring the tray in with you, Ignatius."

"Why didn't you collect the tray when it arrived?" he asked and was obviously a little chagrined that I had not eaten the food whilst it was hot.

"I didn't think it advisable to go out for the tray, as there was someone out there watching the door," I said.

"Well, there's no one there now," responded Ignatius after cautiously looking out again.

I took the tray and settled down to eat the first meal for nearly twenty-four hours. Ignatius was correct. The food was cold but it was also delicious. The wine was hot but that didn't matter either. It was just what I needed.

There was another knock on the door; Ignatius unlocked it and this time it was Silas who came in. This was a different Silas. This was a triumphant and beaming Silas who was almost dancing with glee.

"I've got him," he crowed, "and what's more, Mr. Stewart, I have all your reports. When I confronted him, he said he had put them in a cupboard by mistake and had forgotten to deliver them. 'A total accident,' he claimed. When I said his mistake had been perfectly understandable, he started to smile and agree with me until I added, 'but only for one report, not eight.'"

"Where are the reports now?" I asked.

"I took them to the Governor, and he has cancelled all his appointments so that he can concentrate on them. He asked how long it will take you to prepare your final report, Mr. Stewart."

"I'll have it ready by first thing tomorrow morning," I answered. "What has happened to the clerk?"

"Officially, he is ill and gone home," Silas responded. "Perhaps he's another plague victim. In actual fact, he has been arrested and the Army have him under guard somewhere in the Residence. He'll stay in detention until John Darcy has been dealt with, I imagine. After that, he'll probably go to prison for a very long time."

"That's very good news," I said and yawned hugely.

"We'll leave you to get some rest," said Ignatius and headed for the door with Silas following.

"Thank you," I said and locked the door behind them.

I went to bed and was soon deeply asleep. By the time I woke up it was dawn on what I assumed was the next day. I chanced opening the door slightly and was happy to see that there was no one watching but less content to find that there was nothing to eat or drink waiting for me. I retreated back into the room and, as there was nothing else to do, I sat at the writing desk and started my final report for the Governor.

I had almost finished when I heard a tray being banged down on the table and the sound of footsteps scurrying away. I was delighted that the plague notice was having an effect, but I was still cautious and opened the door only enough to peer outside through a narrow crack after unlocking it. I had just started to squint through the crack when the narrow strip of light suddenly darkened and the door slammed back, hit my forehead, and sent me flying back across the room to sprawl on the floor semiconscious. The next second, a heavy weight descended heavily on my thighs and strong fingers grasped my throat. My muzzy brain registered the fact that I was about to die, and a strong feeling of sadness came over me as I realised I could do nothing to prevent it, and then everything went black.

I opened my eyes and saw a white-faced and panting Silas staring down at me with a very worried expression and a big reddish lump over his right eye. I tried to get up but Silas pushed me back down.

"It's all right, sir, you're safe now," he said.

I lay back and tried to make sense of the various aches and pains I was feeling. Predominant was the pain in my throat, followed by my aching forehead, and then my sore back.

"What happened?" I croaked.

"You were attacked," Silas announced rather unnecessarily. "But I arrived just in time to stop him strangling you."

"Is that how you got the black eye?" I asked, as I wondered how Silas had been able to overpower my assailant.

"I was just coming to collect your report," said Silas, "and I saw him crash into the door and disappear inside. I rushed to help you, calling out for assistance as I ran, and fortunately for both of us a guard was passing by. Between us we managed to pull your assailant away from you, and as we were struggling to overpower him, the guard managed to hit me in the eye with his elbow. A very hard elbow, I might add."

"Where is he now?" I asked with some trepidation as I massaged my sore and aching throat.

"Under guard," he said as he inspected my face. "You'll have some lovely bruises on your throat, Mr. Stewart, and a nice lump on your forehead that will match my black eye," he added with more amusement than pity.

I was sitting up on the floor by this time and Silas helped me to stand and then supported me as I staggered to one of the beds and sat down again.

"You'll feel better when you have had something to eat and drink," Silas said. "Did you complete the report?"

"Not yet," I said. "I was hoping to have breakfast and then finish it but this happened," and I fingered my aching throat reflectively. "It won't take long to finish, but I would appreciate having a guard to keep strangers away whilst I do so."

"I'm going to stay until Ignatius arrives and we can organise something. Clearly, someone found out about our ruse and Darcy tried to eliminate you again. First of all, Mr. Stewart, you must have something to eat and drink…If you can swallow," he added reflectively.

I got up from the bed, walked unsteadily to the door, and looked out cautiously. There was no one in sight so I picked up the tray, carried it to the writing desk where I put it down on top of my unfinished report and flopped into the chair. I was exhausted. With difficulty I managed to eat a little, but I was able to drink rather more, as liquid slipped down my bruised and swelling throat more readily. When I'd finished, Silas took the tray away and then stood guard near the door whilst I finished my report. This was quickly done as I simply summarised the body of the final report in a few sentences.

I wrote,

From my recent observations in New Zealand, I have concluded that there are no grounds for the Government to invest large sums of money in the manufacture and shipping of telegraph equipment and suggestions to the contrary fly in the face of the facts. Whoever is promoting the expen-

diture has no knowledge of the extent of Maori unrest in the North or the sparse extent of settlement in the South. Investment will be required in New Zealand in future, but with the speed of technical advance any equipment manufactured using current technology will be out of date long before it is needed.

I signed and dated the report and handed it to Silas.

"Now what do I do, Mr. Stewart?" he asked rhetorically. "Should I go to the Governor with your report and leave you unprotected or risk the Governor's anger by staying here? I wish Ignatius would come."

"It's better to take the report to the Governor. The quicker this business is finished, the sooner we'll all be safe. Particularly me," I added with feeling.

"I think you're correct, Mr. Stewart, but what will you do whilst I'm away?"

"Leave the door open and sit where I can see someone approaching without being too visible." I touched the lump on my forehead and winced. "This is the second time in two weeks that someone has hit me with a door, and I do not intend it to let it happen again."

"Very well, sir. I'll be back as quickly as possible," said Silas as he hurried away with my report in his hand.

I moved the chair to the back of the room where it could just be seen from the area outside the door. I arranged a couple of pillows and a blanket and then crowned the assembly with my hat in the hope it would look like a sleeping person to a casual glance and then made a seat for myself on the floor beside the open door.

I sat and I waited. My backside went to sleep and I tried not to. In order to keep alert, I wracked my brains, trying to remember the multiplication tables I had learnt in school. I was fluent up to seven times seven, but then my memory failed and I had to calculate each one individually—before fatigue made me forget where I was and then I went to sleep.

Fortunately, it was Silas who found me, and when he did he was rather angry. Well! More exactly, he was exceedingly angry.

He shook me awake and said vehemently, "What do you think you are doing, Mr. Stewart? Why are you sleeping with the door wide open? I have this to show for saving you this morning," and he touched the angry looking lump over his eye. "And then you are thoughtless and inconsiderate enough to leave yourself completely unprotected. It's just as well that I found you and not one of Darcy's thugs with a knife."

He was right, of course.

I had been extremely lucky not to have been attacked whilst I slept and the only thing I could do was apologise to my clerk. I would have to eat a very large portion of humble pie to make amends.

"I really am very sorry, Silas," I started. "What I did was stupid and careless and you have every right to be angry after the chance you took this morning when you saved my life."

"Very well, Mr. Stewart. Thank you for your apology," said a still angry Silas.

After a few minutes of uneasy silence, I asked, "What did the Governor say?"

Silas almost squawked with anxiety at my words. "I was so upset I had completely forgotten why I came back," he spluttered. "I was supposed to escort you to the Governor. He wants to talk to you."

"Dressed like this?" I said angrily. "As the Governor remarked, I look like a cross between a thief and a beggar, and I'm now an unwashed one at that. If I'm to come out of hiding, surely I can wash and change my clothes before I'm seen in public?"

"No, sir. The Governor wishes to see you immediately." Silas started to usher me through the open door he was so concerned to find open about a few minutes before.

"How do you know none of Darcy's men are lurking about?" I asked quietly.

"I don't, but hopefully in broad daylight in a corridor leading to the Governor's office you will be safe," Silas answered but didn't sound particularly confident. As it happened, we made the journey without seeing anybody or being seen as far as I could tell.

We went to Ignatius's office first, and as he wasn't present, Silas walked up to Sir David's door and knocked firmly. The door was partially opened almost immediately, and Ignatius's anxious face peered around the edge.

When he saw that it was Silas and me, his expression changed to one of relief and he beckoned us in to Sir David's office. With a finger to his lips to enjoin silence, he directed us to sit on chairs set at the back of the room and then returned to his seat beside Sir David's desk.

Sitting in front of the desk was a small man with a mop of black hair wearing a bottle-green coat. He was so motionless that I wondered if it was a life-size puppet. Who he was I had no idea, and when I looked at Silas interrogatively and pointed at the stranger, he shook his head to indicate he didn't know either.

Sir David didn't acknowledge our arrival and continued to read a document that lay on the desk in front of him. When he finished, he placed the papers on top of the heap near his right hand, picked them up, and squared them neatly before placing them in a neat pile immediately between himself and his primary visitor. Sir David looked searchingly around the room for a few moments as he assembled his thoughts, looked at me directly, and held up a hand to signify silence and then cleared his throat.

"Mr. Darcy," he said, and as the Governor paused momentarily, I thought, *So that's the man who's been trying to kill me.* The Governor went on, "We have had many discussions about the manufacture of telegraph equipment for New Zealand, and it is well known that the manufacturing and shipping companies you are associated with will receive the orders from Her Majesty's Government if HMG decides to continue."

Sir David stopped and stared at his visitor for a few minutes, but Darcy continued to sit without movement. I wondered if his face was as wooden as his body.

Sir David said with heavy emphasis, "If the order is placed by HMG, you stand to become a very rich man, Mr. Darcy. I imagine that would be a very welcome development considering the size of your debts at the gaming tables here. As you will appreciate, they are as well known as the companies you represent."

Again there was a pause, and again the green figure in front of me made no movement that I could detect.

"I was unwell yesterday…"

Was it only yesterday, I wondered.

"And as a result, I was unable to sign the recommendation to HMG that they order telegraphic equipment for use in New Zealand. I must emphasise that the recommendation is based solely on the information about projected developments in New Zealand provided by you Mr. Darcy, and from your many reports it appears to be a prosperous and forward-thinking colony with a growing population."

The mop of black hair tipped forward and then back in acknowledgement of the Governor's words but nothing else seemed to move.

"Unfortunately for you, Mr. Darcy, I have received equally detailed information that contradicts everything you have told me."

In a colourless voice, Darcy said dismissively, "Your informant has misled you, Governor. I should be grateful if we can sign the agreement without more delay, as I have a ship waiting to carry it to London."

"It will not be as easy as that, Mr. Darcy. My informant has travelled extensively in New Zealand whilst you, sir, have not stirred outside Adelaide. Perhaps you can tell me how you have obtained your information. I wish to be fair, and it would be sensible for me to balance my information against yours. I imagine you must have agents or representatives in New Zealand who provide you with detailed information. Is that so, Mr. Darcy?"

"Yes," Darcy responded.

"Can you tell me who they are, Mr. Darcy?"

"No," he responded. "That is confidential information."

"I'm sorry to hear that, Mr. Darcy," Sir David said and started to look through the papers on his desk. I couldn't see clearly, but I thought they were my reports the Governor was looking through.

The Governor lifted one of my reports up so that Darcy could see it and said quietly, "My informant met a man called Gravenor, who represented himself as your agent. I assume Mr. Gravenor is one of the people from whom you get information. Is that correct?"

"Yes," said Darcy.

"And I assume also, Mr. Darcy, that Gravenor was paid to act on your behalf when you needed specific information or some action taken."

"Yes," he responded.

"Do you correspond regularly with Gravenor, Mr. Darcy?"

"Yes, of course. I need information on a regular basis and usually have a report from him every week or so."

The Governor paused for a moment to stare at Darcy, who wriggled a little on his seat, and I thought, *So he can move then.*

"I imagine you must be quite concerned that you have heard nothing from him for some time now," stated the Governor in calm and benign tones.

"Not really," Darcy said. "As you know, Governor, the mails are transported on ships that are dependant on the vagaries of the wind and sea. A telegraph system would be so much more efficient."

Absolutely true, I thought, *but the time is not right yet.*

Once again the Governor fixed Darcy with a stare, but this time it was the fixed gaze of a predator about to pounce, and Darcy shifted noticeably in his chair but couldn't escape Sir David's eyes.

There was a long silence, and Darcy wriggled on the end of Sir David's gaze like a fish on a hook.

"Your man Gravenor is in gaol in Christchurch awaiting trial for attempted murder, Mr. Darcy," Sir David said slowly, and the courtesy title "Mr." was articulated with absolute contempt. "You may wonder how I know this, so I will explain. The man Gravenor was supposed to murder on your instructions is sitting behind you, and his reports have confirmed what I have long suspected—that you were trying to take advantage of the Government for your own gain. I will not be party to such a deception. I am satisfied that there is no urgent requirement for telegraph equipment in New Zealand at present, and I will not sign an agreement for their manufacture."

As Sir David leant back in his chair, Darcy abandoned his static posture and jumped to his feet, shouting, "You've ruined me!"

As he turned toward where I was sitting, he pulled out a pistol and levelled it at me, shouting, "I'll finish Gravenor's job for him!"

I sat frozen in my seat looking down the barrel of a gun held at point-blank range and thought as his finger whitened on the trigger, *I hope it won't hurt,* and then closed my eyes in anticipation of oblivion.

There was a loud bang, and I thought, *I didn't feel a thing,* then realised I shouldn't be able to think if I was dead, so I opened my eyes again.

It was like a tableau in a waxwork.

Silas was sitting stiff and silent beside me! The Governor was frozen in a half-erect position behind his desk! Ignatius open mouthed with horror, standing with his upended chair behind him staring down at Darcy's prostrate, almost headless body lying at his feet. They were all white-faced from the shock of what they had just witnessed.

I wasn't part of the tableau. I wasn't frozen in place. I was shaking from reaction to another close encounter with death and was promptly sick on the floor.

My human failing seemed to break the spell holding everyone else still, and they all started to move and talk at the same time except Ignatius who continued to stand as still as a statue mumbling, "I didn't meant to," over and over again.

Several people who had heard the gunshot came rushing into the Governor's office and were promptly dispatched again on various errands by the Governor, who had collapsed back into his seat. White-faced and shaken, Sir David stood up again. He came out from behind his desk, walked over to Ignatius, and put an arm around his shoulders.

"Ignatius," he said, then more forcibly, "Ignatius, you must listen to me." When he had his attention, the Governor said, "We know you didn't mean to do more than protect Mr. Stewart. Darcy pulled the trigger and it was his misfortune that the gun was pointing at his face when it fired."

Then I understood how close I had really been to death. If Ignatius had not reacted so swiftly and pulled Darcy's gun arm back it would have been me lying on the floor with my brains spread over the Governor's parquet floor, and I was promptly sick again.

TWELVE

Wellington Again

Next morning, I walked into the Residence well before nine and sat at my desk with a profound sense of relief that it was all over.

Nearly strangled before breakfast and then threatened with death between breakfast and lunch, I felt that the previous day had taken on a nightmare atmosphere. It was certainly not a day I would like to relive, although I couldn't stop myself thinking about it. The Governor's refusal to sign the order that would have given Darcy enough money to buy himself out of his bankruptcy proved to be the straw that finally unbalanced his mind. Darcy's attempt to exact revenge on me had proved to be his retribution and the end of my assignment at the same time.

After Darcy's body had been removed and the blobs of blood and bits of hair and tissue cleaned up, Sir David had told me to go back to my villa to recuperate.

"I'll speak with you tomorrow morning," he said and went on to give similar advice to Ignatius, who had largely recovered from his first sight of violent death and a pallid, very quiet Silas.

So I sat on the veranda and looked out at the green expanse of lawn I could see through my office window and revelled in the thought that I was still alive to see it. I remembered Fregattenkapitan Pueckh's comments about my luck and was pleased it still held but wondered how many more times I would survive.

If I have nine lives like a cat, I thought. *I must have used up most of them by now.*

Suddenly, the day didn't seem so bright anymore.

And what about the future? I wondered.

I had finished my assignment with the Governor and didn't want to stay in Adelaide any longer than was necessary to tidy up my affairs and leave.

But where should I go? and that was a very difficult question to answer.

I could go home and settle down to the life of an earl's son and learn how to manage the estate. I had no interest in joining Fairweather, as he would have no need of my help after so many months on his own, and I was no longer as interested in the telegraph as I used to be if I was honest with myself. I could go back to New Zealand and visit Miss Ball, as I had promised, and maybe see how Jamie Marshall was faring as a gold miner on the Lindis River.

Next morning, I returned to my office. As I sat at my desk mulling over the conclusions I had reached the previous day, I realised that there were a number of possibilities open to me, but there was no advantage strong enough to sway me to one or the other option.

My introspection was disturbed by a knock on the door and Silas came in. He was still a little pale and the big blue bruise over his eye made the pallor more apparent.

Before he could speak, I asked, "How are you, Silas? You still look a little pale."

"Better than yesterday, thank you, sir," he responded weakly, "but I don't think I will ever forget what I saw yesterday." He shuddered from the memory. "It was horrible. I was looking straight at him, willing him not to shoot, and then the next moment there was a bang and his head exploded. I couldn't believe what I had witnessed." He paused for a moment, shuddered again as he said in a very faint voice, "I'll never forget it." I just managed to guide him into a chair and push his head between his knees before he fainted away.

After a few minutes, he raised his head, and his face was now even paler than before. He tried to stand but swayed so much he had to sit again.

"You should stay seated until you really feel strong enough to get up, Silas," I said.

"I'm supposed to take you to the Governor, sir," he said weakly.

"I can take myself to the Governor, Silas. You stay where you are until you have recovered fully," I said and patted him on the shoulder as I left the room.

Ignatius was in his office at his desk and reading the top document of a heap of papers when I walked in after giving a perfunctory knock on the open door. He looked up as I entered and gave me a smile of welcome, but I could see from his face that he was still suffering from the horrors of the previous day.

I asked, "How are you, Ignatius?" instinctively abandoning the conventional morning greeting.

"I'm recovering from the worst experience in my life, Mr. Stewart. How are you this morning?"

"Thanks to you I'm alive and able to enjoy a beautiful day." I took his hand and added, "And to help my friends recover from a nightmare, if I can. You saved my life by your quick-witted actions, Ignatius, and I will be in your debt for the rest of my life. I can only say thank you and hope you will not be troubled for too long by your memories."

He shuddered and said simply but very sincerely, "I hope so too."

Ignatius had his fingers intertwined and resting on the top of the pile of papers while we spoke, and in the pause that followed our conversation, he stared at his fingers as they twisted and turned as if they belonged to someone else.

It was a long silence that Ignatius eventually broke by straightening himself in his chair, and with an enormous effort to sound normal he said, "I'll just see if Sir David is ready to see you."

He stood up and, after knocking on Sir David's door, disappeared inside and closed the door. Moments later the door reopened and Ignatius beckoned to me and then stood back so that I could walk directly to Sir David, who stood behind his desk. As far as I could detect from his demeanour, there was no external sign that Sir David had been affected by the previous day's events, and this was born out when he greeted me and shook my hand as if nothing untoward had happened.

"Good morning, Mr. Stewart. You look better this morning, I'm pleased to say. Please come and sit down."

I simply said, "Thank you, Sir David."

He picked up the reports I had written and said, "Once again you have demonstrated your courage and resourcefulness with the result that you have saved the Government a great deal of money and me the embarrassment of a major error of judgement. But I don't think HMG will give you another medal even if I recommended one. They're not so generous now." Sir David stopped for a moment to blow his nose, then went on, "John Darcy appeared to be a trustworthy man. He was certainly very plausible, and for a long time I believed in him. I began to have doubts when information I received from one source didn't tally with the intelligence presented by Darcy. Your firsthand reports crystallised my doubts into certainties. His sudden death was an unfortunate accident, but as the cancellation of the manufacturing contract would have led to his financial and social ruin, it was probably the best end he could have had. As you know, many men in his position would have ended their own lives rather than be stigmatised by bankruptcy.

"To avoid any unnecessary enquiries and particularly to safeguard Ignatius from any possibility of a charge of murder, I propose to bend the truth a little and report that Darcy shot himself. It is certainly true that he pulled the trigger, even if his aim was not what he intended."

Sir David looked at me appraisingly for a long time before asking, "Do you agree with my intention, Mr. Stewart?"

I glanced quickly around the room and was surprised to see that Ignatius was not present. He must have left the room as I was greeting the Governor.

"As I had my eyes shut at the moment the gun was fired, I cannot say what happened, and if I had to give evidence under oath, that's all I could say. It appeared that Darcy shot himself while Ignatius was trying to prevent him shooting me, so I have no difficulty agreeing with your proposal."

"Thank you, Mr. Stewart," said the Governor with some relief in his voice. "We must now consider your position."

"Indeed. Sir David," I agreed.

"You have completed the task I asked you to undertake. and if you wish to leave Adelaide. I will provide you with a passage home and six months' salary as a token of my gratitude. Alternatively, you could stay here as one of my assistants although at present I'm not sure in what capacity you would be employed."

"Your Excellency, I am grateful for an offer of future employment on your staff, but I think I would prefer to accept your alternative option. I'm not sure yet what I will do, but I am quite sure that I would not find office work congenial. Perhaps you would let me know when you wish me to vacate the office and villa."

Sir David consulted a calendar in a pocketbook and said, "It's the tenth of the month today. If I give you leave of absence until the end of the month will that give you enough time to clear up your affairs?" I nodded and he continued, "Very well. You can continue to make use of your office and call on Silas for assistance if you need his help up to the end of the month, and obviously you can live in the villa for the same period."

"That's very generous of you, Sir David, and I am very pleased to accept such liberal terms," I said.

"Good," he said. Changing the subject entirely, he asked, "Lady Megan is keen to see you and hear of your exploits firsthand, so perhaps you would honour us by accepting an invitation to dinner tomorrow night?"

"I should be honoured to accept your invitation, Sir David. May I enquire, sir, if Mrs. Lewis is still here?"

"No," he said. "She left some weeks ago, as she heard that her mother was very ill, but I doubt if she reached Wales in time to see her alive. She was very concerned about the lack of news from you," he added without elaboration.

There was a short silence, then Sir David said in a definite but polite dismissal, "Very well, Mr. Stewart, I'll look forward to welcoming you at dinner tomorrow night."

"Thank you, Sir David," I said and left the office as quickly and quietly as possible.

Ignatius wasn't at his desk when I passed through his office, and Silas was no longer sitting in mine. I sat at my desk for about fifteen minutes and, as I had nothing to do, I decided to go back to the villa, as it was nearing lunchtime.

As I approached the door to the villa, Evan Edwards opened it and then stood back to let me enter. How he knew I was coming I didn't know, but obviously he did.

He said, "Good afternoon, sir. What can I get you for luncheon, sir? I can offer kedgeree or a curry if you are in a hurry, or I can cook a steak if you can wait?"

"I have time, Edwards, so you can cook me a steak. I'll go and sit on the veranda while I'm waiting."

"Certainly, sir," he said.

On the veranda there was a rickety old steamer chair in the shade of the overhanging roof. I sat down on it and it squeaked unmusically and then again as I adjusted my position. To stop it squeaking I had to lie back as quietly as possible. Then I could enjoy looking at the different greens of the lawn and shrubbery and revel in unaccustomed and official idleness.

One step forward, I thought. *I'm not staying here—but where should I go? That's still the question.*

I must have nodded off because Edwards had to shake my shoulder to tell me my luncheon was ready in the dining room. It was delicious, and I relished every mouthful of perfectly cooked beef and the vegetables Edwards had conjured up. After luncheon, I returned to the veranda to sit on my squeaky chair for half an hour before walking back to my office.

As soon as I sat at my desk, I reached for the bell pull, gave it a good tug, and when Silas arrived, said, "As you probably know by now, Silas, I will be leaving at the end of the month."

"Yes, sir. I do know and I am very sorry you have decided not to stay," he said. "Do you know where you will go?"

"No," I said. "I'm still trying to decide but probably back to Scotland to help my father."

"If I may say so, sir, I envy you the opportunity. It will be some years before I return home. I'm sorry, sir. I should have given you this immediately." He handed me an envelope.

"Thank you, Silas," I said, turning the letter over and wondering who could have written to me. There was no clue on the envelope, and the address was written in a hand I didn't recognise.

I said, "Thank you, Silas. I'll ring if I need anything."

"Very good, sir," he answered and walked out of the office, quietly closing the door behind him.

I looked at the mysterious envelope again and realised that the only way I was going to find out what is in it was to open it, and this I proceeded to do. Inside the envelope I found a single sheet of heavy writing paper folded in half once to fit the envelope. It had the look and feel of officialdom and with my curiosity even more active than before, I unfolded the letter and read it with increasing astonishment.

It was certainly official.

It was signed by the Chief Magistrate in Wellington and requested the presence of Jason Smiley Stewart at the trial of Silas Gravenor for attempted murder. The date set for the trial to commence was a little more than two weeks ahead. No response was requested, so I didn't bother to send one.

I was quite relieved that the decision about where to go had been made for me and gave the bell pull another hearty tug.

When Silas arrived, I explained what the letter was about and asked him to arrange a passage on the next available passenger ship going to Wellington. We left my office together, and I went to find Ignatius to advise him that I was going to Gravenor's trial and asked him to advise the Governor. During our discussion, we realised that there would be no reason for me to return to Adelaide, so we agreed that I would vacate my office and, more importantly, the villa and take all my personal affects with me to Wellington. We agreed also that Ignatius would arrange for me to have six months' salary and the passage money to Wellington and then back to England in cash.

When I returned to my office, I sat down with the intention of writing to my father. I should have written before, and that made starting the letter much more difficult than I expected. Knowing that I could have made time to write and hadn't made me feel rather guilty and that inhibited my powers of composition. Whilst I was cogitating over what to say to my father, the unexpected meeting with Mary Thomas came to mind. I wondered about writing to her as well but wasn't sure if I should. We had spent a few hours together recently after many years without contact, but I wasn't sure that our chance meeting was sufficient reason to start a correspondence with the lady. She was undoubtedly very attractive and pleasant but…I decided to ask Lady Megan's advice the following evening and postponed writing to my father at the same time.

I went back to the villa, told Edwards I was leaving, and instructed him to start getting my belongings ready for my departure in a few days. I had dinner, went to bed, and slept until morning.

I arrived at my office at the normal time and rang the bell for Silas as soon as I reached my desk.

"Good morning, sir," said a much more cheerful-looking Silas as he entered the office.

"Good morning, Silas," I responded politely. "Do you have any news about a passage to Wellington for me?"

"Yes, sir," he said. "There is a steamer leaving tomorrow night bound for Auckland and then Wellington. I have reserved a cabin in your name, and if this is convenient I will purchase the ticket this morning."

"Please purchase the ticket, Silas. There is nothing to keep me here, so I might as well take advantage of this opportunity and leave. Thank you, Silas," I said in polite dismissal. I walked along the corridor to tell Ignatius what had been arranged and then decided to return to the villa to instruct Edwards to have everything packed ready for shipment the following day.

In the afternoon, I arranged for a carriage to take me into Adelaide so that I could buy a pocket watch to replace the one I'd lost, and then I had nothing to do until dinner that evening.

Time was hanging rather heavily on my hands already, and I was very happy that I would be on the move again very soon.

I was at home in the villa and just about to change for dinner when a messenger came with a note of apology from the Governor. He wrote that Lady Megan was indisposed and regrettably it was necessary to cancel the arrangement for dinner. I didn't get the opportunity to ask Lady Megan if it was advisable to write to Mary Lewis and consequently never did. And once again I failed to write to my father.

I had a satisfactory but, as usual, a solitary dinner in the villa and went early to bed.

In the morning, I went to the office for the last time. I checked the drawers of my desk to make sure there were no personal items left then rang for Silas. When he arrived, I locked the office door for the last time and handed him the key. Together we walked to Ignatius's office, where I waited for a chance to see the Governor and say goodbye once again. As I sat in one of the visitors' chairs, my thoughts inevitably went back to the last time I had said goodbye to Sir David Tallboy. I was in a hospital in Bombay recovering from a bullet wound that had almost killed me. Inevitably, it would have killed me but for the strength and determination of Joanna Evans. We would have been so happy together if God hadn't decided that I should live and she should die.

God moves in mysterious ways, I thought, but it didn't bring me any comfort.

Through a fog of unhappiness I became aware of a voice calling my name.

I looked up and saw Ignatius staring down at me with an expression of concern on his face and realised when he said, "Jason! Are you all right?" in a worried tone that he must have spoken my name several times before.

"Yes, Ignatius," I answered. "I was thinking of past events."

"Clearly sad ones," he said. Before I had time to respond, he added, "The Governor will see you now."

"Thank you, Ignatius," I said as I got up and walked into Sir David Tallboy's office and sat down in one of the visitor's chairs in front of his desk.

"Good morning, Mr. Stewart," he said. "First of all, I must extend Lady Megan's apologies. She was looking forward to hearing about your adventures but had a severe migraine and had to go to her room. She is still not well this morning, otherwise she would have come down and apologised in person."

"Please extend my best wishes to Lady Megan, Sir David, and tell her I hope her illness is soon over."

"Certainly I'll do so," he agreed.

I said, "As you will know from Ignatius, Sir David, I will sail to Wellington tonight. After Gravenor's trial, I expect I will return to my father's estate in Scotland. I would like to thank you for offering me the chance to assist you, and I have to say that it has been an interesting experience, but after two attempts on my life and a near drowning, I think I will look for a less hazardous occupation for the future."

The Governor chuckled at that and made a short speech in which he praised my abilities and said all the nice things that an employer says when a member of staff is leaving voluntarily.

At the end he stood up and, as he shook my hand, said, "Thank you for all you have done for me and for our country, Mr. Stewart. I wish you all good fortune in future both from myself and also from my wife."

"Thank you, Sir David," I responded and turned and walked from the Governor's office for the last time.

Ignatius and Silas were waiting for me in Ignatius's office, and we shook hands and said our goodbyes. With the farewells finished, I turned away from them to go back to the villa, where I would wait for the coach that would transport me to the pier.

A few hours later, I was onboard the steamer and settling into my cabin.

———

The voyage to Wellington was uneventful in terms of weather, and whilst I made whatever polite conversation was necessary to oil the wheels of sociability, I can remember nothing of note about my fellow passengers. Not even one of their names.

In Wellington, I disembarked in the early morning and went back to the inn I had used previously. Jack Tyler was in the bar just handing someone a tankard of breakfast beer when he saw me.

I said, "Good morning, Mr. Tyler. Can you let me have a room for a few weeks, please? Perhaps you remember me. My name is Stewart."

"Yes, I remember you, Mr. Stewart. You had a run in with that man Gravenor. Is that why you're here?"

"Yes. I have to attend the trial. Well, Mr. Tyler, do you have a room for me?" I asked. "I'll need a lock-up storeroom as well, as I have too much with me to fit into one room."

He kept looking at me as if there was something in the back of his mind that he couldn't identify but said, "Yes, I do have a room you can use. In fact, business is so slack at the moment you can use the next door room as a storeroom free of charge until I get a customer for it."

"Thank you, Mr. Tyler. That's a very good offer, and I'll pay for the first week in advance." I took out my purse and counted out some coins. "Would you put a table and chair in the room again, please?"

"Of course, Mr. Stewart," he said as he pocketed the coins and made a note in a rather grubby ledger.

I went upstairs to my room and only unpacked my overnight case, as I could unpack other items as I needed them. Remembering what had happened on my previous visit, I decided that it was not unreasonable to carry a loaded gun and a sharp knife, so I unpacked them. I put the gun into my coat pocket and attached the scabbard containing the knife to my belt.

I wrote a short note to the Reverend Ball requesting his permission to call on his elder daughter now that I had returned unexpectedly to Wellington and then went down to the bar to ask Tyler to arrange for someone to go to the Mission Station.

When Tyler returned to the bar after sending one of the servants on horseback to deliver my note, I asked him what he had to eat, as it was nearly the middle of the day. As usual, it was Hobson's choice, and I took Tyler at his word when he claimed that it was delicious. It was a mutton stew, and whilst I would not have claimed it was delicious, it was certainly tasty and very filling.

I had finished and was considering what I could do with the rest of the afternoon when I heard a horse and cart stop outside.

Shortly afterwards, a tattooed Maori came into the bar and started to look around. He didn't see me immediately, but I noticed that he was just as careful not to touch anything as he had last time I had seen him. I couldn't remember his name, but he was obviously trusted, as he had chaperoned Miss Ball when she came to see me off last time I left Wellington. Tyler was standing at the bar looking at me, then the Maori, then back to me again, and the look of frustrated memory was bright in his eyes. After carefully looking around the bar, the Maori's eyes met mine and widened. For some reason that I could not explain, he crossed himself then came to where I was sitting.

"I am Joseph Mathew. Reverend Ball wishes to see you. Please come with me," he said then turned and hurried out of the bar as if it was contaminated.

I looked at Tyler, who was still wearing his puzzled expression, and said, "I'm going to the Mission Station to meet Reverend Ball."

"Yes, Mr. Stewart," he responded.

I walked outside, climbed up onto the seat beside Joseph Mathew, and was driven out of Wellington to the Mission Station. There didn't appear to be anything to identify the small group of buildings Joseph stopped at as the Mission Station, but I assumed he knew where he was going. He stopped the horse and cart, jumped down, looped the rein around a hitching rail, and gestured for me to get down and follow him. So I did.

Joseph Mathew walked into one of the buildings and halfway along a stone-flagged corridor he stopped and knocked on a door. A voice called, "Enter," and my guide opened the door, entered, and closed the door, leaving me standing in the corridor. About five minutes later the door opened; Joseph Matthew stepped into the corridor and urged me over the threshold with a push in the back. The door closed behind me.

On the other side of the room was a man dressed in an austere, clerical black suit standing beside a table with his hand on an open book that I assumed must be a Bible.

He was a tall, slim, and athletic man with a full head of hair and a spring in his step that indicated an active man. He had a good complexion and piercing blue eyes.

He strode across the room with his hand outstretched in welcome and said, "I am Reverend Ball. I asked Joseph Mathew to bring you here because you have requested permission to see my eldest daughter. However, your presence is also something of an enigma."

"Why is that, Reverend?" I asked.

"Because Joseph Mathew recognised you as the man he escorted to the jetty with my elder daughter some months ago when you were about to embark on the *Nimrod*."

Reverend Ball paused to collect his thoughts for a moment, then went on, "Some time ago I received a letter from one of the ladies who worships in the Mission church and was a passenger on the *Nimrod* when it sailed from Wellington. I have the letter here." He waved it at me to prove that he did in fact have a letter. He went on, "She wrote that the voyage was uneventful until they had passed Auckland when the ship's engine stopped and all the passengers were ordered into the boats except one. She knew one passenger was missing because the mate kept complaining about Smiley Stewart staying onboard when it was his place as first mate to help his captain and not an ex-seaman and so on and so on. There were several pages about the discomfort of being on a small boat in the middle of the ocean at night, which concluded with the statement that all the passengers except Smiley Stewart continued their voyage on another ship. Is this correct so far, Mr. Stewart?"

"Yes, Reverend," I said.

"I was informed by the harbourmaster that the *Nimrod* had sunk and no one was saved, which is clearly incorrect, as you're standing in front of me. In the circumstances, however, I thought that Mr. Smiley Stewart had perished with the crew of the *Nimrod* and advised my daughter accordingly. She was exceedingly upset by the news and that surprised me, as I believed you did not know each other well."

I was surprised by the news that she was so upset and said, "You are correct, Reverend. Miss Ball and I have little knowledge of each other." Without any prior thought at all, I found myself adding, "But I would like to alter that situation if you will permit me."

He said, "Mr. Stewart, I first learnt of your existence some months ago when my daughter brought your note to me and told me that you had chanced to meet on the *Nelson*. As it turned out, you had to leave before I could meet you and ascertain whether you were an honourable man or simply an adventurer. As I believed it was possible that you might return to Wellington and again request a meeting with my daughter, I wrote to a friend in England and asked him to make some discrete enquiries about you. I hope that you would take the same action if you were faced with the same dilemma, Mr. Stewart."

I thought about that for a moment and said simply, "I think I probably would, Reverend."

"Good," he said. "My friend wrote that there is a young man called Jason Smiley Stewart who has received a medal from our Queen for bravery." He stopped his explanation for a moment and then asked, "Why don't you use the CMG title after your signature, Mr. Stewart?"

"It hasn't become a habit to do so, Reverend, and I forget," I said truthfully, wondering at the same time if I ought to make more of an effort to remember.

"My friend also wrote that you will inherit a big estate in the Scottish lowlands, and you are entitled to use the honorary title of Viscount." He stopped again and asked, "Do you forget to use that as well, Mr. Stewart?"

"Yes, Reverend," I said without feeling the need for amplification.

"From what I have learnt and now that I have met you face to face, I believe you to be a serious and an honourable man, Mr. Stewart. Consequently, if my daughter should wish to meet you in controlled circumstances now that you have returned from the presumed dead, I will raise no objection."

"Thank you, Reverend," I responded, and suddenly it seemed quite important to have this man's commendation, but I didn't know why.

"Now, I must go and tell my wife and then my daughter that you are very much alive. Please remain here, Mr. Stewart, and I will send for you shortly if Miss Ball wishes to renew her acquaintance with you." Reverend Ball walked out of the room and left me to "twiddle my thumbs," as the saying goes, as there were no pictures to look at and no view to admire from the window.

Some time later the door opened again and Reverend Ball beckoned.

"My daughter would be pleased to meet you again, Mr Stewart," he said when I joined him in the corridor outside his room. "However, she is helping some of my Maori missionaries with their English, and as she is due to start a lesson with them very shortly, she will only be able to spend a few minutes with you."

"I understand," I said.

I followed him along the corridor and through a door at the end, which apparently led into the Reverend's private quarters. He opened another door on the right, halfway along another but shorter corridor and preceded me into a comfortably furnished sitting room. Miss Ball was sitting on one side of the fireplace with another lady who I assumed to be her mother sitting on the other. Miss Ball, who was wearing a high-necked dress in a dark blue, satiny material, was sitting demurely on a dark green, upholstered, high-back chair with an open book on her lap. On the other side of the fireplace, Mrs. Ball, who was dressed in unrelieved black, sat on a matching chair and was embroidering something fixed to a frame on a stand. I thought Miss Ball looked the picture of health, and as I had forgotten how attractive she was, I had difficulty looking away from her when the Reverend Ball broke the silence.

"Mrs. Ball," he said, "may I introduce Mr. Stewart to you? Mr. Stewart, may I present you to my wife?"

We shook hands as I said, "I'm honoured to meet you, Mrs. Ball." She responded with something similar, but I don't now remember what.

Reverend Ball went on, "I don't need to introduce you to my elder daughter, Mr. Stewart, as you have already met." He looked pointedly at the clock ticking on the mantelshelf over the fire and said, "Don't forget your lesson, Daughter."

"No, Father," she said dutifully.

Then with an all-encompassing sweep of his arm, he said, "Now, if you will excuse me, I have some work to complete," and left the room.

As soon as her father closed the sitting room door, Miss Ball took the initiative and, indicating a chair, said, "Please come and sit here, Mr. Stewart." When I had seated myself at a decorous distance from her, she added, "I'm so pleased the news about your death was false, Mr. Stewart. I was very upset when my father told me."

"I'm very sorry you have been distressed unnecessarily, Miss Ball, but I have to admit that I'm pleased that you had sufficient regard for me to be a little upset."

"Oh," she said and her cheeks became a little pinker. "I didn't mean that, Mr. Stewart. I was referring to the loss of the *Nimrod* and all her crew."

"I beg your pardon, Miss Ball. I was presumptuous," I said contritely.

"Indeed you were, Mr. Stewart," she said directly, then after a short silence she asked more politely, "When did you arrive in Wellington, Mr. Stewart?"

"I came ashore quite early this morning. I arranged accommodation and then sent a note to your father asking if I could meet you, and here I am. I must admit, I didn't expect to be able to see you so soon."

"So you came to see me immediately. That was considerate of you. Thank you. How long will you stay in Wellington, Mr. Stewart?" she asked. "I hope you will not go rushing off so quickly this time."

"There shouldn't be any need for me to leave so precipitately on this occasion," I said. "The business I was engaged upon for the Governor of South Australia is finished, so I have the freedom to choose when and where I will go next. I will be here for at least as long as Gravenor's trial lasts, and after that I do not know yet what I'll do."

"I see," she said, then looked at the clock and stood up "I must go to my lesson, Mr. Stewart. Please excuse me."

"I hope I may be permitted to meet you again, Miss Ball?" I asked.

"You will have to write to my father and ask for an appointment to meet me, Mr. Stewart," she said bluntly, then in a slightly more friendly tone added, "But I would like to have the opportunity to talk with you again and hear about your adventures."

"Thank you, Miss Ball. I should be pleased to have the opportunity to satisfy your curiosity," I said, and she left the room without a backward glance.

Seconds after she left, Joseph Mathew entered and Mrs Ball said, "I'll bid you goodbye, Mr. Stewart. Joseph Mathew will take you back to your accommodation."

"Thank you, Mrs. Ball. Goodbye," I said and followed Joseph Mathew back past the reverend's working room and out to the cart. We drove silently back to the hotel, and when I jumped down from the cart he drove off without a goodbye or wave of his hand.

Tyler was occupying his usual position behind the bar.

Actually, he didn't appear to have moved since I went out, and his puzzled expression returned as soon as he saw me.

"You look concerned about something, Mr. Tyler. Can I help you?" I asked helpfully.

"No, sir, I don't think so. Your face reminded me of something but I cannot recall what."

"I see," I said and turned away from the bar to go to my room, as I wanted to write to Reverend Ball and ask for an appointment to meet his daughter again but also to think over the conflicting impressions I had gained.

The last time we met she had given me a miniature of herself as a reminder of a friendship that was ending before it had begun. This time Miss Ball didn't seem so friendly, and I wondered why, but I did what I always do with unanswerable questions: I decided to wait until we had spent some more time together then I might be able to answer the puzzle. I wrote to Reverend Ball requesting an appointment to meet Miss Ball at her convenience and took it down to Tyler so that he could arrange for it to be delivered.

In the bar was a man in a merchant Navy uniform.

As he turned away from his conversation with Tyler, I recognised Captain Prendergast and said, "Good day, Captain Prendergast."

"Good heavens," he said. "It's Mr. Stewart, isn't it?"

"That's correct, Captain. You have a good memory."

"You were a passenger on *Nimrod*, if I remember correctly. I wish I knew what happened to her," he said. "Her loss is a total mystery."

"I can tell you exactly what happened, Captain."

"You were a passenger, Mr. Stewart, and the report I received was that all the passengers were transhipped in Kororareka, so I do not believe you can throw any light on the mystery," Captain Prendergast stated bluntly.

"As you like, Captain," I said and turned away.

Captain Prendergast walked out, and I noticed that Tyler was no longer wearing his puzzled expression, but instead looked as if he would burst if he was unable to ask a question immediately.

To help him, I asked, "What is it, Mr. Tyler?"

"I've remembered what was troubling me, Mr. Stewart. You were one of the passengers on *Nimrod* when she left here. I had an uncle and a nephew onboard. They were part of the crew, and even if old Prendergast isn't interested, I want to know what happened to the *Nimrod*. She was a good ship, and old Giles was one of the best captains around."

"I will certainly tell you what I know, Mr. Tyler, but do you have any relations here who would also wish to hear what happened?" I asked.

"That's a good idea, Mr. Stewart. I do have relations in Wellington, and I'll bring whoever is available here in the next hour, if that's convenient."

"Yes, perfectly. Perhaps I can have something to eat in the meantime?" I suggested.

"If you sit down over there," and he indicated a table, "I'll get you some food."

Five minutes or so later, he arrived at the table with a plate heaped with steaming hot food and a large glass of beer. The food was unidentifiable but tasty. The beer had a beery taste but nothing else to commend it, apart from its ability to generate multiple burps.

By the time I finished eating, a small group of people had assembled at the other end of the room.

Tyler came and said, "We are all here when you are ready, Mr. Stewart."

"I'll come immediately," I said and happily abandoned the second half of the glass of beer Tyler had presented so proudly. I got up from the table and crossed the room to meet the family members who could accept Tyler's invitation or possibly were sufficiently interested in knowing what had happened to loved ones to attend.

I said, "We all know that the SS Nimrod has sunk and her crew drowned. I cannot change that fact, but I can tell you what happened, if you wish to know."

Tyler said, "On behalf of everyone here I can say that we do want to know, so please start, Mr. Stewart."

"Very well," I said and related in as much detail as I could remember everything that had happened from the time the propeller and shaft were damaged up to my rescue by the crew of the SMS Novara.

At the end and after some subdued conversation amongst my listeners, Tyler said, "Thank you for telling us what happened, but I'm puzzled, Mr. Stewart. You were on Nimrod as a passenger, but you related your story as if you know the sea. Which is it?"

"Both, Mr. Tyler," I responded. "Before I gave up the sea, I was a cadet and then the third officer of a cargo ship on the Liverpool to Bombay route."

"If I cannot help you any further," I said to Tyler and his group of relations, "I'll go to my room."

They didn't have any questions, so I said, "Good night," and went to bed.

In the morning after a reasonable breakfast, I walked into the centre of Wellington and eventually found the office of the chief magistrate, where I made myself known to a clerk at a desk near the entrance and told him where I was staying. He made a few notes in a ledger then left me sitting at his desk with a brusque, "Excuse me, Mr. Stewart," as he got up and then disappeared through a door behind him. He returned after a few minutes and sat down again.

He said, "The magistrate has asked me to thank you for making the journey to Wellington and to inform you that Gravenor's trial has been postponed indefinitely because the man is ill. He slipped and fell in the prison yard, hit his head very hard on the cobblestones, and is still wandering around in a daze a week after the accident. It would have saved everyone a deal of aggravation if he had managed to finish himself off."

"My sentiments exactly," I responded. "I imagine that there is no need for me to stay in Wellington in the circumstances."

"Exactly so, Mr. Stewart," he answered. "He's safely in prison now, and there is so much evidence against him that if he recovers enough to stand trial, he will simply go back to prison."

I thanked the man, and when I stood outside the magistrate's building in bright sunshine and an artic wind, I wondered what I should do now.

The primary reason for coming to Wellington had just evaporated, and whilst I had some regard for Miss Ball, I wasn't sure that it was strong enough to justify staying much longer. My stomach reminded me that breakfast had been taken some time earlier, so I walked back to the hotel to see what Tyler could produce. I didn't doubt that it would be pot luck again, but so far it had been tasty enough and hadn't made me ill, which was a bonus.

At the hotel I said, "Did you have my note delivered to the Mission, Mr. Tyler?"

"Yes, sir. My lad took it before breakfast."

"And there has been no reply?"

"Nothing yet, sir," said Tyler. "If you sit over there, sir," and he indicated the table I had used the day before, "I'll bring you your food," which he did a few minutes later.

Unlike the previous day, this meal was composed of identifiable slices of roast beef with some vegetables that proved to be overcooked and mushy. It was a generous helping of meat and it had a good flavour so I ate enough to feel satisfied. While I ate and for some time after I finished, I continued with my mental debate about what to do next.

But I didn't reach a conclusion.

I walked down to the pier in the sunshine and chilling wind but was no closer to a decision when I stood looking out to sea than I was when I started from the hotel. There were a few ships in the anchorage, and I noticed that one British steamer was flying the Blue Peter. *If I was on that ship*, I thought, *I could be home in a month or so*, and suddenly felt quite homesick.

I walked back to the hotel and found Tyler occupying his usual position behind the bar. I enquired again but there was still no letter from the Mission, and I had to accept the possibility that if Reverend Ball had gone on a journey connected with his Mission, it might be some time before I did receive one. It really was most unsatisfactory, and suddenly I was disenchanted with the idea of waiting an indeterminate length of time in order to find out when I could meet a young woman in whom I had at present only a passing interest.

I turned to Tyler and said, "Mr. Tyler, would you be kind enough to send your boy to the jetty and have him find out from Captain Prendergast when the next steamer will leave for Britain."

Tyler said, "Yes, of course, Mr. Stewart, but I thought you were going to stay several weeks."

"Yes, so did I, but Gravenor's trial has been postponed indefinitely because he is ill. There is no compelling reason for me to stay here longer than is necessary for me to get a suitable passage home. By the time your boy returns from Captain Prendergast, I will have another note for him to take to the Mission house," and I went to my room.

My second letter to Reverend Ball was quickly written. I said,

Dear Reverend,
I have discovered today that Gravenor's trial has been

postponed indefinitely because of ill health. Consequently, there is no reason for me to stay in Wellington, and I will get a passage on the first suitable steamer that leaves here for Britain. I should be grateful for the opportunity to say goodbye to your elder daughter, but if that is impossible, I request you to extend my good wishes to Miss Ball for her future health and happiness. I also send my greetings to your lady wife.

Yours sincerely

Jason Smiley Stewart KCG

Viscount Strathmilton

I put the letter in an envelope, sealed it, and took it down to Tyler.

The boy had returned from the jetty and was dispatched to the Mission house after giving me a note from Captain Prendergast that informed me politely that the next steamer would leave in twenty-four to thirty-six hours. He also gave me the name of the local agent of the shipping line if I wanted to arrange a passage.

An hour later I had secured a first-class cabin on the steamship *Achilles* bound for Southampton.

I wrote to Jamie Marshall and told him I was returning home and hoped he was doing well with his gold panning. I sent it to him in care of The Commercial Hotel in Christchurch and included my address as Strathmilton Castle, near Carlisle.

I repacked the few items I had taken from one of my trunks and then I had nothing to do except wait for the hours to pass. Tyler wanted to refund some of the money I had paid in advance for the room, but I decided to make him a present of it as some compensation for sending his boy out with messages.

There was no message from Reverend Ball up to the time I said good-bye to Tyler, so I set off for the jetty without anyone to wave a farewell this time. At the appointed time, I presented myself at the jetty and was ferried out to the *Achilles* in one of her boats.

After an uneventful voyage lasting a little less than a month, we docked in Southampton in the late afternoon, and I took the boat train up to London, where I spent the night in a small hotel near Kings Cross Station.

Next morning, I caught an early train north and spent the night in Carlisle. I was tempted to hire a carriage that evening but decided it would be better to arrive at Strathmilton reasonably refreshed after a night's sleep.

In the morning, I hired a carriage to take me to the castle and engaged a carrier to transport my luggage.

We set off about ten in the morning and were in sight of the castle in the early afternoon. I thought that I would be troubled with painful memories when I saw the castle again, but I was relieved to find that I could view it relatively unemotionally. The memories were still there, but they were not so desperately painful anymore, for which I was grateful. My driver didn't have the skill of old Angus, the castle coachman, and managed to scrape the offside rear wheel boss all the way along the inside of the gate house wall with a screeching, grinding noise that set my teeth on edge, although the coachman didn't seem perturbed. I directed the coachman to the main entrance and alighted as soon as he stopped by the steps.

The heavy wooden entrance door creaked open and one of the servants appeared in the opening. He looked at me then turned back into the house, called something I couldn't here, and then Burke appeared and came hurrying down the steps to greet me.

"Good afternoon, Mr. Jason," he said with a smile of welcome lighting up his face. "What a wonderful surprise. The earl will be so pleased to see you, and you are looking very well, if I may say so, sir."

"Thank you, Burke," I said. "Would you arrange for the coach driver to have something to eat and drink before he goes back to Carlisle, please? I have paid for the hire so we do not owe him anything."

"Certainly, sir," he said then half-turned away to listen to something a servant was whispering in his ear. He turned back to me and said diplomatically, "I see you are travelling light, sir."

"Not really, Burke. My luggage is on a cart somewhere between Carlisle and here. It should be here later today or possibly tomorrow morning. Where is my father, I mean, the earl?"

"In his office, sir," said Burke. "Shall I announce you?"

"No, thank you, Burke. I'll announce myself." I turned and climbed the steps to the entrance and then walked through into the hall. A large log fire was crackling in the fireplace, as it almost always did whether it was sunny or wet. I walked through the hall and climbed the stairs and soon found myself outside the room my father used as an office. I knocked, and when I heard the familiar voice call, "Enter," I opened the door and saw my father sitting at his desk, head down studying some papers. I closed the door and stepped closer to the desk.

I said, "Good afternoon, Father. I hope I find you well?"

My poor father leaped to his feet as if someone had stuck a long, sharp pin in his rump and said, "My God, Jason, a shock like that could kill someone," which wasn't quite the greeting I had hoped, for but I had been a bit unreasonable walking in unannounced as I had.

Moments later, he had come around his desk and we were hugging each other and laughing with the joy of an unexpected reunion.

He said, "I'm so pleased to see you and looking so well too. I was very worried when I didn't hear from you. Why didn't you write to me, you young reprobate?"

"I did intend to, Father, but I seemed to be always on the move from place to place and never long enough in one place to have the time to write sensibly to you. I barely had time to write reports for Sir David."

"Sir David?" he said. "You mean Sir David Tallboy?" he added incredulously. "How did he become involved? You went to join Fairweather on some telegraph work."

"Yes, I did, but—" I stopped, realising as I spoke the futility of trying to relate and also make sense of all that had happened in a piecemeal fashion and said simply, "I will tell you all that has happened from beginning to end, Father. It will make much more sense if I do it like that."

"When will you start?" he asked.

"Now, if you wish, Father, and can spare the time from the estate work," I responded.

"I think," my father said, but what it was he thought I never found out, as there was a knock on the door and he broke of his conversation with me to call out, "Enter."

I suppose we were both looking at the door when it opened, but I was astounded by the sight that greeted my eyes.

I said, "Mary. Is it really you?"

"Jason. Thank God you're safe. I was so worried about you." Then almost magically we were in each other's arms and hugging each other so tightly it almost hurt.

I heard a click and was just in time to see my father disappearing through the doorway as he discretely left Mary and me to rediscover our love for each other.

AGAINST ALL ODDS

Volume 1
Jason Smiley Stewart - My Life Story

(ISBN 1–59886–14–7-6)

Brief Synopsis

Jason Smiley, the son of a blacksmith from a small village in south-eastern England, is befriended by a merchant Navy officer, Captain Stewart, and is offered an opportunity to join his ship as a cadet.

Over the next few years, Jason lives the life of a sailor, maturing in experience and emotion alike.

The third officer on the ship, who was assigned to teach Jason seamanship, is drowned near an island in Elphinstone Inlet with a group of surveyors from the telegraph company. Jason is able to make the survey and behaves courageously when he and his two companions are attacked by local tribesmen.

At the Governor's Ball in Bombay, he meets Mary Thomas, the niece of the Governor of Bombay, and finds the first love of his life. When they return to Liverpool, Jason is sent to Third Officer Evans's home to express the condolences of the captain and crew at Evans's untimely death. Jason is treated without respect by Captain Evans and his daughter, Miss Joanna Evans, and returns to his ship. A little later, Jason visits Mary Thomas at the family home in South Wales and spends several happy days in her chaperoned company. On the final night of his visit, Jason is insulted by drunken Desmond Wilcox, who is a rival for Mary's hand. Jason keeps his temper and answers Wilcox appropriately. Wilcox leaves the house in some disgrace, and Jason is prevailed upon to talk about his experiences.

On the next voyage, Jason shares his cabin with Neil Fairweather, who is travelling to Bombay and will supervise the laying of submarine cable in the Persian Gulf and Gulf of Oman as part of the telegraph link from Britain to India. Jason takes advantage of Fairweather's expertise and spends as much of his off-duty time as possible learning about electricity and the electric telegraph, as he feels that it is knowledge that might one day be of value.

The death of Third Officer Evans leads to Captain Stewart being accused of negligence by Captain Evans, and when SS *Earl Canning* docks in Liverpool, Captain Stewart is relieved of his command until the Court of Enquiry has adjudicated.

Just before the enquiry, Jason receives a letter from Mary's father, accusing him of drunken behaviour at the dinner party on the basis of Wilcox's false description of the event, and bars Jason from all future communication with his daughter.

At the Court of Enquiry, Jason is able to prove by reference to his daily journals that the apparently damning evidence introduced into court by Captain Evans QC was false, and so Jason was instrumental in clearing his father's name.

TELEGRAPH ISLAND

Volume 2
Jason Smiley Stewart - My Life Story

(ISBN 1–5988671–4-8)

Brief Synopsis

After Captain Stewart is cleared by the Board of Enquiry, he returns to his command and the SS *Earl Canning* sails for Bombay.

Not long after arriving in Bombay, Jason receives a peremptory note from Lady Megan, the Governor's wife, demanding his immediate presence. He complies and finds that Mary's father has also written to Lady Megan not only complaining about Jason's behaviour but also calling Lady Megan's judgment into question. She is extremely angry, but after Jason presents his version of events, Lady Megan agrees to write to the local vicar, who had also attended the dinner party, and find out what actually took place. Jason finds out also that Mary has runaway from home to avoid marriage to Desmond Wilcox, and her location is unknown.

One day, Fairweather comes to visit Jason onboard the ship and collapses. At the request of the Governor of Bombay, Jason leaves his ship and joins the telegraph company to help Fairweather, as he is too weak from dysentery to cope with the demands of his assignment on his own. Jason becomes more and more knowledgeable about the telegraph and during cable laying remains onboard as the telegraph company representative when Fairweather returns to Bombay. Jason's knowledge and initiative allows the cable to be laid into Malcolm's Inlet and extended over the ridge and down to the Elphinstone Inlet.

On his return to Bombay, Jason is informed that the Government will be recommended to award him a medal for his courageous and informed contribution to the cable laying. At the same meeting, Jason is introduced to Mary Thomas's father and meets Wilcox again. Mr. Thomas learns the truth about the dinner party and rejects Wilcox then apologizes to Jason. Mary and Jason are reunited, but the brief moment of joy is destroyed when Mr. Thomas orders his daughter to leave, informing Jason that he will never be wealthy enough to marry his daughter—the end of a dream.

Jason receives a letter from Joanna Evans apologising for her previous rude behaviour, and Jason responds appropriately. The award of a medal is confirmed, and Jason returns home for the investiture. He meets Joanna Evans and a friendship develops. Before Jason sails back to Bombay, he and Joanna become engaged.

Jason's first task on his return to duty is to go to Telegraph Island. Jason takes over command of the station and soon finds that the superintendent has not been paying the local tribesmen the agreed amount for guarding the cable. In consequence, the cable is being cut periodically.

Jason goes to the Omani village, hoping to see the man with whom he made the agreement but is unsuccessful. After defeating two attempts to invade the island, Jason evacuates everyone as the third attack is launched by the Omani. As he escapes, he is shot in the leg. On the voyage back to Bombay, Jason is in great danger of losing his leg, if not his life. Joanna Evans who has sailed to Bombay to spend time with her fiancé arrives as Jason is taken to the hospital. His life is saved only by the devoted nursing that Joanna provides. When he is out of danger, Joanna and Jason sail for home and marriage.